Easterleigh Hall at War

Margaret Graham has been .... years. Her first .... she has written a further .... novels, and is now working on her sixteenth. As a bestselling author her novels have been published in the UK, Europe and the USA.

Margaret has written two plays, co-researched a television documentary – which grew out of *Canopy of Silence* – and has written numerous short stories and features. She is a writing tutor and speaker and has written regularly for Writers' Forum. She founded and administered the Yeovil Literary Prize to raise funds for the creative arts of the Yeovil area and it continues to thrive under the stewardship of one of her ex-students. Margaret now lives near High Wycombe and has launched www.wordsforthewounded.com which raises funds for the rehabilitation of wounded troops by donations and writing prizes.

She has 'him indoors', four children and three grand-children who think OAP stands for Old Ancient Person. They have yet to understand the politics of pocket money. Margaret is a member of the Rock Choir, the WI and a Chair of her local U3A. She does Pilates and Tai Chi and travels as often as she can.

For more information about Margaret Graham visit her website at www.margaret-graham.com

Also by Margaret Graham

Easterleigh Hall

After the Storm
(previously published as Only the Wind is Free)
Annie's Promise
Somewhere Over England
(previously published as A Fragment of Time)
A Time for Courage
(previously published as A Measure of Peace)
At the Break of Day
(previously published as The Future is Ours)

Margaret GRAHAM
Easterleigh Hall at War

arrow books

Published by Arrow Books 2015

2 4 6 8 10 9 7 5 3 1

Copyright © Margaret Graham 2015

Margaret Graham has asserted her right under the Copyright, Designs and Patents Act 1988 to be identified as the author of this work.

This novel is a work of fiction. Apart from references to actual figures and places, all other names and characters are a product of the author's imagination and any resemblance to real persons, living or dead, is purely coincidental.

First published in Great Britain in 2015 by Arrow Books

Arrow Books
Random House, 20 Vauxhall Bridge Road,
London SW1V 2SA

www.randomhouse.co.uk

Addresses for companies within The Random House Group Limited can be found at:
www.randomhouse.co.uk/offices.htm

The Random House Group Limited Reg. No. 954009

A CIP catalogue record for this book
is available from the British Library

ISBN 9780099567967

Typeset in Palatino by Palimpsest Book Production Limited,
Falkirk, Stirlingshire
Printed and bound by CPI Group (UK) Ltd, Croydon, CR0 4YY

Penguin Random House is committed to a sustainable future for our business, our readers and our planet. This book is made from Forest Stewardship Council® certified paper.

For my fellow grannies of Words for the Wounded
With love and thanks

Acknowledgements

As a child I became aware that my paternal grand-father, an artillery officer, survived the First World War virtually unscathed, along with his four brothers. My maternal grandfather also survived, only to take his life later. War has long and relentless tentacles. As a result I have read extensively about the 1914–18 war since a child and I thank all those books, too numerous to mention specifically.

I founded and administer Words for the Wounded to raise funds for our present-day wounded, and to a great extent it has driven *Easterleigh Hall at War*. The needs of the wounded are pressing, and may be for the rest of their lives, which, given their youth, will be long.

My thanks to the fantastic Wellington on the Strand, especially Michal, Jose and Esther, for the support they have given my lunchtime procrastination in the writing of this novel. Perhaps I should make it respectable by calling it thinking time.

Chapter 1

Easterleigh Hall Auxiliary and Convalescent Hospital, Christmas 1914

Evie Forbes muttered, 'Aye, well, what are we going to do about this kettle of fish?' She and Mrs Moore, the head cook, stood at the huge deal table in the kitchen of Easterleigh Hall, looking across at the two men who were cluttering up the place. Both women were trying not to cringe at the noise as one man stabbed a knife in and out of the sharpener, while the other stood at the range, scraping a spatula across the frying pan as he flipped onions. It was a kitchen in which Evie had been learning her trade as assistant cook since 1909, and nothing had prepared her for this.

Easterleigh Hall had been a private house, pre-war, but the owner, Lord Brampton, eager to be seen to be supporting the war effort, had ordered his daughter, Lady Veronica, to set up the hospital for the war-wounded on the premises. He and his good lady, however, immediately decamped to their more peaceful homes in London and Leeds, to better oversee his steelworks, coal mines, brickworks, munitions, and the resulting profits. Man and wife were not missed.

Evie felt Mrs Moore's touch on her shoulder. 'Well, young Evie, I hear the vegetables calling. They need counting out for luncheon, so I'll leave you to sort out this little mess. Jack's your brother, after all.' She hobbled off, on feet beset with rheumatism, to the vegetable store at the other end of the vast kitchen.

Evie grinned, her hands on her hips. 'So kind.' Her mind was still half on Bastard Brampton, as he was known, who had sent a demand for hampers of Home Farm produce to be delivered to his London house post-haste. This had not yet happened, so no doubt they'd receive a telephone call in the near future. At least that was one problem she would not have to deal with, and Lady Veronica had become adept at clicking the receiver rest and complaining of a terrible line, before hanging up on his bellows.

As Mrs Moore joined the cluster of kitchen volunteers in the vegetable store, Jack, Evie's elder brother, dark-haired, dark-eyed, with a pitman's scars, stabbed ever more savagely in and out, in and out of the sharpener in the corner. How could he not notice that the shrieks were a million times worse than chalk on a board?

But why would he, when he'd spent the last four months playing silly buggers on the front line in Belgium and northern France with God knows what noise and mayhem all around? And what was he really seeing, as he stabbed that knife? Evie shut her

2

mind to it, and instead checked the cooking implements laid out on the table ready for the Christmas luncheon preparations, glancing at the clock, then at Annie, the kitchen assistant, who had just entered with cranberries from the housekeeper's preserve pantry. She placed the jars on the table, shaking her head at Evie, pointing at the clock and mouthing, 'Come on, pet, sort it out.' She hurried out, heading for the preserve pantry again.

At that moment Jack dropped the knife, cursed, recaptured it from the flag-stoned floor, and stabbed once more. Evie knew she must do something but, instead, she found herself staring from her brother to Lieutenant the Honourable Auberon Brampton, the owner's blond son and Jack's superior officer, who was stirring, instead of flipping. Her instructions to him had been to leave the onions alone to sauté gently for the turkey and chicken stuffing.

There was a pause as Jack examined the knife. Then Mr Auberon, as they called him, returned to flipping the onions, which had begun to burn. As she looked, the smoke rose ever more black, greasy and acrid. How could he not notice, staring as he was? Both men appeared absorbed, but in what? Evie felt a huge sadness at their hunched shoulders, their old faces, when they were both only twenty-four.

These two, together with Simon, Evie's sweetheart, and Mr Auberon's valet, Roger, had arrived last evening on leave. They had come to find a bit of peace. It had eluded them. They couldn't rest, or concentrate, or talk at length about anything, or so they had informed Evie at nine o'clock this morning, standing like a troop of naughty boys in the doorway of the kitchen. They said that they'd decided to do something useful, and help towards Christmas, just as everyone else seemed to be doing.

So saying, her fiancé, Simon, had promptly deserted and headed into the gardens to reacquaint himself with his under-gardener chores, and these two had inched further into the kitchen to carry out Evie's hastily invented tasks. Roger, Mr Auberon's erstwhile valet, proposed to clean his master's boots, but no one in their right minds would put sixpence on that being true. He'd be more likely cadging cigarettes from any passing idiot, or pressing himself up against one of the young housemaids who knew no better.

'We must have been mad to agree,' Mrs Moore muttered, materialising next to Evie again. 'Good grief, we've well over sixty wounded soldiers to feed in less than two hours, not to mention nurses, volunteers, the staff, and visiting relatives. We need to sort this out, it's a pig's ear.'

Evie looked at the clock yet again, as though it might magically have slipped back an hour. It hadn't.

At least the turkeys, geese and hams were roasting, but the Christmas puddings needed boiling for a couple of hours, and the mince pies were stacked in the pastry pantry ready to be shoved into the ovens, once there was room. Much, but not all, of the invalid food had been prepared at 5 a.m. this morning, after Evie, Annie and the two kitchenmaids had shooed the mice from the kitchen, then washed the floor and lit the furnace for the ranges.

Mrs Moore repeated, digging her hands into her hessian-apron pockets, 'Aye, as I say, a pig's ear. Come along, Evie, you'll get through to Jack, and well, you're friends of a sort with Mr Auberon. He thinks your cakes are grand and you said he asked you to be a friend to Lady Veronica whilst he was away.'

Evie hushed her. 'I don't think anyone is to know that.'

Mrs Moore kept her eyes on the two men and laughed quietly. 'Oh, lass, it's obvious. You and Lady Veronica are as tight as a drum and run this hospital as though you were both born to be bossy. I put it down to all that suffragette malarkey you have in common but whatever it is, it works. However, wielding responsibility takes practice, so get to it.' Mrs Moore pursed her lips and rolled her shoulders.

Evie pulled a face. 'Oh, that's grand, and who precisely is head cook with shoulders that should accept that responsibility but, dear me, they seem to be too busy being rolled. I presume you're intent on retreat?'

Mrs Moore smiled. 'Absolutely, since discretion is quite the better part of valour and you know right well, our Evie, that we share the role of head cook, what with my rheumatics and all what, so you just

5

get on with it. Now, mind, if the wind changes, your face will stay that way, so think on. The girls are still brushing the carrots free of storage sawdust in the vegetable pantry and you need to use your influence on these two wee lost souls, especially the onion expert who is intent on burning the house down. What on earth were you thi—?'

Evie interrupted, watching the spatula flip once again, and the knife stab. 'I was remembering that our patient, Captain Neave, said all he could smell when he first came here was the stench of blood, mud, and filth. I thought onions might break through that. Clearly not.'

Mrs Moore nodded, leaning against the table, wincing, and Evie knew she needed to sit for a while. 'Evie, what on earth can they see that we can't?' She indicated Jack who was now looking at the floor as he stabbed, and then Mr Auberon who was also staring, but at the white splash-back tiles behind the range, holding the spatula quite still now. The smoke was on the increase and the onions were irredeemably black and blue from ill-treatment. Mrs Moore nudged her. 'Quick now, get them out of here before the rest of the volunteers return from their break, you know how they talk.'

Evie sighed, for a servant didn't approach an owner, whatever relationship they might or might not have, but nevertheless stomachs would need filling. She worked her way quietly round the table, bracing herself, and raising her voice. 'Why not leave this and walk in the fresh air, Mr Auberon. There has been no more snow since your arrival yesterday evening.'

He did not react. Evie touched his arm, flinching as he spun round, the spatula lifted to strike.

'Sir,' shouted Jack, leaping forward, the knife in his hand. Evie stayed quite still as Mr Auberon stared at Jack, and then at her, his thoughts visibly clearing, the colour draining from his face. He lowered his arm. 'Stand easy, Sergeant. Forgive me, Evie. Never would I . . . Not you . . . Never. How absurd . . . And Mrs Moore.' He placed the spatula in the pan, his hands shaking. He examined the onions. 'Are they really supposed to look like that?'

The mood was broken. Mrs Moore laughed, before heading for the scullery. Evie laughed too, though her mouth was dry with shock, and her hands trembled. She said, 'I believe not, or no one would ever have stuffing with their turkey again.'

Jack was placing the razor-sharp knife on the table, looking first at it, and then his sister, and his hands were shaking, and then his whole body. By, they were all at it. Evie wanted to take the war from these two young men who were only three years her senior, and promise them that all was well, which was what her mam always said. But it wasn't, was it? They had to return to the front, tomorrow.

Instead she smiled cheerfully, which was what everyone who worked here was taught to do. 'You both need to stretch your legs, do something active, breathe in some fresh air. There will be peace and quiet as the gamekeepers are only allowed to shoot at a time suitable to the hospital, to save upsetting the patients. Come.'

She moved the pan on to the range's rest corner, leading them out of the kitchen into the bell corridor. Mr Auberon paused, looked at the bells, then at Evie, and nodded, his face even more drawn. She realised he had not seen before that the room names beneath the bells were those of a hospital.

'Everything has changed,' he murmured.

'Not everything,' she replied. 'The cedar tree on the front lawn remains the same.'

He merely nodded slightly, Jack too. Evie headed towards the back door, the men following her down the corridor like ducklings. At the door Mr Auberon reached forward and opened it, stepping aside and ushering her up the steps before him. It wasn't proper that he should do this for a servant, so perhaps he was right, almost nothing was as it used to be.

She reached the top step. Opposite were the garages, which housed the volunteers' children's playroom, run by Evie's mam, Susan Forbes. Raisin and Currant, Veronica's dachshunds that Lord Brampton had ordered to be killed on the outbreak of war, were disappearing round the corner, probably heading for the formal gardens to be spoilt by whatever patients were taking the air. Evie's family had taken them in until the Bastard left, and then they had been returned.

8

Evie stepped on to the cobbles, looking for Simon, who had said he must find a place for the head gardener to plant a rose bush in Bernie's memory. Bernie had been another under-gardener, his friend. He had died of shrapnel wounds at . . . Where was it now? Ypres? Somewhere with rain, mud and cold as well as the bloody guns, Si had said.

He was nowhere in sight. She lifted her head, taking in the grey sky. They only had today together and then the men started on their return journey, and she needed her fiancé to herself for a few hours. Surely that wasn't too much to ask? Then she closed her eyes. Stupid, greedy girl, of course it was and at least he was alive.

To the left of the garage yard the kitchen staff and volunteers were trooping down the internal corridor steps, pinching out their Woodbines. She waited, counting out the seconds, and sure enough within a minute she could hear Mrs Moore shouting, 'What time do you call this? Yes, I know some of you volunteers have given up your Christmas Day to help, but those lads upstairs have given up a sight more than that, and these vegetables won't wash or peel themselves, the table won't lay itself, the game won't find its own way into soup pans and I won't produce a smile until a grand bit of work is done. You, Sally Armitage, can wipe that look off your face, because I, for one, am not living with any more nonsense today. You scullery lasses, I need them pans and I need them now. Remember, soda and elbow grease is the key.'

9

Next to Evie both men laughed. Jack poked her. 'Aye, fresh air and peace, eh, bonny lass? I'll take the gamekeepers any day.'

The snow still just covered the cobbles, though it was scuffed by the footsteps of the volunteers who came from the pit villages of Easton, Sidon and Hawton by day and night as the rota dictated, knowing that it could have been their bairns, husbands, or brothers who needed help. She felt the chill breeze, and watched the clouds shifting fast across the sky, but then she heard her name called. 'Evie.' It was her lovely lad, Simon, hurrying across the cobbles, clutching dried sage and thyme for the stuffing, his face alight with love, his glorious red hair shining even without the sun. He slowed when he registered Mr Auberon, and started to salute, and then stopped, uncertain.

Mr Auberon called, 'No uniforms so no salutes, Simon. We'll have them back soon enough, and that bloody nonsense will start up, but for now they're being cleansed by the laundry, whilst Jack and I are sent for a walk. It appears that we're surplus to requirements, but I daresay you'll make a better fist of helping your Evie.' He laughed, but it was strained.

From the bottom step they heard another voice. It was Lady Veronica, Mr Auberon's sister, in her kitchen apron rather than her VAD uniform. 'Oh tut tut, no disappearing for anyone today. Come back here, all you able-bodied men. Poor Mr Harvey needs help organising the tables as you, Aub, have insisted everyone eats together in the ballroom ward: servants, staff, patients and visitors. This I applaud, but we need your soldierly muscle power to make it happen, or Mr Harvey will resign as butler and the place will fall apart. You too, Jack, but Simon, as a special dispensation, can have half an hour to spend with you know who, or she will quite deliberately burn the turkeys' parson's noses in retribution.'

Jack winked at Evie as he about-turned, his hair riffled by the cold breeze, as he waited for Mr Auberon to precede him. She watched them troop back down the steps, one so dark, one so fair, following Lady Veronica into the corridor. Lady Veronica called. 'Make the most of it, Evie, because though you have thus far only instructed me in the preparation of a roux and a passable cup of tea, I am here to help, so let the real havoc begin.'

'Don't worry, I have just the task, we need more onions chopped.' Lady Veronica's groan and the guffaws of the men wafted up the steps, to be cut short by Mrs Moore's bellow. 'Shut that door. We're not living in a barn.'

Evie heard Simon murmur behind her, and felt his breath on her neck. 'No, not living in a barn here, but in reserve we do. Now, I have half an hour to show you how much I love you, Evie Forbes.' She felt his arm around her waist, his kisses on her neck, and turned into him. He dropped the herbs, but the scent was still on his hands as he cupped her face. He was the same age as the other two and looked as many years older as they did, but she suspected she was no rose any more, if she ever had been. It didn't matter, he was here, he was safe for now, and what was more, he was hers. They clung to one another. 'I love you,' he repeated. 'I love you so much I could drown in it.'

'Don't,' she said against his mouth. 'Don't you dare or I will kill you myself.' They didn't laugh, because time was so short and the future so . . . what? Uncertain? Dangerous? Impossible? When would it end? Who would survive? What would happen if they lost? She buried her face in his shoulder and he rocked her back and forth and she thought again of her mother's endless sayings, which frequently drove those who knew her to want to strangle her. She would say, yet again, 'All will be well.' This time Evie found comfort in the words.

Half an hour later Lady Veronica used her hands to sweep the vegetable waste on to sheets of Mr Harvey's out-of-date *Daily Sketch*. The juice from the carrot tops seeped into the front page, which told of the Scarborough, Hartlepool and Whitby deaths and casualties resulting from the shelling by the German navy. Evie said, 'It's hard to believe, Ver.'

'Nowhere's safe, Evie,' Lady Veronica almost whispered, rolling up the waste and putting it into the compost bucket. 'How is Mrs Green's niece?'

Mrs Moore was passing. 'The shrapnel wounds to her leg are healing and she's home with her mother, and so Mrs Green will be back from Whitby within days to take up her housekeeping duties. She thanks you for the hamper, Your Ladyship, and asks after your husband. I told her Captain Richard is improving but not yet able to function downstairs. I hope you find him improved again today, slightly at least?'

Lady Veronica sat down on a stool, easing her back and wiping her hands on her apron. 'I do believe he is, Mrs Moore. Just a tad.'

Evie snatched a look at the clock before saying briskly, 'Now, enough chat, let's get the roasts out so they can rest. It won't be for long enough, but it will have to do. It'll be a bit of a trudge to get it all up to the ward, so perhaps you should suggest that Mr Auberon and his little troop help Archie and Mr Harvey transport the feast to the multitude, Lady Veronica.' She tried to remember to address Veronica properly in the company of others. She passed her a heavyweight oven cloth. 'You hoy out the turkeys if you wouldn't mind, and Annie, you take the middle range, there should be six geese in there, and watch the fat. We mustn't spill a drop as we'll need every scrap for January. Who knows what food shortages are coming? I'll handle the hams. How's the soup, Mrs Moore?'

Chaos took over for the last hour with only one mishap. Lady Veronica burned her arm. It was dusted with flour, and she was told it was a medal. She promised she'd wear it proudly.

Somehow Mr Harvey had organised the tables in the ballroom ward so that everyone could be seated, though it would be shoulder to shoulder with one's neighbour. All around would be the recovering enlisted men still bedbound; the officers had their own cubicles, created from the many bedrooms on the second floor.

For now, sherry was served in the great hall and helped to ease the social revolution that was occurring. Nicely lubricated, Mr Auberon led the gaggle into the ballroom, taking his place at the head of the long, long table covered in pristine white linen tablecloths. The fact that they were really sheets was ignored. The glasses glistened, the cutlery too. Chrysanthemums on short stalks were arranged in shallow bowls down the centre of the tables, and candles were lit in candlesticks taken from the silver safe.

Lady Wendover, a middle-aged VAD, was waiting to take her seat next to Maudie, one of the scullery maids, another VAD would sit next to Daisy, a house-maid. Evie thought they could discuss the merits of soda in the scullery, or the virtues of sprinkling tea leaves on the carpets before brushing, rather than the usual subject of how lazy the servants were. She grinned as Jack, who sat opposite her, and a few places down from Mr Auberon, raised an eyebrow. He'd always been able to read her like a book. So had her da and mam, who were to Jack's left and chuckling at her.

Mrs Moore leaned into her, saying in a voice meant to be a whisper but which was considerably louder, 'If you feed the beggars well, it will always be an occasion of cheer no matter who has to sit next to whom.'

Perhaps Mr Auberon heard, for not long after, when the turkeys had been carved on the side table, and the main course was about to begin, he proposed a toast to the kitchen, absent friends, and lastly, the King, mentioning that it was a rare occasion for cheer, grinning at Mrs Moore and Evie as he did so. After glasses were raised, sipped and replaced, they sat again, except for Roger the valet, who Evie saw hurrying to the baize door, having said to Simon that he wasn't going to sit opposite 'that monstrosity' for a minute longer. The 'monstrosity' was Sergeant Harris, who wore a tin mask to hide his facial injuries and sat alongside Captain Simmons whose nose had got lost, as he delighted in telling everyone, due to carelessness. He would then stick his thumb between his fore and middle finger and say, 'Good grief, and here it is, after all.'

As Roger stormed off Evie and Jack exchanged another look, this time one of fury. Mrs Moore said forcefully, but for the family alone, 'Then he'll go hungry. There's nothing left downstairs for even a sparrow to peck on, and with the dogs taking up both armchairs he'll have to make do with a stool.'

Evie pretended not to notice Millie, Jack's wife, flush at these words, laying down her knife and fork. Jack sat next to her, his stepson Tim on his lap, with lashings of cranberry sauce on his small plate. Evie smiled. It was a sure bet that this would be the two-year-old's favourite part of the meal. He was a lovely little lad, but was there an increasing look of his father, bloody Roger, about him? Dear God, she hoped not and if there was, that it was the end of any family resemblance.

Simon ran his hand along her arm and it was only then she saw she had gripped her knife and fork so tightly her knuckles had whitened. He nudged her with his knee and whispered, 'Stop fretting; Millie wouldn't jeopardise what she has with Jack to go chasing after the bloke who made her pregnant when she was the kitchenmaid, and dumped her. She's not that big a fool.'

Jack helped Tim to another great dollop of cranberry and shrugged when his mam said it would rot the bairn's teeth. 'Sugar could get short soon enough, Mam. It's Christmas, we'll let him, shall we?'

Soon conversations were fluttering more easily around the long table, and laughter was spreading. Bravo for Mr Auberon, Evie thought. He'd been right, everything had changed, even the nobs, but perhaps it wouldn't take long to get back to the old order once the war was over, if it ever was. Evie whispered, 'Si, we must remember this: good food, good company, and wine. When things get difficult let's just think of it. I prefer it to looking up at a moon dangling in the sky like the poets say.'

He laughed. 'It's because you live and breathe cooking, and I love you for it. One day I'll be home, we'll all be home and you can get on with sorting our dream of a hotel, at last.'

She lifted her glass of chilled white wine, taking a large sip, more a gulp really, but by, she needed it. Within seconds it seemed her shoulders were low, her muscles felt loose, her smile was growing. 'You will sing and fiddle for the wedding parties and we can get Bern . . .' She stopped. Bernie had been killed, so too Jack's marra, his close pitman friend, Mart Dore.

Jack had been listening and leaned forward, stroking Tim's dark hair. 'We'll come back, Evie pet. We'll all come back.'

Mam said, 'All will be well.' The family laughed and Da patted his wife's shoulder. It was then Evie noticed that Millie's place was empty. 'Where is she?'

Jack shrugged. 'She's gone for more cranberry sauce.'

Mam murmured, 'I told her there was some further along by Captain Neave but she was determined.' She mouthed, 'Showing off for Jack, I reckon.'

Evie placed her serviette on the table, and started to rise, her food like ashes in her mouth. 'I'll help her. She probably doesn't know where it is.'

Simon pulled her back down, saying for her ears only, his blue eyes determined, 'Let someone else do something for a change. Every moment with you is precious. She'll find what she's after.'

That was what Evie feared, because the only other person down there was Roger.

Jack was watching and listening, and now he leaned forward yet again, saying quietly, 'Let it go, pet. It's the bairn that's important. Over my dead body will he have Tim, who deserves better, and, by, I don't want to have to keep leaning over like this to calm you down, it's causing havoc with me innards.'

She laughed. Jack grinned, lifting a finger towards the baize door. 'Here she is with the cranberry, so I reckon you've counted two and two and made ten.'

Millie sat, avoiding everyone's eyes, her hair adrift from her cap, and Evie would have bet that nearer ten was right after all. Stupid woman. She always had been and always would be, and why had Jack ever married her? But she knew why, and it was best left alone.

After the meal the nurses sang Christmas carols under Matron's Amazonian conducting, and were joined by several of the wounded, as well as Simon and Evie, and Dr Nicholls, the Medical Officer. It was Simon whose solos brought the audience to their feet, his pure notes taking them from the present to a quieter, more blessed time. Jack told Evie how Simon had stilled everyone's hearts in the trenches, during a lull in the fighting, when he had sung 'Oh for the wings of a dove'.

For that moment she allowed happiness to enter.

Chapter 2

Easterleigh Hall, 26th December 1914

Overnight, light snow had fallen, but that didn't deter Mr Auberon and Jack from joining Old Stan, the head gardener, in the arboretum to drag out the roots of a swathe of old trees cut down a few days before Christmas. Every spare space was to be used for vegetables, Captain Richard had insisted in a memo sent from his convalescent bed to the usual staff breakfast meeting in the kitchen on 23rd December. He had ended, *'The Atlantic is relatively safe for merchant shipping, but for how long? We must be responsible. We must sidestep shortages.'*

In the kitchen, a Boxing Day morning would perhaps have dawdled for Evie in a perfect world, allowing her time for Simon, but it rushed past in the face of the never-ending demands of the kitchen. This was due, in part, to the fact that Mrs Moore, and Evie, had decreed that invalids needed food when their body clocks insisted, not when Matron's chimed. At first Matron had hitched her vast bosom and huffed, but it was a token gesture. Almost immediately she had said, 'I have never had a kitchen willing to put the patients first. My thanks to you and your staff and volunteers.'

At eleven, whilst the turkey stock was simmering, and the calves'-foot jelly setting for invalid support, Mrs Moore and Lady Veronica ordered Evie and Simon to the servants' hall, to sit on one of the ancient overstuffed and torn sofas. 'At once, Evie, and turf those dachshunds out who have tried a different venue. They should be stretching their little legs,' Lady Veronica paused. 'The clock is ticking. Simon needs to see the rest of his family, who I believe are travelling to his parents in Easton for the day. Are you quite sure you won't go with him? If you do, I will follow Mrs Moore's instructions to the letter, I promise, and to prove it, I will now obey her and make the mayonnaise for luncheon.'

'Must you?' Evie said, grimacing. 'Just a drop of oil at a time, remember. We don't want another disaster.' Lady Veronica sniffed. 'It wasn't that bad. Now will you go with Simon to Easton?'

Evie longed to, but their lives were not their own at the moment, and he had said he needed time with his family, and that her patients needed her. She shook her head, and Lady Veronica ordered, 'Get along with you, then.'

Mrs Moore was opening the door into the central corridor as Simon tugged Evie along. Mrs Moore waved them through. 'I'll leave a bundle of carrots by the back door for Old Saul, that lovely old pony of your da's, lad. Aye, he does grand work carting in the volunteers. There're a few bits for the table and all. Now, go.'

Simon kissed the cook, hugging her ample body to him. 'You're a belter, Mrs Moore. If I didn't already love Evie I'd be after you.' He earned a twisted ear for his pains. Mrs Moore called the dachshunds, who scampered into the kitchen after scraps, and far from stretching their legs they took over the armchairs again, scrabbling amongst the knitting. The door was slammed behind them. Evie and Simon crossed the central corridor into the servants' hall, which was empty, presumably on Mrs Moore's orders. It was a wasted effort though, because as Evie nestled into Simon's arms there was no comfort to be found against his braced body.

She lifted her head and saw that he was looking from one oozing horsehair tear in the sofa to another. She waited, so used was she to recognising the signs of anguish in their patients, to the point where, a few weeks ago, she had suggested to Dr Nicholls that she should ask new patients about their favourite foods, and produce it for them. It had helped some to connect again with the normal world. God bless food; the sight of it, the taste and smell. It could ease aside savage images, and reclaim better times.

Simon removed his arm from around her and leaned forward, his elbows on his knees, his hands clasping and unclasping. 'The tears are like wounds that I can smell and see. It's what we live with. Will it be me next? Will I lose my face? It's so easy, you

21

see. You're in the trench. You peer over. Bang. Shrapnel takes your face. Bang, you're dead.'

He stood and paced before her, and Evie wondered if it had been the best idea to mix these lads in with the wounded for lunch yesterday. She stood, taking his hands. 'We'll walk. You must show me where Old Stan is to plant the rose for Bernie.'

She hurried him through the kitchen, noting that Lady Veronica was adding the oil drop by drop, and Mrs Moore and Annie were embarking on the vegetables. She snatched her coat from the hook in the bell corridor and his khaki greatcoat from his pack by the bootbox, heading up the steps into the snow-heavy wind.

She shrugged into her coat, pulling the collar up around her neck. He did the same, lifting his head, sniffing the air as gardeners do. All sounds seemed muted as they walked arm in arm, sometimes slipping and sliding in the snow, round the back of the house and into the formal gardens. A few hardy soldiers and airmen, who were almost fully recovered, were slapping their hands and puffing on their pipes, or smoking their forbidden cigarettes.

Dr Nicholls, who had been the district's doctor before he had been seconded into uniform to head the medical staff at Easterleigh Hall, harangued them almost daily on the disgusting habit. 'Soiling your lungs, dammit, after we've spent time and effort putting you back together.' He became so red-faced on the subject that Evie and Lady Veronica felt that one day he would burst with indignation, though Matron said it would be from too much pudding.

Evie told Simon this as he headed for the southern face of the garden, and he laughed in reply. A sergeant called to her. 'Great meal, Evie. Marry me and we'll live like kings.' Another, Colonel Masters said, 'Stand down, Sergeant. She'll choose me if it's anyone.'

Evie called, 'You're all out of luck. It's Si who'll get fat around my table.'

They reached the rose bed Simon and Bernie had dug, manured, and planted. Simon slipped his arms round her and held her against him. 'Here, Old Stan will plant it, here. Bernie was our rose expert. Loved the buggers, he did. Do it for me too, will you, next to his, if . . .'

There was a long pause, because there was little point in telling him it wouldn't happen. She said eventually, trying not to cry, 'I'll do it for you, but we must hope. We truly must.' It was easy enough for her to say, when she was just picking up the pieces, and not in jeopardy herself.

They walked on, round the wall surrounding the nursery plants and back past the stables which had been turned into winter quarters for the pigs after the horses had been taken by the army. Evie's da and Simon's helped to tend them, but today it was Sergeant Harris, in his face mask, carrying a bucket of vegetable peelings, together with a couple of corporals whose wounds were healing more quickly than they would have liked. Simon squeezed her to him. 'Poor bugger.'

They returned to the warmth of the kitchen and she shooed Lady Veronica back to the acute cases ward where she had begun to work, under the eagle eye of Ward Sister Annie Newsome. It had taken a syrup pudding from Evie for Matron, and the threat of no more, ever, for her to agree to allow Lady Veronica to move on from VAD dusting, sweeping and sterilising to try her hand at proper nursing. The acute cases ward was to test her dedication, Lady Veronica suspected. Auxiliary hospitals were not originally intended for serious cases, but this war was determining otherwise.

Evie called, gathering up the cocoa and milk, 'You'll be late, Lady Veronica. It's almost eleven. Matron will have your guts for garters.' She left.

Mrs Moore was either in the cold pantry or resting in her room. Evie and Simon sat on stools side by side at the table, drinking cocoa. He wiped the moustache from her top lip with his thumb and kissed her. She tasted his cocoa and all fear, all worry faded for that moment. She opened her eyes and saw the clock. It was time. His parents, together with his aunt and uncle who had walked in from Hawton, would be waiting for him at home. 'Come with me after all,' he said, kissing her hands.

She shook her head. 'I want to, but I can't, I have the patients to feed. Mrs Moore did the back shift and needs a rest.'

He kissed her mouth again, heedless of Millie who slipped past them, heading for the kettle. It was time for a brew of tea for the laundry staff, and as Millie lifted it on to the range hotplate she said, 'It's all right for that old bag Mrs Moore to put her feet up, then? I was awake all night with your brother shouting when he slept, pacing when he didn't, and was I allowed to slip to my room like Mrs Moore? Well, no, what I've had to do is work solidly since I had to hike to the crossroads for the pickup cart, and Old Saul clopping through the snow as though he's a ruddy snail. I'm right worn out and not in the right way. I expected better from a husband I haven't seen for months, I'll tell you that for nothing.'

Simon's grip on his mug seemed to tighten. 'It's the guns and . . . well, everything, Millie. It gets to you. You can't sleep in the quiet, and when you do sleep you hear them and . . . Well, everything. You could try being understanding.'

Millie put her hands on her hips. 'Well, what about understanding me for a bloody change? The uniforms are ready, hung up in the laundry, well away from the boiling coppers so they won't be steamy and damp. Disgusting they were, alive with lice, stinking like a lav. Right worn out we are, too.' She strutted back to the laundry, which was off the central corridor. Evie rested her head on Simon's shoulder. 'What would it take to change her? Should I lock her in the coal cellar for a year?' For the first time that morning she wondered where Roger was.

They collected Simon's uniform. It was pristine and louse-free and smelt of soap. Evie felt a flicker of gratitude towards Millie. As Simon left the laundry to dress in the nurse's changing room Ethel called across, 'It was Dottie and me who worked right hard on those, Evie, and an honour it was too.' Millie flushed and returned to the kitchen to make the tea.

On Simon's return he looked grand, from his ankle boots and puttees right up to his cap. Evie walked with him as he wheeled his bike through the garage yard and past the stables with only Tinker, Lady Veronica's pony, to snuffle his farewells, against the sound of pigs rooting in the straw. Sergeant Harris waved. 'Keep your head down, lad.' His voice was muffled by his mask.

Evie and Simon walked on to the gravelled drive and stood outside the front of the house. In the centre of the huge lawn was the cedar tree. 'Just as strong and unmoving as ever,' Simon murmured, his arm tight around Evie.

'In spite of breathing in all that smoke day after day,' Evie laughed gently, because there were her favourites, Captain Neave with his almost healed broken femur, alongside young Lieutenant Harry Travers with his crutches and one leg, both smoking for England and keeping a permanent lookout for Dr Nicholls. 'You'll be left with a twitch, young Harry,' Evie called. He laughed. 'Keep your head down, Simon,' he shouted.

Simon waved, but turned to Evie. 'God, I miss you every moment we're apart,' he said into her neck. 'I don't know when my next leave will be. You'll write?'

'Always,' she said. 'Just think of yesterday when you need strength. Think of the chatter, the laughter, the warmth, and your friends. Remember singing for us all, and most of all, remember me.'

They clung to one another until he tore free and cycled through the snow, head down, pack on. Evie watched him until he reached the gate at the end of the drive and turned left for Easton. She felt empty, her legs heavy. In the distance she could see Stunted Tree Hill looming over Farmer Froggett's farm, near to which was her family home. She dragged her shawl around her shoulders, waved briefly at Harry and John Neave and hurried back to the kitchen.

Jack and Evie ate lunch in the servants' hall with their mam and da, Tim and Millie and the rest of the staff, including Roger, who had apparently been kept busy by Mr Auberon, polishing his boots, belts and anything leather, and brushing down all the clothes in his dressing room. Perhaps his master realised that Roger was not the most popular person below stairs?

There had been very little turkey left, but enough to create a splendid soup, served with the barley bread with which Evie and Mrs Moore were experimenting in case of wheat shortages. It was accompanied by cheese from Home Farm dairy, Mrs

Green's tomato pickle, and the remains of the goose and ham. Lamb stew had been sent up for the patients, and wheat bread, which they preferred. Two young men had had special requests. One was scrambled egg, and the other was liver and bacon. This was encouraging, because they had both been listless and unaware until Evie visited them late last night to see if she could stimulate them into showing interest in eating. They were sitting up today. It was a crucial first step.

The volunteers had laid up the table in the servants' hall under the footman's eagle eye. Archie had been asked by Mr Harvey to delay volunteering for the war, as the butler needed support with his duties, but how long he would stay, who knew. He was now laying up the beer that had been sent down by Mr Auberon, who was lunching with his sister and brother-in-law up in Lady Veronica's suite. Mr Auberon would be meeting up with Jack and Simon at Easton Miners' Club, and would take them to Gosforn station in old Ted's taxi. Ted's driving was hit and miss but somehow he got people to where they needed to be, usually in one piece though the taxi was increasingly battered, and the hedgerows showed ever more signs of damage.

It seemed no time at all before Evie was out again by the cedar tree, waving farewell to her brother, alone, because Millie had said she couldn't face seeing Jack leave. Her mam and da had hugged him tight in the kitchen, where he had insisted they stay.

Tim had followed him up the steps into the garage yard, clinging to his leg, crying, until Mam had eased him away and carried him down with the promise of a biscuit.

As Jack walked away, following Simon's tracks, heaving his pack up on to his back, Evie called softly, determined that he must have some joy, some good memory to take back with him, 'Jack, please go to the beck, for me. It's important that you do. Trust me. You need the beauty.'

He turned, and waved. 'Bonny lass, I need to get to Mart's to see his uncle and mam, to tell what I know about his death.'

'Promise, Jack. Do it for me.'

He shrugged. 'For you, lass, but you should walk there, too. It would be grand for you to get away from the kitchen once in a while.'

He saluted, and began to walk away again. Evie ran after him, snatching at his arm, her shawl slipping from her shoulders. She said urgently, 'You joined up with Mr Auberon's North Tyne Fusiliers to kill him for causing our Timmie's death when he deliberately put him in a dangerous area in the pit, but he's still with us?'

He grinned down at her, shaking his head. 'Such an elephant you are, you never forget the rubbish I talk. He was a lad like the rest of us, put in to manage a pit by his bastard of a father. He had no experience and he made a mistake, letting his feelings get the better of him because I was a union man, a thorn in his side. Aye, pet, he punished us for my activities by putting the Forbes family in poor seams, but hate gets to be a habit. It's a dark and dismal bugger and takes up space inside your mind and maybe . . . Ah well, we'll see. You've moved on past it, I can see you have. Besides, there are enough shells banging about without me getting involved.'

She blocked his path. 'That's no answer.'

He moved her to one side. 'I've got to go, Evie.' He stooped and kissed her, his dark eyes the same colour as his hair, coal dust embedded in his skin, blue scars on his brow, and she could hardly bear to let him go, but she did, watching as he walked on, looking at the cedar tree. He called back over his shoulder, 'I'm going to see our bonny lad first.'

Evie nodded. 'Of course you are.'

He waved and walked on, hearing her call, 'I've slipped a package into your pack. Have a look and deliver it when you're in France.' He just waved again.

Jack felt the gravel and snow shifting beneath his boots, heard Evie add, 'Be safe, be lucky.' There goes the pitman's prayer, he thought and it works as well for a soldier. He dragged in deep breaths, but all he could smell was France. He reached the road, turned left and almost immediately right, down the rutted lane with its iced puddles, and the deeper snow drifted up against the hedge. The gate was snow-crusted, and looked much like Evie's Christmas cakes, if you stretched the imagination a mile. It screeched as he shoved it open, the snow banking up behind it.

The churchyard nestled several fields away from the Hall, but was still in the grounds. It was the Protestant village church, and there was no way his mam would have had Tim laid to rest in chapel land. At the time of the funeral Jack had objected to Timmie being buried on Brampton land, but where else was there?

The snow had almost covered the many footprints that led the way to Jack's brother. He added to them, knowing he could have found his way blindfold. He reached the grave, it too was cloaked in snow. He stood looking down, and when he could speak he said, 'Well, bonny lad, I forgot what a fine spot it is here. Quiet. Bit of birdsong, and there'll be violets in the spring. You'll be liking that. It's a damn sight better than being tossed into them great graves with a mass of others with no birds, just bloody artillery blasting overhead. Remember you thought you'd heard a cuckoo in February, or was it earlier? Bloody great pigeon, wasn't it?' He stopped talking, feeling his voice shake.

He looked back at the church where the burial service had taken place and he and Millie had been married, in that order, with Parson Manton presiding. 'Well, lad, what else could I do but marry her after she had been brought to us by Evie to have the bairn? Better than the workhouse by a mile. Millie named him after you, and that helped Mam, it did. So, as I say, what else could I do and what the hell does it matter?

'Aye Timmie, it's all a bit of a bloody mess, wouldn't you say? Your lead soldiers were simpler, bonny lad.' He surveyed the landscape: the hills that hid Easton's Auld Maud pit, the Stunted Tree hill. He slung off his pack, hunkered down and wiped the headstone clean of snow. He traced the words chiselled by Da: Timmie Forbes 1897–1913.

'At least you're with your lead soldiers and your marra.' He nodded hello to Tony, who lay beside his family's lovely lad. He liked to think they were riding Galloways, the pit ponies they had loved, across fields in another world, not this crazy one. 'Bad was it, Tony, man? But they brought you back from the Marne to the Hall. You wanted to smell bacon the night you were dying, our Evie said. So she cooked it for you and you died with your mam by your bed. I thank whatever bloody idiot thinks he's God, for that. So much bloody life left unlived for you two, eh. Perhaps the rest of us can live it for you if . . .' He stopped.

At the base of the gravestones, jam jars held holly. The water had frozen but not cracked the glass yet. Jack had sworn he would not, but he cried, brushing the snow from both graves, until his hands were red, wet and numb.

He took a lead soldier he had bought in Southampton from his pocket and placed it by

Timmie's jam jar. 'Not like the ones you painted, but it'll last even if I don't. But look, Timmie, I have to tell you something, it's difficult and I'm not sure what you'll think, but I'm finding it hard to carry the hate for the Bastard's whelp any more. I know, I know, lad, but I think that the cart that killed you would have run away in any seam, on any slope. I punched him in the front line when he stopped me going to find Mart's body, but he let it go when he could have had me shot. It was then I felt . . .'

He waited a moment, wanting permission to let go of the hatred he had felt for Auberon, but knowing he was bloody daft to expect a voice to boom out and give it. He patted the headstone one more time, and rose, hauling up his pack, wiping a freezing wet hand across his face. The wind was getting up now. Had Timmie understood? 'We're not marras, you know, me and him, but we're something. Perhaps it's just that we're soldiers? I call him Auberon now, in private. Not a lot of the bosses allow that.' He looked down at the grave again, and left, saying once more at the gate, 'Aye, we're something.'

He marched quickly, turning at the Cross Trees crossroads, glancing at the middle spruce, which was where they'd hung highwaymen not that long ago. An hour later Jack reached the turn-off to the beck, where he and all the local bairns had dammed the stream to create a pool for swimming. He checked his watch. Why not, he had time? He hurried along the track, slipping through Froggett's ploughed fields to cut off the corner. Last time he'd been here, with Evie, there had been a kingfisher. Did it still come in the summer? Why not, there were still trees – here. 'Why not' seemed to be something he said too often.

He slipped through the gate on to the path and along the bank towards the dam, and remembered the feel of the water on coal-slecked skin when they were older and coming straight from the pit. He could feel the plunge into the dam, then the calm of the sky as he lay on his back watching the clouds scudding, the tug as Mart took him underwater, the bugger. He laughed. Aye, he'd been a bonny bugger all right. He reached the beck, picked up a stone and tossed it into the water. 'For you, lad.' Another stone. 'For you, Timmie,' he whispered. Another. 'For you, Tony.' One more, for Grace. God keep her safe. He watched until the ripples died, squatting on his haunches. He stayed, and stayed, rising at last when his legs hurt and his back ached. Aye, it was beautiful here, Evie was right. She usually was.

He made for the road again, his boots muddy, his puttees too, damn and blast it. He walked into Easton, past the parsonage. He would not look, he had promised himself he would not, but of course he did. The windows were dark, but they would be. Parson would be on his rounds and the parson's sister, Grace, was nursing in France. It was as well. He marched on, facing front. Ahead and around were the conical slag heaps, seething and fuming, the winding engines glinting in the sun, and over everything hung the smell of sulphur. Now he was really home.

Lieutenant the Honourable Auberon Brampton watched from his bedroom window as Evie waved to Jack's departing back. Her shawl had slipped and one end was trailing in the snow. She would be shivering. Behind him Roger opened the door from the dressing room. Auberon turned. His valet was in his private's uniform and had therefore metamorphosed into his batman once more. 'I have your clothes ready, sir, and your boots have a high gleam.'

Auberon nodded. What a bloody silly way to fight a war, with gleaming boots, and one's servant alongside to cater for one's needs, and what a servant. He tried not to let his distaste show, remembering the stories he had heard from below stairs. He dressed quickly, allowing Roger to brush his shoulders, spotless though they were. His uniform belt was buffed. Had he used spit as well as polish on this, likewise the boots? The thought of going to war with Roger's spittle accompanying him was so utterly bloody ridiculous that he had to walk to the window and look out again, or laugh in the harsh manner that overwhelmed him all too often. It was all so damned surreal. He pushed the window further open and breathed in the icy air. Evie had gone, back into the warmth. Jack had disappeared.

Roger coughed behind him. Auberon closed the

window. The room became quiet and it was too strange, this silence. He said, still looking out but this time across the lawn to the hills beyond, and then back to the cedar tree, 'Best finish the packing, then, Private.'

Auberon was unsurprised at what he had overheard between Evie and her brother. If Jack, as boss, had used his power to do the dirty on him and it had resulted in the death of Veronica, he would have wanted to stick a knife in his gullet. He had been that boss, an arrogant, angry, bloody fool, and who knew if it was over between them? But it was only in Jack's provenance to declare a truce. He leaned forward, resting his forehead on the icy windowpane, feeling strange, out of place. He was torn between wanting to be back there amongst the normality of chaos, screams, the sudden laughter, the sense of belonging, the comradeship and grief, but also desperate not to be.

Behind him Roger was packing his silver-backed brushes. Silver brushes, for God's sake. Auberon checked his battle-scarred wristwatch. Too much time had passed, and he had things to do. He hurried down to the second floor, moving steadily to his father's study, hearing the noises of the hospital all around: the groans, a laugh, a scream, a 'Hush'. A nurse hurried past with a kidney bowl covered in corrugated paper. Veronica was working in the Acute Injuries Ward, and who on earth would have thought it? Well, his mother, for a start, God bless her good democratic heart. How she would have applauded Ver's suffrage activities.

Another nurse, Sister Moss, came from the Blue Sitting Room, now divided into a Rest and Recreation area for officers and nurses. The VADs had their own area in the servants' hall.

Sister Moss was checking her watch, which was pinned above her heart. He smiled at her hurried greeting, then opened the door into his father's study, a place that had held such misery for him in the form of beatings too numerous to count. His father might be a lord, created by the Liberals in 1907, and his appalling stepmother a lady in her own right by virtue of her poverty-stricken aristocratic family, but you couldn't remove the inner man and woman.

He shut the door quietly behind him, leaning against it. The aura of the man remained, though his father had not been here for months, not since he had slammed his way here, having brought the back of his hand across Veronica's face at dinner when she dared to mock him, or so she had told Auberon when they met at Newcastle Central station as he and his men were embarking for the Front. He shook away the memory of the bruises she had exhibited on her face. That time he had not been able to take the beating for her.

He turned the key, checked that the door was firmly locked, and strode across the Indian carpet to the vast walnut desk in a way he could never, perhaps, have done, had he not killed his fair share of men. Some he had killed at quarters close enough to smell and touch them before ramming his knife into their guts, looking into their eyes. No, he would never let that bastard lift a hand to anyone again. Instead he would probably kill him. But he wouldn't think of that now.

There was a window overlooking the side of the house, and another at the front. The clouds were thickening. Was there more snow on the way? Would it hold up Ted in his taxi? Would it make bivouacking in France and standing there in the trenches that were being dug everywhere even more of a bloody misery? He must hurry.

He dragged a piece of paper from his pocket, checking the numbers Miss Wainton, their beloved governess and his dead mother's friend, had given him before he left for Oxford University. She had advised him to keep it safe, and secret. It was the last time he had seen her alive. But he wouldn't think of Wainey now. He had work to do.

He skirted the two large sofas set either side of the fireplace, which was laid with the best coal from Auld Maud, but not lit. Auberon removed the oil painting of London Bridge hanging to the right of the fireplace, revealing the safe. He turned the combination lock, hoping it remained the same. There was a click, then another until it was done. He turned the brass handle and pulled the door open. Auberon found he was holding his breath. He made himself suck in air, right down, and again. He steadied his hands and took out the stack of papers, carrying them to the desk, shoving aside the blotter, making space.

He returned to the safe and pressed the right-hand corner of the back panel. He pulled it down. Inside there were many more papers. He carried these to the table, and laid them down, too. His hands were shaking. He drew in more deep breaths, and steadied himself. It was like going over the top of the sand-bagged trenches into the rattling guns. He removed the folded parchment deeds, laying them to one side; these were not what he needed.

Outside the snow was falling in earnest; it darkened the room. There was enough light for him, though. He leafed through the papers. Please don't let him have taken it to one of his other lairs. He had seen the letter on the desk during a beating for failing to prevent the parson and the Forbes family buying Farmer Froggett's houses; the only independent houses in the pit village. He had seen the letter, and the letterhead, but it had held little interest until the war began. Now it could hold the power to change his and Veronica's future security and the well-being of everyone under this man's thumb, especially the miners.

He reached the end of the pile. God damn it. It wasn't here. There were the usual figures on the Leeds brickworks, the steelworks, mines and the new armaments and netting factories, which were possibly legitimate, but they were of no interest to him. He swung round to scan the safe. Had he left anything? No. He rubbed his hands over his face. Think. Think.

He made himself begin again, slowly, slowly, turning the papers face down as he started a 'seen' pile. And there it was, halfway through, the letter with a German factory address, and another, more recent, dated 5th August 1914. How had he missed them? He held them up towards the window, to read in the weakening light. He scanned the fractured English of both, quickly. He replaced the earlier one, but placed the more recent letter on the blotter. It contained the name of a German company, and one in the Dutch port of Rotterdam. He read the recognisable words 'acetone' and 'cordite', not enough to bring his father down, but it was a start.

He sat at the desk and wrote a letter to Veronica, blotting it and tearing the blotting paper from the pad, ripping it into strips so that nothing could be deciphered. He burnt the strips in the metal waste-paper bin. He put his letter and the most recent one from the German firm in an envelope, sealing it with wax. How dramatic. But it must only be opened if he died or became totally insane, which seemed to him a distinct possibility. He laughed. He must be mad to prefer northern France to England.

He put everything else back as he had found it, then locked the safe, replaced the painting and shoved the envelope in his uniform pocket. He retraced his footsteps to the door and unlocked it, slipping out into the corridor. He was shaking, but that might not be because of his father; it was something that was beginning to happen with monotonous regularity. It comforted him that Jack sometimes shook when they wrote their letters of condolence in the dugout by the light of a candle.

One of the irritations of the front line was the lack of jam jars in which to stick the bloody candles. Auberon's captain, Alan Bridges, similarly regretted that the supply was so limited. 'Glass shatters so easily these days,' he would say, tutting at the German artillery which frequently fixed their position accurately and rocked the ground around them, causing the jam jar with its candle to crash to the ground, plunging them into darkness. 'Mother wouldn't like the mess.' It was funny, really and truly funny, every time he said it.

Auberon made his way to his sister's room. On the door was the label *Lady Veronica*. Inside, though, would be Captain the Honourable Richard Williams, who had returned some time ago, severely injured. His progress had been slow but now, under his wife's care, he was improving daily. He knocked gently, knowing that Ver was downstairs, making yet more beef tea to be available day and night for the badly wounded. He had gathered that rum was also on the menu and probably did a damn sight more good, but he hadn't shared that information with any of the kitchen staff. His bravery had its limits, and getting on the wrong side of Evie, Mrs Moore or Ver was beyond the call of duty. 'Come.' Richard's voice was weak but at least he was speaking.

Auberon entered, making his way towards the bed where Richard was sitting against heaped pillows. The curtains were drawn back and weak sun entered. The snow shower had ceased. Richard lifted his remaining arm, the right, in a sort of wave. His left leg had been amputated below the knee. What remained of his left ear was jagged. His cheek had been scorched and torn by the shrapnel. Once he had been handsome but now he was not, though he was loved. He had told Auberon on Christmas Eve that he much preferred the latter.

Auberon sat on the easy chair beside the bed. 'Ver's doing her bit in the ward, then?'

Richard laughed. 'Indeed she is. I'm sorry you're going back and bloody glad I'm not.' The two men exchanged a glance. 'It's worse now, isn't it?' Richard asked.

Auberon smiled. 'It's never been a picnic. You were right, it's an industrial war and absurd to think in terms of a short conflict. We're entrenched, deep in mud, blood and shit, and the war of movement is finished. It will be a rotten hideous slog and we've a chance of winning if the generals realise that attacking is absurd; it's sitting it out defensively that will bring most of us home in one piece. Or so say I, and what do I know? I'm glad you're out of it, and that Ver's come to her senses and is pleased you're here. It was all the years with Father, you see. Well, you know what she's told you about the beatings he gave me. I think she saw you as capable of the same violence, perhaps also that you would stop her doing what she wanted.'

'I know, old chap. We're getting our lives . . . arranged.' Richard eased his back, moved the stump of his leg. 'It's as well she is a determined woman with a mind, a proper mind, because look at me. But I like the fact that she and Evie didn't approve of the violence of the suffragettes, nor did the parson's sister, Grace. But, for all that, they make a frightening trio, you know. Grace was home on leave two weeks ago and supported Evie's campaign to let Ver loose on the patients by telling Matron that when Evie gave her word, she kept it. So no more pudding meant just that. I'm pleased that at last Ver has a couple of proper friends, especially in Evie, which is a strange one, in this day and age. Light me a cigarette, would you, old lad, bloody difficult one-handed.' Richard's hair was long, and fell into his eyes. His face was drawn.

Auberon did so, then lit his own, snapping shut his silver cigarette case. Richard looked at him through the spiralling smoke. 'Grace Manton found me in a clearing station and I was on that bloody train before the surgeon could stop her. Straight to Le Touquet. Evie shoved Veronica on a train this end, in spite of her protests. You know, old lad, I thought she might not come and I wouldn't be able to say goodbye. I loved her but knew she didn't love me. Your stepmama and my mama are a formidable force, you know, and pushed the poor girl into the marriage.'

Auberon nodded, feeling uncomfortable. One didn't usually share such things. It was women's talk, but the wounded were different. He had heard this from Richard before, several times, but the wounded man's memory was strange and he repeated himself. Dr Nicholls said it would perhaps improve and then had shouted, removing his pipe to do so, 'If you'd had a mighty crack on your thick head, wouldn't you be a bit knocked sideways?'

Auberon had replied, 'Probably. By the way, it's one rule for the men – no smoking – and one for you, is it?'

Nicholls had grunted, 'Pipes are different and enough of your impertinence.' He had charged on his way to the next crisis.

Richard was muttering again, waving his cigarette in the air. 'I believe Ver has a cause, you know, with the hospital, and I think that it makes her happy. All I have to do, it seems, is to step to one side and let her work, and her love will continue to grow. Or so Evie said. I think I should get a cauldron for all three of them, but especially . . .'

Auberon reached for the ashtray on the bedside table and held it beneath the growing ash on Richard's cigarette, and then his own. Both of them tapped, the ash fell. 'Evie,' Auberon finished for him.

'Yes, a cauldron might be good, but nothing bad would be created, just some of her special magic.'

Both men laughed.

Auberon stubbed out his cigarette in the ashtray he had laid down on the sheets, and dug into his pocket. 'I have this letter. I need you to keep it for me, safely. If I don't return, I need you to pass it to Ver for me. Make her use it. You'll need additional information, from Father's deposit box in a bank in Rotterdam. You won't understand at the moment, but I repeat, make her use it, and help her to do so. Now where can I put it that you'll remember, but where it isn't obvious?'

Richard pointed towards his portmanteau, his cigarette almost finished. 'There's an inside pocket. It contains my will. Put it there, then it will be found if either of us pops our clogs, old lad. Now, have I told you that we have bought you boots with a heel that contains a compass? Did I? I know I forget. Your batman has packed them but you must wear them in action.'

'Yes, you have told me, but it's unlikely I'll need it. Not done to be caught by the Hun, better to die.'

Richard's ash fell on to his pristine sheets. 'Sister Newsome will murder me, that she will. Calls it a fire hazard to be smoking in bed. Don't be bloody silly, don't die, think of Veronica. If there's nothing else for it, you must stick your bloody hands up and surrender, others do. Yes, you'll have to fill a bloody form in on your return giving a damn good reason

45

but sometimes there's no alternative, or so my general said, so hands up, live. Then use the compass to get yourself back to the lines, pretty damn quick. They should insist we all carry one. Well, now you do. Now, have I told you how I thought Ver might not come to fetch me?' Auberon smothered his sigh and lit them another cigarette. If he stayed much longer he'd *ask* for a bullet in the brain. 'No, what was that then, Richard?'

Auberon had half an hour before Ted and his taxi arrived. He had promised himself tea and fancies in the kitchen, just as he and Veronica had done before the war. They'd probably be in Evie's way but if they were, she'd tell them. The very thought amused him.

He headed through the green baize door and along the internal corridor, his boots ringing on the tiles, and into the kitchen. Veronica had the tea ready and the fancies. She laughed at his face. 'No, don't worry, Evie made them, not me.'

But that wasn't why his smile had faded. Veronica said, 'Evie thought we'd like time to ourselves, so they've all taken their breaks and Sister Newsome has given me half an hour.' Auberon looked at the servants' hall, and there they all were, knitting something khaki. The war was everywhere. Evie was knitting a balaclava for which someone would be thankful.

Ver was pouring tea into enamel mugs. 'You don't

mind a mug do you, Aub, but we haven't time for niceties.'

He laughed. 'And we have, out there?'

Behind her the pan of beef tea was almost finished, except for skimming the fat. The tea poured, he watched as she reached for a sheet of greaseproof paper, stood by the range, laid it on the pan's surface, soaked up some of the fat, placed the paper on a plate beside the pan. Again and again she did it until it was fat-free. They talked of nothing of importance, except for the fact that Ver was trying to knit a pair of socks, and would use Kitchener's stitch to create a seam-free finish. 'Hopefully fewer blisters,' she muttered, nodding towards her needles stuck into the ball of wool on the armchair. Raisin and Currant were curled up beside it, asleep.

He said, 'You've no idea how blessed you will be by some soldier out there. Keep at it, keep making them, trench foot is a bastard and blisters are harmless but bloody painful. I have a feeling our mother would be doing exactly the same. Do you still miss her?'

Ver smiled at him. 'Always. She died too young, and she'd know that we knit because we're so worried, all the time. Grace writes to us from her VAD perspective and here we live amongst some of the results. But then again we don't *really* know. We can only imagine. What more can we do for you all, dearest Aub? How do you get through it?'

He sipped his tea. 'Do you remember Saunders, my old tutor? He always talked of the River Somme, which is Celtic for tranquillity. He'd fished it. Said it was a slice of heaven. I think of that. One day, I'll go, when this is over. But in the meantime, Ver, there's a sense of it here, tranquillity I mean. It's partly because Father's absent.'

'Partly?'

He said nothing more but looked into the servants' hall again, seeing Evie, the tilt of her head, the frown of concentration. Then it was time to go. Ver walked with him through the great hall and down the steps to where the taxi waited. Roger sat in the front, the luggage in the boot. Auberon said, 'It seems better with Richard, Ver.'

'Aub, I love him. It's as though everything is beginning to settle. He drives me to distraction with the repetition, but it is improving. Evie's father and Tom Wilson, the blacksmith, are making him false limbs for when Dr Nicholls says his stumps can cope. Simon's father helps too. It's wonderful. We're all working together and the mood is good, but then of course there are times when we have to telegraph a relative with the worst news. We send telegrams to the enlisted men's families too, though the army doesn't. Did you know that, Aub? Their families have to wait for letters and it can take weeks.'

Auberon could not bear to hear more. He kissed her hand. 'Be happy, Ver. You and Evie look after one another. I will try and see Grace Manton if I can.

You must write, please, if you can spare some time. I love to hear news of you all.'

He hugged her then, looking over her head towards the house, and the old stables, but Evie had not come.

He turned, opened the car door, and at last Evie's voice rang out. She was standing at the entrance to the stable yard. 'Mr Auberon, be safe, be lucky.' The dogs rushed at him, barking. He stroked them. They tore back to Evie.

He took a moment, and when he could be sure his voice would be steady he called, 'Thank you, Evie. I will bring your Simon safely home, and Jack, if I possibly can.'

She waved. 'And you, you come back too, bonny lad.' Then Mrs Moore shouted, 'You'll catch your death, lass. Come in here this minute.' Evie waved again and disappeared.

He and Veronica laughed, and then he left. Yes, he must bring Simon back, because Evie's happiness was everything to him, and at last she'd given him the marras' farewell.

As Ted drove down the drive Auberon wondered if his father would ever accept that he employed a Forbes as his cook. Probably not, so Evie must continue to be known on the books as Evie Anston. How absurd it all was.

Chapter 3

Northern France, early March 1915

The North Tyne Fusiliers were in deep reserve, well to the west of Rouen, after a winter that was supposed to have been quiet as far as the war was concerned. Some bloody hope. Jack and Simon took a last puff on their roll-up stubs before tossing them away, each pulling the strands of tobacco from their lips. The strands clung, as though reluctant to follow their brethren on to the damp ground where the stubs hissed, then died. The men leaned back against the door to the barn, out of the wind, shoving their numb hands into their pockets, watching the reinforcements right wheel, left wheel and every-thing in between. They'd been recruited after Kitchener's *Your Country Needs You.*

'Well the bugger isn't far wrong there,' Jack muttered to himself, eyeing the tumbling dark clouds barrelling over the old oaks, and the village a kilometre distant, hearing the distant sound of shells. The road running between here and there and onwards was busy with lorries that churned through the mud, men marching in single file, carts carrying shells, and ambulances.

'What's that you say?' Simon tipped back his cap, and shook his head at the training troops.

At least the rain had stopped, for now. Winter had been a bugger, not just because of the noise, the crash and groan of shells, the snipers, the forays, but it was the day-in day-out sheer bloody misery of the the snow-drenched trenches, worse if you slid off the duckboards, so you pretty soon learned not to. Even when they were in the second line it had been little better, huddled in disintegrating billets with shells plummeting down just to keep them alert. Here, in deep reserve, none of them had rid themselves yet of the sense of chill, though they'd been here for almost a month. At least the Auld Maud pit had been bloody hot.

Jack jerked his head towards the men who were kicking up mud and spray on the field Captain Bridges had commandeered along with the billets. Bloody luxurious they were too, as they all had roofs and walls without holes. 'I was just thinking we need this lot of buggers, bonny lad, good, bad and indifferent though they are. But they'll not be up to proper fighting scratch for a while, and likely be dead before they have a bloody chance to be. Look at the roads, crawling they are, like a bloody ant run. There's something brewing.'

Captain Brampton appeared around the corner and called, 'You've your sunshine face on again this morning then, Sergeant?'

'Just telling it as it is, sir.' Jack shuffled upright,

saluting. Auberon had just been made up from Lieutenant and for a moment he and Si had wondered if it would go to his head. It hadn't. 'Stand easy for God's sake, Jack,' Auberon told him. 'Well, let's do our best to look after this lot when we move up to the front, if we move up, especially the Lea End crowd. You've done well, Jack, put them through hell and back again, which I feel you enjoyed to the full?'

They all laughed. Auberon continued, 'Now I'd pit them against any Glaswegian or Canadian company, let alone the Huns. So let's blow the clouds away, and find that little Mr Happy I know you have hiding somewhere.' Auberon grinned at both men and walked across to Captain Bridges who was conferring with the company sergeant major, kicking up spray and sinking into the muddy field until he reached the duckboards.

Jack slumped back against the barn, smiling in spite of himself. By, those buggers could fight like heathens, but he and Si had known that way back when they'd fought them while sea-coaling. 'That was a grand barney on Fordington beach that day, wouldn't you say, bonny lad?'

Simon knew exactly what he meant. 'Aye, what a damned fool Parson Manton was. Our Evie says he can't cross the road safely, so high are his thoughts, so how he fancied he'd trot along the beach, Bible in hand, and convert that drunken lot, God alone knows. The only result was always going to be a ducking. Would have done for him an' all if you and Timmie hadn't led the charge to send 'em packing, and then gone in after the fool.' They were watching as the two captains stood together now, discussing something. Perhaps they were on the move again? Jack hoped not, but then touched Evie's package in his pocket. Well, perhaps it wouldn't be the worst news.

Simon continued, 'Not done a lot of that, have we, charging I mean? But we're pretty bloody good at hunkering down in trenches and shell holes and getting better at keeping our tippy-toes dry, and trench foot away, and our heads whole. So, are you taking that package to Grace Manton, man? You can't keep putting it off.'

Jack stared at the Lea End men who came from beyond the Sidon pit, and even from beyond Hawton and Easton collieries, as they made fours. Their marching was neat, very neat. It had taken a few goes behind the barn with his fists to show them the error of their ways but yes, the buggers were far from the pregnant camels they had been. In fact, Auberon was right, they were the best of the bloody intake bunch. They put him in mind of the Canadians. Nobody's yes men, but fighters to the last man. He just had to make sure his Lea End men lived long enough on the front line to be as safe as they could be. They'd make their own luck. Yes, *his* men, dammit.

Simon was laying tobacco along his cigarette

paper, which he then rolled, licked and lit, blowing the smoke up into the wind. 'You've been carrying the damned package about for months. How it survived Ypres, God knows. Get a grip, man, and give me some peace from our Evie's letters. Just let me tell her you've delivered it, please, or do I have to get on my knees in this mud?'

He made a show of getting down until Jack hauled him upright. 'Give it a rest, Si. I'm going'

Simon shook his head. 'Why she didn't just send it to the woman, I don't know. They're friends after all and most things get to where they need to be by the postal service, for Christ's sake. Women? I just don't understand them.'

'You never used to swear, young Si. Your roses wouldn't like it, so think on.' Jack started to walk away, but stood to attention, throwing a salute as Auberon ambled over from Captain Bridges, flagging him to a stop. 'Surprised to see you're still here, Jack. Shouldn't you be on your way? Please give Miss Manton my best wishes, and Ver's, though I expect they're in regular contact. You deserve a few hours off camp, you've worked damned hard.'

Jack threw a look at Simon. 'Thank you, sir. Corporal Preston did his little best with the men too.'

Auberon laughed. 'You heard that then, Corporal? Faint praise, but praise indeed.'

Simon stood to attention. 'I heard it all, sir. How'd

you manage to get him to agree to shift his arse and get the package to where it should be?'

Auberon laughed, and tapped the side of his nose. 'Bumped into a friend of Ver's who is also one of the Very Adorable Darlings and asked if they had a Grace Manton. One gets so tired of letters from home asking if Jack's delivered the wretched thing. My sister doesn't seem to understand that the VADs are a movable feast and could be anywhere, and what's more there's a war on and we actually have more important things to do than fulfilling Evie's wishes.'

Simon shrugged. 'Don't tell her that, or we'll all be buried six foot under.' Captain Bridges was standing watching the new intake again, as the sergeant major yelled at them to get a bloody move on.

Auberon laughed. 'Wouldn't dream of it, Corporal. But miracles happen, and this VAD said that Miss Manton is here, or as near as dammit, just a few miles or so away, near the railway station at the camp hospital. I suggested to Jack yesterday that I find and ask this particularly attractive VAD to deliver the package but our Jack refused, wanted to make sure it reached her himself. I daresay that was one of Evie's directives. So I was denied a reasonable excuse to make contact with the most recent apple of my eye.'

Jack listened to the pair of them behaving like little girls. Daft buggers. Around them bugles played. It would be the same over at the camp hospital as the nurses skidded along the duckboards, just as the men did here.

He let them light up yet more cigarettes, and blow the smoke away across their shoulders, saying nothing. Why should they know that he always knew just where Grace Manton was, because he asked every nurse or VAD he came across.

Auberon wagged a finger at him. 'Why are you still here? Surely you've remembered I suggested sixteen hundred hours in my message to Miss Manton, at the *estaminet*, but she has officer status and you have not, so sit at the back where you are unlikely to be seen, there's a good lad. And think about taking a commission as Bridges suggested. We'd all support it.'

'What, and have to buy my own bloody uniform and mingle with the bosses?' Jack retorted.

Auberon laughed. 'Not sure the bosses are ready for it, but he'd look good in long boots, wouldn't he, Simon? Then you could have his stripes and before we knew where we were we'd have you buying your own uniform too. Just a short step to you two running the ruddy war, each with a batman like Roger.'

They all laughed. Jack said, 'Over my dead body.'

'Highly likely, Jack.' Auberon's tone was dry, their laughter was loud. They seemed to do a lot of it, but not deep down.

The *estaminet* was well over an hour's walk, Auberon had said, or he could grab a ride on the ration lorry.

Jack refused. Why meet sooner than they had to? 'Once there,' Auberon said, 'you'll see a narrow road that leads from the square, dominated by the church. It leads to Le Petit Chat.'

Auberon shrugged when Jack asked if there actually was a little cat. 'You'll have to wait and see, and for God's sake, man, get there, give the package over and only after that may you head for the cellar at Rogiers'. Yes, I know you can get good beer there, but it's as good at Le Petit Chat, I've tried both. Bear in mind that I'll tear your stripes off myself if you retreat before hand over. Just give us all some peace from home, there's a good lad, and let's be done with it.'

Jack made his way to the exit, passing the Lea End lot who had been dismissed and were scrounging amongst the tents and stores, looking for hand-bomb-making material no doubt, to supplement their personal armaments: jam tins, bits of metal and screws, and fuses, all of which Aub and he knew from experience worked a treat. Soon, the rumour was, the factories back home would come up with something better, but who had time to wait?

He took to the road, thinking of war, not his meeting. It was easier. And another thought came to him. Those Lea End buggers could certainly throw, bowling out the Newcastle recruits within minutes at the winter cricket match. It had earned them beer from Captain Bridges. Not a good move because Jack and Simon, plus Eddie and Frank, who had come out in a January draft, both hewers, had had to round them up and herd them back to their billet and sit on them till morning, or have a raging fight on their hands, not to mention the whole lot on a charge.

Jack stuck to the verge as the ammunition carts rumbled onwards, to the station probably, or towards Ypres perhaps? The Front was so extended that every conceivable form of transport was used. The lorries with red crosses were as busy as ever, heading either to the Front or away towards Rouen and the base hospital, or Le Touquet, or even to the ships, if someone was lucky enough to have a wound that would get them back to Blighty. Taxis and buses had been called into service too and all around, carried on the wind, was the crump and muted roar of artillery, the stutter of machine guns. Often there was the crack of a solitary sniper. With every step nearer the Front the noise would increase, and added to it would be the sound of the men, and the blast of hand bombs. ·

He was striding on mud-splattered cobbles as he entered the village, splashing through swathes of surface water, even though it had stopped raining by nine hundred hours or thereabouts. Bloody hell, what about some warmth, and sun? But it was only March. Nuns were scurrying children along the edge of the road towards the church spire. Were they off for Mass? He didn't know and didn't care because God was a lot of baloney, but if it kept the poor buggers happy, so be it. It was their country being wrecked and how did one cope with that? He didn't dwell. Why would he when it dragged him down?

Cars and lorries revved. A horse neighed as its driver sat astride and urged it forward with its cart-load of shells. Now he could see the church ahead, and the long line of children entering through its massive doors, being shepherded by the nuns. There was a market set up in the square, with people buying, talking, bartering. It was comforting, in a way, that life went on within the sound of warfare. It meant that one day sanity could prevail because some people would remember the sense of normal life. He couldn't, not any more.

He headed straight for the turning Aub had mentioned. It was shaded here and the cold pene-trated deeper. He slowed, looking left and right, and there it was. Le Petit Chat. He stopped, feeling in his pocket for the package. Damn Evie. He squared his shoulders and took a deep breath, and then another. Damn Grace. Damn her to hell for what she had done.

Inside Grace Manton sat at the back of the café, near the swing doors leading to the kitchen. An elderly waiter in a long white apron glided past, his tray held high on the tips of his fingers and thumb. How on earth had he retained such elegance? Didn't his back ache, his feet throb, or was he a better man than her? Never had her feet been as swollen, her back as sore, her knees so agonising. She sat back, enjoying this moment of rest. The *estaminets* were the lifesavers of the nurses and VADs, away from the noise and smell of the hospitals, and the coffee was just heaven, usually. Le Petit Chat didn't disappoint and she'd already ordered one, and a beer for Jack. Both would be served on his arrival.

The waiter had told her when she arrived two weeks ago that the proprietor had bought many barrels from the cellar Rogiers' for les Anglais before Christmas, as the war would not end for many months. She had replied, 'If there is money to be made and throats to slake, then one must.' As she had spoken in French she was now his best friend.

Grace pulled her coat belt tight. There was no need to make her VAD status obvious, though there were usually no bearers of tales here. Usually being the operative word, for some of the new officers could be stuffy about enlisted men breaching their sanctum. At the front of the café officers cluttered up the tables, but today they all had that unmistakable look and pallor of old hands. At the back were several enlisted men, some with VADs, some with officer friends they had known at home.

The doorbell tinkled. She looked up but it wasn't Jack, only Major Sylvester, an American surgeon who had come across the Atlantic on his own initiative to work at the camp hospital. He was introducing them to the wonders of blood transfusions, which would save many lives, God bless his good heart.

He saw her, and waved, weaving his way between the tables towards her. 'Gracie, all alone?'

Behind him the door opened again. It was him, Jack. She half rose. Major Sylvester hesitated, turned. 'I see you're not. Later, perhaps?'

Jack had stopped, and was closing the door carefully, searching the room. He saw her immediately, and Major Sylvester. The colour rushed to his drawn face, his poor tired, thin, drawn face, and he swung round on his heel, reaching out for the door. 'Jack Forbes, don't you dare.' Her shout silenced the clatter and murmur of the room. Major Sylvester laughed quietly. 'I'll leave you to your prey. Be gentle with him, he looks in need of tender care.' He tipped his cap and sauntered in that long-legged way of the Americans over to a distant table.

Grace saw Jack hesitating, his hand gripping the door handle, then it was as though he gave up. He strode towards her, weaving through the tables, his head down, his weight forward as though he was approaching the enemy. Surely that's not how he thought of her? Had she been wrong all this time? She stood tall, refusing to doubt.

He reached her, and half bowed. She sat. He looked anywhere but at her. 'Oh do sit down,' she snapped, as disappointment drained courtesy from her.

He did. She said, drawing off her gloves, 'I have ordered a beer for you, and a coffee for me.'

'Thank you, Miss Manton.' He laid his cap on the

table and groped in his pocket. Miss Manton? Had he really forgotten those last looks they had exchanged before he embarked? Yet again, as she did every evening before she gave in to exhaustion, she berated herself for all her mistakes.

He stopped fiddling in his pocket at last, and drew out the package that Evie had spoken of in her letter. A letter which arrived in the new year, when she was at the base hospital in Rouen. Dearest Evie, she knew how much she loved Jack, she had always known and was determined that somehow the situation must be resolved. 'God, I was such a fool.'

She didn't realise she had spoken aloud until Jack looked up, startled and said, 'You've never been a fool.'

He looked down again immediately, studying the package as though it was something curious he had never seen before. It was two inches by three, and battered. The ribbon had once been silver from the look of it, and now it was dirty, but stained and precious because it had been with this young man since Christmas. At that, Grace paused. Yes, young man. He was twenty-four, she thirty-two, no wonder he had forgotten. The waiter glided to their table with coffee and a beer.

He placed the coffee before her, reverentially, and the beer before Jack. '*Il n'y a pas de frais,*' he said. Jack replied, in French. 'Oh no, of course we must pay.'

Grace said at the same time, 'You must make a living.' The waiter nodded, smiling. 'For those who speak our language, and protect our families, we insist, especially for those who speak as one. War is a time for lovers, you must never forget this, for time is short,' he told them.

He swept away. Grace and Jack stared at the package, neither speaking. At last Jack pushed it across the table. 'From Evie, Miss Manton, and I need to tell you . . .'

'Yes?' She knew she was too eager.

'That the French you taught her to help her career as a cook and hotelier has been of value to me here, because of course she passed on the lessons.' He took a deep draught of beer, wiping the back of his hand across his mouth.

'Of course,' she said. 'That's our Evie.' How formal they both were, she thought, her heart breaking. She untied the ribbon of the battered package. Inside was a squashed white cardboard box. She removed the dried and cracked greaseproof-paper package within it. The waiter had moved nearer to their table, watching, a benign smile on his face. She removed one layer, then another, and another until she reached a light grease-stained package tied again with ribbon. It was shapeless, it felt like – beads? Sand? What on earth was it? Evie had refused to say. She undid the knot, opened it and there was yet more greaseproof paper. This she opened, and there lay a piece of Christmas cake, or rather, a mass of crumbs.

Jack flung himself back in his chair. The waiter, who had perhaps expected to see a ring, just shook his head and muttered, *'Les Anglais?'* He shrugged, and banged back the swing doors as he escaped to the kitchen.

Jack spluttered, 'Bloody Evie, all this way for crumbs? What d'you think of that then, Grace?' He laughed, reached forward, pinched up some crumbs and held them towards her mouth, she opened her lips, his fingers touched her tongue. It was as though electricity passed through her. At that moment he snatched his hand away. 'God. Sorry.'

He shook his fingers free of the crumbs and seized his beer, finishing it, reaching for his cap, but Grace clutched his hand, holding it vice-like to the table. 'Oh no you don't, Jack Forbes. You damn well don't.'

He tried to pull away. She held on. 'Do you think I'm about to let you go? I've worked with men out of their minds and wrestled them back on to their stretcher, I've removed crawling, bloated, greedy maggots from wounds, bleached my hands a million times a day so I carry no infection from one to another. I've cut off clothes until I have corns on my hands from the scissors. You, Jack Forbes, are a lightweight. I have muscles where I didn't know I had places, my hands are so rough, tough and gnarled I have the grip of a prizefighter. So you will listen.'

The touch of his fingers on her tongue had told her that her love for him was all-consuming. It always had been, but she had made a mistake and had withdrawn. She had been at the Froggett house, comforting his family on the day of Timmie's death, and told him she would be there whenever she was needed, and she had failed him. Today could be the last day, for one of them. Even here in the *estaminet* she could hear the guns.

She said, 'I might have been Evie's first employer but we all became friends after you saved Edward from the Lea End mob, you and Timmie. Is that right?'

She still gripped his hand but he was no longer fighting her. Instead he was staring at his empty glass. Well, he could damn well wait if he was after another. She'd spent too many weeks rehearsing what she would say when he arrived with the package to waste time ordering another beer.

Jack nodded. 'Aye, lass.' He still looked at the glass.

'Do you remember that cart ride out to Froggett's farm to secure the three houses, two for Edward and me to use as emergency and retirement homes for the miners, and one for you? You almost had the money, but not quite. We were able to thank you for Edward's life by loaning your family the balance. It meant you could pursue your union work without fear of eviction from your miner's house. Do you remember? Do you? What about when I tied the gate behind us to stop Auberon getting there first?'

Jack nodded, and this time he looked full into her face. 'Aye, of course I remember, Miss Manton. You were good to us when our lad died, too.'

'You've just called me lass, and now it's Miss Manton, but it was Grace then. We were friends.'

Jack's face was bitter now. 'Aye, and I helped you repair your houses once we had them, as well as our own, and dug your garden, and planted your bloody potatoes with you, and you held me when I cried for Timmie. I loved you, lass. I loved you and I thought you felt something for me, and then the next day when I came to get me hands grubby for you, you said you could manage "perfectly well, thank you", in a real posh voice, and that you didn't need me. I was to go about my business and get on with my life. So I got on with it. I married, I have Roger's son who is a little belter and who I must protect, as I couldn't Timmie.'

The waiter brought another beer, removing the empty froth-smeared glass, tutting at the untouched coffee in Grace's cup. 'For you, madame, I will produce a further coffee.'

'This time, we pay,' they said together, their eyes fixed on one another, not on the waiter. Grace loved Jack's eyes, so brown and dark, so like Evie's, and his almost black hair, so like his da's and Timmie's. Evie's hair was a riot of chestnut curls like that of her mam.

'Perhaps,' the waiter murmured before removing the cup and backing through the swing doors.

Major Sylvester rose from his window table. Grace saw him looking at her clutching Jack's hand. Fraternisation with enlisted men was forbidden. Well, let him do his worst. He tapped his cap and smiled but said nothing. She knew his worst would not happen.

Grace remembered all too well holding Jack at the front gate of his parents' house, soothing him as he sobbed for his brother, knowing finally what she had suspected for weeks, which was that she had met the love of her life. But she was older, she was boring, she was the parson's sister and Evie's first employer. He was adored by women, a rising union leader, a strong and respected hewer, a glorious young man who would have been appalled had he known the riot of her emotions. She had ridden her bicycle away feeling that she must put distance between them or she would do untold damage to everyone, and take advantage of the vulnerability of his grief.

It was only when the North Tyne Fusiliers were embarking from Newcastle Central station, and she had gone in Edward's place to wave them farewell, that they had, for the first time, really looked at one another again, and that was when she saw that his love matched her own. But it had all been too late because on his arm was Millie, his wife. It was still too late, but he must be told how very much he was loved. He must take that back to the trenches.

It was this that Grace told Jack now, and she felt him turn his hand beneath hers and grip, tightly. At last he smiled, at last his shoulders slumped with a release of tension, at last he met her eyes and allowed her to see that indeed she had been right. There was love between them, a huge bloody sea of it, a bloody great seam of high-grade love between her and this precious man. There really was.

'I was wrong,' he said. 'You have been a bloody fool to think you would be taking advantage, bonny lass, for you're all I've wanted for too many years.'

Another coffee arrived, and this time Jack dug in his pockets for francs, saying to Grace, 'You will let me do this for you and you will let us have this moment, because it is all we can ever have.'

Grace knew that. 'I had to speak of it. I couldn't bear to not tell you of my feelings, because Evie felt that you were so unhappy and felt so unloved. You are not, my darling. You never will be.'

'Oh, Evie,' Jack laughed. She smiled, but couldn't bear to think of his hurt. He gripped both her hands, lifted them, held one against his cheek and kissed the other. 'And did she tell you that I loved you so fiercely that sometimes I felt it burned me up?'

Grace shrugged. 'She said that she thought you loved me. She didn't mention anything about burning.'

They both laughed this time. She drew his hands to her mouth, kissing them, seeing the blue miner's scars, the more recent wounds. They were the hands of a man, not a lad. She searched his eyes. She traced with her finger his crooked nose and swollen ear, damaged from his early bare-fist fights which had helped earn the money for the Forbes' house. She traced his lips, longing to kiss them.

She asked about Mart, feeling Jack's breath on her fingers as he said against them, 'I can't believe he's gone and there'll be no more humming which drove me bloody mad, or him saying, when we were in the thick of it at Mons, "like a home from bloody home, lad". He meant just like the pit, danger at every turn. Daft bugger must have dropped his rabbit's foot and that's why the shell got him. They never found him. Decapitated, Bernie said, but there was no body when they went to gather them up, just a bloody great mess of shell holes and bits.'

He stopped for a moment. 'I haven't been able to talk about it properly till now. Grace, for God's sake, why the hell did you cut me out?'

She kissed his hands. 'Because I hadn't the sense I was born with. But this time, when I say if you ever need me I will come, I mean it from the bottom of this wretchedly battered and foolish heart. I will love you for the rest of my life, dearest Jack Forbes.'

'And I you.'

Her coffee grew cold again, his beer remained untouched. They just sat gripping one another's hands, aware of others coming and going, but taking no notice until the clock in the square chimed its tinny sound and Grace withdrew her hands. He said, 'You're right, your hands are not so soft now, bonny lass. And the better for it.'

'Ah Jack, I've scrubbed floors so clean that they would even meet with Evie's approval and would knock Ver's efforts into a cocked hat. I've helped at operations, would you believe, such has been the need for someone, anyone, who had the first idea of what to do.' She looked at her coffee, drank it cold but didn't taste it.

Jack downed his beer. 'Aye, I would believe it.' He left francs as a tip on the table. Together they left and walked to the square, holding hands as though they'd never be prised apart. In the square she pointed to the left, he to the right.

'It's time,' he said, replacing his cap. Around them the market was packing up. A cart passed loaded with empty wooden boxes, and a few turnips. The wheel caught in a ruck, the driver swore, the old horse neighed and a turnip tumbled to the ground to be scooped up by a young boy who ran off with it. 'Bravo,' Grace whispered.

Some VADs were heading for the café. Two officers passed on horseback, en route to heaven knew where, but she had a good idea it was the front, or perhaps a new one, because the hospital had been clearing the wards, sending the Blighty cases, those serious enough for treatment at home, to the ports by the trainload, and the walking wounded, patched up, were being sent to their units to free up beds. New beds were being delivered, and put together by swearing orderlies in the marquees. Bandages were being stockpiled, masses and masses of them. New contingents of orderlies, nurses and a few VADs were arriving. Dear God, the obscenity of war was about to blast in on them again as some wild scheme was concocted by those at the rear to bring about a breakthrough. In their dreams, perhaps.

She felt him pull his hand free but then his arms were round her, and they kissed, at last they kissed and it was as though nothing else existed. 'I love you and it's grand that you still smell of lavender, even here, in amongst all of this. And it's grand that I can smell it now.' Jack sighed.

She murmured, 'That's what deep reserve and fresh air does for you, dearest Jack.' She was crying and had promised herself she wouldn't, and she could barely make out the sense of her own words as he pulled away, and she held him back, just for a few seconds more, whispering, 'Be safe, be lucky. Live. I know not for me. But live, and know that you are loved.'

He held her again, forcing her head up, holding her chin, kissing her savagely. His breath was beer-tinged, 'If I live, it will be for you, Grace bloody Manton. I always have, and I always will love you, and damn you for letting me go, back then. Damn me for allowing it.'

His next kiss felt as though it bruised her mouth, and she was glad of it, and he said, his lips still on hers, 'I'll find you when this bastard mess is over. Somehow I'll work it out. It isn't enough. It will never be enough but I have my lad, my Tim. Oh God in heaven . . .'

It was he who cried now and Grace knew that she must draw on something resembling courage, but she wasn't sure that she had enough. She eased away from him, wiping his face with her hands, making him look at her. 'Jack, you have a child and his mother is your wife, and the war could create a great change in Millie. We know what we feel and that is more than I ever thought possible. It is enough for a lifetime. It truly is, Jack Forbes. You go on with your war, concentrate on that, and get back to your family. Know that I'll love you every day for the rest of time, just a call away if you need me. But never will I come between you and what's right.'

He didn't speak. He just wrenched her hands down, turned and strode away, then started running, almost into the path of a cart. The carter yelled, '*Attention!*' Jack stopped, turned, waved, barking a sort of laugh. 'That'd make a good memorial. Killed by a cart. You be safe and lucky and remember what Mam says, all will be well, all the bloody time. I'll let you know I'm safe, after each push. I'll make sure you hear.'

Then he ran on.

She watched him until he was out of sight behind carts, stalls, lorries, an artillery limber, then another, and another. Dusk was falling fast. She headed back to the camp hospital past shuttered houses with steep tiled roofs, and dogs that hurled themselves round corners chasing cats. She was on duty at twenty hundred hours. She dug her hands deep into her coat pockets, torn between longing and a strange calm. She was loved. She loved. What more could she ask from a life which was adrift in something which should have been over three months ago, if the newspapers could have been believed.

She caught up with Angela Feathers who was walking ahead of her, her collar pulled up, mud splatters on her coat. She was a VAD from Hull. Grace slipped her arm through hers. 'Will it ever end, Angie?'

'Better had, but what then, eh? Back to tending the hearth, bearing brats, adoring our menfolk?'

'No, never any of that, for me.' Grace felt her voice shake and pressed her lips together, hard. Shut up, shut up.

Angie squeezed her arm. 'You saw him then? About damn time, but don't let's even think about what comes after. Let's just try and get through. You heard Sister Merryweather was killed shipping back some wounded from some little spat?'

'Poor bloody woman.' Grace brought out the box of crumbs. 'Christmas crumbs, from Easterleigh Hall, made by a very special friend, they'll be delicious. We'll share them round, just a crumb each but I'll write and she'll send more, direct this time.' Both women smiled.

Chapter 4

The same day

As he entered the camp, seeing shadows flitting in the dusk from tent to tent, to latrine, to barn, Jack was met by Auberon, who motioned him to one side, leading the way to the lee of the barn, out of earshot of everyone else. 'We're on the move, six hundred hours tomorrow, Jack, out of deep reserve. All I know is that we're heading to an area, here.' He held up a map against the side of the barn, lighting it with his torch, tracing the route they were to take.

'We'll entrain to here.' He stabbed at a junction. The right-hand corner of the map folded down. Jack pinioned it back, looking closely as Auberon traced the way to the embarkation point. 'We'll march to here and await further orders.' He stabbed again. 'I know nothing more, except that the Indians are on the move too. Get your men together and ready, but I don't need to tell you that. And keep your mouth shut, though why anyone would think there was nothing going on with all the damned movement, God alone knows. The Huns will have their reconnaissance planes up, tracking everything.'

Auberon switched off the torch, tugged the map from beneath Jack's hand, folded it, and tucked it into his pocket. 'Could be close contact, could just be festering in bloody foot-rotting trench. Be prepared for anything. But again, I don't need to tell you. I've sorted beer for the men. It'll be at the pigsty at twenty hundred hours. Keep an eye on the Lea End mob, only a pint each, there's a good chap. They seem to prefer it to rum.'

Auberon dragged out his cigarette case, offering it to Jack, who took one. They were better than roll-ups any day. 'At ease, Jack. Mufti time.' They leaned back against the barn. Jack struck a match, lit both, flicked the match away. Soon they'd be at the Front and they'd not be hanging about lighting too many matches. He'd have to remember to remind the lads. Thank God he made it to Le Petit Chat, thank God for so many things about today.

He stared up at the sky. It was beyond dusk now and the stars were out. Auberon said, 'Did you deliver the cake?'

Jack nodded, drawing on his cigarette, exhaling, seeing the smoke rise in the chill air. 'Aye, I did that, Auberon.' Was that the Milky Way? He was right bad at stars. He asked, 'Bloody sweepstake on it, was there?'

'I won it.' They laughed and Auberon added, 'That's why there's beer. There'll be rum first thing tomorrow.'

Jack looked at him. 'A boss couldn't do anything else, could he really?'

'More's the pity. I'd have liked to go to Le Petit Chat myself if my Very Adorable Darling was available, but as you say, best to roll out the barrel, bought I might add from Rogiers', the other *estaminet*, to leave you in privacy. Not even time for a drink for myself.'

'My heart bleeds.' Jack drew again on his cigarette.

'I'm hoping it doesn't, Jack. I'm hoping that things . . .' Auberon trailed off as Jack stood away from the barn. 'Sorry, none of my business,' Auberon said quickly, though he remained lounging.

Jack said, 'A while ago someone called those three women, Evie, Veronica and Grace, a monstrous regiment. Can't remember who but I reckon they were right. Veronica's been writing about it to you, so you knew it was cake, and chose not to tell me? Well, Auberon, you can write and tell that "regiment" that we've met and we understand one another and the whole thing has been resolved. Is that enough for now?' He relaxed against the barn again, looking back at the stars. Aye, he was sure it was the Milky Way.

Auberon replied, 'I truly hope that you were both able to say what needed to be said, and that you know that you are cared for very deeply, as I believe you are, from Veronica's letters on the subject.' Jack started to interrupt. Auberon continued, 'No, Jack, let me say this and I am not under their orders to do so, but we're going into action so I feel I must. You should know what I already know, that Grace Manton loves you and love is precious. Hold it close to you. It's all that matters in the long run, d'you hear? Who knows, perhaps something will happen to work things out without pain to others. It's such a strange bloody world, at the moment.'

Auberon paused. 'Do you think that love finds a way?' His tone was urgent, and he was grinding his cigarette beneath his foot as though it was a Hun. 'Oh, forget my ramblings, and now I've embarrassed myself enough, and you too, so I'm off to catch up on orders, and you should get along to the men. They need you. Talk them through all that matters again, including the knuckledusters that I'm sure they carry with them. Make sure they carry wire-cutters and knives, too.'

Jack watched his captain slip and slide through the mud towards Colonel Townsend's tent. He grinned. Each day Roger had been beavering to keep those boots gleaming, and himself as far as possible from the drills. Lucky bugger, and no worm deserved it less. His own cigarette was smoked to the utter stub and he flicked it through the air in a way that he wouldn't be able to in a few days' time. He watched Auberon salute the guard at the colonel's tent, lift the tent flap and enter, and was filled with a welling of peace. 'D'you understand, Timmie?' He looked once more at the Milky Way, nodded and made his way to the tents that housed the Lea End mob. Only one pint, eh? Captain the Hon. Auberon

Brampton should know better where that lot were concerned.

The next morning, 8th March, they fell in and marched to the train. It was raining. Of course it was, Auberon grunted to himself. The Lea End lot were quiet. They travelled in cattle cars all morning and then it was to be Shanks' pony. The horses were unloaded, skittering down the ramp, and the officers mounted. He headed for the front of the C Company column on a horse that Richard had arranged to be delivered from England. It wasn't Prancer, but it would do. He slowed as he came upon young Lieutenant Barry marching at the head of Jack's section. He kept pace as he introduced Jack to Lieutenant Barry, who had arrived late yesterday evening. He looked like a boy. He was.

Jack and Auberon locked eyes. 'Lieutenant Barry will be accompanying you, Sergeant Forbes. He's fresh from Britain by way of Officer Cadet Training at one of our major public schools and then the usual route. I know you'll keep an eye on him.' Jack nodded. Auberon shook his head slightly. They understood one another perfectly. Another chick to try and keep from harm until he'd learned the way of the world.

Auberon told Lieutenant Barry, 'If you listen to Sergeant Forbes you've a chance of reaching the age of twenty, d'you hear me?'

'Sir,' shouted Lieutenant Barry, snapping to attention.

The section stumbled to a halt behind him. Jack and Auberon sighed together. 'Save your energy, sir,' Jack murmured. The boy looked confused.

All morning they marched, then an order was passed down the line and Jack told the men to fall out at the side of the road. They flung themselves on to piles of stones, logs, whatever they could find to keep their arses out of the mud. They ate their rations. The Lea End mob were rallying after their hangovers, because of course the one pint had become many. They moved on again and this time their grumbles reached Lieutenant Barry, who half turned. 'We should stop them,' he told Jack.

'You start to worry if they're saying nothing, sir. When they're grumbling on the first day of the march they're alive, they're functioning. When they're silent, unless it's the most bloody awful hangover, which this morning was, it means they're brewing some trouble. Tomorrow though, they'll be quieter, the blisters will be bursting, their legs will be aching, then maybe we'll get Corporal Preston here to give us a song.'

Si, who was marching the other side of Jack, grinned. 'How much is it worth, Jack?'

'A clip round the ear, bonny lad.'

Eddie, their lance corporal, muttered, 'And I'll clip the other one just to keep it all balanced.'

They arrived at the billets, which did not reach the high standard that Lieutenant Barry had clearly expected. He limped off to the officers' roofless outhouse. 'Sending us bloody kids, they are,' Jack cursed.

'Nothing new in that.' Simon had hunkered down beside his pack and was rolling them both cigarettes. It was dark when Auberon found them crouched around a fire behind a pigsty, the men having been fed and watered. He squatted down with them, checking that there was no one around. He shone his torch on his map. 'I thought this might be on the cards. We're to stay in support, on the flank of the Indian Corps. There's a big push. We're to arrive at our destination here, let's say in couple of days.' He stabbed at the map. 'Neuve Chapelle. We'll be here.' Another stab. 'Poor bloody Indians will be taking the brunt. We'll be fannying about but perhaps won't be needed. I'll tell you more as I know it. There'll be the usual barrage, but perhaps we'll go out under an artillery creeper when we go over the bags, if we go over.'

He rolled up the map. They stood. Simon offered him a roll-up. He pulled a face. 'I'd rather die.'

Simon and Jack said together, 'You probably will.'

Auberon tapped his cigarette case, which was in his breast pocket. 'Never smoked as much as this before, just like bloody chimneys we are. Dr Nicholls would protest.'

The next day they marched past wild flowers beginning to bud. Above them the Royal Flying Corps were like gnats on a body as they buzzed forward. Jack told Lieutenant Barry, 'They'll be doing reconnaissance, finding out what's what with the Huns. Soon the barrage will start. Be ready, it'll be worse than any bloody railway station run amok.' He no longer really noticed the continuous shellfire, rifle fire, sniper fire, hand bombs, though they became more and more obvious the closer they drew to the Front, because it was a home from bloody home, as Mart had said. No one else who'd been there any length of time seemed aware of the noise either.

The barrage started within two hours, and young Donald Barry marched in a sort of crouch as the screaming shells roared and pounded to break the wire and mangle the Huns' trenches. Jack bellowed, 'Stand up, lad. They'll not hit you. They're way up high. Well, most of the time.' He ducked as a shell fell short over to the right of them, throwing debris high into the air, and along with it the smell of cordite.

By lunch they were breaking stride and walked single file along the road as artillery limbers passed, and ammunition carts, ration carts, ambulances, Uncle Tom Cobley and all. They marched a few hours more before receiving the order to fall out, by which time the artillery was deafening, the smell of explosives was being carried back from the Huns' trenches, and they were shouting to be heard

Auberon trotted back, his horse twitchy and side-stepping as he reached Jack, who grabbed the bridle and held the horse steady. 'Prancer would never have clowned about like this, dammit,' Auberon complained.

Jack said, 'He'll be over the hills and far away if he's any damned sense.'

Auberon growled, 'Nearly there, Sergeant. Captain Bridges is taking his company over the left, we're to the right. Bring your section and follow me. You doing all right there, Donald? Feet not too much of a problem? Never fear, not much more marching.' He wheeled away. 'Follow me.' A German retaliatory shell came over, close. No one ducked, not even Barry. Jack clapped him on the shoulder. Donald Barry muttered, 'And what does he know about feet? Stirrups rub, do they?'

Jack grinned. 'Ah, he's learning the way of the world already, Corporal Preston.' Auberon called back, 'I have ears, Lieutenant Barry.' Barry coloured. Jack shook his shoulder. 'He's on your side.'

They followed in the footsteps of their master, and stopped when Auberon flagged down a ration truck. Jack heard the private driving it yell over the noise, 'Go on till you get to the three dead mules, turn right, right again. Keep going till you reach the two, or is it three dead 'uns, men that is. Bit puffy they are. Then turn left, sir.'

Lieutenant Barry paled. Well, Jack thought, he'll hear and see worse before the day is out, and God help him tomorrow, or would it be the next day? Poor bairn.

That night Jack, Lieutenant Barry and Auberon sat in the dugout in one of the forward trenches.

Auberon was puffing on his pipe, filthy thing, as though the air wasn't bad enough with all the trench muck and blood and shit. It was the one he used before an action, so not long now, Jack thought. He eased himself on an old ammunition crate. Hard as bloody nails it was, and splintered. Auberon picked up his pencil, pointing it at Jack. 'Told your men to get their letters written?'

'Aye, even the Lea End mob are at it, tongues between their teeth, though a couple asked me to write theirs for them. Let's hope we don't have to write too many of the other kind when we get back.' They were writing by the light of a candle, which stood in a jam jar found by Roger, which was the first helpful thing he'd done on the march. The flame juddered with each salvo.

Jack wrote to Evie, Mam and Da, Millie, saying much the same thing. He took more time over his letter to Grace, speaking of his love, of his content-ment, his happiness now that he knew how she felt, telling her not to mourn but to make a life, telling her that he felt no fear. That last was a lie; the tremors in his hands and guts were a dead giveaway.

Young Donald Barry was writing to his parents, and one other, perhaps a sweetheart? Jack wouldn't ask. He hated to see a boy of that age writing a letter to be read in the event of his death.

He watched as Auberon wrote one letter, to his sister, and then another. He did this every time. He watched as he reread it, and tore it into the smallest pieces. Jack never asked.

Auberon caught him looking but said nothing. He merely nodded. 'The barrage will stop just before dawn. The Indian Corps will go over, we will wait our orders. Now, young Donald, you stick like a limpet, do you hear me, a damned limpet to the sergeant's side, and if not him, then Corporal Preston. You do what they say and that way we might just get you home, is that quite clear?' Donald Barry nodded, jerking with every explosion, every shudder of the ground, every fall of debris from the roof, every judder of the flame. 'Now lad, get some sleep. There's the cot there. If you can't sleep, rest at the very least. I'm off on rounds. Jack?'

'I'm with you, sir.'

Every evening before an advance, or even a patrol, the two of them would visit their men. It helped to settle them and with the reinforcements yet to be blooded it was as well to remind them of what to expect, of what to do, of how to empty their minds and follow orders.

Just before dawn the next day they ducked out of the dugout with Captain Bridges and young Barry. The ladders were in position against the side of the trench, the rum ration had been round. Auberon checked his watch, shook Jack's hand. 'Remember we're to reinforce the right flank. We'll go over with the whistle and let's try the small groups, as we discussed. There'll be machine guns waiting to cut us down and anyone who thinks otherwise is a bloody fool. The barrage didn't take them out at Ypres, they haven't been taken out at any time since, so don't let's give them an easy target.'

There was a cracking blast. They crouched down low on the duckboards. Dirt, stones and dying shrapnel fell around. The three of them hunkered down. Captain Bridges tipped his cap.

'So the colonel's approved it?' Jack raised an eyebrow, shouting above the thundering and crashing shells. Bridges moved on.

Auberon shouted back, 'Let's show him it works first. I've written down my orders so you're covered.'

Jack shrugged. 'D'you think I'm worried about that?'

Auberon looked past Jack at Lieutenant Barry, who had a hand on the trench wall and was stooping, not hunkering. Jack followed his line of sight as Auberon said, 'I think you'll find that our sergeant has very decided views, young Donald, and worrying about the opinion of his bosses isn't one of them.'

Lieutenant Barry looked uncertain and finally hunkered down. Auberon said quietly, for Jack's ears only, 'Quite right too, when one remembers I put Timmie in the wrong place at the wrong time just because I could.'

Jack was surprised. 'We've had this out before, at Mons. We've both made mistakes in the past. We'll make a few more but hopefully we'll keep our bloody heads on straight.'

Auberon eased himself upright, leaning for a moment on the sandbags which stopped the trench from falling in, and added greater protection for all within it. Roger was still in the dugout. 'Get out here, Roger, for God's sake. You're a soldier too, you know, and we need every man, and his pack,' Auberon ordered, adding quietly, 'Though man is taking things a little far, I fear.'

Roger appeared, ashen, struggling with the webbing of his sixty-pound pack. His hands were trembling fit to bust. Jack cast a look along the trench. Every man was where he should be, and he'd kept the Lea End lot with Frank, Eddie and Simon. Simon should be as safe as he could be with those fighters in his wake. He had to get back in one piece or Evie would have Jack's guts for garters.

Auberon was saying, 'Never ever be tempted to look over the top, young Donald. It's the easiest way to a third eye or a tin face mask. Not something that will thrill the girls.' The barrage seemed louder, but then it ceased. Along the line came shouts. Auberon and Jack nodded to one another. Auberon checked his watch and headed down the trench to the left to lead B platoon out. He blew his whistle.

Jack roared to the men, 'Be safe, be lucky.' He gripped Lieutenant Barry's sleeve and dragged him along the trench as the bullets rattled and zipped. 'Lance Corporal, take six and go over the bags now.

The rest in four-second intervals and dodge, remember the plan. Lea End, think of the Fordington charge, dodge and weave, don't walk into the mouth of the bloody guns. Make it hard for 'em.' Jack shoved the arse of one of Frank's men, Ted, a small bloke weighed down by his pack, then pulled him off the ladder, stripping him of the pack. 'Now go, have a fighting bloody chance at least.' Ted roared up the ladder, and over.

The screams had begun, the machine guns were upping their chatter. Bugger.

Eddie was lying on his back in the trench, staring at the sky, staining the duckboard red. 'Steady, lad,' Jack shouted as Lieutenant Barry moved two paces to the ladder. Simon knelt on the duckboard, checking Eddie. Shook his head at Jack. All along the line the call was up. 'Stretcher-bearer, stretcher-bearer.' Simon went over with his group. Jack's group comprised five of the newest and youngest. 'Keep with me, dodge, weave, keep your head, think, charge. Hit the ground and get up and have another go, do not run straight into those bullets, do you hear me?'

'Sarge,' went the roar. They followed him up the ladders, over the parapet, dodging and weaving, crashing to the ground, across ploughed land with early wheat, and mud which dragged at them, slowing their advance, pulling them earthwards, weighed down by their packs. Machine guns nipped and zipped at the men, the earth, the air. Jack was down on one knee. 'Remember to dodge.' His voice cracked. He swallowed, looked back, waved them forward in a lull. Had a shell hit a machine gun? They ran on. He spied Lieutenant Barry running on, calling to his troop, 'Be men, keep going.'

Jack screamed, 'Dodge, duck, do as I said.' He watched the boy spin round, and drop, half his head gone. The men faltered, then ducked and weaved onwards, hitting the ground, waiting, rising when the bullets seemed to lessen, making ground.

Jack yelled, 'Dodge, fall, go again, for the love of God.' He waved his men down. The noise increased. Shells burst. Auberon caught up with him. 'It's the Huns' artillery.' The crashing was shattering, mud and shrapnel were flying. 'Keep going, Jack. We're halfway there, one of the machine guns is out.'

Roger was at Auberon's heels. Simon veered towards Auberon, yelling, 'I've lost my men, all of the buggers. Stretcher-bearers. Stretcher-bearers.' The bullets were still zipping, the shells still exploding. They were pounding through winter cabbage. How bloody ridiculous. Cabbages, Jack thought. He could smell the buggers. The breath was catching in his chest. Maybe this time they'd turn the tide. About bloody time too. He kept running.

Grace had no time to eat, drink or think as the new beds were filled, the stretchers with their burdens stacked up on the ground in triage, as a French orderly called the assessment area. Ambulances rolled up with more, the Red Cross lorries with even more. They could hear the guns over everything, even the screams and calls of the injured. Angie was labelling the wounded. Grace was washing, cleaning, calling. 'Orderly, here, now. Emergency.' Another life might be saved.

The earth shook even as far back as they were, but it wasn't so much the noise of guns but of the victims of those guns they saw and heard now. And it was the victims' blood they smelled. She stared at her hands, just for a second. Blood is so very red, she thought. Blood has a particular smell, all-pervading. She bent to her task again, her mind running along its own path, chattering, chattering. It kept her sane. Blood used to make her feel sick. Now it did nothing except fuel her rage. A soldier on a stretcher was singing, 'Hitchy koo, hitchy koo, hitchy koo.' Another moaned, 'Shut him up. Just shut him up.'

An orderly moved Mr Hitchy Koo into a marquee at Sister Saul's request.

'Manton, in the transfusion area, now.' Sister Miller grabbed Grace as she was reaching for a sterile bandage for a corporal's ruined face that bubbled as he tried to speak. She administered the bandage, and hoped for his sake he died quickly. He grabbed her hand as she went to rise, but all she heard was gurgling. 'I'll be back,' she soothed, 'in a moment. If not me, someone. You're safe now. You will be all right, trust me.' She pressed his hand between both of hers, bent and kissed it. It was what his mother would have done.

She hurried along the duckboards towards the transfusion area, wiping her mouth with her hand, but feared that all she did was to smear more blood. A passing orderly threw her a clean dressing. 'You look like a vampire, Gracie.' She wiped her mouth again and tossed the soiled dressing in the bucket before entering the tent.

Major Sylvester was transfusing a pre-operation patient direct from a flask of matching blood. When Slim Sylvester arrived two weeks ago he'd shown the British surgeons and a good many nurses and VADs how to add blood to the sodium citrate solution already in the flask. This was then transferred from the flask to the patient via a pipe, once it was matched. The sodium citrate solution prevented the blood from clotting. Lives had been, and would be, saved. Lives that would previously have been lost.

Grace could see that the patient had lost his legs from mid-thigh down, and was still losing blood. The loss just had to be slower than the blood going in. He was heavily sedated. She tended him while Slim Sylvester moved on to the next patient. It was midday and just the beginning. Was Jack in this push? Of course he damned well was, why else had they entrained. Dear God, be safe, be lucky.

Chapter 5

Easterleigh Hall, 21st March 1915

On 21st March there was the customary morning meeting of the heads of department around the kitchen table to discuss the hospital's daily orders and requirements under Lady Veronica's nominal chairmanship, as the daughter of the owner and therefore commandant. Today, as he had for the last few days, Captain Richard, as they called him, attended also, which was a welcome sign of his continuing recovery. Over mugs of tea, the dietary requirements of Matron and Dr Nicholls, as regards the patients, were noted, as were any special measures that would be required in general. On the armchairs the dogs snored.

Dr Nicholls reported on the economic situation. The government paid three shillings per patient per day, and Lord Brampton paid an extra ninepence per patient per day; this sum was becoming insufficient. Lady Veronica had written to her father asking him to consider increasing his funding, as it had been his directive to set up the hospital. She had hinted that it could only enhance his reputation to be more generous, a generosity that might result in a second ammunition contract. So far there had been no reply.

Evie reported on the demoralised patients who were, or were not, responding to personalised meals, Mrs Green's problems with housekeeping and laundry were solved by shuffling around the volunteers and releasing more storage space in the basement. Mr Harvey outlined today's administrative procedures; the head orderly, Sergeant Briggs, made a note of who would be leaving and what convoys of wounded were expected. The most pressing problem was left until last.

'It's the dressings,' Matron declared, tapping her pencil on the table. 'I said it yesterday and say it again today. Since the Battle of Neuve Chapelle began eleven days ago, convoys of wounded have been arriving steadily. Our dressings are diminishing, with a mere week's worth left, and no more to be had for love nor money. Well, of course not, because demand has far exceeded expectation. It's this damned war, it's demanding too much from the suppliers, nothing is steady.' She flung down her pencil and everyone watched as it rolled to the edge. Mrs Moore caught it just before it fell. In the background the furnace rumbled.

Matron and Dr Nicholls then bickered over which Peter they could rob to pay Paul. Mrs Green and Mr Harvey argued over what linen could be ripped into bandages before being sterilised in the laundry, while Ver and Richard sat in sulky silence because Richard had just said, yet again, 'I seem to have forgotten what it is we need, did someone say dressings?'

To crown it all Millie slammed her mug down, slopping tea on to the table. 'So, you want us to boil and sterilise strips of sheeting? You all seem to think the laundry has nothing better to do with its coppers than fulfil your requirements.'

In the silence that fell, the tension threatened to overwhelm Evie. She felt a great heat, a boiling rage that roared until she could bear it no longer. Where the hell was Si? Why hadn't Auberon telegraphed with his usual message of survival to Veronica so they knew all was well? And how could bloody Millie go on being such a typical cow? 'Well, yes, that is, in general, the role of a laundry,' she shouted, banging the table so that the wretched girl's tea slopped again. The dogs woke, and barked once, then settled.

Veronica's kick caught Evie on the shin. Millie sniffed, glared, gathered up the tea towels, and left her tea for someone else to clear up as she slammed from the kitchen, along the corridor, and into the laundry where her minions were working hard, which was something she never quite managed.

Evie's mam, Susan Forbes, sat between Mrs Moore and Captain Richard, representing the needs of the children's nursery. She shook her head at Evie before preventing Tim from bashing Captain Richard's false leg with his toy car. The rage drained from Evie, leaving the gnawing, repetitive anxiety. They always heard after a battle, and not only that, Veronica heard weekly. Weekly, dammit. She forced herself to sit on her stool, when she wanted to be pacing. She listened to the worries, the irritations, she looked at Veronica's furrowed brow, her mam's too. She wasn't the only one who was longing to hear; she must pull herself together.

She made herself listen as her mam told Tim that on the next warm day they would go out for a picnic on the moor. She watched as her mam removed the car from Tim's hand, smiling her apology at Captain Richard, who shook his head and ruffled Tim's hair. The moor? Mrs Green and Matron discussed whether flowers were a good idea in the wards. 'It's extra work for the housemaids, and volunteers. We have to keep replacing the water,' Mrs Green protested. Matron snatched back her pencil from Mrs Moore. 'They induce calmness. They are light in the darkness.' She was tapping the pencil again. 'They are removed at night so the wards are not deprived of oxygen.'

The moor? Her mam used to take them out to the moor when they were bairns. What was it they picked? Mrs Moore was pointing to the teapot, a question in her eyes. Evie took no notice. What was it? She remembered the cold of the . . . What?

Veronica slapped her hand down on the table.

'Enough about flowers. It's the dressings that are the priority.'

'Dressings?' Captain Richard queried.

'For God's sake, Richard,' Veronica shouted. The stockpot was boiling, much like the committee, when it should have been simmering. Evie slipped it on to the resting shelf. Flowers? Dressings?

She returned to her stool in the silence that had fallen, but she barely noticed because there was something nudging her memory. The wind had been in her hair, she'd been very young, and had stooped to pull up something. Yes, it was in water. It was something her mother needed for Grandfather, who was . . . What? That's right. He was hurt in a fall in Hawton Pit. Yes, she felt again the water running down her arm as she pulled up something. Her feet were wet, sinking into . . . mud? Jack had hauled her out.

Evie looked up now into the silence that still hung like a cloud. 'The bog. We picked something, Mam, years ago, for your da. It was a plant, yellow. We picked some, kept some, sold some.' Her mam was staring at her, then she smiled. 'Sphagnum moss, that's what we need.'

They all looked at one another. Captain Richard said, 'Moss, did you say? For the vases?'

Her mam smiled at him, and handed the car back to Tim. 'Not for the vases, Captain Richard, but it's what we used as dressings when times were hard. Aye, pet, you're quite right. I should have thought of it, but I'm too tired to think these days.' Her eyes were sunken and dark, emphasising her words. She continued, 'There are sphagnum bogs out behind Stunted Tree Hill. Evie, you're a canny bairn, you must have been really young and somehow you've hoyed it out of your memory.'

Dr Nicholls was slapping the table. Evie did wish people would leave it alone. What with the tapping, the slopping and now the slapping, the poor old thing was getting a good bashing today. His face was alight as he said, 'Good God alive, of course, yes. They've been using it a lot in Canada just recently. I read a medical paper on it, the other day. It has perfect absorption, it's like a sponge and can soak up, oh, twenty times its own weight. Scotland is the main supplier, but if you say you've used it . . . ? I never connected it with here. You say it's here, definitely?' He was rubbing his hands, and Matron was beaming. The dogs had woken, and jumped down to settle in front of the ranges.

Evie's mam removed the car from Tim again and hid it in the fold of her plump arm so that he tugged at her, and left Captain Richard in peace. 'Yes, I do say it's here, you've just heard me, haven't you. Or are you having trouble with your hearing, Dr Nicholls?'

He laughed, everyone did. Captain Richard said, 'He's deaf, is he? I didn't know that.'

Veronica snapped, 'Do shut up, darling.'

Evie smiled at her mam, loving her. Susan

continued, 'The thing is, can we collect enough? It needs to be picked clean of all bits, dried, then placed in muslin bags with room to let the moss expand, and there you have your dressing. It's naturally sterile some say, and worked a treat for us, but you've sterilisers, so use those to be quite sure. How could I have forgotten?' She raised her hand to her forehead.

Captain Richard poured himself more tea. The teapot lid wobbled. Mr Harvey reached across Dr Nicholls and held it down. Richard smiled his thanks. 'Sphagnum is Greek for moss. All rather interesting really . . .'

'No it's not, Richard,' Veronica said, her voice becoming a shout as she shoved her VAD uniform sleeves up. Captain Richard ignored her, and finished pouring, placing the teapot within Evie's reach. She shook her head as Veronica continued to shout, 'What is interesting is getting dressings into Easterleigh Hall by the quickest possible route. We're being inundated with casualties and for God's sake, we still haven't heard from Aub and he damn well promised to send a telegram every week so just be quiet and let the bloody Greeks go and Greek themselves.'

There was total silence, again, until Matron said, 'My, if that isn't worthy of the playroom I don't know what is.'

Dr Nicholls roared with laughter, and Evie turned to him. 'You can put that revolting pipe out and all.

Don't think I didn't see you picking that piece of tobacco off your tongue and dropping it on Annie's clean floor.'

Mrs Moore took another biscuit. Evie saw. 'You don't need that. Dr Nicholls said you had to cut down.' She stood, stared around, and then sat again. There'd been so many wounded, so many dead on the lists. Damn. Damn. Where were they?

Mrs Moore finished her biscuit and gathered up another, patting Evie's knee. Evie gripped her hand. She just had this feeling. There had been so many on the casualty lists, so many coming through their doors, needing their bandages, dying, crying. Matron straightened her shoulders and her vast breasts, her face drawn with exhaustion. In Evie's pocket was the pencilled note from Grace she had received two days ago, sent via a VAD who had accompanied a Red Cross convoy to Newcastle.

She had hoped it contained good news and that was so, in a way. Grace had enjoyed the crumbs; more would be welcome, but preferably in a single slab. She said that she and Jack had spoken and knew that their lives had moved on, that there was a nice American surgeon at the camp hospital, and Jack was happy with Tim and Millie. She and Jack both recognised there had been love, and that Evie was not to worry any more. She had added that she was to be Jack's homing pigeon and convey news of his safety to his family at the end of each push, though she knew that Auberon telegraphed too.

When she heard from Jack, she would also send a telegram. But the note had been written on 11th March. There had been, so far, no telegram.

Captain Richard had made enquiries yesterday at Veronica's insistence, and been told by his former adjutant Potty Potters that the Fusiliers had been decimated, that splinter groups had joined up with other regiments, that it was chaos but he would let him know any news when he had it. The general anxiety had risen.

Matron said, 'Do we have your undivided attention, Miss Evie Forbes?' Evie realised that everyone was looking at her. 'If so, perhaps I may continue, because you have just saved the day as you do annoyingly often.' Matron's smile was luminous and she did indeed continue while Evie forced herself to concentrate. 'If you have used this moss before, Susan, and are familiar with the process, I will be relieved and delighted if you would lead a team out to the bog. I believe, Dr Nicholls, that the moss can hold exceptional amounts of pus and other liquid discharges, far more than cotton, and will therefore be invaluable.'

Mrs Moore replaced a fourth biscuit, uneaten, and shuddered.

Richard eased his left arm stump and nodded. 'Excellent. This would mean that in due course the cotton can be used for armaments.'

'Be quiet, Richard,' Veronica snapped. It was all she seemed to be doing today.

Evie released Mrs Moore's hand and drank her tea which was almost cold, feeling proud of her mam as Susan said, 'It's excellent for burns, and the moss dressings don't heat as much as the cotton. I'm sorry, I should have remembered it earlier.'

'My dear, we haven't needed them earlier.' Matron said quietly, avoiding Evie and Veronica's eyes. Mrs Moore squeezed Evie's hand again.

The next morning Evie patted Old Saul while the dogs yapped until Mr Harvey called them into the house. Evie then allowed Sergeant Briggs to hitch the horse up to the cart, which was jointly owned by her family and Simon's. 'Beautiful old boy,' she murmured into his cream mane. Alongside Old Saul was a space for Grace's mare, Sally, and the Manton cart, which Parson Edward Manton, Grace's brother, had said he'd trot over. He arrived in a flurry, leaping from the cart. 'So sorry I can't stay to help, Evie. Parish business.' He hoisted down his bicycle from the cart and tucked his trousers into his socks.

Evie's smile was the genuine article as she led him to the kitchen for a quick cup of coffee, sidestepping Annie and the scullery maids as they cleared breakfast, and Daisy who was after used tea leaves for the sweeping of the sitting room. The thought of dear Edward, with his two left feet, his wayward sense of direction and tendency to drift off into the heavenly ether, trying to help, was not comforting. Far better that he went about his hand-holding.

Her smile died as Richard arrived, standing blocking the doorway to the central corridor. He shook his head. 'No news is good news,' he said, leaning on his walking stick and trying to throw his false leg forward without falling over. He had forbidden anyone to help. Relieved, she left Edward and Richard together and returned to the carts.

Veronica was to drive her trap pulled by Tinker, with as many volunteers as she could cram in. The others would ride bicycles as far as Froggett's farm and then hike round the base of the hill to the bogs. Harry Travers, with Captain Neave, who had been pronounced fit yesterday and would be returning to restricted military duties at the end of the week, would drive Sally's cart and be responsible for stacking the hessian sacks of moss in it, while Evie's da, who was on the back shift at the pit, and Ben, his marra, would drive Old Saul's cart and stack it. Everyone else with two legs and two arms would gather up the moss from the pickers. The gatherers would include Stanhope, who had lost all his fingers when a hand bomb blew up too soon, and was dextrous with his thumbs. Sergeant Harris with the face mask and Captain Simmons without half a leg and his nose would heave the moss on to the carts.

It took an hour to drive to the bog, Evie travelling with Captain Neave, and all the time the wind swirled. Along the verges the primroses struggled in the cold of early spring. In a few weeks there could be cowslips. The hawthorn blossom was about to emerge. Once there, the women hitched up their skirts, the men rolled up their trousers, and everyone removed their boots and waded out, barefoot. It was icy and slimy and Evie's toes sank into the peat. She had left Mrs Moore and Annie to prepare luncheon. It was rabbit and bacon stew with herb dumplings, and tons of carrots, in line with Richard's anti-extravagance initiatives. It was the same meal that Evie and Mrs Moore had provided the previous week, but if it helped Richard to feel he was breaking new ground by issuing orders about economy, building his confidence as a result, then they didn't mind.

Why should they trouble him with the fact that they occasionally added wine that Mr Harvey 'rescued' from Lord Brampton's cellars as per Mr Auberon's instructions, when last home at Christmas. He had the written permission in his desk should Lord Brampton visit and want to see the wine-cellar audit.

Evie's mam explained that they must just yank up the top layer. 'Like this,' she instructed. Evie reached into the bog, tugged at a clump of moss, pulled it up and wrung it out, just as her mam did and as she now remembered doing, with Jack at her side, bonny, bonny Jack. The water ran down her arms and into her sleeves. She threw the moss to the waiting collectors, feeling energy surging to replace that which had seeped from her as they had fed one another's panic and anxiety. 'Come on, Evie, you're lagging behind,' Captain Neave called from the cart. Jack was strong, he would live. She would believe that. She must.

John Neave looked so much better and his shrapnel wounds had healed, his femur too, with Dr Nicholls removing the last of the splinters from near his spine a month ago, rendering him fit for service. Nicholls had kept him back for as long as he could, and had been heard to say to Matron that the boy had done his bit. The powers that be couldn't afford the luxury of letting their experienced officers sit out the war, apparently. 'You can just mind your own business, bonny lad,' Evie retorted. 'I'm a fast finisher.'

She retied her shawl and set to with a will. She'd show him. Again and again she yanked out the moss, wringing it as dry as she could, feeling the debris scratching. It didn't matter. She laughed across at Veronica, and then her mother, knowing that there was a race on. She snatched a look at the piles. John Neave was shouting at her looking at the Forbes and Preston cart. 'Come on, we're losing.' He was stacking her pile in the front of the cart, and Harry was piling more at the back. Her mam's and the other volunteers' harvest was going into the cart her da had charge of. She glanced over. Ben was gazing across the moor. 'Thinking of your next painting, Ben?' she called.

'Aye, lass. I thought the servants' hall could do with some brightening.'

'You're not far wrong,' she replied, easing her back.

John called, 'Away with you, bonny lass. Fill that sack.'

She and her da laughed. 'You're no Geordie, lad,' Evie told him. 'So try again.'

John yelled, 'Get a move on, old girl.'

Her da called, 'Much better.'

Evie went back to work. The sun was creaking through the clouds, giving a weak warmth, but warmth nonetheless. They were moving along the bog, the carts keeping pace. Her hands were sore, but what did that matter? The moss was needed. Harry Travers called, 'We're winning, Evie. Keep going.'

She straightened her back. 'Easy for you, bonny lad. We're the ones with cold feet, sore hands and wet sleeves.' At last it was midday.

They had sandwiches huddled in the lea of the Forbes' cart, and it was as though they were sea-coaling, but instead of wet coal heaped in the cart, there was springy moss in the hessian sacks. Veronica said, 'Mrs Green is setting out the apple store as a picking platform. Old Stan is replacing some of the roof felt with glass so it'll heat up when there's some sun and help dry it, and the draught when the opposing doors are open will help too. He's also drawing up a rota for the moss to be turned by volunteers and patients who want to help. They will also pick it free of debris. Some of the villagers are coming up later today and tomorrow to start off the picking. Others are sewing gauze pockets. The best moss is for dressings, the intermediate for dysentery pads, splint pads, and we chuck the worst.'

Harry said, sipping tea from a mug, 'The sterilisers in the hospital wing are going to do what is necessary, aren't they? I was thinking that perhaps it would do Captain Williams good to have a project, like trying to get more sterilisers to us, and working out where they can go.'

John Neave tossed a crust at him. Harry ducked and laughed. John said, winking at Evie and Veronica, 'Not just a pretty face, eh?' He tossed another crust at Ronald Simmons. 'Whereas, you, my lad, are definitely a pretty face, with or without a nose.'

They all grinned. Matron had heard of a Canadian doctor in the south of England who thought he could do something with faces, and she was trying to find out more.

'Good idea, Harry,' Veronica said, pushing away from the side of the cart, and dusting off her hands. 'We'll install Richard in Father's study. Evie and Mrs Moore will have their kitchen back, and I will stop being a harridan.'

'Oh no, you won't,' came the cry from them all.

The next day Captain Neave's taxi drew up at the door an hour before luncheon on a bright and shining morning, with a sky so blue the birds were soaring for joy. Mr Harvey carried his portmanteau down the steps as he did with all those leaving, regardless of rank. Evie walked with John Neave to the taxi. He kissed her hand, then he smiled, holding out his arms. She hugged him. 'Be safe, be lucky.'

He said, 'I have been up to now. Just being here has been something that has changed my life. When I think of all the people I've met – you especially, Evie – it means so much. Trust that your men are safe, Evie Forbes. Trust that they are, until you hear different, and don't let go of your dream of a hotel. The problem will be that your guests will never leave your kindness and your cooking.'

Matron came to them, crunching across the gravel. She shook hands. Captain Neave held out his arms. She drew herself up to her full length and breadth. It was impressive. 'That's quite enough of that, young man,' she told him. Captain Neave laughed and was still laughing as he threw his captain's obligatory stick into the back of the taxi and bounded in after it. They waved as the taxi roared off down the drive. Matron called, 'Be careful, young John. You just be careful. I won't have our work undone.' Tears were running down her face.

Without turning to Evie she told her, 'You will say nothing, do you understand. You will say nothing to me.' With that she dragged her hand across her eyes, set her shoulders and marched back inside.

Evie waved again, and saw Norman, the telegraph boy from Easton, cycling, head down, up the drive. He passed the taxi, which stopped. She saw John lean from the window and look at the boy's retreating back. Norman was pushing hard on the pedals, trying to make speed on the gravel. Evie could hear him panting as he drew near. He skidded to a stop, looking over her shoulder as he had taken to doing, because he said he couldn't bear to look in people's eyes any more.

He dug into his leather pouch. 'Here you go, Evie, hoy this beggar to Lady Veronica.' He licked the lead of his pencil and thrust the telegram at her. She signed for it. He stuffed the docket into his bag, swung his bicycle round and pedalled back down the drive. John Neave had climbed out, and now flagged the boy down.

Norman stopped. They spoke. Evie took the telegram into the hallway. There were men on stretchers on the floor in the rest room that had been put aside for visitors, and on mattresses in the billiards room, which was for the recreation of all ranks. Neuve Chapelle had taken its toll on all establishments. An orderly was passing. Evie gave him the telegram. 'Let Lady Veronica have this, would you, Sid.'

He grinned. 'This'll put a smile on her face. She's been waiting long enough.'

Evie hurried to the back stairs, heading for the kitchen. She must trust it was good news. She must. She must. Potty would have told them if it wasn't. Yes, that was it, of course, and she was glad that today they were breaching Captain Richard's orders and creating a golden soup, to be removed by Home Farm pork with sautéed potatoes and spring greens from Easterleigh Hall land. This would be removed

107

by honey sponge and custard. The men had been informed. Excitement was in the air, and Captain Richard would have forgotten his instructions.

She leaped down the stairs. Honey sponge had been suggested by young Derek Hayes, just eighteen and here to convalesce. His war was over, his foot left somewhere in France. Had he shot himself? Who the hell cared, Dr Nicholls had said to Evie as they sheltered from the wind beneath the cedar, 'It's far better than losing his mind.'

Mr Thomas, the Hawton bee-keeper, said there was a greater demand for honey as people were still stockpiling, and he might not be able to supply as much as the Hall needed on a regular basis. Nevertheless, the sponge would have an extra few spoonfuls today.

As Evie hurried down the corridor she remembered that Harry Travers's family had beehives. When he got going it was the only time that the young man was boring, such was his interest in the little beggars. She must remember to suggest to him that he sell them jars from home, because he'd be heading back there soon. The false leg Da and Tom, the blacksmith, had made for him was working well, if yesterday's efforts at the bog were anything to go by. He'd be back, of course, because the stump would shrink and adjustments would need to be made.

In the kitchen Annie was up to her elbows in flour, and Mrs Moore was chastising the vegetable volunteers for being lax with their washing of the leaves.

There was a rich smell of tender pork, pumped up with several bottles of Merlot, thanks to Auberon and which Richard mustn't know about. For a moment Evie could see Auberon's grin, his blonde hair falling over his forehead, his eyes that were even more violet than Si's. Aye, the lad had changed into a good, good man. She felt happier than for such a long while, and she started to sing, 'If I was the only girl in the world, and you were the . . .'

She saw that Mrs Moore was looking at her, but no, not at her, behind her, Annie too, and Mrs Barnes from the village, who had stopped chopping carrots. She fell silent, and turned. It was Ver, holding out the telegram, her face alabaster. Captain Richard was behind her, holding on to the door frame, his face rigid.

'Take it,' Veronica told Evie.

'Read it,' Evie insisted.

Captain Richard limped forward, using his cane, and snatched the telegram. 'Mrs Moore, kindly help Veronica and Evie to the stools. Annie, tea at once. Mrs Barnes, would you be so kind as to continue preparations for luncheon. Life must go on.'

Mrs Moore took each woman by the elbow and urged them to sit down. Evie remembered Simon coming to tell her that Timmie, her lovely lad, was dead. Timmie. Tim. Millie. 'Someone fetch Millie,' she said, her voice even and level, but it didn't sound like hers.

Mrs Barnes left the potatoes she was washing in

the zinc sink in the scullery, for there was no peeling of them any more. Every ounce of goodness must be saved. Evie watched as she hurried to the laundry, her pale blue uniform stretched around her ample body. They heard the shriek as Mrs Barnes delivered the message, the running feet, and here Millie was, grabbing Captain Richard, nearly knocking him over. Mrs Moore shouted, 'Sit down, Millie.' She reached for Captain Richard, and set him upright as though he was a bowling pin, Evie thought. A bloody bowling pin.

The telegram was from Potty, not Auberon. 'Captain Hon. Brampton missing believed killed stop almost certain to include Sgt Forbes stop Cpl Preston stop Francis Smith stop my condolences.'

Evie heard someone screaming. Then a slap. The screaming stopped. Mrs Moore rubbed her hand, so swollen with rheumatism. 'You must get a grip of yourself, Millie.'

'Francis?' Evie said. 'Francis?'

Millie was howling, sitting rocking on a stool. 'Roger, you bloody fool, Evie. His name is Francis Smith, little you know about anything.'

Veronica said, 'Father insists on every valet being called Roger, every footman James or Archie. God, oh God.' She was gripping Evie's hand. 'I can't bear it. I won't bear it.' Annie was pouring tea into enamel mugs. She gave one to Evie.

Evie passed it to Veronica. 'You can. You must. We all must. Somehow.' It was she gripping Ver's hand now. Be safe, be lucky, what a bloody laugh. There was a knock on the kitchen door. It was John Neave. 'I spoke to Norman. I wasn't convinced it was quite Auberon's usual message. I will go to your parents, Evie, and to Simon's, shall I?'

Evie pulled away from Veronica. 'Take me, too. They need that.' She looked at Mrs Moore, who nodded, saying, 'Pour more tea, Annie. Captain Richard, brandy if you will, from Mr Harvey, quick as you can. Off you go now, Evie.'

John Neave and Captain Richard muttered together. Evie felt as though she was no longer physically present, her mind was fixed so strongly on the word *believed*. Only believed. Believed. She said it aloud. 'Potty only believes. Remember that. Those who told him don't know. They need a body to know.'

Richard and John said nothing and she knew they thought of artillery, of shells that destroyed, of shell holes full of mud that drowned. She remembered Mart, gone, never found. But the telegram said believed. She reached for Veronica's arm, squeezed it. 'Potty said "believed".'

Chapter 6

Easterleigh Hall, 25th April 1915

On 15th April Tyneside was bombed in a Zeppelin air raid, and the newspapers carried a follow-up article on 25th April. In Richard's study Ver stood close to her husband, feeling his arm around her. 'I love you so much,' she said. 'We're lucky, we have our lives ahead of us, not like these Tynesiders, not like those at Ypres, not like . . .' She stopped. 'Disaster is all around us, darling, it's found our men and now it's coming for us.'

He kissed her hard. 'No, it's not targeting us, you, Evie. It's war, just war, but I think you're overtired, you have rushed and bustled ever since you insisted on returning to duty after your collapse, too early in my opinion.'

They were in Richard's study, looking at the map of the progress of the war pinned up on a board to the left of his desk. A few days after Potty's telegram, while Veronica was in bed, numb and ill from shock and despair, he had sent for his old desk and filing cabinets from his parents' home in Cumbria. He was unwilling to remain in Lord Brampton's study which he had found too repressive, too full of the sense of the beatings Auberon had endured at his father's hand.

Richard had explored the basement, finding many large disused storerooms which he felt would be needed for administrative purposes as the war progressed, but which required electrification. He had chosen the one nearest the servants' hall for his study and purchased what sterilisers he could find for the spaghnum moss, all the while making the arrangements for the electrification of the basement and the attic. He used his own money for all of this, and severely depleted his resources, insisting that it must be done, saying that it was the least he could do for the war effort. It was as though Potty's news, and Veronica's collapse, had jerked him on to a different level, and even improved his memory. Or was it, Veronica wondered, that they all felt that if they worked hard, and were very very good, they would somehow earn the survival of their men? When she finally reappeared in the kitchen after two weeks, she was given cocoa by Evie, and honey cake, and a big hug. 'All will be well,' Evie had said. Somehow one half of Veronica believed her.

Now she held Richard's face between both hands and kissed him. 'Work makes the days pass, darling, and stops me winding myself up like a great spring about everything. But then something breaks through, like the news of the gas the Huns have used at Ypres, which means we'll use it, and then where will it end?' Her head ached from tiredness, but also perhaps from the drilling in the corridor, as the workmen brought electrification to their subterranean world.

'You must try to sleep, darling.'

She smiled. 'I do, sometimes, after . . .' She kissed him again, flushing, remembering the pleasure of those dark hours now he was so improved. 'But it feels wrong, when Aub has gone, when another convoy is on its way here. So many broken minds and bodies, day after day.'

Richard held her close, kissing her neck. 'I know I've said it before, but moments of happiness are not a crime. I know I've also said that you've been on the acute ward for three weeks now, so should you ask Matron for fatigue duties?'

Veronica shook her head. 'I'm useful, I'm learning. I'm needed. I prefer it to dusting, of course I do. It keeps . . . Remember that Evie said they only "believe".'

He kissed her forehead. 'She's right. There's room for doubt. Think of that, not anything else.'

'How can there be doubt about all four? One shell would be enough.' Veronica made herself stop. It did no good, only harm. She shrugged and Richard loosened his grip, turning to the desk. He handed her the costings that Dr Nicholls had produced before going on leave. 'Here, this is what you came for, darling girl, as requested by Nairns. You said Evie would take them up with the kitchen figures,

114

didn't you? I've checked over them and agree with you that they are accurate.'

The temporary Medical Officer, Dr Nairns, was imposing himself and his ideas on Matron, and had just this morning badgered Veronica as commandant for up-to-date accounts of hospital expenditure. 'He seems uncommonly interested in our costings, and far less concerned with the patients than Nicholls,' Richard remarked.

Veronica flicked through them. 'I suppose everyone has their different methods, and we are cutting it very fine with the hospital budget. But at least the funding you're trying to raise for the work programme isn't his concern, so he can keep his nose out of that. He really does seem to be everywhere, like a bad rash, or so Evie puts it. Have you heard back from any of your contacts yet? I know it's difficult, as one hesitates to approach those who are grieving, but needs must. We do have tea parties and a fete planned for the warmer weather, but that's for the hospital.' She drew a quick breath, seeing her husband's patient smile, but she had to keep talking, keep interested, and working. It was what Evie did, but what didn't she do? She was a force of nature, that girl.

There was a bang from the corridor, a shout. 'Watch it, man. That nearly hit me foot.' The drilling resumed.

It was Evie who had suggested that Richard use his skills to produce money for a work programme at Easterleigh Hall when he had finished preparing for the electrification. This had followed his attempts to help in the kitchen, and then a return visit two weeks ago from a partially disabled army corporal and his wife, who could find no work and had no money. They had work now, at Easterleigh Hall, and were being paid, but there were many other ex-patients who had been in touch, their disability pensions proving inadequate. Something had to be done. Money had to be raised, work must be found.

There was a knock on the door and Captain Simmons poked his, she couldn't say nose, round the door and announced, 'Mr Harvey has just taken a phone call from Sir Anthony Travers, Richard. Clearly Harry bent his ear on his weekend home, and he'd like to speak to you at his club in Durham within the next few days, if we'd like to telephone him. Can you manage Durham if I come with you? Didn't say what it was about but it could be some help with funding for those without work. He's a good chap, Sir Anthony is. Or so Father says. He'll put something into the pot too, but I told you that.'

While Ron was speaking Richard had returned to his chair, and was now pushing some papers around, not replying. Veronica beckoned Ron in. She knew that in spite of coming so far, so quickly, her husband still lacked the confidence to leave the confines of Easterleigh Hall and it was becoming a problem, one that Ron had been discussing with Dr Nicholls. He had obviously been discussing it with others too, because he and Harry were as thick as thieves and just as devious. Ron nodded at her, and she spoke her prepared lines, written together with him and Evie first thing this morning.

She said, 'It would be ideal, Ron. He'll need someone with him the first time to circumnavigate any obstacles, as long as you don't mind. People can be cruel, I know they stare, and it won't be easy for you.'

She felt the heat rise on her cheeks because she had never before brought up the fact that he presented himself to the world with facial injuries, but he'd insisted on this when they prepared her words.

Ron said, 'We'll have a high old time, won't we Richard? The two of us out on the town together.'

Evie had suggested that Richard would feel honour bound to accompany a man who dared to face the stares in order to act as support. There was a pause as he continued to tidy the papers on his desk, placing one on top of the other, lining them up exactly. He looked up finally, and grinned. 'I now know that there are absolutely no lengths to which my wife and my friends will go to do what is best for me, so how can I refuse?'

'Splendid, old man. I'll reply in the affirmative.' Ron winked at Veronica and limped out of the room. Veronica reached out and held Richard's outstretched hand, saying, 'Excellent, now the electrification can progress into the study in your absence, giving Evie the time she needs to properly prepare an alternative kitchen before the electricians rip the old one apart.'

'Good God,' Richard said, kissing her hand. 'You two really are witches, as Auberon said. All this Durham business just for that.'

For a moment their smiles faltered. Auberon. Where was he? But Richard was levering himself to his feet, reaching for his cane. 'Will you help me pack?'

There was a knock on the door, and Ron looked in again. 'You can't hear above the noise, but Evie's calling for you, something to do with the pastry for lunch.'

Veronica snatched up the figures and rushed to the door. 'I forgot.'

'Then you are damned for ever. Try telling her that it is your off shift and you are bestowing a great kindness on her,' Richard called after her. 'And I suppose I must pack myself?'

Veronica rushed along the corridor, calling back, 'If you don't mind.' She slowed to step over wires, avoiding men who were drilling holes and wielding screwdrivers. Someone was singing in the laundry. It was Millie, for God's sake. It was as though she had leapt into widowhood with alacrity and pleasure, appearing in black the day after the news, tripping through the kitchen, her hair damp from the early morning mist, her face the picture of someone bereaved. Veronica had thought that Evie would strike her, but Mrs Moore had stepped into the fray, giving Millie a flea in her ear for jumping the gun, shouting, 'Believed dead, you silly girl.' She had then shoved her down the corridor and into the laundry.

Since then Millie had remained firmly in black and asked daily about some money to help eke out her earnings, but as Richard pointed out, she was still receiving her allotment at this stage from Jack's wages. He had also emphasised that Potty still had no more news that would alter the fact that they were 'believed' killed. Mrs Moore had said, more diplomatically than usual, that shock took people in strange ways and perhaps this was the case with Millie.

Veronica slowed to enter the kitchen where all was cheerful bustle and seeming chaos, with the usual discarded knitting guarded by the dogs on the two armchairs by the furnace, ready for the night shift to work on between providing what food and drink was needed. It wasn't chaos of course, but it was cheerful. It had to be, it was the rule of the house. Evie looked up and jerked her head towards the pastry waiting on the marble slab. 'You wanted to learn how to do this, so stop messing about in Richard's cubbyhole and get to it, young lady. It needs to be cool, hence the marble. It does not need to be kept waiting in the heat of the ranges.'

Veronica placed the accounts for Nairns on the dresser and snatched a white cotton apron from the hook by the door. She had half an hour before her shift began in the hospital, just time to roll out the pastry and learn how to line the pie dishes, but she couldn't stop looking at Evie who had such dark circles under her eyes, and was even paler than yesterday, and the day before, and before that. Fear clutched at Veronica. This girl's fiancé and brother were missing but nonetheless she never slacked, never failed to smile, or run the kitchen to its full capability. As if that wasn't enough she played with Tim over in the nursery her mother ran, and was always ready to laugh and joke with the men, but what if one day she did stop? What would they all do?

As though Mrs Moore could read her thoughts, she heard the head cook say as she came in from the central corridor with tea towels heaped in her arms, 'Good, you're here, Lady Veronica. Then we will have a bit of a sit-down in my parlour, if you please, Evie. We have those kitchen figures to go through, those that Dr Nairns has requested. He's requested every single invoice, if you can believe that, Lady Veronica, as though Mr Harvey hasn't been in charge of our accounts since time began.'

Mrs Moore put the tea towels next to Veronica's accounts, picked these up and waited, watching Evie, who was ignoring her and instead was checking the Home Farm lamb that was slowly casseroling in all three ranges, with an overload of carrots, turnips and parsnips to eke it out, as everyone agreed they should, as shortages were beginning to occur. 'Now,' Mrs Moore bellowed. The kitchen staff froze. Evie straightened and wiped her hands down her apron, saying, 'Keep your hair on.'

She raised her eyebrows at Annie and Veronica as she followed Mrs Moore out of the kitchen. They passed Mrs Green, who was almost running from the airing cupboard to the stairs. A fresh convoy had just arrived, this time from Ypres where what was being called the Second Battle of Ypres was taking place. Poor Canadians, bearing the brunt, poor all of them. Soon they'd be arriving, after every push it was the same, and in between, with the steady attrition, it was the same.

Veronica wielded the rolling pin under Annie's expert eye.

In his study, while Ron was upstairs phoning Sir Anthony, Richard stared at his portmanteau. Was now the time to give dearest Ver her brother's sealed letter that was to be opened in the event of his death? It was a question that didn't linger, because hope hadn't left the building. Not yet. Not yet. But soon common sense must take its place because Richard had been in northern France, he had lived here, at the hospital, and who could not be a realist after all of this? These women, that's who: this monstrous regiment who might waver, but would hold on until the absolute end. Grace had written, and she, too, would not let hope fade.

In the parlour Evie sat in the armchair, opposite Mrs Moore, watching her flick through the paperwork. She couldn't sit, she really couldn't. She leapt to her feet. 'Sit down,' bellowed Mrs Moore, pushing her spectacles up her nose, peering over the top. 'Just stop this endless activity. You have to be well for the patients, and for Simon and Jack when we know where they are. Now stop it or Matron will be down again, worrying over you. I just wish Dr Nicholls hadn't taken it upon himself to go on leave, because I'd get him down to check you. That's men for you.'

Evie sat down. 'There's no need for worry.'

'What do you call wobbling all over the place in the kitchen the other day, if it's not cause for worry?'

'The heat from the oven took me by surprise.' The door into Mrs Moore's basement bedroom was open and Evie wondered, not for the first time, what it must be like to sleep in a room with no windows. At least up in her attic room she could see as far as Fordington, and the sea, in between the folds of the hills, with not a sign of the pits. It was just country-side, and sky.

'Nonsense, you need to get some decent sleep. Your mam thinks so too, and I heard her telling you only yesterday.'

Evie said, 'I could be the only one left, Mrs Moore. First Timmie, now Jack, and Simon. It's lonely, Mrs Moore, and I can't bear it for me mam and da, or for me.' She shut her lips on the words she had refused to voice before, which had somehow bubbled to the surface. But they must sink again, because everyone needed her to be strong.

Mrs Moore wiped her glasses. Evie watched her. Mrs Moore said, '"Believed dead"', remember that. You can't keep everyone else's spirits up but ignore hope yourself, Evie lass.'

Evie started to rise. 'They will be back from the bog with more moss. They will need hot drinks.'

Mrs Moore gestured her to sit, and snapped, 'You have trained your staff well. Trust them to manage. You are almost, but not quite, indispensable, so lean back and do as I say.' Evie took one look at her and did as she was told, feeling the air leave her body quite suddenly as it had started to do recently. It was as though she was a balloon that had been pierced when the telegram came. It was just a tiny hole, one she could almost see, and each day the breath left her body a little bit more and was not replenished. Sometimes, though, it just gushed from her and left her limp, empty, and weak, as it had last week, so that she wobbled like a jelly, daft beggar that she was.

Now in this chair, in this room which she loved as much as the woman sitting opposite her, she struggled for breath, found it, nurtured it, her limbs as heavy as lead, lost it again, searched and found traces. She panted it back into her lungs. For a moment all she could see was black.

Millie's black dress.

Every day, Jack's wife came in that black dress.

But Potty had said, 'Believed dead' Evie had told her. 'Grow up, Evie,' Millie had said.

It was at night when Evie had time to think, lying in her bed, wondering where they were, or how they had died, seeing the long years ahead with everyone gone, or not. Perhaps hurt, or not. They were her lovely lads, Simon, Jack, Aub. Perhaps she'd never see Si's red hair again, feel his soft lips, perhaps he was out there buried in mud, shrinking into a skeleton, perhaps there'd be no more burned onions from Aub, she could almost smell them, see the smoke, no more screeching knives from Jack.

Yes, she was tired but she couldn't sleep, and every day, and night, there were more convoys, every day now there were electricians and spirit stoves to organise, and today the accounts must be taken upstairs to placate Nairns, and what was Bastard Brampton up to? It was such a strange thing, this world at war. It seemed unreal, but wasn't. It existed, and was like a wheel that went round, and round, picking up bits, dropping them, leaving its filthy tracks wherever it went, on whatever it rolled.

Mrs Moore fanned herself with Dr Nairns' papers, then tossed them on to the table. 'I know I usually say that work is the answer in a crisis, but within reason. A body can't go on and on, even if it belongs to a pitman's daughter. You must accept the need for rest, in order to be strong. Do you understand me, Evie Forbes?'

Evie had watched as Mrs Moore's lips framed the

words, and slowly she nodded. 'Aye, I do understand. It's what I tell myself, so you're right.' She made herself smile, as Mrs Moore laughed, but what Mrs Moore did not understand was that the one thing she could not be was weak, because everyone depended on her strength. 'I believe and hope, I do really, Mrs Moore. I mostly do. Sometimes though it just goes out of me, like the air.' Mrs Moore looked puzzled, but Evie continued, 'I can't tell you how long I will go on hoping because I don't know, but I won't stop for a long while. We owe it to them, to the lads.' She sat straighter, feeling the breath restored inside her again, and the blackness fading, as she groped for more of the words that Mrs Moore wanted to hear. 'I don't feel that they've gone, not here, inside me.'

Mrs Moore just nodded. 'If the time comes when you have to accept the darkness, then you will manage, just as all the other poor souls are doing. In the meantime we have many a young man who will only want beef tea tonight after arrival, or calves'-foot jelly, or egg custard, but you won't be on shift. You will be sleeping. If not sleeping, resting. Tomorrow you will do the rounds of your poor wee new boys to see what are their favourites, and together we will produce them. On the ranges at the moment, and on spirit stoves later.'

She crossed her arms. 'Now you will rest. If you can sleep, well and good, but if not, then you just lean back and close your eyes. All I want you to do

125

when you wake is to take these accounts to Dr Nairns, and then have a gentle walk in the fresh air. Your mother and I have discussed this and she is of the same mind, so nice and easy does it.' Mrs Moore heaved herself up from her armchair, then glanced down at her side table. 'Oh, but best read this letter Nairns sent down for you, which is probably some nonsense about more finicky stocktaking that we can deal with together. I gather the wretched man is a member of the same club as Lord Brampton and came here on Brampton's orders, but why, one wonders?' She stopped. 'The ramblings of an old woman. Forget my words.'

Evie felt the prickle of the upholstery under her hands as she gripped the arms of her chair. Nairns knew Brampton? She breathed deeply, looking at the letter Mrs Moore was placing on top of Nairns' papers. Mrs Moore said, 'Not now, Evie. Instead, see, I have a new photo.' She was pointing at the frames above the fireplace. Evie saw the usual photograph of Grace, Mrs Moore's first employer, on the wall. Next was another, one she had not seen before. It was of herself with Mrs Moore, taken at Christmas beside the tree. Standing behind them were Jack, Auberon and Si in civilian clothes, smiling. She leaned back in her chair, watching them until she slept, and all the while the tears ran silently down her face, soaking her collar and uniform.

When she awoke Mrs Moore had gone. She checked her watch; two hours had passed, more than she had slept in weeks. Nairns' papers were still on the table. On the top was the envelope addressed to her, in black ink, with a sloping hand. She reached forward, pushed her finger under the flap and ripped it open. She read, and then read again. As she did so she felt the air rushing in, stretching her balloon thinner and thinner. Who did this man think he was? How dare he?

She crushed the letter and left the room, returning immediately to collect the papers. She looked neither to left nor right as she headed along the hall, the words in the letter dancing in her head. She pounded up the stairs, through the baize door and into the grand hall, almost floating in the air that stretched and thinned the balloon. Lance Corporal Samuels, the orderly on duty, stood up at his desk. Ambulances were arriving, all was activity. Orderlies, nurses, VADs and Matron were hurrying across the hall, into wards, down the steps to the ambulances, then back up the steps alongside the stretchers. Steve Samuels had a pencil behind his ear, and another in his hand. Did he know he had two? Did it matter? 'All well, Evie?' She could see herself in his boots, and even his putties looked pressed.

'Soon will be, pet,' she gasped. Steve Samuels reached out, concerned. 'Evie, what is it?'

She spun away, weaving between these people who were bent on saving lives, but so too was she. She entered Dr Nairns' office without knocking. It was one of the anterooms, the one that Dr Nicholls had commandeered as the hub of the Medical Officer's empire. Nairns was drinking a cup of coffee. She dropped the papers on his desk, and then the letter he had sent. It was still crushed. He looked up, his lips thin. 'Did I hear a knock?'

She said, leaning forward, taking her weight on her hands, forcing him to withdraw sharply against his chair, 'I doubt it, unless it was my head banging on my kitchen table at your ridiculous time-wasting shenanigans. We haven't time for this rubbish, you absurd little man. How dare you send paperwork asking for specific numbers of knives, forks, spoons, cups, and instigating a weekly stocktake of said items as though we are overrun with kitchen thieves? As for demanding sterilisation of all cutlery, mugs and God knows what else, Maud, our scullery maid runs a tight ship, and there has been no history of stomach trouble since we started the hospital. Unless, of course, you count those who have half their guts hanging out when they arrive.'

She had moved even closer to him, and he was pale by now. His sandy hair, which he swept over his bald pate, had plunged over his wire-rimmed spectacles. He put up a hand. She slapped it down, actually slapped it. She saw the shock on his face and it only fuelled her fury, and was the only thing that seemed to reduce the air inside her. 'We are short of all supplies so where are we to get yet more sterilisers? Captain Richard has obtained as many as are available and is moving mountains to fulfil the needs of the hospital as it is. Where are your priorities?'

She was panting, air was rasping in and out, hurting her chest. She must draw more in. She stood upright. 'You require invoices from us, figures that balance. Mr Harvey provides Lord Brampton's accountant with these, so why must he copy them out a second time, for you too? We're busy here, rushed, tired, with always more to do.' Dr Nairns rose too, his mouth open. She put up her hand. His mouth closed. She continued, shouting in her rage. 'We run our kitchens to the commandant, Lady Veronica's, satisfaction, and also to that of Matron and Dr Nicholls. I will suggest that we cut up those papers into squares and hang them in the latrines, and you may use your imagination as to their further use, but buttocks come to mind. Is this quite clear? If there is any more fuss, then beware the food you eat. Who knows what will be in it for the few weeks that you remain here. Now, as for the letter, if you dare to order the dismissal of Mrs Moore and Annie, to be replaced by volunteers under my control in the interest of economy, then you are missing a great many brain cells. Mrs Moore is essential, Annie too.'

The air was leaving her, coming out in great bursts along with her words, and none was replacing it. She knew tears were not far behind, but no, she would not allow them to come. 'I repeat, Dr Nicholls and Matron, and Lady Veronica, our commandant, have no reservations about the running of the kitchen

129

and until they do, nothing changes, because you, as a temporary Medical Officer, have no authority to dismiss anyone. Nothing changes. Do. You. Understand?'

Dr Nairns walked out from behind his desk to her side, towering above her, a piece of paper in his hand. She faced him as he waved the paper and began to speak. 'I care not what Dr Nicholls, Matron, or indeed the Lady Veronica have to say on the subject. Here I have a directive from Lord Brampton. In it he explains that he has arranged for Dr Nicholls to be transferred to a new auxiliary hospital outside Newcastle and I am to remain until this . . .' He waved his hand towards the grand hall. 'This chaotic sloppy informal mess is under control and that means more volunteers and fewer paid servants, and strict rules of hierarchy. Those that remain must pull their weight. Your Mrs Moore does not, and Annie's work can be taken over by any flibbertigibbet from the village.'

'The kitchen is the powerhouse . . .'

'You stupid little girl.' He sliced the air; the directive fell fluttering to the floor. Evie forced herself to stand firm, feeling his spittle on her cheek as he roared, 'The government pays three shillings per patient per day. It costs this establishment three shillings and ninepence, but that is rising. His Lordship is not prepared to shoulder the burden of the extra cost any more, but instead is opening another hospital nearer Leeds, a smaller establishment, the upkeep of which is to be shared with an influential Member of Parliament. We either close, or we make the changes and operate within three shillings per patient per day. To do this, we must lose staff, and if you wish to keep Mrs Moore, then do so. You however, will be off these premises by the evening, and perhaps this will encourage you to treat your betters with respect. One must hope that Mrs Moore will last the course without you, or die trying. Do. *You*. Understand?'

Evie stared at him, feeling the weakness threatening. He had spittle in the corners of his mouth, protruding nasal hair, and thin lips. For the first time she noticed that he was old, drawn and tired, with an air of grief and fury so tangible that she could almost touch it. Had he lost someone? What did anyone know about anyone else?

He pressed closer. She smelt the coffee on his breath. She would not move. She transferred her weight on to the balls of her feet, as Jack had done when he was fighting. She breathed deeply, and again. 'I will leave, but I will return as one of the volunteers.' Her voice was totally calm. She turned and strode to the door, wrenching at the handle. It opened. He said, 'You will not enter these premises again. Do you understand? You have caused trouble, and I will not tolerate it. Be gone by this evening.'

She turned on her heel, exiting into the entrance hall. There Matron and Sister Newsome stood, transfixed. Behind them stood Lance Corporal Samuels, his mouth hanging open. Evie smiled, breathing, refilling the balloon. 'You'll catch flies, young man,' she told him. All around people were working, helping the patients, carrying stretchers. There was the odd shout, the odd groan.

She managed to walk to the baize door without faltering, though the balloon was still punctured, the air easing out, slowly, steadily, and the weakness was building. She descended the stairs, walked to the back door, the one that the volunteers used when going outside to smoke their Woodbines. She must climb the steps and breathe in the air, and walk home, to the Forbes home, where she could sleep, just for a moment. She just needed to sleep because her head was bursting with his words, words which were jumping and juggling.

She walked across the yard, then down by the yew hedge, through the birches where the cowslips splashed yellow against the grass, past the thatched bothy where she and Si used to meet. Sometimes they would kiss, sometimes they would take their bikes and cycle to the sea at Fordington. Sometimes . . . Or never again?

She stopped, returned to the bothy, pulled out her bike from amongst the rest, including Si's. It was rusting. She must clean it in case . . . But not now. Now, she would ride to the sea. There she could breathe. She pushed hard on the pedals; the right one squeaked. One, two, three, one, two, three, again, and again and steadily the squeak lessened and there was just the call of the thrush, somewhere a wood pigeon, the shout of a pheasant. She turned at the crossroads, and head down she passed the hedges in full May blossom, on past the turning to the beck. Now the stream ran alongside, slecky and turgid, then into Easton, past the parsonage. She wanted to stop, to be where Grace had been. She didn't, she kept going through Easton, in the shadow of the slagheap, smelling the sulphur, seeing the winding gear of Auld Maud. People waved. She did not. Her hand was too heavy. Out of Easton, still on Brampton's tarmac road and now the squeak had disappeared. One, two, three. On and on, gliding on Brampton's smooth road. Brampton. Brampton. But the Bastard had no right to the space inside her head. Brampton. Brampton. He had money. How could he cut his support when it was his idea in the first place? She turned left as she and Simon had done, on to the track, over the bridge towards Fordington. It was cold but soon she would be able to breathe, and inflate the balloon, mend the puncture, somehow.

On and on she rode until she reached the sand and felt the wind that whipped at her, the waves that pounded and roared, the smell of salt. It was so clean. She dismounted and let the bicycle drop and walked along the sand, stepping over the sea coal scattered the length of the bay. She shaded her eyes and looked towards the Lea End section. By, that had been a glorious day when Timmie and Jack had swum to save Edward. Silly Edward, what would he think of the Lea End lot fighting alongside Si, Jack and Aub? Yes, fighting with them, because they were still alive. She needed to say the words in case God was listening. They would come back here and they'd all be friends together. No one would be thrown into the waves again.

She walked on, the sand slipping beneath her boots. There weren't many waves today. It must be grand to float, to feel the water, to be rocked until you slept. Where was Si? Where was Jack? Where are you, Aub? Stop the fighting for a moment and let's find them. Aub promised, you see, to keep them safe, all of them safe, him too.

She lifted her head. Above her the gulls were wheeling and crying as the water rose to her knees, dragging at her uniform skirt, but why should the gods and Aub keep all her loved ones safe, when she had not protected Mrs Moore? She had thought she could come back without pay to help her do the job that was now beyond her. It had not worked. It never worked against the bosses, they crushed you, just as they crushed Timmie. But no, Jack said they hadn't. He could have died anyway.

The waves were breaking on her, lolling against her waist, pushing and pulling her, lifting her off her feet, then setting her down again. She forced her legs to move towards the horizon though she could no longer feel them, and the air was clean, it was deep in her lungs and it was time to sleep, to be rocked beneath the wheeling gulls and the pure air.

She leaned back, watching the gulls, and sank into the sea which carried her as though she was a feather, the water soothing her face, again and again. She coughed. Jack had swum, how he had swum to save the parson. Her skirt dragged, she couldn't move, her legs were gone, just absent, her arms too, but that was right canny, right grand, because all she wanted was to sleep, just sleep.

Oh, how Jack had swum. In and out of those hurtling waves and then he had dipped below them, and above, and then below and had sunk. Timmie had caught him up, laughed in his face, and together they had brought in the parson. She had watched, seen, heard about it later after they had brought the daft man back together. Together.

'Jack,' she called. 'Jack, stay with me while I sleep, I'm so tired. Jack, don't leave me alone.' The water was in her mouth, it caught in her throat, strong salt, the gulls were screaming, screaming her name. She shut her eyes, and now there was no water on her face, but it was drawing her down, holding her safely.

'Evie, Evie. I'm coming. Swim to us.' Jack was swimming to her, she could see him, and she smiled, but the voice called again, and it wasn't his. Whose was it? It was there, in the distance, calling and calling. 'Evie, Evie.' It was kind, and she knew it, needed it. It was all she wanted. Jack, Timmie and Simon were coming, there, through the water, swimming, smiling. She reached out but they were swept away by the current. They called, but there was another voice too, the voice of someone she must find, the voice of someone who would save her because her lungs were full. Quite full and he would come and take her where she could sleep, with him, for ever.

She moved her arms, because he was over there, but she couldn't see him. She tried again, tried to reach out, almost. She was on her side, tumbling with the sea, her lungs bursting, she must open her mouth, she must call to them, as they were calling to her. 'Come on. Try. Swim. Come on.' It was Jack, Simon and Timmie

She was so tired, too tired, and her clothes were heavy, clothes that were her uniform, but it didn't matter, she didn't need it. She could sleep and so she let the sea take her, down and down. She was rolling, gently, and she could hear them, Jack, Simon and Timmie, but over there, behind them, was the blue, the blue of violets. There was his voice. Jack was reaching for her, smiling, but he, the other, was coming, she knew he was, and now there was a flash of yellow. She reached out, past Jack, past Simon and Timmie, and he was coming. Soon she'd see him. Soon.

But then she felt hands, digging into her shoulders, another snagged her hair, pulling. Her arm was gripped, pulled. She turned over, because that lovely voice was calling, 'I'm coming, Evie.' She smiled, reached out, and then there was pain because her arm was yanked up, she was leaving the voice, leaving him, because someone was pulling, pulling. Her shoulder screamed with pain, popped. Her lungs were too full. They were bursting. There was someone holding her, kicking, kicking upwards, someone else was hurting her arm, her shoulder, the sea was snatching at her, wanting her to tumble with it, play with it. Her arm was pulled, harder. The pain. She screamed. Choked. Swallowed.

She couldn't breathe, of course she couldn't breathe, she was under the bloody sea, and now she was fighting because the pain was tearing at her, and she was kicking in her boots, and clinging to the man. Her arm was still being pulled, and her hair. Her arm was released, the man held her tighter, and was kicking harder, and now there was air, and the sound of gulls, and two men, and wind, and salt on her lips and she was choking, coughing, spitting out water and saliva. Pain roared in her shoulder and down her arm and it was Ron Simmons holding her, laughing, turning her on her back, and stroking for shore, with Steve Samuels helping. Ron Simmons was shouting, 'Fine day for a swim, our Evie. Fine bloody day, you daft girl. Take your damned boots off next time. Thought we'd let you go, did you?'

They were in the shallows now, and Samuels was hauling her by her armpits over the sand and the sea coal, while Ron Simmons did a funny doggy paddle alongside, right into the shallows, and then he crawled. 'Had to take the bottom of me leg off,

Evie, the only thing it's not good for.' Samuels was taking her weight as her skirt clung and made life difficult as they struggled through the surf for the last two yards. 'Heard the lot, I did. Bloody bastard, that little worm is. Needs to be dealt with, but that's for another day.'

They were out of the water, and Evie fell to the sand with Samuels on one side of her and Simmons the other. Both men were laughing. Simmons panted, 'We came to find you in the kitchen but you'd gone. Parson phoned after you'd passed him like a whirling dervish, looking fit to commit murder. Your mam guessed you were heading for the sea.'

They were both without their shirts, pale and shivering with the cold. Evie struggled upright. Samuels held out his hand to Simmons, and hauled him up. Simmons hopped, then his good leg gave way. Samuels took his weight as Simmons laughed again. 'Ooops-a-daisy.' Water ran from the nasal holes in his face. He wouldn't look the same with a nose, Evie decided.

Veronica and her friend Lady Margaret, who helped look after the recovering facial injuries, were running towards them with towels, which they wrapped around Evie, holding her close but avoiding her arm. 'Matron gave us leave, busy though we are. I will pay for this, mark my words,' Veronica shouted above the surf and the wind. All the time they were rubbing and Evie felt warmth returning, and with it came even more pain. She said, 'I needed to sleep.

I got confused.' She looked out to sea. He was gone. He? He?

Lady Margaret said, 'I remember a time when I was confused, after hunger-striking and suffragette campaigning. I think that you are just extremely sad, worried and tired, like I was.'

Lance Corporal Samuels was grabbing towels from the pile that Lady Margaret had dropped and threw one to Ron, who was sitting on the sand. They both rubbed their hair dry, and slung the towels, sopping wet, round their shoulders. 'Heave ho, me old matey,' Steve said, hauling Ron to his feet. Ron had his false leg in his other hand. Lady Margaret picked up their clothes, and together they stumbled along towards the Rolls-Royce, which was pulled on to the beach as far as was safe. Samuels said, 'You need to get confused nearer home another time, Evie. In the pond would be good.'

She looked out to sea again, hearing the gulls, feeling the wind, the cold. She said, 'Thank you for saving me.' She thought she meant it, but wasn't sure.

They drove towards Easton, sitting on towels with Lady Margaret in the driving seat, through the pit village, and straight to Evie's parents' home under Stunted Tree Hill. Her mam and Tim were there, and the range was stoked. Dr Nicholls had been sent for. He was at Fenton House near Newcastle and would fix her shoulder, which Lady Veronica announced was dislocated. They felt it best not to ask Dr Nairns, as if they did, either Evie or he would not live to see the end of the day.

Ron Simmons sat next to Evie on the sofa, wrapped in a blanket. 'What are we to do? How do we get Evie's job restored? What say you, Lady Veronica?' His holes were still running and he held a handkerchief to them that Evie's mam had given him.

'It's bigger than just me though, don't you see,' Evie said, her mam sitting on the sofa arm and gripping her hand as though she would never let her go. 'How can we protect Mrs Moore and the hospital from your father, Ver? How can we make the economies he wants?'

Lady Veronica was collecting up the towels, folding them to take them to the laundry at Easterleigh Hall. She had given Evie a sedative because the pain was ripping through her body. Lady Margaret was sitting at the table, fiddling with the strips of material waiting to be incorporated into Susan Forbes' latest proggy rug. Veronica replied at last, 'Steve told us all he had heard and Captain Richard is working on that now, and it's something we all need to think about. *We*, Evie, not just you. And somehow we must get Dr Nicholls back, too, though the most important thing is for us all to somehow bear the waiting. Just as everyone else must.'

'Talking of time, which we weren't altogether,' said Lady Margaret, looking at her watch, 'I need to get back to my patients, I really do. It's the dressings, you know. The moss is helping the pain of their faces but they like people with whom they are familiar to attend them, especially Major Granville.' She flushed.

Evie's mother was now pouring tea, using the best china. 'There is time for a cup of tea, and don't fret, all will be well,' she said. Everyone laughed but they were all so far away, Evie thought, and drifted now, down into the water, searching.

Veronica received Auberon's kit on 28th April, the same day that letters arrived telling the enlisted men's families that they were missing in action, presumed dead. Their kit accompanied the letters. Lance Corporal Samuels took control at Easterleigh Hall and carried Auberon's kit up to Veronica and Richard's suite. He said nothing, just saluted, and left.

Veronica insisted that it was she who unpacked. Her fingers struggled with the cracked and dried leather straps. The dirt of Neuve Chapelle fell on to her carpet. She took out Auberon's spare uniform, his boots. They smelt of war, and filth. They were lice-ridden. Why? No one had worn them recently? His letter to her, written on the eve of the battle, was here. It had not been posted. So no one thought he was dead? Or had it simply been overlooked?

She read it. He spoke of Wainey, their nanny, and their mother, how he had loved them, how he had learned at last their lessons of fairness, of responsibility. He spoke finally of his love for her, his hope that she would find happiness with Richard, who was a good sort. He ended, 'Your ever-loving brother, Aub.'

Right at the bottom, alongside his scarf knitted by Annie, and a pair of spare socks Veronica remembered Evie wrestling with, was his diary. She looked at Richard, who said, 'It is up to you.' While she read his last entry aloud Richard checked Auberon's boots, pulling at the heels, which did not move. He seemed pleased. He said, 'He's got his compass, otherwise it would be in one of these heels. He stands a chance of getting back if . . .'

Veronica interrupted. 'Listen, Richard. Listen to this. "Of course, the sun rises and sets with her but as long as she is happy and loved by him, then what more is there? I suppose this is the height of love, something that does not require fulfilment of self. Please God, he lives through this mess, and that I can help in that objective. For her sake."'

Richard reached across and took the diary from her. 'I think we must not read any more. It is not ours to know.' Veronica stared at her hands, at the dirt that engrained her skin. She hadn't cried for some days, but now she did.

Chapter 7

Near Neuve Chapelle, 20th March 1915

Jack and Auberon shambled ahead of Roger and Simon. The German uhlans, cavalrymen who seemed to have misplaced their horses, had cut their packs from them, and all their webbing, including their belts and chucked them into a pile. Captain Brampton had retained his leather straps and belt as behoved an officer, and as such to be respected, or was it feared? The Germans had ripped watches from the enlisted men's wrists, but Auberon still had his.

The rain drizzled down as it had when they were captured a few hours ago; kicked to consciousness around the edge of the shell hole, up to their bloody eyes in mud and guts, with the noise of the flies, gorging on the bodies, overhanging everything. Jack had thought for a moment he was in amongst a meadow of bees. Hadn't Evie talked of bees in a letter? Something about honey sponge? Another kick had brought him back to the noise, and stink.

A guard menaced them with his rifle as they kicked up mud, the noise of battle still all around, the artillery pounding, the machine guns chattering,

'*Schnell*,' he bawled, hate in his eyes. Well, who wouldn't menace the enemy who had sent over a barrage for hours and then advanced, death and hate in *their* eyes. When you thought of it, they were bloody lucky they hadn't been run through where they'd lain. Jack wiped his mouth with the back of his hand; they damn well would have been if Auberon hadn't shouted, 'Throw away your weapons. Do it now, Jack, or I'll shoot you myself.'

Jack asked him now, as they were jeered by other Huns weighted down by their packs, marching to the Front, the dusk lit by great balloons of orange, the ground shuddering beneath their feet, 'Would you, Aub, would you have shot me?'

'Of course I bloody would. Right through your heart, you bloody fool, Jacko.' He was grinning. Jacko? Jack realised then what he'd called his captain. 'Sorry, sir, can't think straight. Won't happen again.' He snatched a look around, but no one had heard, they were too busy stumbling along, either side and in front and behind, a lot of Tynesiders amongst them, some Indians, poor buggers. Too bloody cold for them. Too bloody cold for any of them.

Auberon slipped on the mud. Jack caught him, shouting as the guns became rapid, and vicious. 'Because I called you, well, you know. Aub. It's just that . . . Oh, I don't know, I don't get knocked off me feet by a shell every day and kicked awake to find a bayonet pointing at me gut.'

'It's not a problem, Jack, good to have friends from

144

home. Best not in front of the other men, though, eh?'
Jack felt blood trickling down inside his collar. The
shell burst had created shrapnel that had sliced above
his ear, and he had shrapnel splinters along his arm,
back and ribs as had they all, he reckoned. What was
more, he'd lost time, they'd all lost it when the blast
knocked them down like bloody skittles, ripping their
clothes and flesh and sending them into the land of
Nod. But at least they weren't dead, as those who
had been to the left were. No, they were disgraced,
they were cowards, they'd surrendered. Jack felt sick.

'*Schnell*,' the elderly soldier said again, hitting Jack
with his rifle butt. Jesus, it hurt. There was shrapnel
in that shoulder, too. 'Jack,' warned Auberon. 'Do
nothing. Just keep going.'

Each step hurt, jogging his wounds, light though
they really were, and his head felt full to bursting.
He glanced over at Simon. 'You doing all right, lad?'
Simon was helping Roger, who was limping and
groaning. Jack dropped back, took Roger's weight.
'Go ahead, stay with the boss.'

He heard Auberon's laugh as Simon nodded. 'Aye,
bloody heavy, he is. Almost a dead weight, but when
isn't he? How much of it is real, Lord knows, but
he'll be stabbed if he falls.'

Jack grunted. 'Don't tempt me.'

They struggled on, mile after mile, and three of
the Lea End lot were here too, Jim, Dave and Mike,
and they took turns to help lug the batman along,
soon to be joined in the effort by Auberon, which

astonished the uhlans. It astonished the prisoners too, the long stream before and behind them. Roger seemed almost unconscious, though there were few visible wounds. As their sergeant, Jack shouldered the lion's share of the waste of space. It seemed a good penance for capture. The shame of his surrender hurt him more than the shrapnel.

On they slogged, through the dusk and into the night, and now Roger was a dead weight, requiring two to drag him along. Jim and Jack took their turn as the guards alongside were joined by horse-mounted uhlans now with lances, who jostled them as they marched, the bits and bridles jingling in the pauses between shells. 'Jack,' warned Auberon, as he lifted his free arm to beat back a lance. He continued to put one foot in front of the other but his stomach thought his throat had been cut, so hungry was he, so thirsty too.

He hitched Roger up, but young Dave had caught him up. 'Give over, Sarge, I'll have him for a bit. Mike'll take over from Jim.'

Jack slipped back one pace, keeping his eye on the uhlans, easing himself out just a foot so that he'd be nudged by the bloody great horse, not the lad. On they plodded, lit by just the moon. He could hear the clink of the horses' bridles, the guns, coughs, curses, a muttered conversation. Jim behind him was saying, 'Never thought I'd be here. Thought I'd be in bits, or home. Not this.'

Jack hadn't thought it either, he'd *known* he'd die

fighting, but to be lying there in mud and stink, looking up into the eyes of the enemy holding a bloody great bayonet at his throat . . . Why hadn't he fought, God dammit? He'd done nothing except shake his head, try to make sense of it, his ears whooshing, his head thick and stupid. He'd done nothing except struggle up, then look around, and finally his hand had gone to his knife. It was then Auberon had given his order. It had been the right one. The Huns would have killed the lot of them.

Soon he took over with Roger again, and Si took the other side, but Auberon dropped back, his face drawn in the weak moonlight, the snow falling. 'I'll take him now.' He pulled him from Jack. 'Never thought this would happen. Never, ever.'

'You heard my thoughts, Aub.' He walked alongside his officer.

'That's right, Jacko.' They laughed quietly. The marching didn't stop. The prisoners opened their mouths, letting the sleet, for that was what it was now, moisten their throats. At last, at midnight, they were halted and herded into a wheatfield, its emerging shoots and soil chewed by stray shells. There were shadows in the distance, probably trees. There was barbed wire, higher than a man, being snagged on to makeshift posts by the guards to corral the column.

'Water? For the wounded?' Sergeant Major Dawson asked. The guard shook his head. '*Nein.*' The prisoners sank down into the dank earth. Near Jack there was a youngster, his head on his knees.

His sniper's badge was visible in the moonlight. Jack inched across and ripped it off. The lad jerked awake, his face tear-stained. 'Hey,' he yelled. Jack hissed, 'If they see that, they'll more than likely shoot you. Spread the word. Machine-gunners, snipers, hand-bombers, get rid of the badges.' The lad was no more than eighteen, if that. Jack pressed his shoulder. 'Poacher back home, eh, got a few rabbits with an airgun? Did well myself. Stay with us. It's better in a group, always. Where's your section?'

The lad inched back with Jack and settled down next to him. 'Overrun. Charlie's my name. I'm a gamekeeper, well learning to be. B section, North Tynes.'

Some of the men had carried injured pals on groundsheets. Auberon asked for water. Two buckets were brought, having been filled from the animal trough. There was nothing else, except the water that would have been present at the bottom of the shell holes, and God knew what else was down there, or who else, or how many. Jack looked round: there must have been over eighty men in the field. Auberon was sitting nearby with Simon. Roger was lying at their feet. Jack said, 'Had to be a boss who got us water.' Auberon laughed. 'Just open your mouth, Jack, and let something in, instead of letting moans about the bosses out, just for a change.'

Simon laughed. 'That'll be the bloody day.'

Roger moaned. Auberon sighed. 'Where are you hurt?'

148

Roger muttered, 'It's my feet, I've got blisters.'

At this no one said a word, but when they were rousted again at dawn Auberon ordered that he walked, or he fell. 'It's up to you, Private.' They marched, or straggled, along straight roads, with poplar trees and grazing land either side. As they fell out at midday, another group of prisoners caught up. A voice called, 'If it isn't the poor bloody infantry.'

'It's Tiger, and more from the North Tynes. Over here lads, let me make sure you behave,' Jack called. Tiger was ragged, bloodstained, and it was clear he had fought well. Only four out of thirty of the Lea End Lot were prisoners, or at least, prisoners here. Some might have survived and be back at the lines. God, Jack hoped so.

After two days of being jostled repeatedly by the uhlans who rode the line, pushing in with their horses and lances, they were herded into a barbed-wire square in a field so far behind the lines that it was untouched by shells, and the sound of war was quieter. Not quiet, but quieter.

Here, as on the last two nights, teams were organised on Auberon's orders to dig latrines. Who wanted typhus to add to the situation? As the men dug, supervised by the sergeants, who were supervised by Sergeant Major Dawson, they were gawped at by German soldiers on their way to the Front, poor buggers. Jack could barely look them in the eye, so deep was his shame. As he supervised the men on fatigues he pulled out his tin of roll-ups which he'd

149

managed to shove into a rip in his waistband just before he was searched. He smoked as the men dug. 'I thought I'd die fighting,' Dawson laughed grimly. 'Never thought I'd be here, like this. Glad I haven't a mirror, couldn't look myself in the face, I couldn't, but the missus'll be happy.'

Jack had been trying not to think about home, Mam and Da, Evie, Tim, Millie, and especially not about Grace. They would know nothing, or perhaps they would have been told they were missing presumed killed in action.

He dragged the smoke down into his lungs, and looked up at the sky as he exhaled; the stars were bright, there was little cloud. Where was Grace? He heard Simon singing. *'Nein, nein,'* came the order The singing stopped. Near the far end of the field he could see the officers grouped together. Some men were walking the wire, searching for weaknesses, but there was no way out, Jack and Auberon had already checked.

'Dismiss,' Dawson ordered. The latrines were finished, and the men limped back, their shoulders slumped in exhaustion. Jack walked the wire again. A German soldier patrolled, coming towards him. He gestured with his rifle. Jack stepped back. The soldier beckoned him forward. Back and forward again. He laughed. Jack didn't. He was gestured back again. Jack stood still. The soldier lifted his rifle, cocked it. Jack still stood. Auberon appeared from nowhere, standing in front of Jack, saying in

German, 'I am his superior officer, you will withdraw, you will show this sergeant the respect his rank deserves.' For a moment none of the three men moved, then the German walked on.

Auberon clapped Jack on the shoulder. 'The Germans respect rank, unlike you, my lad. No need for thanks.'

Jack smiled. 'None given, sir. But thank you.'

They marched the next day, still thirsty to a point where they could have groaned, had they the moisture in their throats. It had been drizzling overnight and raining with the dawn, and close to midday the rain stopped, and the sun emerged. They steamed in the sun. They had not eaten for three days but there was a war on and no one cursed their captors; they understood.

At thirteen hundred hours they walked and limped through a village and then into the outskirts of a town, before they reached a railyard. Jack's wounds were infected, but whose weren't? Engines huffed and puffed as they edged along the track. One halted and German soldiers streamed down the ramps from the carriages, staring at them. Some were marched off, but a small group were gathered up and marched to the Uberleutnant who was in charge of the prisoners. He was an old man, but it was the uniform the troops respected, and the salutes were smart. Within half an hour all the sergeants were called to a wagon and handed cards to be given out to their men. They were to list basic details of name

151

and battalion and say that they had been captured and were not injured. This would be true, because the wounded had been carted off in trucks the day before. The cards would be forwarded to Britain via the Red Cross, and in due course food parcels would be sent, their own officers told them. It was this information that cast a hush over the men, because it hit home that this situation was not a temporary one; it would last until the war was won, or lost.

Jack hunkered down, drawing out his pencil, feeling bleak and despairing and wondering how he would survive his shame. Simon said, 'Evie will be pleased, she'll want me safe.' Jack said, 'And you?' Simon nudged him, grinning. 'Better than the alternative, isn't it, bonny lad.'

Jack smiled. 'Aye, you could say that.' But he knew that he never would speak or think those words. At that moment, he missed Mart more than he ever had.

Dry biscuits were given out as the men were formed into squares of forty, Charlie staying with Jack, and a bucket of clean water was dispatched to each group. Jack nodded his thanks to the German who brought theirs. In an open field there was none but trough water and the Germans, no more than the British, had wands to wave. Everyone understood.

The cards were collected. An engine arrived pulling cattle trucks. The wheels screeched as it ground to a halt. The air was full of smuts and the smell of sulphur was similar to that of Auld Maud. Jack smiled and saw that Auberon and the Lea End lot were grinning too. They exchanged a nod. 'Home from bloody home,' he could hear Mart say, as loud as though he was here. Steps were brought and they were gestured up into the trucks, forty to a truck. Jack heard Auberon being ordered by Major Dobbs to travel with his fellow officers, but Auberon shook his head. 'I'll stay with my men. I have one in trouble, my batman. If you don't mind, sir, of course.' The major turned away, red-faced with rage. Roger had not stopped grumbling since he had had to walk on his own, even though Auberon and Jack had hauled a stocky branch from a hedge and passed it to him to use as a walking stick. He still grumbled as he limped up the steps.

They travelled with no water, or food, and only one excrement bucket, not knowing when it would end, or where they were going. They feared it was Germany. Jack sidled across to Auberon, who was hunkered down as far from the bucket as possible. It had been on the point of overflowing until Sergeant Major Dawson and Corporal Vance had hoisted Jack up to the small barred window at the end of the first day. He had tipped out the contents, but the wind had thrown back a good percentage all over him. He smelt like a cesspit and to save anyone else having to undergo the same trial and have more soldiers stinking, it had become his job.

'I don't remember volunteering to empty the bucket, sir,' Jack told Auberon. All they could hear was the clattering of the train. The sound of the guns was fading with every mile as they powered away from them.

Auberon was sitting with his arms on his knees. Charlie was beside him in the same pose. Jack and Auberon had taken him under their wing. 'In the army volunteering is not a decision you necessarily make yourself, Jack.' Auberon grinned, so did Charlie.

Jack sat as close to his captain as he could. 'I expect you're rethinking your response to Major Dobbs, aren't you, sir?' he murmured. Auberon nodded, his face as filthy and drawn with tiredness as the rest of them. 'You've read my mind, Sergeant, now perhaps you'd move away, at least a fraction.' They were both laughing. 'You are no violet, and I simply fail to believe that I couldn't smell burning onions at one point, so sensitive does my nose seem to be now.'

Jack inched as far from him as possible, but came up against the corner. He had moved barely six inches away, but better than nothing, or so Auberon seemed to think. Everyone else had left a circle around them, preferring close proximity rather than the smell of Jack. Auberon had clasped his hands together, and Charlie followed suit. Jack smiled to himself. Auberon muttered, 'I wonder if Ron Simmons has a sense of smell?' Jack made no reply. 'What must they be thinking?' Auberon said. 'They'll have been told Missing in Action, believed killed.' They lapsed into silence, listening to the rackety-rack of the wheels on the track. 'What will they think when they know?' Jack murmured.

Two day later they were all herded into a transit camp, but it was in Belgium, not Germany. They had thought something was amiss because the sound of artillery had grown louder and louder again. Unknown to them they had been rerouted back to where labour was needed, Auberon had discovered. As they detrained, they could see flashes in the dusk. It was chaos at the camp: captured soldiers, French, Indian and British, were all milling about. Jack stripped and had bucket after bucket of fresh water thrown over him by Simon, Charlie, the Lea End lot who were delighted to get their own back for the Fordington rout, and Auberon. Jack then doused his uniform, shivering.

He dressed again, in soaking clothes, but what else could he do? He lay in the old pigsty they were allotted, on the bare ground, and shivered all night. In the morning it was still damp and cold, though it was only drizzle that fell. They were told they had to start work immediately, the officers too. Major Walker, Dobbs' friend, spluttered, 'This is against the Hague Convention.'

The officer in charge said, through Auberon whose schoolboy German was improving with each day, 'Once in your proper camp, rules will be observed. Here, there are no rules. Officers will work. No one expected so many of you, so many months of war. We have no proper place. You must work.'

The major replied, through Auberon, 'We should not help your war effort.'

The officer sighed, and broke into English. 'You are filling in roads, you are not handling munitions. Work.' He was as tired, worn, drawn, as the Allies were.

'You will transport munitions over those roads,' Major Walker protested. The Uberleutnant spun on his heel, his revolver in his hand. 'You chose disgrace over death. I can oblige you with death now, if you prefer?' There was no feeling beyond impatience in his voice. Auberon and Jack exchanged a look. Walker capitulated, avoiding everyone's eyes as he turned away. They all felt the same shame.

There were boulders in the nearby quarry to be split and crushed for road repairs. Auberon worked alongside Jack, Simon and Roger, wielding a sledge-hammer, while most of the other officers supervised, and not a word of complaint was made by any of them at the end of the first day. Auberon tore off some of his shirt to make rags to wrap around his blistered and bloody hands once they straggled back to the camp, a camp which was strung around with barbed wire, not once, but twice. Their guards watched them all closely and escape seemed far away.

'You'll get out of it soon enough, into your officers' camp,' Jack told Auberon as he undid his bandages, washed the wounds and redressed them, finding it hard to be sympathetic, because it was true, the enlisted men were to be workhorses, but did any of them deserve better? They were out of the firing line. They had surrendered. They were safe. He still couldn't believe it. He had to get out, get back to the lines, and at least they were near the Front, from the sound of the guns. It should be possible. 'I won't go,' Auberon protested. 'It's better I stay with you men, keep you out of mischief.'

The next day they worked slowly on the roads, because lorries bound for the Front were passing, and how could they justify working hard for such a cause?

That evening they all poked at one another's embedded shrapnel, as the sick-bay orderly had advised. Auberon had collected all the medication that had been missed by the searching uhlans, and gave out a little iodine to share. Some shrapnel was near to the surface and working its way out and it was like getting out splinters, but much worse. The pus gushed, along with blood. 'It's a good thing,' gasped Auberon, as Jack dug into his back. 'Gets rid of the poison.'

Jack dressed Auberon's hands again, and that was when Auberon told him of the compass in the heel of his boot. 'We should get out while we're still near the lines,' Auberon muttered. Jack laughed. 'You don't need a compass, just follow the sound of the guns, bonny lad.'

Out on the road the next day his group watched the changes of the guard, checking for any moment that would give them a chance. There were none. That evening Jack strolled the perimeter again and again. Another fence had been created, and the wire was coiled and wicked, with prongs fit to rip a cow to pieces, let alone a man. They knew all about that from the advances they'd made, when the wire should have been cut by artillery. He paused where the ground rose in front of the perimeter. What if coats were thrown over the wire? He stood looking over the countryside. There was a wood half a mile distant over the thick clay of the early barley field. They had a chance if they reached the trees. He inched closer to the wire, looking both ways along the length of it for possible breaks.

There was a thud, a grunt, and he was shoved hard into the barbs, and pushed again and again with the guard's rifle butt. He was ripped and torn, and he screamed. He was knocked again, the barbs digging deeper. He strained to keep his face from the wire, his eyes. God, not his eyes. There were shouts, British shouts. 'Leave him, you bastard.' It was Sergeant Major Dawson. Another shove, and the barbs tore deeper. Jesus, the pain. He heard Auberon shout, 'Enough, God damn you.'

There was a shot. The Oberleutenant yelled in German, 'Put down that rifle. Put it down. Get him off the wire.'

Hands hauled at Jack. He groaned quietly. 'Gently,' Auberon shouted. 'Gently with him.' Slowly now, Jack was unhooked, and held up by Lea End Dave and Simon. Auberon gripped his face, looked closely. 'Pain, or worse?'

'Pain,' Jack grunted. 'Take him to the sick bay,' Auberon ordered, Charlie his shadow behind him. 'Swab those cuts.' Jack pushed Simon, Dave and Charlie away. God, it was a ruddy party. 'I can walk.' He couldn't. They half carried him, while behind he heard Auberon berating the Oberleutenant. 'I will not have my men hurt, do you understand? I hear you when you say the guard's brother has just been killed, but that is no excuse.'

The sick-bay tent was humid, and smelt of grass and guts and dirt. Several men were laid out on groundsheets. An orderly came to meet them. Dave said, 'Daft bugger's had an argument with a bit of wire, no more than he deserved for punching me lights out on Fordington beach a while ago.'

Simon laughed; the orderly looked at Dave blankly. Later, in the sick bay, Auberon sat next to Jack. 'It is, of course, a sufficient excuse to want to avenge a brother as you and I well know, after Timmie,' Auberon said. 'If you wish to complain, the commandant will listen.'

Jack was shrugging into his shirt, the jagged rips in his flesh covered by corrugated paper bandages which would only last a few hours, but would soak up the blood. 'We've gone past that, Auberon. The guard'll get over it too, so no complaint.' The two men paused, looked at one another, and nodded. Jack continued, 'There's a wood, you know, Aub, just half a mile away. We could use coats to throw on the barbs when it's a moonless night, and go over the top.' Auberon handed him a cigarette from the dwindling supply in his silver cigarette case, which he had somehow retained. 'My thoughts exactly.' They headed off for the potato-water queue which served as an evening meal. 'Evie would not be best pleased by their food standards,' Auberon muttered. 'Take what bread you can manage tomorrow. We could need it. Let's make it sooner rather than later. Tomorrow night, eh Jack? Talk to Simon and see if he's coming, but on the other hand, he'll be safer here, behind the wire.'

Jack stared at him. What the hell was he talking about? They were soldiers, and should want to get back to finish this bloody war off, shouldn't they?

The next day, after the pushing and shoving in what was supposed to be an orderly queue to grab a slice of black bread, the men gathered for the forced march to the quarry. Every muscle in Jack's body ached, every tear ground deep, but he'd managed to grab two slices and stuff them in his tunic top. His stomach hurt with hunger, but excitement roared. They'd be back in the line soon, holding their heads up, but not Simon, he wanted to stay and keep an eye on Charlie. Jack had said the four of them could go, but Simon thought it too risky for the lad. Perhaps he was right. He shot a look at his sister's fiancé. He was kind, no doubt about it, or . . . He left it; things were complicated enough as it was.

As the roll call proceeded he saw that there was activity near the exit. The Uberleutnant was issuing orders, some lorries were parked, their engines idling. The major was being escorted to the Uberleutnant and a discussion ensued. As the roll call continued, all the men watched. Jack felt a fury like nothing he had ever known sweep over him. Had someone escaped? Where, how? How could they have missed the chance? The guards would be on alert, how could they get away now? He snatched a look at Auberon, who stood at the front of the North Tyne roll call square.

Major Dobbs called his officers together. Auberon looked at Jack, and then shouted, 'Sergeant Major Dawson, keep control, you too, Sergeant Forbes, no matter what happens.' He hurried towards Dobbs.

The guards were unhitching their rifles around the group of officers. What the hell was happening? What were they going to do, shoot the buggers? Jack waited, outwardly calm, inwardly in turmoil. He moved to stand alongside Dawson, who whispered, 'What do we do? We've no weapons.' Jack shrugged. 'We wait.' He was on alert as he'd never been before as more guards moved to stand around the perimeter.

The British officers dispersed, back to their men, all except Auberon, who appeared to be arguing with the major. Finally the major drew himself up and actually stabbed his finger at Auberon's chest. Auberon saluted, and left, walking towards his men, his head down. As he drew near he straightened, and looked at Dawson first. 'The officers are to be transported to an Offizier Gefangenenlager, or to you and me, a prison camp for officers. Roger will accompany me as batman. Inform the men, please, Sergeant Major, and good luck to you all.' Jack felt the shock. He was going? But they were escaping together, they were friends, weren't they?

Auberon returned Dawson's salute, and watched as he marched away. He turned to Jack. 'I had to go, but I have a plan and I will get you out, I promise you. And Simon.' He reached out his hand, his face pale, his eyes pleading.

Jack stared past him at the men who stood in their squares, deserted by their officers. 'I'm so sorry, Jacko. I wanted to stay,' Auberon whispered. 'I wanted to escape, with you. To go back, together.'

'Then why didn't you say no?' Jack also whispered, keeping his voice steady, though the anger made him create fists of his hands. 'Your men need you, you've said so yourself.'

'I did say no. It did no good.' Auberon's hand was still stretched out towards him. The North Tynes were watching. Jack saluted, ignored his hand, and marched back to their square, saying nothing, feeling the disappointment like vomit in his throat. He was going, when Jack had thought . . . He shook his head. What had he thought, stupid bloody fool? Of course Auberon was going, that was what bosses did, they were never your friend, they just went off to a nice camp, with a nice bloody servant.

The officers started to pile into the lorries. The guards still stood at the ready. Roll call was over, and the enlisted men lined up at the eastern entrance. Simon caught up with him. 'That wasn't fair, Jack, to ignore his hand in front of everyone too. You know bloody well he's a good officer and that he has to do what the major says. He's argued enough with him, sat in the cattle truck with us, had to put up with you smelling of shit. I bet theirs smelled of roses. He hacked at the quarry with us, when the other nobs stood supervising.'

'Shut up, Corporal. I should have killed him when I had the chance.' Jack heard the lorries revving, heard Major Dobbs shouting, 'For God's sake, Brampton, get a move on.' Above it all was the sound of artillery, and below them the shuddering of the ground.

Behind him he heard Auberon calling, 'They can wait one moment, sir. Corporal Preston, here a minute.'

Jack stared ahead as Simon was allowed by the guard to speak to his officer. Later when they were marching to the quarry Simon slipped him Auberon's cigarette case. 'It's to barter with. We can get bully beef from the Feldwebel sergeant, as they call him.'

'I'd rather starve.'

Dave and Charlie said together, 'We already are.' Those around them laughed. After a pause, Jack grinned, and laughed too. It was what they did or they'd go bloody mad.

Chapter 8

Easterleigh Hall, 21st May 1915

Evie read the Red Cross postcard from Jack that the postboy had just delivered to her mam's home on her afternoon off. Tommy's face had been almost split in half by a grin. 'Thank God, bonny lad,' she whispered. 'Thank the Lord, Jack.'

It was as though the sun had come out and warmed the earth, and all the ongoing problems of Easterleigh Hall had disappeared. The postcard was addressed to Millie as next of kin but she wasn't here, she was at the hall, busy on laundry duty, or sneaking off with Sergeant Pierce for cigarettes, or some such, some said. But all that mattered was that Jack was safe, and did that mean that so was Simon? Evie scrambled for her bike in the back shed and pedalled into the wind, down the track to Easton, and the Prestons' house. She met Ethel Preston, her shawl tight round her shoulders, striding out of Easton, heading towards her, the slag heap seething off to the left, with the foreshift hurrying to work. When she saw Evie she waved the postcard she held. 'Safe, he's safe. Our lad is safe.' Her face was alight with joy, but no more so than Evie's.

'I must get to Mam and Da, they're at the Hall. Nairns won't see me, he thinks I'm still laid up,' Evie told her.

Ethel laughed. 'As you should be, lass, not sneaking off to help Mrs Moore at every given moment still with that dicky shoulder, and don't forget to tell Millie, she should be first to know. She'll have to come out of black now, and stop nagging Captain Williams about extra money to cope with widowhood. I'm off to the pit to get a message to the old bugger.' Ethel spun on her heel and Evie could hear her singing as she hurried off, and calling the news to the friends she passed. 'Aye, Simon and Jack are safe.'

'Mr Auberon?' called Mrs Wilson, the blacksmith's wife. 'Me old bugger is right fond of the whelp.'

'Evie will tell us when she knows,' replied Ethel, striding past the gossiping women.

Evie laughed all the way to the Hall. They were safe and if they were, surely so too was Auberon, not to mention Roger, or should they call him Francis? The bluebells jogged in the breeze and brightened up the verges, and she breathed in their scent as a cuckoo called. In the fields on either side lambs jumped, their mothers calling them to heel. The lambs ignored them. Quite right too.

She tore into the drive, slipped to the bothy and left her bike. She ran through the silver birches, jumping the clumps of bluebells. They were safe. Was Aub? He must be. Jack had said in one of his letters that they were all a pretty tight gang. 'Safe. Safe.' She was shouting it as she ran alongside the yew hedge, and then fell silent but continued to run, taking no notice of her painful shoulder. It was only a little bit swollen, and she could use it. Everyone fussed so. For heaven's sake, how much sleep and rest did one person need?

She hurried along the bottom of the walled vege-table garden, emerging at the garage yard. The volunteers were hanging up washing, as they invar-iably were. One nipped down the stairs when she saw her, to check that the way was clear. It was. Evie ran across the yard, down the steps, into the kitchen. Mrs Moore turned. 'Wasn't expecting you until eleven, bonny lass, but now you're here . . .'

She had her recipe bible open on the table. Enid was straining mushrooms through the hair sieve, a task Evie loathed. For luncheon it was mushroom soup to start, they'd decided yesterday, to be removed by bean and rabbit stew, removed by stewed plum pie from Mrs Green's preserve pantry. There was sufficient milk for custard today, but there would be only enough for tea tomorrow.

Tending the furnace was Kev Barnes, the bootboy, who'd left to go to war and arrived back here with an injured and useless hand, something to do with a bullet going through his wrist and cutting the main nerve. Evie's father had made a brace, with the help of Alec Preston and Tom Wilson, to Sister Newsome's instructions. Sister Newsome had spent some time in an orthopaedic hospital and her advice was invaluable, Bob Forbes told Evie.

Richard had created a position for Kev, voluntary at the moment, until they had found more people like Sir Anthony Travers to help fund the programme, but all food and accommodation found. His particulars were held on a list quite separate to any seen by Dr Nairns. Everyone was getting so wise in the ways of war, wounds, and their aftermath, and the idiots who sat in judgement.

Evie was already moving through the kitchen. She waved the postcard. 'He's safe, so is Simon. Safe. I need to tell the others, I need to see Ver. Has she heard?'

Mrs Moore held out her arms. Evie went to her. Mrs Moore squeezed her until her shoulder was in danger of popping again. She had been making pastry and the kitchen smelled of wheat loaf. 'That's the best news, bonny lass. Quite the best news.'

Evie said, 'Wheat, not barley?'

Mrs Moore laughed, releasing her. 'We're preparing for the latest convoys from Ypres. Easier on their stomachs, or so we think.'

Evie replied, 'Then shall we try a mixture? The baker in the co-op says that the wheat is really needed for the ordinary people in the area because barley is too much of a change for their minds, not their stomachs.' The ranges were up to temperature, she could tell from the rumble.

Enid had dropped the sieve and was patting her back, pulling her away from Mrs Moore. 'Good idea but even better, we need a party, but first we need to see about Mr Auberon.'

Betty, one of the volunteers, called from the end of the deal table where she was forcing more mushrooms through a wire sieve, 'Millie's not in the laundry. Perhaps she's hanging out the clothes?'

The voluntary scullery maid, Sylvia, called through from the sink. 'Perhaps a blackbird will peck off her nose, it might make her behave.'

Evie wanted to find Ver, but she needed to tell Millie first. Mrs Moore pre-empted her, and Evie suspected she knew the reason why. 'Betty, go and find Millie. Quite likely she's having a fag in the top tool store. Your mam's in the new children's nursery near Captain Richard's study, now the electricians have finished. They moved in yesterday and I have to say that the lights in there are a treat, too. The captain likes the sound of children. Your da's in the garage which is now the limb place, did you know that?' Mrs Moore was rolling the pastry with gusto. It would be dead and buried at this rate. Evie hurried into the scullery, washed her hands and took over the rolling pin. 'Sit down, you'll be exhausted.'

Mrs Moore did so, fanning herself with her hand. 'Aye lass, you're quite right. It needs your light touch. Ah, Evie, such a day we had yesterday, people rushing here and there, moving furniture and whatnot. You go along and tell your mam the news, and the captain will know where Lady Veronica is. She might even be with him now she's banned from the acute ward until she stops plummeting to the ground in a faint, now she's having a bairn. She can return when she's three months gone. This news will be just the right thing for her, if, that is . . .'

She stopped. Evie looked at her. 'Surely she's heard?'

That evening, once Dr Nairns had retired to his quarters in the cottage where the under gardeners had once lived, a party was held in the servants' hall to celebrate the news that their men were safe. Roger had addressed his postcard to his son Tim, at Easterleigh Hall. Evie would not let the information enrage her any more than it had done already, because this evening was a time of happiness.

She and the kitchen staff had prepared simple food, to be served once the patients' dinner was cleared. Ver brought down her gramophone and she and Evie sat together, talking of their relief, but words couldn't describe their feelings. Tim had been put to bed in Mrs Moore's room for now, and Mam and Da danced to the music of ragtime. It was embarrassing, it was funny, it was wonderful.

Ronald Simmons danced with one of the nurses, most ably even with a tin lower leg. Mrs Moore whispered, 'They seem to spend much time together. It warms my heart.'

Harry Travers was swinging Lady Margaret around in some approximation of a dance which would not have altered much had he had two proper feet, Captain Richard groaned to them all. He clapped the dancers, then clasped his wife in a display of love that warmed everyone's heart.

Lady Margaret sat now, next to Evie, on the over-stuffed sofa, fanning herself, alongside Major Granville. He was adjusting to the metal face mask created by the 'improvement' department, which was what her da called his unit. Evie smiled at her, saying quietly, and noting how Lady Margaret had touched Peter Granville's hand on her return, 'You're busy these days?'

'No more than you, Evie. But I don't have to hide and rely on the discretion of others. It is a measure of the respect in which you're held that no one has even hinted to Dr Nairns that you are back, albeit as a volunteer.' Lady Margaret leaned towards her, whispering, 'I don't like to ask, but can you manage financially? Can I help? I would deem it a privilege.' This time it was Evie's hand she touched.

Evie remembered the woman who had supported votes for women of property rather than universal suffrage, the woman who had set fire to the Easterleigh Hall stables while the horses were inside, the woman who had been broken by too many forced-feeding ordeals in prison, and who had been ignored by her family but not by Easterleigh Hall. Sometimes war changed people for the better.

Evie grinned across at Mrs Moore. 'My boss is

still being paid, and we share. It is enough, and it is what she wants. But thank you.'

Those in wheelchairs had been brought around to the back of the house and carried down the steps. Though they were paralysed or legless, they could still clap their hands together, or if they only had one, they could slap it on the arm of their chair. Access was a constant problem and Evie wondered if there was room to create a ramp up the front steps, so that those patients situated on the ground floor could leave the building on their own. Or perhaps it would be easier to create a route out through the conservatory doors? Was there room for a ramp from the garage yard down to the kitchen? Did they want them in the kitchen? She laughed quietly. It all needed thinking about, and she'd talk to her da and Tom Wilson.

After half an hour the nursing staff swapped with those on duty, including Matron, who dragged young Kev in with her, scooting him off to the younger VADs before joining Mrs Green and Mr Harvey as they sipped sweet sherry and kept an eye on 'Mr Manners', as they had warned the younger members of staff they would.

While Evie directed the clearing up at eleven that evening, Mr Harvey completed his rounds, having checked the windows and locked all the external doors, except for the grand hall. The keys were positioned in various places in case of fire though the huge double doors remained unlocked at all times, and an orderly was on duty at the reception desk because ambulances could arrive at any time.

Evie watched Mr Harvey, finding comfort in his steady walk, his upright posture, his pristine suit and shirt, his polished boots, his permanently unflustered demeanour, as he checked the vegetable storeroom skylights. The sky could fall and he would bear its weight on his shoulders. At that moment, just as she was putting on her coat to slip away home, in the boot hall the telephone bell jangled, positioned just below the room bells. It was the one thing that disturbed his stateliness. She watched as he braced himself, and advanced on the enemy before it could stop ringing. The telephone was fixed to the wall. Mr Harvey lifted the earpiece off the rest with two fingers, as though it was destined to explode. 'Easterleigh Hall,' he pronounced into the mouthpiece as though he was in the pulpit, so solemn was his tone.

He listened, his shoulders drooping further and further: Evie stood in the kitchen doorway. She heard the ra-ta-tat of the voice, but had already realised that it was Bastard Brampton, shouting.

Mr Harvey replaced the earpiece and sighed, unaware, clearly, that he was observed. 'Bugger,' he murmured. Evie stepped back, slipping into the scullery. She had never seen the butler so disturbed. She knocked a pan into the sink. 'Hello,' Mr Harvey called. She bustled out. 'Just finishing, Mr Harvey, and then I'm off home. I do just wish I could use my old room, but best not to tempt fate, as you said the other day. We don't want any surprise check-ups by Nairns.'

He smiled, absent-mindedly. 'Evie, Lord Brampton is arriving after luncheon tomorrow. It is to be a flying visit, in response to Lady Veronica's news regarding Mr Auberon, and he mentioned something about changes at Easterleigh Hall. I think perhaps it is to do with the budget, and dare we hope for good news? I gather he will visit the mines too.' It was as though he was thinking aloud.

Evie replied, 'I thought he sounded rather . . . well, loud.'

Mr Harvey raised his eyebrows. 'Ah, you could hear that in the scullery, could you, young lady? Well, let us just say that I fear that even the news of his son's safety has improved his mood little from last week, when his steelworkers went on strike to prevent him paying German prisoners of war at a cheap rate. Have you heard that there is a similar move afoot in his pits here, should he employ such men? You must be away from here, Evie, by midday. You know his habit of surprises and I suspect he and Mr Nairns confer more, rather than less. There is supposed to be only one cook here. Annie must fade into the background also.'

Evie arrived at her usual time of 5.30 a.m., wishing that she was back properly because although this cycling was helping her recover her fitness, it wasted time which could be better spent at the Hall. She wouldn't use the pickup trap or cart because then she was involving others in her disobedience, as Matron called it, kissing her on the cheek in gratitude. It was Mrs Moore who walked the wards, talking to the new patients, or indeed anyone who needed some food-fussing, while she stayed hidden below stairs. The patients, though, sent messages to Dr Nairns' study demanding Evie and Annie's return, to his fury.

Breakfast was the usual bustling procedure, followed by the morning meeting round the kitchen table. Captain Richard announced that there had still been no movement on Dr Nairns' position over the kitchen staff, and that the doctor had drawn up yet another document, which listed others who should be dismissed. He produced it, and Evie checked down the names. This time the garden staff was targeted, with Old Stan as the bullseye at the head of the list. Evie stared into the distance. How bloody dare he? For the hundredth time she wondered how they could stop all this.

As though he could read her mind Captain Richard reminded them that he was to travel to Durham again for a further meeting with Sir Anthony Travers, who was now in talks with others who might be agreeable to funding the shortfall over and above Lord Brampton's ninepence per patient per day. Not only that, but they were interested in the work scheme for ex-patients.

But when would we know, Evie wanted to ask, but instead she smiled. Richard was to travel alone, leaving Ron Simmons in the office this time. Bravo.

Richard now said, 'I have informed Dr Nairns, who insists that this funding possibility still allows for no movement on the employment of Evie Forbes, though it could ensure the reinstatement of Annie.' He peered across at Evie. 'Is she likely to leave Gosforn Auxiliary Hospital do you think, Evie, to return here?'

Evie shrugged. 'No idea, Captain Richard.'

Richard exchanged a look with Veronica and then continued, 'Indeed, Nairns has made the point that Miss Forbes' absence had caused no problems whatsoever, as the standard of service has been maintained.' He grimaced, Veronica groaned, the laughter of the head servants was wry. Mrs Moore muttered, 'It's not only the troops in the trenches who have to learn not to poke their heads over the parapet, my dear girl. Keep your head down, bonny lass, from now on.'

At the close of the meeting, hurried at the end because of Veronica's inelegant rush for the door, her hand to her mouth, Evie and Mrs Moore embarked on luncheon preparation. It was to be lentil soup, removed by casserole of fowl and dumplings with the usual overload of root vegetables, removed by apple pie and cream. There would be beef tea, fish simmered in milk and egg custard for those who were on light diets. Evie couldn't stop glancing at the clock, her stomach clenched in a way it had not been for a long while. Why was the Bastard coming? Why?

By eleven the kitchen was full of the aroma of casserole and stockpot and the ranges were humming, the furnace gurgling. After glancing at the clock once more, Evie said, 'Aye, lasses, it's quite time for a cup of tea and soon I must hoy myself out of the door. He said after luncheon but you never know with him.'

Enid broke off from cutting up the root vegetables that would be added to the casserole in half an hour, gathered up some enamel mugs and placed them near Mrs Moore. 'You be mother, pet.' They were the same age and had been friends since Mrs Moore had cooked for Grace at the parsonage.

Mrs Moore laughed. 'Be stretching it a bit to be your mother, our Enid.' Evie placed the kettle on the hotplate. As though she smelled the tea, Veronica joined them for some company and to take her mind off her sickness. Tea was one of the few things that she found acceptable. She stood with Enid at the end of the table nearest to the scullery and started to chop up the carrots, staining her fingers orange as they all discussed the rabbits that two of the youngsters from the village had promised but which had not yet arrived. They were destined for the lunch table tomorrow.

'If we don't get them,' Evie said, 'how about rissoles for the staff out of the remains of the casseroles today, but what for the patients?' Embarking on the dumplings, she rubbed suet into wheat flour lightly with her fingertips. 'I'll need some herbs from Old Stan's store at the bottom of the veggie garden, Joyce, when you have a moment.' Herbs would perk up the dumplings no end. 'We've some bits of streaky bacon which I'll add also, do you think, Mrs Moore?'

Joyce was chopping up the apples for the tart, leaving the skins on because every scrap of goodness was needed, not to mention bulk. Some were already beginning to brown but just as Evie started to say something, Joyce scooped them up and dropped them into the bowl of water she had ready. Evie smiled. Aye, like a smoothly oiled machine, they were.

The apples were stored in a shed that Old Stan had converted, now that the sphagnum moss was dried in the former apple stores. The war had rejuvenated the old boy, and his energy was prodigious. Mrs Moore tapped her recipe bible, her spectacles on the end of her nose. 'Bacon, you said, Evie? You've reminded me of quiche Lorraine. We haven't made that for a while so we'll let the rabbits hang, if they ever arrive, and put quiche on the menu for tomorrow. Now, how's that dratted kettle coming, Evie?' She looked over the top of her glasses from Evie to the kettle on the range behind her. It was then that they heard a car in the garage yard, the slam of a door, rushed footfalls on the steps. Raisin and Currant leapt off the armchairs, barking.

177

Veronica paled even further than usual, if possible. 'Oh God, Father's early. I'll leave the chauffeur to you and go and head him off in the grand hall. Evie, you need to leave the dumplings to Enid, and go. Take the dogs. He thinks they've been put down. Quick, for heaven's sake.' She slipped from the stool as Enid dropped her knife and started round the table towards Evie. Veronica had reached the door into the corridor when they heard the back door burst open. Evie spun round, her hands sticky with dough. The kitchen door had slammed back, crashing into the end of the row of ranges. They all froze as Lord Brampton entered, taking in the room at a glance.

'Just as I thought,' he roared, striding to the table, slapping his cane under his arm and tearing off his gloves and homburg, which he threw amongst the prepared carrots and turnips. His grey hair was in disarray, his pale blue eyes barely visible in the fury of his crunched-up face, the astrakhan collar of his black coat dappled with drizzle. He shoved aside Joyce, who dropped the chunks of apple she was about to put into the bowl, staggered, but managed to catch hold of the end of the table, shock in her eyes. 'Just as I bloody well thought,' he ground out again. The dogs whined and hid under the table.

Mrs Moore sat on her stool, slumped as though the air had gone from her body. Evie could hardly breathe. Automatically she rubbed the dough from her hands back into the bowl. None must be wasted.

Lady Veronica stood motionless, one hand on the door handle.

Brampton threw his cane on to the table, knocking two sieves, several spoons and some knives to the floor. Pushing aside Enid he reached for Evie, gripping her shoulder and swinging her round. The pain almost made her cry out. She smelled the alcohol on his breath. Lady Veronica shouted, her hands gripped in front of her now, as though protecting her child, 'Her shoulder is healing, leave her alone, Father.'

He flung Evie back against the table; the bowl of dough juddered. Her shoulder throbbed. He stabbed at her with his forefinger. 'You're a Forbes. Do you think I wouldn't recognise the name when that fool Nairns sent me his list? We employed you as Evie Anston and you, Veronica, you knew about this, and why aren't those dogs dead? Bloody Hun creatures.' He glared around the kitchen. Maudie was standing in the scullery doorway, gripping her hessian apron. She darted back out of sight. Mrs Moore reached out her hand. 'Please, Lord Brampton . . .'

He roared again. 'You, you old woman, should not even be working, so useless are you, so just be quiet.' The kettle was boiling, rattling the lid. The range was belting out heat. He was close to Evie now; she could see the pores on his nose. 'You were ordered not to cross the threshold again, but here you are, with everyone knowing, thus making a fool of me. I will not have a Forbes in my employ. Your brother led strikes, and bought the houses that should have been mine. What might you be bringing about here, and what about the mine? Are you encouraging a strike there? Too much of a coincidence, isn't it, bloody Forbes everywhere, like a plague? Hey? Hey?' His spittle pitted her face.

Evie forced herself to stand erect, her shoulders back, her head up, ignoring the stabbing in her shoulder and Mrs Moore's pull on her skirt, her whispered, 'Evie, take care, lass.'

'I cook, that's all I do, for the patients that come to the hospital here in Easterleigh Hall, which as you might remember you insisted your daughter establish. She is the commandant, not Dr Nairns, and it is she who should be running it.' She had kept her tone even and calm, though her hands were fisted to such an extent that her nails dug into her skin and the sweat of fear ran down her back.

He stepped even closer, so that there was barely an inch between them, and now the lid of the kettle was rattling fit to bust. 'How would you know what I have insisted, unless my daughter has shared more than she should with a minion? A minion that confronts and abuses the Medical Officer in this establishment, just as any Forbes would.'

'Father, leave her.' Veronica was as white as a sheet, her hand to her mouth.

Enid and Joyce were stepping away from the table, fear in every shaking step. He bellowed, 'Did I give you permission to move?'

Veronica spoke again, opening the door into the corridor and gripping it so tightly that her knuckles were white. 'She confronted Nairns because he was dismissing staff we need. You weren't here. You don't know what happened.'

Her father didn't even look at her, but kept his eyes locked on Evie. 'I know that I have the pleasure of a nest of Forbes under my roof. Not only his sister but his wife, his parents, and his child on these premises. I will not have it. I will not be disobeyed in this fashion.'

He swung round then and looked towards Lady Veronica, who had her hand to her forehead, wiping the sweat from it. Oh God, she's going to vomit, Evie thought, before calling for a bowl.

Mrs Moore rushed to the scullery and back again, a damp cloth and a bowl clutched to her. She placed them on the table, and she and Enid forced Lady Veronica to sit at the table, fanning her. Evie went to Veronica's side.

Her father stared, moving back to the end of the table. Veronica shrank from him. Mrs Moore whispered to Enid behind his back. Enid nodded, grabbed Joyce, and they were out and up the steps to freedom. Brampton leaned on the table, putting his weight on his hands. 'Am I to understand that you and your cripple of a husband have managed to start off a child at long last?'

There was a gasp from Maudie, who was standing in the doorway of the scullery again, but no sound

181

from Evie, his daughter, or Mrs Moore, who knew this man too well. He continued, 'Well, at least that is some sop, but only some, to make up for the sheer disgrace your pathetic brother has brought to this family. How typical that he preferred shame to death with honour, and taking a Forbes with him too. Cowards have no . . .'

Evie shouted, standing between him and Veronica, 'Auberon is no coward.'

Lord Brampton lifted his hand to strike her. 'Address my son correctly.' Evie shouted again, 'Touch me and I'll rip your heart out.' She snatched up one of the knives he had not managed to knock to the floor. It was the vegetable knife Jack had sharpened all those months ago. It was still as sharp as a razor, and she would use it. 'Roger tried to hurt me when I wouldn't give in to him years ago, and do you think I'll let you or anyone do it again? Do you think I'll let you hurt your daughter again? Do you, Bastard Brampton? Put your hand down.' He didn't. She lifted the knife. Mrs Moore called, 'Evie. Lord Brampton, please.'

At that moment Captain Richard spoke from the doorway, but Evie would not take her eyes from Lord Brampton, or he would strike. 'Evie, put the knife down. If anyone is going to kill him, it will be me.' She looked at him now, and saw that his rage had caused his lips to thin, his colour to rise. 'I received Enid's message, Mrs Moore. I doubt she's moved that quickly for many a year. Now, Lord

Brampton. It is time you left or it is I who will fillet out your heart, God help me, I will.'

At this Lord Brampton laughed, a drunken, frenzied sound. 'You wouldn't have the guts because if you take one step towards me I will cease *any* sponsorship of this establishment, above and beyond the government grant. I will insist you pay for the upkeep of the Hall. After all, you live here only because I allow you to. Or shall I just close the whole hospital down, and make you and everyone else homeless? How would you like that, eh? What's more, I'll have this bitch arrested and see how she likes that.'

Captain Richard limped towards his father-in-law, his walking stick steadying him. Evie saw his eyes, and they chilled her. 'You will do none of these things, or your reputation will suffer at this time of your country's need, no matter how many lesser establishments you start in Leeds or wherever else. Come with me, Lord Brampton. Come with me out into the yard and I will tell you exactly what position you are in, or do you wish this discussion to take place in front of your staff?'

Lord Brampton hesitated, unsure, probably for the first time in his life. Evie felt more proud of Captain Richard than she had been of anyone for a long while. Richard stood so close to his father-in-law that it seemed as though they were about to take part in some bizarre dance. Evie almost laughed. Everyone stood or sat motionless, staring. There was only the sound of the damned kettle lid to break the silence. Maudie still stood in the scullery doorway, horror on her face.

Richard rested his walking stick against the table and tried to take the knife from Evie with his one hand but her fingers were locked around the bone handle. Dough had dried on her fingers. She stared down at his hand on hers. He said, 'I apologise on behalf of my father-in-law for his behaviour towards you, Evie. He will not interfere in the running of this household again, nor touch anyone within it, and you will be reinstated immediately. Do you hear that, Veronica? He will not touch anyone, ever again, within the walls of Easterleigh Hall.'

Evie looked at Veronica, sitting slumped over the bowl next to her, and said to Richard, 'I saw Aub's poor battered face before the war, again and again; the first time at the stables. I saw Ver's, you saw it too, when she came to see you entrain . . . Fathers shouldn't . . . Bosses shouldn't . . . We need to help our patients, we can't stop doing so, not on the whim of a bully.' She nodded at Lord Brampton who looked dazed now, and confused. He muttered, 'Aub? Ver? How dare you?' But the heat had gone out of his voice. Sweat dripped from his face on to his astrakhan collar, and the stink of drink was worse, seeming to ooze from the man.

'He's a menace,' Evie whispered, looking up into Richard's face. He smiled, eased the knife from her and threw it to the table, where it skidded and fell to the floor. No one picked it up. 'Maudie will have to wash it,' she said. Her shoulder hurt.

Captain Richard picked up his cane and nudged Brampton's arm. 'We'll leave now,' he said. Brampton tried to thrust him off, kicking at his cane. Richard staggered, his balance always precarious. Veronica vomited into the bowl. Evie left her to Mrs Moore and went to steady Richard. Still the kettle lid clattered.

Mr Harvey entered from the corridor; perhaps he'd been there for some time. She watched him walk over to them in his stately fashion, his shoulders back, his demeanour as calm as usual. He said, 'May I assist you, Captain Richard.' It wasn't a question. He armlocked Brampton and moved him towards the door, while the captain smiled and followed, treading firmly now, saying, 'Look after Ver for me, Evie, if you wouldn't mind.' It was the first time they had shared the use of Ver.

'This way, Your Lordship, up the steps with you,' Mr Harvey said. 'Geoffrey is waiting with the car for you in the garage yard, but there's time for Captain Richard to have that little word, probably within the automobile, I suggest.' It clearly wasn't a suggestion. Evie realised that it wasn't only Captain Richard of whom she was proud, it was this wonderful elderly man too.

Lord Brampton stopped as they reached the door, and shouted, 'This isn't the end.' He sounded close to tears.

'May I suggest that you are just overtired, and in need a bit of a rest? Perhaps a lie-down in a darkened room,' Mr Harvey said, propelling him into the boot corridor.

'You're dismissed, do you hear, damn you Harvey. Ouch.'

'Just a tweak of the arm, Lord Brampton, it helps things along.'

Ver vomited again. Mrs Moore sighed. 'It's a good sign, bonny lass. Means the baby is strong.'

Ver groaned. 'How long will this go on?'

'It'll run its course,' Mrs Moore soothed. No one knew if either woman meant the baby or the situation.

Evie took Veronica to her bedroom, calling in on Lady Margaret in the facial injuries suite and asking her for a moment of her time to keep Ver company, if she wouldn't mind. She wouldn't. Evie returned to the kitchen. Maudie came from the scullery, saying, 'I didn't know Roger had hurt you?'

'He was a fool and wanted what I wouldn't give.'

Maudie crossed her arms. 'Is this what happened to Millie, then?'

Evie shrugged. 'In a way, I suppose. He charmed her, made her love him and had free use of her. I warned her but she wouldn't listen, and she was by no means the first.'

Mrs Moore had removed the kettle from the hob at last, and was pouring tea into the mugs and pushing them towards Evie and Maudie. Joyce and

Enid joined them, hurrying in from the corridor where they'd been hiding. Maudie asked, 'Does she love Jack?'

'Oh, I just don't know.' Evie's thoughts were chasing about in her head. Maudie took her tea into the scullery, saying as she went, 'How can a father beat his son like that, and lift a hand to his daughter?'

Evie just shook her head, fearing that the man would never change, fearing what this would mean to them all. Mrs Moore eased herself on to her stool. 'Anyone would think we didn't have a luncheon to serve. Evie, sort out these dumplings please. Enid, the vegetables need to go in the casseroles, and Joyce, the apples. Chop chop, the enemy is on our back.'

Evie looked at the clock. It was eleven forty-four. Had their world changed in just three quarters of an hour? Were they to close down?

Grace straightened, checked the transfusion tube, and stroked the corporal's hand. He was unconscious but might feel the comfort. He'd been washed, but grime and the stench of war still clung to him. He needed blood before surgery. Her back ached but she was pleased to be back at base camp, because at least last night she'd been able to change her uniform, and shower. Here the guns were loud, but not *as* loud, and though the ground shuddered from the effects of the barrage it didn't throw up dirt and shrapnel. Here it was bugles she heard, not whistles indicating that soldiers like this poor boy were scrambling out of the trenches into the mouths of the guns. Never had she thought she would be so close to the Front. Could she bear to be again?

She held the corporal's hand. He stirred. She soothed, 'It's all right, you're safe.' He relaxed, still unconscious. Yes, he was safe, and so was Jack. Thank God. She touched the telegram from Evie which had at last reached her, brought down by Angie, who was replacing her at the casualty clearing station, such was the rush and shortage of orderlies.

Outside, trucks ground their gears, a horse neighed. The tent seemed to ooze damp, but of course it did, for the rain was unceasing. A letter had arrived too, with the news of Veronica's pregnancy. Grace smiled as she checked the transfusion, and the lower-legs blood loss. When would they all refer to her by her title, Lady Veronica? Perhaps never? Perhaps at the end of all this? But would it end? If so, how? Would any of these young men be left alive, let alone whole?

For now, none of that mattered, nor the ache in her legs, her back, her neck, nor the blisters on her heels from boots that had rubbed as she rushed around the aid station, treating the minor injuries, and sending others on to the casualty clearing station. Jack was safe; Tim had his father, Millie her husband.

'Penny for them, or should I say a dollar?' It was Slim, standing too close to her. 'Maybe I can guess. He's safe and perhaps you're thinking we can go to the *estaminet* to celebrate?'

The corporal groaned. 'Hush, you're safe,' she

soothed again. 'I'm tired,' she told Slim. 'There's a lot of work to do.'

He moved to the foot of the bed, checking Corporal Young's chart. 'You said you couldn't meet with me until Jack was safe. He's safe, Gracie. Can't you let me in?'

She stayed by the transfusion stand and could feel the telegram in her pocket and knew what she had really known all along, and her pride in Jack grew with each word she said. 'He's safe for now, but he'll fight, like our Evie with that damned Brampton. Our Jack will carry on fighting. He'll make their job difficult, and he'll escape, or die trying. That's our Jack. So I can't come to the *estaminet* to celebrate, because he'll never be safe until this war is over, or perhaps not even then, if he goes back in the mine. I'm sorry, Slim, really sorry. You're a lovely man and a wonderful doctor.'

'You don't mind?' His voice was gentle.

She smiled, holding the corporal's hand, because he was awake, but talking to Slim. 'Of course I mind, but I wouldn't have him any other way.'

He said, 'I'll keep trying. You're a special woman, Gracie, and you deserve better than to go through life alone.' He left. Grace stared at the tent opening. Alone? The thought chilled her, but then she touched the telegram again. With Jack alive in the world, she wasn't alone.

Chapter 9

Northern France, behind German lines, late August 1915

In a field not too far from Lille, Jack, Simon, Charlie and three of the Lea End lot, Tiger, Dave and Jim, hunkered around the empty can a German guard had tossed to them, and which they'd suspended from a makeshift tripod over a weak fire made of sticks they'd collected. 'Dawn's too bloody early this time of year,' Charlie grumbled. Around them everyone was doing the same, on grass that was dry, and flattened by the prisoners, who slept beneath the stars. A few had tents, a few were in the barn, but that comfort was confined to those who were sick. When the water was passably hot they tipped in the camouflage coffee, which was burnt barley, and let it brew.

The dawn chorus was the usual rattle and roar of the guns, even two kilometres behind the lines. The star shells, used by both sides to spot wiring parties in no-man's-land, had ceased with the dawn.

Simon nudged Jack. 'What d'you reckon we'll be doing today, Jack?'

'Whatever our masters tell us, but what you lot won't be doing is eating the crusts you should have kept for your five-course breakfast, but which you ate last night, again, before slipping between your linen sheets and wool blankets.' The men hooted. Si grunted, 'Chance would be a fine thing.'

Dave poked the fire with a stick, watching it smoulder, before ramming it into the ground. 'Should have been born an officer then, laddie. They'll be waking up between sheets that their batmen will have washed, dried and spread with rose petals, won't they, Jacko boy?'

Jack dug into his pocket and brought out his bread, so hard it could have doubled as a hammer. He soaked it in his coffee, then shared it out. 'This is the last time,' he warned. Charlie muttered, 'You say that every time. Doesn't your stomach lining stick to itself at the end of the day then, Jack? Mine hurts.'

Dave cuffed him, and gave him half of his small piece. 'That's because you're a growing lad whereas we're just canny raddled old men.'

Si laughed, cramming his piece into his mouth, and licking his fingers. 'Speak for yourself, bonny lad. I'm in me prime.'

The Feldwebel, who spoke a little English and had worked as a waiter on the Strand, approached. Jack asked him where they were to go today. Gerhardt looked around, eased his rifle on his shoulder. He was nearly sixty and relieved to be too old for the front line, he'd told them. 'The dye works again.

You break up the machinery, legally this time, Jack, so you won't end up punished for sabotage. It must all be in bits. No use, no more. They will watch you close, in case you try to get to your lines again.'

Simon said, 'What about work in the field party? Did you tell them I was a gardener, not a basher, like these pitmen?'

Dave looked at him and frowned. Gerhardt shook his head and leaned forward. 'You must not speak of pitmen, Corporal. The mines and salt mines are not places to work, and if it is heard that . . .' He walked on.

Jack kicked Si. 'You need to keep your mouth for eating because if we go, you'll go, Si. They think you're one of us. Those mines are in Germany, and then how do we escape? Come on, we'll be late for roll call.'

Simon flushed. 'I *am* one of you.'

Dave stood, drowning the dregs of his coffee before swilling his cup out with water from the bucket. 'Then act like it, you daft beggar, and it's not the bloody first time we've told you. I'm sick of hearing about your gardening, your need for the soil. We live, eat and sleep on the bloody soil, whether it's wet, dry or indifferent, what more do you want?'

After roll call they marched to the factory, and again they bashed apart perfectly good machinery for scrap metal to be transported back to Germany to make more guns. The concept stuck in their throats and they worked as slowly as they could but still their backs were near to breaking, and their heads close to bursting, but they were safe. The thought of all that was happening not too far from them, beneath the shells and the machine guns, made Jack determine to find a way back, somehow.

Turnip soup was waiting for them as evening fell, or was it mangel-wurzels? Even Simon didn't know but at least it wasn't maize soup, which tasted like paraffin. No matter how hungry Jack was, he could never finish it.

Every day he, Dave and Charlie scanned the wire entanglements which surrounded the field. They did the same that evening. Every day they were alert on the march to and from the factory, the railway yard, or wherever they were to work, for any escape opportunities. Only one had occurred, and it was Gerhardt who had clubbed Jack to the ground, saving him from the uhlan's lance. It had earned him a kicking, and solitary for a week in the pigsty.

No further opportunity had presented, so the most he and Dave had been able to do was tip coal out on to the tracks after derailing one of the carts, which was easy enough with a piece of pig iron. The first derailment had earned Jack and Dave a beating and two days' loss of bread for their group. No one had minded, because others had shared their rations. The same thing happened the second time.

Jack's ripped skin from the barbed-wire incident was long healed; his shrapnel was either lying still or had been eased out. It was the same with the others. They were hungry and exhausted, and because they moved billets constantly they had received no mail or parcels, so they didn't know if their relatives thought them dead. It was this that kept some awake at night.

All week they bashed apart the machinery and on the evening of 28th August, thirty of them, including Jack, Simon, Dave, Frank, Danny and Jim, were called to stand out at the front and herded off to one side, guarded by several uhlans. They were told they were moving on. Jack noticed that all but Simon bore the blue scars of the miner, and swallowed his anger at his marra's big mouth. Charlie stepped forward out of the ranks, panic in his eyes. He called, 'Ask them to take me, Jack.' Gerhardt came abreast, his rifle across his chest, pushing Charlie back.

'Jack,' Charlie pleaded. Jack called, 'I suspect you'll be better here, bonny lad.'

Dave nudged him. 'Poor wee bairn, let him come, we'll take care of the little bugger. We can't leave him, he's your bloody shadow, you know he is now the captain's gone. It might not be a pit.' Jack took a moment, then sighed, and stepped forward to salute Uberleutnant Bauer. The man was standing in front of the hundred prisoners, watching the proceedings as though they were specimens in a jar. 'Permission to speak, sir.'

The larks were singing above the fields. How

strange these birds were, somehow impervious to the guns, which seemed muted this evening. Somewhere a lamb bleated, because it was far enough from the front line for there to be fields which contained something other than prisoners. God, he was so tired, so hungry. He mentally shook himself.

Uberleutnant Bauer was nodding at him. 'Carry on, Sergeant.' He had been at Cambridge University studying some sort of science, so the story went, and his English was impeccable. Jack said, 'Permission to include Private Meadowes, sir.'

'Ah, the one who called out?'

Charlie stepped further forward. 'Private Meadowes reporting, sir. I'm part of them, sir.'

Bauer tapped his swagger stick against his leg. His gaze swept the troops lined up in squares of twenty for ease of counting, then back to Charlie. 'You are young and are not strong. Where your friends are going, you need that strength. You should choose to stay, Private Meadowes.'

Charlie stood ramrod straight. 'I choose to go, sir. I am stronger than I look.' Jack started to shake his head. 'No, Jack, I don't want to stay here without you all.'

Bauer seemed to be looking at the larks, watching as they swooped. Jack followed their movements too. The lamb bleated again. Bauer looked for a long moment at Charlie, then raised his voice. 'I need one of the thirty to step back into line.' Behind him, Jack heard Simon step forward, then someone from B Company marched quickly back to the line. The moment was over, and Jack wondered what he would have done if Simon had tried to duck out of a situation he had caused. He wanted to smash the bugger.

Bauer strolled across to Jack, coming close, his voice no more than a whisper. 'Our young friend is your responsibility now. Protect him well and perhaps you'll get him home in one piece. I pray so, and that we all survive. It is a ridiculous situation, do you not agree? And perhaps tell your young gardening friend that he talks too much, so now he too is bound for the salt mines in Germany, though you would perhaps have gone anyway at some stage. Blue scars are like a badge, sadly, Sergeant Jack Forbes.' He nodded, looked down at his immaculate boots. 'It was my decision to include Corporal Preston, I fear that he has not half the internal strength of even this boy, Meadowes. You will need to be on your guard, my friend, with that one. His thoughts are seldom far from himself, not quite the sort I'd want for a friend whether I was man or woman.'

Bauer moved on, his hands clasped behind his back, his swagger stick under his arm. 'Carry on, Sergeant,' he ordered Gerhardt. Jack stepped back. Had Simon heard? He didn't care, because they were moving back from the lines, making it more difficult to escape. He saw that Dave was thinking the same, and cursing Simon under his breath.

They travelled in cattle trucks, but this time, however, there was more room, and stops for the emptying of latrine buckets. They travelled for days, it seemed, and they slept, Charlie tight in with his marra group, for that was what Jack realised they had formed. They were not just friends, they were to be pitmen, and marras. They would watch one another's backs, they would take one another's loads, and because Simon was the love of Evie's life, he would be enclosed within their group. What did Brampton have, in his comfy cosy camp, that came close to that?

They disembarked near the Hartz mountains, miles from the front line, into pure air devoid of the crash and grind of guns, with towering peaks and searingly blue skies. Here there were wooden houses with balconies, flowers hanging from them. How the hell would they get back to the front line?

'Bloody salt mines,' the men cursed as they marched along the roads. The people, thin and tired, looked at them warily. Simon was quiet, but the men ignored him. Dave marched alongside Jack. 'Makes you thirsty, I expect, all that salt.'

Jack shrugged. 'I expect you're right, bonny lad, but doubt it's as hard as coal.' He didn't know, and what he didn't know frightened him. Would it be white, friable, easy? Would they be shovelling, not hewing? Simon marched beside him. 'I've told you before, and will tell you now I'm right sorry. Me and my bloody great mouth. Jesus, Jack, I'm right sorry, man.'

Jack slung an arm round his shoulders, and pulled Simon to him. 'Don't go on and on, Si. We've all got gobs on us. We'd have ended up here anyway, and you might still get to a garden.' If he forgave him so would the lads, and he was too bloody tired to do anything else.

Simon grinned. 'Aye, maybe you're right. But let's get through this day first.' He pulled away. 'What say you, young Charlie? One day at a time, eh?' Charlie was grinning as Dave joshed him about something. 'Who knows, I might get some rabbit snared here. Better than potato-peel soup?'

They arrived at a small town at eight in the evening. The sun had gone behind the mountains and there was a chill in the air, even though it was still August. What would the winter be like? Would they bivouack in fields? If so, they'd bloody well freeze. The guards who were, like Gerhardt, too old for service, marched them to a building which it became clear was an old school.

Their boots rang on the wooden floors as they entered a dormitory with narrow beds. 'Real beds,' sighed Charlie. 'Aye, and a roof,' Dave added, guarding their corner from incomers. 'Nah, get your own space,' he muttered to some Welsh pitmen. Danny, Jim and Frank joined them in the corner, with Simon dithering on the edge. There were no mattresses, just bare boards, and gaps in between those. There was one grey blanket per man, but who needed more? They were off the ground, the dirt, the mud. It was bloody heaven.

Guards approached. *'Schnell.'* They were led to the ablutions, basins and toilet stalls, then to a kitchen with the luxury of a cooking range and huge pans. They were told that they would collect their own wood for cooking, under guard, tomorrow after work. For tonight they were given black bread, two slices, and potato-peel soup.

They marched to the mine the next day, and entered a world in which the air was clean. It was remarkable. There was none of the smell of a coalmine. They took their tokens, and a lamp, and then plunged down in the darkness of the shaft. Simon and Charlie stood between Dave and Jack. Jack yelled above the rattling and crashing of the cage, 'Think of those larks, lads, and that blue sky. Think of the forest because that's where we'll be picking up the wood when we're out of here. Mart used to hum. Have a go yourselves, and remember the larks, or whatever, or whoever, takes your fancy.' All the while his chest was constricted, his heart beating too fast, because they were bloody falling. That was the nub of it.

They reached the bottom of the shaft. There was no white salt, glistening and ready to be shovelled. Instead there was salt deposited in old seabeds, which looked like granite. They worked in a huge cavern. 'It is your task to drill, blast, cut it out. Once your work is done, it will be removed and crushed,' they were told in halting English. They were to work with an equal number of civilians, to prevent sabotage. We'll see about that, thought Jack. Si gripped his arm. 'Listen to him, Jack. We can't do anything here and it'll be short rations for the rest of us again, if you try.'

They worked for ten hours without stopping, or eating, though they were allowed to drink. Jack and Dave bore the brunt of the work in their group, hewing whilst Simon and Charlie collected the broken-up rocks into carts. 'They say the air is good for you,' a skeletal figure muttered as he brought water to them. He was from the Nottingham coalfields. 'They say salt heals, and I reckon it does, but so does food. Trouble is, they don't have much themselves, our blockade is too good, poor buggers.' He took the leather water flagon on to the next group.

Within three days Simon and Charlie had abscesses on the palms of their hands from the non-stop shovelling of the rock salt, though the pitmen fared much better, so hard were their hands. On the fourth day Jack received the first of his beatings, for derailing a cart. The beating took place in the cavern, the pick handles and rifle butts slamming into his curled-up body. The other pitmen stopped work. Charlie was held back by Dave. 'He knows the score, lad, let it be.'

'*Schnell*,' the guards called, threatening them with their rifles, and they began work again as Jack was dragged to the cell carved out of the rock, with an oak door. Normally it would hold picks. Now it held recalcitrant prisoners. He was locked in solitary for twenty-four hours, in pitch dark. Dave banged on the door as he passed at the end of the shift. 'Keep strong,' he said quietly. Charlie, Jim, Frank and Danny echoed him.

The guard banged on the door with his rifle butt. 'No food for your men. This your fault.'

Jack crawled to the wall and dragged himself into a sitting position, his arms resting on his knees. His bruises would heal, and his back, where it had bled, would scab, but the others would go hungry. How long could he carry on the fight while his men also paid the price? Perhaps Simon was right? The seconds, the minutes and the hours passed, and as the darkness pressed in on him he cursed Auberon, who had promised he would get them out. And then he cursed him again for leaving them, because he was part of the group, wasn't he? And he cursed the bloody war, and the endless movement of his group. They had still had no letters, because no one knew where they were.

He cursed the bloody dark, and bosses, and the crashing and blasting and hewing that continued day and night and was making his head split, or was that because of the rifle that had crashed into the back of his skull, or the thirst that was driving him mad? He cursed the civilians that stumbled past his door, free, with a water bottle on their belts, and bait in their tins, and he cursed himself for hurting his own marras. Charlie's stomach would be aching, his hands throbbing, his abscesses bursting. He buried his head in his hands. The salt on them stung his eyes. He should never have brought the lad. He should never have derailed the cart. Shit, shit.

They let him out after twenty-four hours. His bruised hips and ribs had stiffened and he could barely stand. He was handed his pick by the overseer, his sleeves rolled up, muscles rippling. 'You work.'

He was led to his men, and his shame for their suffering meant he could not meet their eyes. But they met his and came to him, heedless of the guards, and the civilians who busied themselves elsewhere, calling the guards to them. After all, they were miners too, and they spent minutes pointing out faults on the wagons and the carts while Charlie handed him a flask of water, which he gulped down, then bread. 'The Welsh miners shared theirs with us. Here.' Dave had barley coffee in a bottle. Cold, but coffee. Jack shook his head. 'No, it's yours,' he croaked. Dave grinned. 'What's ours is yours, except for the beatings. You can have those all to yourself, bonny lad.'

'Aye, he can an' all,' Simon said, handing him a crust off his bread.

They worked for the next ten hours, each with their civilian minders, who never spoke. The skeletal Nottingham miner brought water at regular intervals.

They worked while the civilians broke for lunch, eating black bread and some spicy sausage. With each hour Jack blessed his years as a pitman because he could do it, blindfold, and like a machine. He could do it, and he kept telling himself this until the shift was over.

As he stumbled back to the cage the civilian miners handed them each some of the sausage they had saved, and one gave Jack three cigarettes. 'You brave man. You need these.' The man's hands were scarred, his forehead too. 'My son in war. War bad.'

Jack nodded, unable to speak for a moment. 'Yes, war bad. *Danke.*'

They travelled up in the cage, Jack slumped against the side, drifting, hearing the larks, seeing the blue sky, then the cedar tree at Easterleigh. So strong, so solid, and the memory of it made him stand up straight. At the school he broke the cigarettes in half and shared them with his group, ate mangel-wurzel soup, grieved for the prisoners who had died that day in a roof fall, or from illness, as so many did throughout the camps apparently, and slept as though dead.

Every day they worked, then slept. They grew thin. At the end of September, Charlie, Dave, Simon and Jack were marched back to the station, shoulders hunched against the icy wind. They were shepherded on to a train which was already getting up a head of steam. They were locked into the last carriage, a proper carriage, with slatted wooden seats. There were only two guards. Was there a chance of escape? Jack stared out of the window, and at the door, but the guard reached across and waved his hand. '*Nein*,' he warned.

They travelled all day with bets being taken on their destination, passing ploughed fields, haystacks and stooks, and slowing to go through towns. They suspected they were going to a mine, but which sort? They arrived at a railyard as the sun was lowering. Close by they could see winding gear, and coal was heaped high in the yard. Dave took his IOUs and stuffed them into his back pocket. He had bet on a coalmine. They were escorted into a camp with wire and posts, and barracks with the smell of sulphur overlaying everything, and coal sleck on the roofs. 'Home from bloody home,' Jack murmured. Dave laughed. 'At least Mart's out of it now.'

There were vegetable patches between the barracks. Si said, 'It's a proper camp, we'll get mail, we can write too. Must have been an army barracks.' They felt they had reached heaven. The light was dying. They were taken through into a white-tiled room and told to strip. They did, and were given a black uniform with KG in red, for Kriegsgefanger, a prisoner of war, on the back of the tunic, and their POW number on the front in red, with a yellow patch on the sleeve and a wide yellow strip inserted down the outside of each leg. Their cap was black with a vivid yellow band. They kept their boots. 'This is who you are now,' the Feldwebel said, pointing to the POW number. They didn't mind. They were within an established culture, there would be order, there would be mail. Yes, letters. They grinned at one another, and Charlie poked Jack. 'See, I told you I was right to come, man.'

'Aye, lad,' Jack said, 'but you've not been blooded in a pit yet.'

Dave smoothed his uniform. 'Neither's Simon, but we'll take care of you, aye, that we will. Do we wear this fancy dress while we're hewing, d'you reckon, Jack?'

Jack was saved from answering, as they were given singlets and shorts. 'That answer your question, bonny lad?'

They were given black bread and barley coffee and put into a small room, with beds with no mattresses but a base of chicken wire, and a blanket. The wire was more comfortable than the bare boards in the school had been, and they slept like logs. The next day they were roused before dawn and quick-marched out on to a lorry with several French and Belgian prisoners, who told Jack they had been there almost a year. They said there was a routine, there was mail, there were food parcels and some had put on weight, just a little but enough to make a difference.

Dave nudged Jack. 'You're the one speaking French, so ask if there are dancing girls?' Jack did and everyone laughed and no one bothered to answer. Charlie and Simon examined their abscesses. They were almost healed.

As they approached the mine and the seething slag heaps, the smell of sulphur grew stronger. At the shaft head they queued ten by ten to take a lamp from the cabin, and a token from the board to be returned after the twelve-hour shift. Charlie moved confidently, Simon less so, towards the cage. Jack stood close to them. Coal was a different beast to salt and an outsider would need to be supported, or he'd not make it. After the banksman had rapped three times, they squeezed in with the smell of the coal all around. The last time he'd been in a coalpit was with Mart, and his gut twisted, and he could almost see the silly bugger, almost hear him.

Jammed like sardines in the cage, Jack felt his chest constrict, as it always did. At two raps they were almost ready to fall through the air. They waited, he swallowed. To his left, crammed against him Charlie was humming, remembering Jack had said it might help. To the right, Si closed his eyes and said, 'I'm thinking of the larks. It's not helping, I'm still scared shitless.' Dave agreed. 'As are we all, bonny lad.'

One day, Jack thought, he might not mind. One day his breath might not catch in his throat, but he wouldn't place a bet on it. Charlie was still humming; it was getting louder and louder. 'Shut your noise,' someone yelled from the back. Charlie muted it, but didn't stop. Jack grinned at his balls. Bauer was right, the lad had inner strength. He glanced at Simon, and waited for the last single rap. It came. He braced, and down they went, rattling and heaving. Dave eased his water bottle, and the packet containing two pieces of bread, which he'd attached with wire to his shorts waistband. He knocked against Jack. 'Sorry, lad,' he said, but his words were almost drowned by the creaking and clashing.

With a jolt they were down, in the dust and the heat. It smelled of Jack's world. He snatched a look at Si, and then Charlie. It was as well they'd been in the salt mine as some sort of preparation, though here there'd be no huge caverns, just seams, just noise, just heat and dust. Soon he'd be able to read it as he'd done Auld Maud: the creaking of the pine uprights, and the coal, the roof, the movement of the air. Soon he'd be able to almost taste her moods.

They waited for the lower banksman to come and release the barrier. The lamp hung from Jack's hand. A few of the others talked, some cleared the coal dust from their throats. Some were silent, like Charlie and Simon. Guards waited with rifles over their shoulder. In the following cage would come the civilian miners, for yet again the prisoners were forbidden to work without a German beside them to forestall sabotage. Jack stared around, wondering how he'd blow up a seam, for that was what he'd decided, and how would he get the workforce clear, for he'd not take any lives with it, and where were the explosives? But that was not for today, or next week. It was for when an opportunity arose, and before that he might have managed an escape. It was a bloody long way back to France, so he'd have to head for neutral Holland. Bugger Auberon. His captain's German was coming along grand, and if they could have escaped together . . . Well, he'd just have to work on the language and do the best he could.

Jack could see that their picks were in a pile near the cage. Their guards were strolling about. An elderly banksman with a limp unlatched the civilians' barrier. Dave nudged Jack. 'Howay, man, takes you back a bloody lifetime, doesn't it.'

The barrier went back.

Simon elbowed past them, sweating, his face pale. He leaned down, his hands on his knees. 'You all right, Si?' Jack held his shoulder. Simon coughed, straightened, and grimaced. 'Just loving it, Jack, bloody loving it. Me and my mouth. It's not bloody fair.' Jack sighed. Dave shook his head.

The civilian cage was down. They were motioned towards their picks, and the foreman pointed ahead. They started their single-file trudge to the coalface, one behind the other with a German in between. Charlie was kicking up the coal dust, and Simon too, and they were shouted at by the German miners just behind them. '*Heben sie ihre füsse.*'

Jack called, 'Lift your feet. Just lift your feet the pair of you, or we'll all choke to death before we reach the face.' He repeated the German phrase in his head. Yes, he'd bloody learn to speak the bugger, then he'd have more of a chance.

Miners were streaming towards them on the other side of the coal road, back towards the cage: prisoners, some like skeletons, and the better-fed Germans, their eyes visible, their faces black, their shoulders hunched. Jack and his file pressed themselves against the sides as the full coal wagons passed, shoved back to the cages by putter boys and prisoners. It was the end of one shift and the start of another. There would be trappers on the doors, controlling the flow of air. Timmie had been a trapper, then a putter, driving the wagons heaped with coal, as the men were doing. But Timmie and Tony had Galloway ponies to do that, except when they carted coal out from low seams to meet up with the wagon.

Their lamps cast light only over the immediate area. Rats scurried, dust rose, the roof sighed, men shouted to each other above the clatter of the wagons. There was a lull. More prisoners were coming up behind them. Charlie was slowing the line down. A prisoner just behind him called, 'Pick your feet up and get along, man.'

Jack called back, 'Leave him be, he's young and only a gamekeeper. He'll learn.'

They plodded on, and in the continuing lull the man behind Charlie called again. 'Is that him humming? Bloody hell, I've been here a month and I get the bloody hummers. There's a bloke down in C seam who got here a day after me and then another couple from three weeks ago, who hum for bloody

England. They should open their mouths and sing, then they'd choke to death. Geordie thing, is it? Thank Christ I'm from Nottingham. One of 'em says it made his memory come back, coming here. Didn't have a bloody clue who he was but the Germans guessed he was a miner from his scars. They're getting us all here, all the miners. It's a pit they've just pumped out. The C seam chap's on about losing something, some foot or other, but he's got both of his, and never stops bloody humming.'

Jack stopped dead. A German miner pushed Jack from behind. '*Schnell*, hurry, hurry, work to do.' A guard came alongside and shoved at his shoulder. Jack dug in his heels, calling back to the German, 'Stop your pushing. I know you speak English. Ask if I can go to C seam, it's me marra, friend. I think it's him, but he's dead.' The guard was shoving him again. Jack repeated, 'I think he's my friend. I thought he was dead. Ask if I can go, I'll give you my cigarettes.'

The Nottingham miner called in German to the guard, who pulled at Jack's singlet, and shouted something and shook his head, and just pushed him forward. Simon said, 'It can't be him. He's dead, Bernie saw him, you know he did. The foot could be anything. Get a move on, Jack.'

Jack and Dave hewed for six hours with their German minders while Simon, Charlie and the German putters shovelled the coal into the carts. Their hands became swollen, the abscesses flared up and made Charlie groan but he never stopped, not for a moment, not until they broke for a drink, and bread, black bread. 'All of you, just chuck your picks,' Charlie said, sitting down and chewing. 'Use me bread, it'll be harder.'

They laughed. Simon threw a piece of coal at a rat scuttling along just outside the lamplight. 'Hate the bastards.' He muttered to Jack, 'You feeling better now? Went a bit strange back there for a moment, didn't you, lad?' Coal dust trickled from the roof. Jack counted the uprights. There weren't enough. He pointed at them, and then nudged the German miner, counting out the number needed on his fingers. The miner nodded, grimaced and shrugged. He said something, which Jack didn't understand, but no doubt it was 'Bloody bosses'.

He leaned back, closing his eyes. It would have been too good to be true. Mart was gone and one day soon he'd have to really feel it, deep inside, where belief lay. He'd told Grace he couldn't feel it, and that was the bloody trouble. He couldn't, not even here. Many hummed, of course they did. He worked for the next six hours and by the end his legs were shaking. Guided by the civilian miners, they took this shift-end slowly or they'd have never made it, but at last it was over, and they shouldered their picks and almost crawled back down the seam, towards the cage. It seemed further than on the way out. The glow from their lamps bobbed along the walls, and as before they passed miners, incoming this time, and were joined by others heading for the cages, some staggering under the weight of their picks.

Jack listened for humming in the lulls, and continued to do so even as the noise picked up, and how bloody silly was that? Charlie was lifting his boots as he walked. He was a canny lad, a right quick learner. The cage was ahead, but there was a queue. Dave said, 'Same old stuff, the world over.' Jack and he leaned against the wall, letting their picks drop to the ground. Charlie and Simon sagged, their heads down. Here it was quieter, and as Jack examined the abscesses on Charlie's hands he heard someone call out, 'If you don't stop that bloody humming, I'll do for you.'

'Sorry man, don't know I'm doing it. Can't hear too well, since the shell. Nearly took my bonce off, it did.'

Jack straightened, letting go of Charlie's hands. Another man shouted above the banging and clattering of the approaching lift, 'Sorry, man, didn't know. Been here long?'

The cage landed. It was quiet. 'Just a few weeks. Lost me memory but they knew I was a pitman from me scars, when they collected us up from the farm. Minute I got here I started to remember. It's like a bloody home from home for me.'

Jack was moving now, Simon in his wake. 'It's him,' Jack said. 'I know it's him.' His German partner was with him, pulling him back. Jack shrugged him off. Simon hauled on his arm. 'Come back, man. You'll get us all into trouble. God dammit, Jack.' Jack shrugged him off too. Dave called, 'Howay with you, Jack. Find him.'

He was almost running along the queue, pulling round one man after another, checking their faces, yelling, 'Mart?' again and again. Men were cursing him as he blocked their way from the cage to the start of their shift, shoving him to one side. A guard unslung his rifle, stopping him. Simon pulled at him again. 'For God's sake, come back man.'

Dave was there, armlocking Simon. 'I told yous to leave him be, you bloody bugger.' He turned to the guard. 'And you can stop poking me with that bloody rifle or I'll stuff it up your arse.'

Another guard made for Dave, who called, 'Get on with it then, Jack. I'm not doing this for the sake of me bloody health.'

Jack hurried along the line, being patted now by the prisoners, one of whom shouted, 'Good luck.'

A German miner put up his hand to a guard, saying, '*Sein freund ist hier.*' The guard hesitated, blocked him for a moment longer and waved Jack on.

Jack continued searching, grabbing shoulders, swinging people round. 'Mart, Mart,' he called repeatedly. 'Mart.'

'What the hell . . . ?' one man shouted.

'Mart, Mart, is it you? Mart?' A figure stepped out from the line. 'Jack?'

Jack stood quite still. He'd know that bloody idiot's stance anywhere. His shoulders weren't the same height. The miners in the queue fell silent, though those heading away from the cage continued, heads down. 'Mart? Mart, we thought you were dead.' He broke down then, running towards his marra, who threw down his pick and met him halfway. Jack picked him up, slapped him on his back. He was so light. Mart pounded his shoulders. 'I've found you,' Jack said, his voice muffled. 'I've bloody found you.' Mart was sobbing, clinging to him.

The queue moved forward but the guards said nothing, just bypassed the pair of them. Jack could feel Mart's ribs, the backbone, the shaking that ran through him. He saw the mouth that drooped on the right side, the scar that sliced across his brow, his cheek. He rubbed Mart's hair. 'Look at you, you messy bugger. Got to get some food in you, lots of lovely black bread, and then get a letter off to your mam and get some parcels from our Evie.' He drew his marra to him again, and whispered, 'Then we'll get you home, my bonny lad. Never fear, we'll all get home.'

Mart stepped back, gripped Jack's shoulders. 'Aye, that'd be grand.' Tears were still running down his face, just as they were down Jack's.

Auberon stood to attention at the start of the second hour of the punishment roll call or appel as he now called it. It was the end of November, so not surprising it was snowing, with the wind whipping across the square, but did it have to bloody snow and blow quite so hard? He felt it on his eyelashes, in his eyes, down his collar, and he thanked God for his cap. Saunders, his boyhood tutor, had told him the head was the greatest area of heat loss and to keep it covered. As he swayed, just as his neighbour had done a moment ago, he grabbed on to a thought, any thought, to keep him upright. The cedar tree. That would do; strong, and immovable. He was a tree. He shifted his weight from his toes to his heels as Jack had told him to if he ever had to stand for a long time. It could stop you fainting, he said. Well, you would faint wouldn't you, standing like this with all the blood sitting down there, not up here, in his head, leaving a damn great space which was wobbling about all over the place.

All the prisoners of the Offizier Gefangenenlager were standing to attention as a punishment for Colonel Mathers' complaint about parcels and mail being withheld without cause, and the insistence that the prisoners continue to write innocuous letters home to allay the concern of relatives. Mathers' adjutant, Captain Crawford, had had a bash at the Kommandant, Oberst Habicht, first, standing to attention like some naughty bloody schoolboy he'd said later, spouting that it was totally against the Hague Convention, but was chased from the office. 'Chased, you understand,' he'd exploded in the mess hut, 'with a bloody bayonet up my backside but what can you expect from some jumped-up clerk, made up to maître d'hôtel for God knows what reason.'

Auberon thought it might have done the arrogant sod Crawford a bit of good had he had his buttocks pricked, but it was bad form, nonetheless, and what was worse, the rations were then cut, and no one was allowed to buy from the village, or have access to their parcels. Crawford had ordered a hamper from Fortnum and Mason, so he could kiss goodbye to that for a while.

Mathers had taken it on next and was now in solitary, and they were standing here. It was a bloody disgrace, but the Kommandant was a nightmare and even the guards were nervous and on their toes all the time, likely to get a belt round the ear for nothing. German officers had a right to lay hands on their men, and that was a bloody disgrace too, and wouldn't be tolerated in the British army.

Auberon swayed again, and grabbed on to the cedar tree, taking himself under the lower branches, laughing alongside young Harry Travers, and John Neave, and waving Jack and Si into its shade. For he had brought the sun into his head, just as it was when he imagined the whir of his fishing line, the light catching his fly as it descended to the reaches of the river Somme which were well back from the front line, because that was his first stop after this bloody war. It was his road to tranquillity, for tranquillity was what everyone had come to realise was what they most longed for.

His neighbour pressed against him, whispering, 'Can't be for much longer, old chap, surely?' Smythe was a good sort, a former Territorial Force officer, and therefore a bit beyond the pale, as Auberon was. Not proper army. Well, as Frost, another former Terrie who shared his quarters said, in the front line he couldn't see much ruddy difference.

Major Dobbs had kept his eye on him on the journey here, and subsequently, disapproval in every glance, but why should the officers leave their men? This was what Auberon had said, and that was the stain on his reputation now, all put down to his Territorial roots. Dobbs had said they'd find a way to get his blokes here as orderlies, but so far there had been no opportunity. What was needed was an upsurge in prisoners. Well, the one certainty in this bloody war was another futile push, so that was a definite possibility.

He transferred his weight from toe to heel and back again, and straightened his back as Uberleutnant Baader inspected and counted them, yet again, followed a step behind by Krueger, his hauptfeld-webel, a sergeant major whose boots were like mirrors, even in this weather, and whose every stride squeaked as he compressed the fresh snow. But his boots squeaked whether there was snow or not. Another inch had fallen since the last roll call an hour ago. Back to the cedar tree, *toute suite*, he ordered himself as he started to shiver again. He was just so damned cold, and wet. But so were they all. This time Veronica was there, with the baby that had been born in October and named for him, using his second name, James. Evie had taken over her commandant duties as well as the kitchen with Mrs Moore while Veronica was so busy with James, and worked hand in hand with Richard. Evie. He rolled the name round in his head. It was getting crowded now, under the branches, no room for her. No, it was safer that she was kept away.

What other letters awaited him in the mailroom? They had received none for a month. Was there more news about his men? Veronica had written that they had been taken to the mines and at last could write; were they still safe? He should have seized Dobbs by the throat and made him request them as orderlies there and then, when the officers were taken off and brought here. Why the hell hadn't he? He shook his head. Actually he had, but not in so many words and perhaps that was the problem. He really should have throttled him. It was what Jack would have done. Shame enveloped him.

The Uberleutnant was in front of him now, looking as cold, if not colder than Auberon felt. '*Achtzig*.' Eighty, dear God, another seventy men to go. The Hauptfeldwebel ticked him off on his clipboard chart soaked by the snow, his fingers white from the cold, and Auberon wanted to wrench the clipboard from him and beat him to death with it, beat them all with it, and in particular Dobbs, but how easy it was to be brave after the event.

Thank God he had a dry uniform to change into when they were dismissed. What a war that allowed officers to send to their tailors, but of course the Germans demanded that the prisoners be correctly dressed in order to salute their masters. Civilian clothes were also permitted, but only with the insertion of the yellow stripe. However, what one tailor could do, another could undo for escape purposes. He'd requested a grey uniform from his tailor, which might have surprised him, but khaki would have been a giveaway when he finally escaped.

They were also permitted to have contact with their banks and the money enabled him to buy food from the village, though the entente blockade was causing increasing shortages. Within the camp they had to exchange their money for that issued by the camp. He snatched a look at the orderlies in their squares. They had only their one uniform. He must check with Roger that he was sharing the blankets Auberon had bought off the baker in the village but it had to be said, never had the little brat been so helpful. He was determined not to be sent back to a work camp, because he had a relatively easy life here.

Auberon leaned back against the trunk of the cedar tree, looking up at Easterleigh Hall. He had been twenty-five in October, ten days after the birth of his nephew. With that birthday had come the release of his inheritance from his grandfather, his father's father. He had instructed his bank to allow it to be accessed by Veronica and Richard for the upkeep of the Hall and hospital. That, with the fund-raising efforts of Sir Anthony Travers and his friends, had helped to make up the shortfall now that his father had totally withdrawn his support after that appalling drunken fiasco. Thank God for Evie and Richard, standing up to him; the upset could have caused Veronica to lose the baby. What about Harvey, too? The old boy deserved a medal.

Things were still difficult, however, as Sir Anthony hadn't yet provided extra funds, so it seemed that weird and wonderful tea parties, and sales of work were under way to help, as well as many and varied economies. Auberon made himself remain unemotional as he thought about all this. His father would be dealt with, at an appropriate time.

The snow was lighter, surely? He looked ahead at the barracks opposite, and the steep roof that allowed the heavy snow to slide to the ground. Lieutenant Rogers had collapsed into the snow, and his friends either side were hauling him to his feet. He was unconscious, but perhaps that was preferable to the sheer misery of this. Auberon's sense of powerlessness was growing, his rage too, and finally he understood Jack, and all the other pitmen, who had known that a strike couldn't succeed, but had to do it anyway, just to be heard.

He stared ahead, straight at the Kommandant,

who had come out of his office in which would be a stove throwing out heat. He strutted backwards and forwards, safe in the knowledge that he had total power. Or ruddy had he? Auberon thought of the union reps, Jack and Jeb, and now that held him, not the cedar tree, mulling the strike over, then creating detailed plans. At last they were dismissed, and once in his warm dry uniform, he marched to Major Dobbs' room.

'We need to strike,' he said, without preamble, standing briefly to attention.

The major sat in his chair, his legs crossed, his novel on his lap, his pipe tamped but not lit. His nose was still red from the cold, his stove plentifully supplied with wood bought from the village.

'We need a salute, old chap,' Dobbs drawled, moving to his desk, laying his book and pipe neatly side by side.

'You're not wearing a cap, old chap, even Terries know that,' Auberon snapped. 'We need to strike to bring about a change of Kommandant. We should refuse to write home, to order uniforms, to contact our banks. We have sufficiently well-connected families who would be concerned enough to ask questions of their tame politicians, which would create waves, and even make headlines. The powers that be will then ask questions via diplomatic channels, and something will be done. We need the action to be universal. We don't need strike-breakers.'

Dobbs was listening, but at this he barked, 'We're

not a load of your ruddy miners, for God's sake, we're officers and gentlemen. Pull yourself together.'

'I'm quite together, but I repeat, we do need to take action, and the only way we can do this is by striking. I repeat, we don't need strike-breakers.'

Dobbs' smile verged on contempt. 'Ah yes, I was forgetting you are in trade and understand these things. I gather your father obtained his peerage through the good offices of the Liberals, no less.'

Auberon strolled around the desk, sat on it, and leaned so close to Dobbs there was a mere inch between their faces. 'Do you, or do you not, want to rectify this situation and bring about the removal of Habicht? If so, forget your damned airs and graces, and remember what I said. Then you can trot to the adjutant to get a message to Mathers and present it as *your* idea, and earn a few points to buff up your sense of self-importance, not that it needs it.'

Dobbs leaned away, speechless it seemed, so Auberon proceeded to tell him what he had said, all over again, and the detail of what the major needed to do, and left.

The next day the order came round via the adjutant forbidding contact with home, bank, or tailor. By January 1916 Kommandant Habicht had been removed, and Kommandant Klein installed. Mail was released, and letters could be written again.

On 12th January, when work had begun on an escape tunnel under the dining hall, which doubled with the concert hall, to head out beneath the foundations of the barrack wall, Auberon entered Major Dobbs' room again, and plonked himself down on the edge of the desk before speaking. 'I have repeatedly asked for your support in my request for the transfer of my men. You have refused to take it to the colonel, though you promised before I agreed to leave the transit camp. I was told that to remain with my men would set a bad example. I know exactly where they are now, thanks to letters they have written home. We have had many more officers join us, many without orderlies, such are the hardships of war. Colonel Mathers will just have to hear whose idea the strike was, unless you explain to him that we have need for more orderlies, but more importantly, we have need of miners for the tunnel.'

Dobbs laid down *The Thirty-nine Steps*, borrowed from the camp library, and found his voice. 'Get off my desk, and we dig our own tunnels. It is a matter of honour, and how dare you blackmail me?'

Auberon ignored him. 'I repeat, my men are miners, there are four of them, these are their names, and the stalag where they are being held.' He slapped the paper on Dobbs' desk. 'My sister, Lady Veronica Brampton, has been in touch with your family, to be supportive, you understand. If you do not, in turn, support this request they will hear of your duplicity. My men will be brought here as orderlies by the end of January, they will also help in the digging of the tunnel which should prevent falls as happened, last week, and injured Captain Frost. The existing orderlies will assume their duties. My men will, of course, be amongst the escapers.'

He stood now, his shaking hands deep in his pockets. His heart was hammering so hard he was surprised that Dobbs could not hear it. Throttling the bastard would not achieve anything, but doing so metaphorically could be extremely productive. Still keeping his voice level, he continued, 'Finally, of course, this is your initiative, your idea to seek advice from such men, in order to expedite the work. Who knows, it could raise you to Lieutenant Colonel, especially if a remarkable number effect an escape from a well-built tunnel.'

He sauntered from the room, hearing Dobbs almost scream, 'You bloody Terries, you have no sense of what is good form.'

Auberon whirled on his heel, and re-entered. 'That reminds me. Smythe and Frost will be in the escape party. Frost's arm should be healed by then. It will take a long time to tunnel, such is the subterranean composition of the ground.'

As he left he heard Dobbs' high-pitched voice. 'Go to hell.'

Auberon slipped and slid across the icy square where some officers had created skates and were twirling. No doubt he would do as Dobbs said, but at least hell would be warm. He entered his hut. Frost was lounging on his bed, his arm strapped, and Smythe was writing a letter. They looked up. 'Well?'

Auberon grinned. 'Carrot and stick. Now we wait, but he's had a bloody bayonet up his backside and I reckon it will move him. He feels we have no sense of good form.'

'Hooray to that,' Smythe laughed. 'If you could have gone straight to Mathers it would have been different. He's a good sort. Let's see now.'

On 30th January Auberon was called into Mathers' office. He stood to attention. Major Dobbs stood at Mathers' side and Auberon nodded, but let his body relax out of attention. Mathers said, chewing on his empty pipe as he always did, 'Sit you down, Brampton. Now I hear Dobbs discovered that you have some miners whose expertise we need. As you know we normally do our own digging, but getting around the foundations has thwarted too many attempts, and the rocks beneath these barracks have proved insurmountable. We need a miracle.'

He tapped his pipe on the desk, and replaced it. It was extraordinary how easily the man could speak with it gripped between those teeth.

Auberon wanted to punch the air, but instead smiled. 'Jack Forbes is used to pulling those out of a hat, trust me.'

There was no heat coming from the colonel's stove. He would only light it as the sun went down as part of his war effort; the other was to organise as many escapes as possible. Auberon wished he wasn't quite so principled. It was bloody freezing.

The colonel continued, frowning, 'Ah yes, Sergeant Forbes.'

Auberon's heart sank. What the hell had Jack done now?

'The problem is that I have already contacted him, and word has just reached us that Sergeant Forbes has refused, therefore so have Corporal Preston and the two privates. It would have been a good idea, but as it is, it is a balls-up and time-waster.'

Auberon felt his jaw drop, saw the fury in Dobbs' eyes. What the hell was Jack playing at, the stupid bugger? He'd told him he'd bring them out. He coughed. 'Was a reason given, sir?'

Mathers scanned a note on his desk. 'It seems that there's a fifth miner, Corporal Mart . . .' He strained to make out the name.

'Dore,' said Auberon. 'Of course, Mart Dore.'

'Unless he's included, they won't come. It seems that an order is not an order in this man's army. Another strike on our hands, I feel.' Mathers' tone was dry.

Auberon wanted to laugh with relief. Bugger Jack, bugger him for being as strong and awkward as he'd always bloody been. It meant he was fit and well. He said, 'Mart Dore worked with them back home, I had forgotten my sister's news on that. They've all been drafted into this mine that's been reopened. There's a shortage of coal in our enemy's house, it seems, though knowing Jack he's slowed production up a bit.'

Mathers threw the letter down. 'Not sure we want trouble-makers here.'

Auberon felt like crossing his fingers as he lied, 'Oh no, not Jack. Never caused a moment's trouble in his life, just doing what we have all been ordered to do, a bit of sabotage and try to escape.'

Dobbs wriggled, because he was one who had declined to join the escape, preferring, Auberon was pretty sure, to sit out the war playing chess and reading novels. But who could really blame him?

Mathers pointed to the note. 'Deal with this immediately in the affirmative, Dobbs. We have a huge intake of officers and we can't have them denied their servants, can we?' He shared a glance with Auberon, one of distaste, or was it despair. Perhaps it was both.

Chapter 10

Easterleigh Hall, March 1916

Evie heard the lorry being driven into the garage yard, and snatched up her shawl, following Annie who was back at Captain Richard's request, her loyalty to Easterleigh Hall firmly in place. Together with Mrs Moore they ran out of the door and up the steps to meet Harry Travers, and his bees. As they reached the top step they heard Harry's voice. 'Steady, old chap. The bees are on their sofas having a snooze.'

They grinned at one another as he jumped out of the lorry, or hopped perhaps, because his weight was on his proper leg, not his wooden one. Their rush towards their favourite returning 'son' was overtaken by the laundry girls, who had been loitering over the task of hanging up the washing, waiting for him. 'Mr Harry,' Sally called, a wet sheet bundled up in her arms. 'Grand you're back, and not just because we all like honey.'

The other girls laughed. Harry used just a cane nowadays, his father had told them when he had laid down the conditions under which the consortium of fund-raisers would help to support the hospital and convalescent home. He had explained to Richard and Ron Simmons that his son had not settled at university, because he felt it full of children. 'All he wants is to return to Easterleigh Hall to do something to help, so that is the first of our conditions, well, mine, as I am the chief, and most willing, contributor: that he is allowed. The other conditions are of an economic nature, and basically we insist that any extraneous expenditure is discussed with the fund-raising committee before being implemented.'

Evie called over the heads of the laundry girls, 'Wonderful to have you back, Harry. How have the bees travelled, do you think?'

Annie was slipping round to the rear of the lorry. Raisin and Currant had found their way there, and were yapping. One of the volunteers carried them back to the kitchen. 'Lock them in, will you, Lily,' Evie called. 'Can't have them upsetting new visitors.' She and Mrs Moore waved to Harry.

The tailgate was pulled down by Arthur, the elderly driver, who worked as a gamekeeper on Sir Anthony Travers' estate south of Washington pit village. Harry joined Evie and Mrs Moore after weaving his way between the laundry girls. His hair had been tousled by old Mrs Webber. He slapped his gloves against his good leg, and straightened his hair. 'They should be all right, we've taken it steady, haven't we Arthur? Arthur's going to help me erect the hives if we can have a few helpers to get all this to the meadows. The honey will taste much better if the bees can gather pollen from flowers, rather than down near the ha-ha, which Richard thought might be the best place.'

Mrs Moore smiled as he clasped her in a bear hug. 'Right glad to have you back, we so need the honey, bonny lad. The food shortages are mounting . . .' She patted him and he moved on to Evie, holding her tightly, replying to Mrs Moore over her head.

He nodded. 'Yes, I passed the queue outside the co-op, and nowhere else is any better. Why the hell the government don't take control I don't know. They could use the Defence of the Realm Act to set up ration rules, surely?'

'When you're ready, Harry,' Arthur called, climbing up into the lorry and shoving one of the bee carry-boxes towards the tailgate. Harry released Evie, landing a smacking kiss on her cheek. 'So damned glad the lads are with Aub. Excellent, excellent. Just need the bloody government to sort out the food . . .'

Evie waved him to silence. He laughed, as he said, 'Sick of hearing it are you, Evie?'

'You could say that, our Harry.'

Harry smiled as he grabbed Evie's hand and they hurried through the girls to the lorry. He took one end of the box, and, helped by Evie, lowered it to the ground. She could hear a humming, and a slight vibration. Harry touched her arm. 'It's quite safe, and I checked that we've a queen in each. They've weathered the winter well and will be eager to feed. I didn't need to give them sucrose, which is marvellous. Let's get 'em set up and settled, and within days they'll make a rush for the meadow flowers, you mark my words. I've brought three cases of honey too. And Mother is packing up more from the hives at Searton. You said you were looking for an alternative sweetener?'

Evie touched his sleeve. It was strange to see him in mufti. He looked even younger. 'You are an angel, Harry. Yes, sugar is short, everything is, and we should be able to supply as much as we can ourselves, surely to God, with Easterleigh land, and Home Farm. Those poor beggars ploughing across the Atlantic and heaven knows what oceans in supply ships are going to get picked on more and more by the submarines, and what's available should go to those without means. Or so our Richard says. Bangs the table he does.' Harry roared with laughter.

Evie continued as Arthur shoved another box along to the end of the lorry. 'We've more volunteers coming every day from the villages, and we have German POW patients who are recovering and want to help.' She and Harry shared the load again, and settled the box gently on the ground. Mrs Moore tapped his shoulder as he straightened up. 'Oh Harry, pet, you'll be billeted in the under-gardeners' cottage, or what used to be theirs, and Evie's right, the Germans are champing at the bit to do something.

We've got some of our facial injuries too, who are being eased out into the sunshine by Lady Margaret to try and build self-confidence.' As she said this, the sun went behind a cloud, and the wind seemed to freshen.

Annie was helping Harry lower another box to the ground. 'Millie's nipped off to fetch the prisoners out. Matron's given them permission to escape for a moment to help with the bees. It's her they're afraid of, not the guards.'

Mrs Moore laughed as she chivvied the laundry girls back to their pegging out. 'Not surprised, the two old boys guarding them must be sixty if they're a day, and still in the reserve for heaven's sake. Imagine if they were in the front line. Now I don't want to hear a word out of you girls about that silly old duffer who thinks he's God's gift to cooks, and brings flowers every day. Pinches them from the nursery bed, he does, young Harry. Now, Evie, let's get back to the coalface. Annie, go and hurry Millie up, she'll as like as not be dawdling along with that young Heine she's taken a shine to. No need to speak German it seems, sign language is doing the job just grand, it is for too many of them, including young Maudie.' Mrs Moore stalked off, and stopped at the top of the step. 'They're the enemy, after all.'

Evie hurried after her, waving to Harry, calling, 'They're also young men who've been hurt, you old witch.'

'Enough of your cheek.' Mrs Moore's words ended

on a roaring laugh. In the kitchen they checked that the mixed-grain bread was rising nicely. It was Home Farm barley and wheat, though their own winter-sown grain was doing well and the harvest should be good in the fields around the church, arboretum, and all land in between. The land south of the cedar tree and beyond the ha-ha had been planted with potatoes and the early crop could be lifted any day now, and many more rows earthed up in land behind the stables. Spinach was sown in fields along the lane to Easton, plus spring greens. Old Stan and some of the prisoners had just started tomatoes in the glasshouses, and a whole swathe in the conservatory below the grapevine.

With the coming of spring more and more land was being given over to food production, as part of Richard's plan. Pigsties had been set up in three fields and lambing was under way, under the eagle eye of Trotter, of Home Farm. Froggett was trying to train Richard and Ron to handle sheepdogs for next year, because no one could believe that the war would be over by then. They had tried their whistles on the dachshunds, which had provided an hour of hilarity but little progress.

In the kitchen Dottie was mixing the butter from Home Farm with mashed potato. 'What the eye don't see, the stomach won't mind,' Mrs Moore muttered. 'We've got to spin it out, but only for the staff, mind. The wounded get the proper butter or I'll want to know the reason why.'

'Even the Germans?' Evie wondered. Mrs Moore pursed her lips. 'They're someone's son, or husband, or brother. It's our duty. It's not our duty to like 'em, or whatever else these silly girls have taken into their heads, especially that wretched Millie.' Mrs Moore stopped, coloured, then said as she reached for her recipe bible, 'Sorry pet, didn't mean that, not really. Well, you know, I'm just an old witch, as you say. She's just happy that your Jack is with Mr Auberon now, and out of the mine, you can tell she is.'

Evie busied herself checking that the pulses and beans set to soak two days ago were sprouting. One of the Indian patients had told them that this treatment of the beans produced something more nourishing and digestible. It seemed that the starch was converted into maltose, allegedly more nutritious. Even if it wasn't, soaking softened the beggars, and they took less time to cook, which in view of the industrial need for coal, and the shortage on the domestic front, was all to the good. Best of all, they created less wind, which pleased the nursing staff who complained that they had to bend to tend the patients, with catastrophic results all round.

She poked the beans. 'Are you sure you agree with introducing them today in the mutton casserole for the patients?'

Mrs Moore was checking the ovens, all of which contained either the casseroles or the jam-sponge puddings.

At that moment, there was a knock on the internal door. Evie waved in Veronica, with baby James in her arms, and Richard, who was walking with more confidence, and who had asked that the upper servants call him by his forename. He, Tom the black-smith, and Evie's da had devised a way for Richard to kick his false leg forward which seemed to make walking easier. Veronica saw the beans and her face fell. Evie wagged a finger. 'Enough of that, there's a war on. How is the lord and master today, Ver, and how is Mart's mam managing as nanny?'

Veronica smiled, kissing her son. 'Angela was named correctly, she was born an angel. We manage together very well now I'm back nursing in theatre. It was inspired, Evie, to ask her to come. You can see that she has this energy, which you say is new, but why wouldn't it be, if a son has been recovered. Thank heavens he is a prisoner and has a chance of surviving this terrible war.'

Richard slid on to a stool and stared hard at his wife, who ignored him, saying, 'I thought I'd just walk James in the garden while the sun is out.'

Richard continued to stare at her. Evie and Mrs Moore looked from one to the other, and at Mrs Green as she came in with tea towels, freshly aired, and piled high in her arms to a point where she could barely see. Richard went to her, his arm outstretched. 'Let me help.'

Mrs Green shook her head, her expression saying as clearly as her words would not, 'It's not seemly, you belong above stairs.' Yet again Evie wondered if this changed attitude of the ruling classes would outlast the war. But what world would they be living in by then, and would these German POWs be their masters? Would there be any young men left, from either side? So many questions and no answers whatsoever. Richard was still staring at his wife.

Evie slid on to a stool herself, checking the clock as she did so. Ten thirty, with breakfast a distant memory and lunch looming too quickly. Daisy and her fellow housemaids would be down for yesterday's tea leaves for the carpets before ten minutes were up. Veronica said, 'I'll be back in half an hour.'

Her husband said, 'You'll be no such thing.'

Evie and Mrs Moore said at exactly the same time, 'Come on, out with it, you two.'

Out it came, with Veronica settling herself down, and talking into James' hair. 'Lady Margaret's friend has been injured, amongst others, in an ammunition factory where she's been working. Margaret wonders if Easterleigh Hall could manage to take in wounded women too, and I wondered what you think, Evie?'

'There is quite a bit of wondering going on here, and why should it concern me?' Evie replied.

Richard was smiling. 'I told you so,' he said to Veronica. 'Now I've done the sums, you can do your own dirty work.'

His wife glared. Mrs Moore asked, 'Sums? So is there enough money? Have you discussed it with Sir Anthony? We won't get the government subsidy, will we, and where would we put them? Can't be in the wards, just imagine the hanky-panky.'

Richard looked aghast. 'I hadn't thought of hanky-panky, and I would think it would be the last thing on anyone's mind.'

All four women sighed, and Evie muttered, 'Shows how much you know about anything, but of course they can't share a ward. I imagine you're asking me where I think they could go?'

At that point the housemaids rushed in for the tea leaves. Evie dragged out the bucket from the end of the ranges. The furnace was gurgling and could do with more coal; she fed it. Daisy rushed her ducklings out again.

Mrs Green followed in their wake, calling, 'I'll leave you to your problems, but perhaps the conservatory? We have spare drapes we could hang from the ridge. We could then tuck them in at guttering height, leaving sufficient material for them to fall to the floor. There is already a stove in there, and a sink, water, and pipes running along the bottom of the walls to keep the vines from freezing, so I feel sure it is within the imaginings of man to create a haven for women.' She shut the door.

Richard was beginning to assume the hounded expression that was becoming more frequent these days, and usually ended with him muttering about cauldrons and monstrous regiments. Evie remembered something. 'Old Stan's tomatoes. They will have to share with them, but the smell is nice.'

The laundry volunteers came clattering up the internal corridor from the yard, the empty clothes baskets on their hips, stuffing their Woodbines in their pockets. Suzy called through the open door, 'The POWs are helping to get the hives to the meadows. Millie is directing operations.'

Evie was busy organising the table with cutlery, and longed to snap, 'I bet she is.' Instead she called through to the scullery for Dottie to make sure the large porridge pan was ready for use for yet another load of potatoes, this time for lunch. She rejected one of the vegetable knives as too blunt. 'Right, if that's that, off you go for your walk and Richard, Sir Anthony called, though I expect Mr Harvey has already told you. When is Ron back from Aldershot? Has he written with news of the rebuilding of his nose?'

Ver was still here, rocking James, who was crooning in response. Evie eyed the clock. 'I'll take that as a no, as neither of you are answering. Don't worry, he'll be all right, whether it works or not. He's such a wonderful young man. Now, Richard, I'm sure you have work to do, because Mrs Moore and I most certainly have.' Mrs Moore was pulling mixing bowls from the cupboard at the end of the room near the scullery. Richard shook his head at Veronica. 'Speak,' he commanded.

Veronica glared at him, again, then looked at a point above Evie's head. 'The thing is, Dr Nicholls agrees that we should take the women, Lady

Margaret's trust can fund it, but no one has quite got around to asking Matron . . .'

There was a crash as a mixing bowl fell to the floor. 'Bugger,' said Mrs Moore, and yelled, 'Dottie, we need a brush.'

Evie looked from Richard to Veronica. 'So . . . ?'

Mrs Moore shouted, 'Don't be stupid, Evie, she wants you to beard the dragon in her den, that's what this is all about. No one else has the courage to actually ask, not even Nicholls, even though he's right glad we've hooked him out of that other place.'

Veronica was smiling tentatively now, and inching towards her husband. 'You know very well you're the only one she listens to, Evie. Please, please would you tell her what we've managed to sort out, and that includes funding for another three nurses, and two VADs to concentrate on the women, and they can sleep in the storage room beyond the wine cellar which was electrified along with the rest of the basement, and I've spoken to Millie who isn't happy but will for an extra ten shillings a week . . .'

Evie put up her hand. 'For the love of God, be quiet. Yes, yes. Now will you go, because we have to feed the multitude, and I will not expect that unpleasant look on your face from either of you when I produce the casseroles complete with these beans.'

Richard was staring at Veronica again, and then nodding towards Evie. Veronica, knowing Mrs Moore was now in the pantry, sorting the vegetables, came round the table to stand close to Evie. James was beginning to cry. Evie rubbed his back. 'And?' she asked quietly, disturbed by the worry in her friend's face.

'And,' whispered Veronica, 'Margaret is pregnant and will not marry Major Granville, though he longs for it. She feels that women need to make a point. She has her own money since her aunt's death and could adequately provide for her child herself.'

Evie replaced the spoons she'd been examining, and wiped her hands down her hessian apron. James was crying properly now. She said, 'Take him for his walk, and let me think. Richard, will you go with her, or perhaps stay here with me, but someone do something. This needs to be dealt with.' She knew her voice shook. Pregnant? Another one? What about her? When would it be her turn to have a child? She felt a mixture of rage and pain.

She turned to the range. The kettle was boiling. Tea was the answer. The leaves had been used once this morning, but never mind. Veronica leapt at the chance of escape. Evie made the tea and stirred the pot. Mrs Moore came from the pantry, a large bowl full of carrots in her hands. She slapped it on to the table. 'We'll need that tea sooner rather than later, Evie pet. This is a damn sight more serious than bearding Matron over a load of women, this is a child's future being hoisted on the petard of its mother's ridiculous principles.'

Richard swallowed, and then the laugh burst from

him. 'I thought you were in the scullery, Mrs Moore. Ears like an elephant, that's what you have.' Mrs Moore picked up a carrot and threatened him with it. 'It's no laughing matter. We need to sort it. Evie, what are we to do?'

Evie looked from one to the other. She'd slap the silly woman if it was up to her, but not because of any affront to society. It was because Lady Margaret was blessed, it was because Major Granville had lost his face and had to live his life behind a tin mask, and struggled every minute of every day to find some sense of self-respect. How would her refusal be perceived by him? Oh for God's sake, why couldn't people just hug their wondrous moments and treat them as the gifts they were, for surely the war had taught everyone that no one knew how long good fortune would last. 'Where is the silly girl?' she asked Richard, and was horrified to hear the shake in her voice.

Mrs Moore shook her head at Richard. 'Now Evie, keep calm. We need to think this through.'

Evie was already heading for the door. Good, they thought it was rage. But part of it was. 'I'll leave the tea to brew and will be back shortly. Perhaps you'd like to get your recipe bible open at wedding cake, because I'm not having this. There's Verdun blasting men to pieces, men dying in Italy, the Zeppelins are causing mayhem over us all, our men are limping back to Blighty so we can repair them, only to send them back. No, I'm not bloody well having this nonsense about principles when that lovely man needs a wife. Dear God, he's not going to live for more than a year or so Matron says, so what's the stupid lump of a lass thinking?'

Evie headed up the stairs and through the green baize door, waving to Sergeant Briggs, and making a course straight for the Facial Room off to the side of the great hall. On the way, she heard Lady Margaret organising the VADs in the anteroom, and peeked in. A few extra years had not altered the woman's looks, which still resembled those of a thoroughbred racehorse. Would the child have the appearance of a foal, or look like its father? That was difficult, because no one here knew how he had looked. Lady Margaret was pale. Well, she'll be a damn sight paler in a moment, Evie thought, her hands rammed into her apron pockets so she wouldn't be tempted to strangle her.

She strode into the Facial Room, used to the remnants of faces. She smiled and waved, and spent time talking to each of them, asking if any of their visitors had made use of the overnight rooms that had been created in one of the cottages on the estate. Several had. She had to concentrate on Tom very carefully because the left-hand side of his face was gone, and though she could see the exposed raw mechanics of his jaw and tongue as they produced speech, it was hard to hear what he said.

Major Granville was reading to one of the corporals by the open window. He waved at her, his tin mask reflecting the light, even though volunteers were painting them as close to skin tone as possible these days. The window was open because the men liked to listen to the birds, preferring to hear them from the sanctuary of their day room rather than outside. Lady Margaret had tried to have Major Granville transferred to Aldershot's facial hospital but it was too late, and his injuries too bad. The good news was that some patients with facial injuries were now going to the Aldershot hospital from the ships, though some still went later. Soon it would be the turn of these young men too. Evie waved, said she'd come again, and only then did she enter the anteroom, gripping Lady Margaret's arm, and escorting her into the passageway along from the hall.

There, in words of great clarity and force, she told Lady Margaret her opinion of her decision, stressing the need to think of a child in this world as it was now, to think of the father of that child, to think of Mrs Moore who would be denied the chance to make a wedding cake in this time of shortages, and to consider her patients who would wonder why the lovely confident Major Granville was to be denied the role of husband and father, in the eyes of the law.

Lady Margaret tried to interrupt several times. This was a mistake, because it gave Evie fresh impetus. It was only when Lady Margaret held up her hands in surrender and said, 'Very well, I can see your point, Evie. I will marry Andrew for his sake, and my child's, and for yours, because your anger moves me, and because you drew me back from the darkness when I came to Easterleigh Hall in ruins, after repeated imprisonments. I know how hard it must be because your friend Veronica has a child, I am pregnant and you are not yet able to marry Simon.Therefore, mostly I will do it for you.'

It was almost as though the woman had rehearsed her capitulation. Evie shook her head, silenced for a moment, but not for long. She gripped Lady Margaret's arms, both of them this time, shaking her head repeatedly. 'No, Margaret, you will not do it for any of these reasons. You will do it for yourself, do you understand? To want something for yourself is not shameful, it's natural, and that is why you must do it, if indeed you do love Major Granville. If not, would you please tell us so I can get Mrs Moore to close her recipe book and let us all escape the misery that will be waiting for us in the run-up to the wedding.'

Lady Margaret leaned against the wall now, covering Evie's hands with her own, her almost black hair streaked with grey, though she was still in her twenties. 'You know, damn you, Evie. You know why I don't want to marry him, don't you?'

Evie leaned against the wall next to her. 'Yes, I think perhaps I do. But it won't make any difference, Major Granville will die anyway, within a year or two, or so Dr Nicholls feels. By choosing happiness you aren't tempting fate. Be brave, Margaret. This is harder than any forced feeding, any imprisonment. You are opening yourself to love and you will receive pain, but you will anyway. You deserve this happiness, all these men deserve to see it.' Evie could say no more, because her voice would have failed her.

She squeezed this awkward, difficult and wholly admirable young woman's arm, for they were now both weeping. At last though, all was agreed and she left to seek out Matron, who huffed and puffed in the entrance to the acute ward and then agreed to accept women patients. But of course she did, Evie told herself as she left, because she was an angel who thought she hid it well behind a uniform and a massive bosom. 'Well, bonny lass, you don't,' she whispered, then shouted over her shoulder, 'You're an angel, a big one, but an angel.'

Matron did not even break stride as she swept into the acute ward, saying, 'You, my girl, are a bossy and impossible commandant.' Sergeant Briggs on the reception desk pulled his pencil from behind his ear, pointed it at Evie and grinned. 'Nah, Evie, don't tell Matron anything nice. She'll breathe fire today just to cover up. Talking of fire, Dottie poked her head in here a moment ago with a message for you. Apparently Mrs Moore is breathing it down in the kitchen, because the clock is ticking and you are still absent.'

Evie stared at him. 'I have never managed the art of being in two places at once. I will just pop on a pair of wings and flutter back.' She spun on her heel and stamped to the baize door, slamming it behind her, then smiled. The staff liked a pantomime from time to time. As she hit the internal corridor and drew level with the laundry she met Millie, a clipboard in her arm, a frown on her face as she ticked off items. When she saw Evie she said, 'Well, I think it's disgusting.'

Evie sighed and tried to sidestep her sister-in-law, but Millie rammed the clipboard across her chest. Evie stopped. 'What is?'

'Lady Margaret.' Millie's pasty face was twisted with distaste.

'That's rather rich from you, Millie. I seem to remember that you had a bun in the oven when you married my brother. Have you written to him, by the way?'

Millie shook her head, her mousy hair lank. Behind the girl the coppers were boiling on the ranges while the staff stirred them with wooden poles. 'Not the baby, for God's sake, Evie, but that face. How the hell can she face what's under the mask every night?' The girl paused for two seconds while Evie studied her, wondering if she could possibly be any more loathsome.

Millie suddenly smiled, as though a light had switched on. 'Ah, that's right canny. He's going to pop his clogs, isn't he, any day? She'll be rich then. Really rich.'

Evie hated her more than she ever had before, and

slapped her, right across the chops. The crack echoed down the passageway, followed a beat later by Millie's howl. Evie shoved her clipboard aside and strode on, storming into the kitchen, with Millie's voice calling after her. 'I'll pay you back, Evie Forbes, you see if I don't.'

No one said a word. Mrs Moore merely lifted her head from the recipe book and muttered, 'Cake?'

'The best we can manage,' Evie said, changing her apron for a clean one, her hand stinging, and proceeded to tell Mrs Moore what had happened, and even Mrs Moore was silenced.

On Tuesday 4th July 1916 Major Granville waited with his best man, Captain Richard Williams, in the front pew of Easterleigh Hall's chapel. Edward Manton stood in front of the altar in his cassock, looking older, his hair quite grey though he was only thirty-two.

Lady Margaret's parents had decided to attend, to Lady Margaret's displeasure, and sat in the front on the left-hand side of the church, accompanied by Lord and Lady Brampton, to everyone else's displeasure. All four looked as though they'd sucked on lemons, and there were no others from their circle in attendance. On the right-hand side sat plain Mr and Mrs Roger Granville and a large number of their friends, many in mourning. The rest of the church was taken up with VADs, Lady Margaret's friends, many of whom had shared imprisonment with her,

Major Granville's friends, John Neave who had snatched a few hours out of his weekend leave, and a good smattering of patients, men and women, including Ron Simmons, who had returned to take up his post alongside Richard as the assistant financial administrator of the work programme and the hospital. He was complete with a reasonable nose now, and a pretty VAD on his arm. Sir Anthony Travers had sent his apologies but Harry was there, of course, and not alone. He was surrounded by all the laundry staff and numerous VADs, not to mention two nursing sisters.

Evie had grinned when he had slipped into the chaos of yesterday's kitchen as though he had the troubles of the world on his shoulders, and shared with her the fact that not only Annie, the laundry girls, and the housemaids wanted to hang on his arm, but also the VADs and nurses and he didn't know how to choose. 'Take the lot of them and one day someone will steal your heart and that will be that. Until then, make all their worlds happier,' she had advised.

Mrs Moore, Annie and Evie sat in the back pew with Mrs Green and Mr Harvey, as good servants should, and besides, none of them wanted to meet Lord and Lady Brampton. Several from the facial unit slipped into the pew in front, to be joined by Sergeant Briggs. He turned round and whispered, 'It will be you, one day, Evie Forbes, but we've got to get Mrs Moore hitched first and that could take some while. She's so choosy. She turned me down only last week.'

Mrs Moore slapped his arm as the pianist lurched into the wedding march, and in came Lady Margaret, with her carefully designed dress hanging in such a way as to disguise the child she was expecting in three months' time. She looked beautiful, her hair fell in soft folds, her face was fuller, more gentle, loving, and Evie felt a tug at her own heart, and called silently for a miracle, for life to be extended for Major Granville, who had just been decorated for his bravery. He had been standing beneath the cedar tree as Evie passed this morning at dawn, on her way to the hives, just to check that the bees were still there. It was what she did, because if they hadn't left, no one would die today. She had walked towards him. He had held out his scarred hand, and gripped hers.

'You have read the newspaper? You have seen the lists?'

Evie had nodded. 'The Somme is supposed to be a place of tranquillity,' she murmured. 'We are expecting the convoys of wounded soon.'

He had said, confused, 'Tranquillity?' His eyes, within the mask, searched her.

'Aub told me that the Somme is Celtic for tranquillity.'

He took her other hand. 'I thank God he is safe, and your brother, Simon, even Roger. You will tell Auberon, when you see him, that I had a great admiration for him, a great love. He is one of the best young men I know.' His voice was urgent. 'You see, there is so much I want to do, and say, but I know I haven't the time. I know that Easterleigh Hall will look after Margaret, Veronica has promised that. I ask you to help too, Evie.'

She did not belittle him by denying the need. She merely agreed, and passed on her way. Please, bees, be here, day after day.

Now Lady Veronica followed, as Margaret's Matron of Honour. Harry and one of the Germans had worked with Old Stan to create the bouquets of white roses, with some pale pink blooms from Bernie's rose, planted by Simon at Christmas. They had also worked on the church, and decked it in the tranquil colours of green and white. Myrtle had been included, for constancy.

Though the service passed quickly, the kitchen staff left before the end to put the final touches to the wedding breakfast, which had been a trial to produce, as Lady Margaret insisted that the restrictions that Evie and Mrs Moore had set in stone for the staff should be maintained. There was a preponderance of rabbit, which would please Lord Brampton, whose favourite it was, but practically no one else, since they felt that they were beginning to grow fur, and their two front teeth were lengthening of their own accord. Harry had muttered, 'Don't even mention my ears, they are elongating and they twitch, I swear they do.'

The situation hadn't been altogether helped by Major Granville announcing that carrot patties would just make his day, though the red cabbage fricassee had helped somewhat. Mrs Moore had put her foot down at the mention of nettle soup. Instead Evie had got hold of cow-heels and between them they produced Italian soup, as herbs were plentiful. There would be no dessert, but Mrs Moore's cake would come into its own.

She and Evie had used only honey in the cake, which was sponge. After test-tasting they declared it practically inedible, as somehow honey wasn't sweet enough, crestfallen though Harry was at the news. It was now a multi-layered jam sponge, thanks to the greengage jam from Mrs Green's pantry. Mrs Green had arrived with her bounty on a tray and a puzzled expression on her face. 'I must check my record book,' she had said. 'I seem to be missing several jars. But perhaps I forgot to note it.'

At the wedding breakfast, set up in the marquee on the lawn, John Neave joined their table, looking strained and preoccupied, as did most soldiers on leave. He raised his glass to Evie. 'Wonderful effort, as always, Evie. Mrs Moore too, of course.'

Within seconds, he was joined by Harry. Evie groaned. 'The incorrigible duo are back together.' They laughed and John told them of his need to leave within the hour, if he was to catch the train. 'Get your foot blown off next time, old man,' Harry said, 'then you can help me with the bees. Much more conducive to a quiet life.'

'Nothing would please me more,' John said, grinning across the table at Evie. 'Then we can annoy old Nicholls by smoking under the cedar tree again.'

Everyone served themselves from the buffet table, at Lady Margaret's request, as it seemed the quickest way. Mrs Green slipped on to the seat next to Evie. 'I see that you signed the greengage jars out in May. I do wish you had told me, Evie.'

Mrs Moore looked askance. 'Evie, that is Mrs Green's empire, and well you know it.'

'I didn't, unless I was sleepwalking,' Evie responded, but was then distracted by Veronica, who touched her shoulder. 'There's to be dancing after all, Evie. We have the fiddler from Easton arriving in half an hour, and then Old Stan's nephew too, but we need someone to sing.' They all thought of Simon, but Evie shook the image from her mind. 'We have the dinners to prepare, Ver. Surely there's someone else.'

John Neave called across the table, 'Just half an hour, Evie. It will be a happy memory to take back to France, there's a good girl.'

Harry nudged him. 'After you, Evie, we can ask Susan from the conservatory ward.'

Susan Forbes agreed. 'She has the voice of an angel and is feeling well enough. I asked her earlier. It's just the first half-hour when she is having her dressings changed that she can't manage.'

Evie laughed. 'Ah, so I'm just the finger in the dyke.'

'Definitely,' Veronica said, smiling at them all and returning to her son and husband.

The dancing continued for two hours only, for there was a hospital to run, patients to tend, meals to prepare and perhaps convoys to expect. Evie, Annie and Mrs Moore clattered into the kitchen, confident that the cake had been the success they had intended, and there they found Lord Brampton's chauffeur, with Millie, filling wicker hampers with pheasant which the old gamekeeper bred for all-year use, hams, eggs, and preserves from Mrs Green's pantry, plus two sacks of sugar and heaps of vegetables. Mrs Moore placed herself between the chauffeur and the hampers. 'Just what do you think you are doing?'

The chauffeur explained that Lord Brampton had given him orders to fill the hampers with stores from Easterleigh Hall, and that Millie had agreed that he could. Millie stood quite still, her hands in her apron pockets.

Evie was hurrying upstairs to find Richard even before Mrs Moore called to her to do so. She saw Lord and Lady Brampton heading down the stairs, making for the main doors. She stood in their way, her arms spread wide. 'I am acting commandant and you will not take food from these patients,' she said quietly. 'You will not, do you hear me?'

Lord Brampton pushed past her, his wife too, clutching her skirts to her as though the very presence of a cook would contaminate her. They hurried through the doors and down the steps where Margaret's parents waited to say farewell, their Rolls-Royce at the ready. Evie flew past them, and across to the marquee. 'Richard,' she shouted, her voice so high that he swung round mid-sentence. Mr Harvey turned too, breaking off from instructing the young pitmen who were lining up the chairs around the edge. This was where they would triage the injured from the Somme when they arrived, today, tomorrow or next week.

Richard limped to Evie as she explained, and she and Mr Harvey followed as he hurried past the departing Rolls-Royce, nodding to Margaret's parents as he did so, and then on, into the old stable yard, hot on the heels of his parents-in-law who were heading towards their car. The engine of the Bramptons' Rolls-Royce was running in the garage yard, the chauffeur was behind the wheel, and the blacksmith, and Evie's da, Bob Forbes, stood in front of the car, preventing him from driving forward. Mrs Moore rushed up the steps, pointing to the boot of the car. 'Captain, they've taken hamper after hamper of food that we need for the patients, though Evie told them not to. I asked Bob to block the car.'

Lady Brampton was climbing into the back seat while Lord Brampton was trying to push aside the blacksmith, who was in his Sunday best, hiding the muscles which usually terrified any potential opposition.

Richard held up his hand, and the blacksmith stepped back. Richard took his place. 'Please, Brampton, this is no way to behave. I will ask you to agree that we may remove the hampers from your car. It is unacceptable that you should deprive those in need.'

Lady Veronica was running up the kitchen steps, her hair escaping from her bun. 'Father, we need every bit of food. We have convoys of wounded that could arrive at any minute over the next few days. How can you? And Stepmama, what are you thinking? You have your reputations to consider.'

Evie was already heading towards the boot. She turned the handle, opened it, and started to drag out a hamper which was so heavy it could have fed an army. Veronica helped. They dropped it to the ground, and took another. Lord Brampton pushed at Richard, whose balance was much improved. With Bob Forbes' help, and the blacksmith's, he stood his ground.

Brampton shouted, 'This is my house. I insist on taking what is mine.'

Richard shook his head. 'It is not yours for the duration of the war, or have you forgotten that you have passed the running of it all to me, and your daughter? We need this food for our people, and now I suggest that you remember who you are and leave with as much dignity as you can muster, yet again. This is becoming too much of a habit.'

The blacksmith was helping to empty the car now. He carried a hamper on either shoulder down the steps and into the kitchen. Evie followed with another, and Lady Veronica yet another. The blacksmith returned for more.

Millie had disappeared. Evie went in search of her, dragging her from the laundry and into Richard's office in which Ron was doing paperwork. He looked up, registered the look on Evie's face and left, closing the door quietly. Evie held Millie by the shoulders. 'If you ever forge my signature again, I will have you dismissed. You will repay the money you received for the greengage jam you stole in May. You will replace whatever you have put into your pockets when helping the chauffeur. I will check that you do. Now get out of here and watch your step. It is only because you are Jack's wife and Tim's mother that I am saying nothing.'

Millie pushed out her chin, opening her mouth, her eyes filling with tears, which Evie ignored. Crying was just another of Millie's ploys.

Ron knocked on the door. 'The convoys have arrived, Evie, so all hands to the pump. We need to finish clearing the marquee.'

Evie thrust Millie in front of her, out through the door and almost into the arms of Mrs Moore and Mrs Green, who grabbed her and marched her to the cool pantry. Evie heard them shouting at her, accusing her of taking the jam. She heard Millie's reply. 'You'll all be sorry, you mark my words. You're just horrid to me, you always have been and Evie said you'd never know. She's a liar.'

Evie hurried through the kitchen and up the steps, running through the stable yard but slowing to a walk once she was crossing the drive. To run spread panic.

The stretchers were being offloaded as she slipped into the marquee. One man was walking around in circles, with that strange shell-shocked shake and staring eyes. Stan led him away, to the quiet ward in one of the estate cottages. Triage would be waiting for him there. In the marquee, magically it seemed, the floor was clear, and the pitmen had finished lining up the chairs around the room. The triage team were waiting in a bunch at the entrance. She thought of her men, and thanked God they were out of it for now, though as Grace had written, they'd be thinking of escape every day. Evie wished with all her heart that they wouldn't. There was the hoot of a horn, the crunch of gravel, and the Rolls swept through the bustle taking Brampton and his wife away, thank God.

Ver stood on the front steps holding Richard's hand, gripping it very hard. 'What will he do with our home when the war is over, darling?'

She and Richard watched the Rolls until it disappeared out of the drive. He said, 'We'll have to wait and see. We just can't even think of it, Ver. We simply can't, there's too much to do now.'

Ver looked at the cedar tree. It was still strong, calm and a haven for the smokers. She smiled. All would be well. Indeed, all must be well, because she and Evie were responsible for everyone. She said, 'I wish we'd let them have their wretched hampers now.'

Richard put his arm round her shoulders. 'It's done now and the new patients will be fed well, as our beloved tyrants Evie and Mrs Moore insist. They would not have been, had your father had his way, because he would have been back for more, and Evie knew that. One problem at a time, Ver, don't you think? It's the only way.'

They watched as yet more ambulances arrived. There was work to do. Tomorrow must take care of itself, but Ver saw the worry on her husband's face, and knew it was reflected on her own. 'Smile,' she insisted, 'it's what we must do, and thank God for Evie.'

Chapter 11

Offizier Gefangenenlager, Germany, July 1916

Jack used his elbows to wriggle along the eighteen-inch wide, twelve-inch high tunnel, pushing the enamel spoil bowl before him as silently as possible. The candle was stuck to the bottom of another bowl with its own wax and the flame flickered with every movement, but at least it was still flickering, he thought. He was slithering over rock, jagged from their narrow chisel marks created from stolen cutlery. He clutched the freshly sharpened knife and spoon that the tunnel committee had 'released' from the guards' kitchen store. They were wrapped in cloth so filthy it was as hard as board, but it prevented telltale clinking.

It had been easier working in clay but now they were through that and it could be back to rock, chipping away with sharpened cutlery, using the cloth to muffle the sound. They'd padded the communal mining clothes he'd changed into at the mouth of the tunnel, but nevertheless he and the other five tunnellers had open sores on their elbows and knees.

Jesus. He caught his elbow on the edge of the rock they'd failed to smooth properly in the left wall last week, and it tore through the padding. Well, it bloody would, wouldn't it? It took more than half an hour to get to the face now that the tunnel extended to 70 yards. The poor air gave the tunnellers only half an hour once they reached it, and then they had to slowly ease backwards to the mouth, but it was a damn sight better than it would have been. The air pump he, Dave and Mart had devised had wiped the smile off the supercilious bastard who had refused to let them fitten up when they had first arrived. Prancing into Aub's room, he had told him to get his orderlies back to making beds. Major Dobbs was his name, and he wasn't coming anyway.

Jack grinned now, hauling himself onwards as the tunnel sloped upwards, remembering Aub's roar as he backed that overfed major into a corner while Jack had sat, hungry and ill, not yet used to his new surroundings. Aub had threatened all sorts of things, making Dobbs drop his bloody book he carried everywhere. He'd blustered and carried on and then Captain Frost and Smythe had entered, and between them they'd lifted the daft bugger out in the passageway and just dropped him.

They'd heard no more.

It had taken a good four weeks to get him, Charlie, Dave, Si and Mart up to full strength, using the escaping officers' food parcels. The fact that the guards who doled out the goods from the parcels insisted on opening the tins and mixing the contents together on the pretext of searching for hidden escape tools was neither here nor there. He'd become quite used to custard and tinned ham, all chopped up together.

The guards had even done it to the parcels from Easterleigh Hall which had started arriving the moment Evie knew they were safe. Jack forbade them to write that news to Evie or she would come out here and sort 'em out. 'We must tell her immediately, then,' Auberon had spluttered, eating with them, as he so often did, along with Smythe and Frost.

Jack took even greater care now, only about five feet from the surface. The officers on the tunnelling rota a month ago had reported that they hadn't been able to hack through the stone that had blocked their passage. Jack had checked and agreed they should go over the top and boarded the roof tightly. He was on the downward slope now, back to the depth of eight feet or so, where any noise he made would be less audible. The candle was still flickering, so all was well, but the headache was beginning. Mart would be pumping the bellows, taking turns with Dave. Charlie and Simon were on shift tomorrow, but helping Roger today with the work the 'orderlies' had been recruited for.

Jack inched forward, the sweat falling into his mouth. He thought of the cans they'd collected while they built up their strength, pinching the empty biscuit tins from rooms, much as they 'borrowed' the bed boards from everyone without asking. Secrecy was everything. Only those escaping must know of the tunnel.

He'd shown the toffs how to create an air pipe by linking the cans together and feeding the result with air from the bellows they made from a 'borrowed' leather jacket and a few bits of wood. The pilot had never got to the bottom of his loss, and the toff tunnellers had accepted them from that moment on.

It didn't stop the headaches at the face, because you couldn't create a silk purse out of a sow's ear, or good air out of bad, but you could make it possible to continue the tunnel into the rye field. Colonel Mathers had agreed that this was the right place to come to the surface. At that thought Jack increased his pace; within weeks the rye would be the right height to hide their exit, but by Colonel Mathers' reckoning harvesting would begin within a month. It would be tight, as they only had three hours available in the day and approximately two yards to go. Appel finished at 11 a.m. after which they dispersed, changed their clothes and tunnelling could start. The Germans stopped for lunch from midday to about three o'clock, and the second appel was at four. Jack squinted at his tools. They'd laugh at Auld Maud to see these two little beauties, but with patience, it was surprising what could be achieved.

Finally he reached the face. They'd broken through

into clay two days ago, on his shift, so progress was quicker but he had to prop and board tomorrow. What if the roof came down now? What if they hit rock? So near and yet so far? Had Aub had any luck 'releasing' any more bed boards?

He filled the spoil bowl, raising his body, easing it under him, wincing as the edge caught at his hip bone, pushing it free of his body, tugging on the rope for Dave to pull it back. There was barely room for the men to reach the bloody tunnel mouth because of the bags of spoil, which were stacked in the cellar. An officer had discovered the disused entrance right at the back under the stage of the concert hall when he'd chased a rat in there, trying to beat it with a broom.

They'd hidden the entrance by 'borrowing' a saw from the civilian carpenter who came on a regular basis to maintain the old army barracks. Lieutenant Brothers had cut out several of the wooden boards that lined the back of the space beneath the stage, removed the nails but kept the heads in place so they looked untouched. He'd then replaced the boards, using two bolts on the inside to secure everything in place. Bloody clever, some of these bosses.

They'd be going out during a show, and rehearsals were under way, covering the noise and movements they made. Simon was in it, but an understudy was taking his role on the night so he could come too. Fifteen men would be going, and the tunnel would remain open for another lot to use when Colonel Mathers gave the go-ahead.

Jack felt a tug on the rope and pulled the bowl back. He'd loosened a mass of spoil and his head was splitting. Three more bowls and then his time was up, he'd go back with the last one. He worked on, mentally ticking off the escape requirements. They had their clothes ready, grey, dyed, borrowed where necessary, brought in by the new lot from the Somme. What a bloody disgrace that was, all those lives. He was attacking the face aggressively now as his anger grew, and his doubts. Should he make Charlie stay here? He didn't want him in the line, not again. But he wasn't a child and wanted to come.

The bowl was full again. Sent it off. Back it came. One more, and then it was time to go, taking his bursting bloody head with him. He smiled, tasting his dirty sweat. He backed down the tunnel, wriggling, hating the pain, and the bloody rats. He lay down, pressing his head into the ground as one whose eyes had glinted at him from the darkness ran over him to get out of the tunnel first. Bastard. Another one for the lieutenant to chase but they should be grateful to the creatures, because the youngster had realised that the rat had gone somewhere, and had been determined to find out where.

The air was fresher nearer the mouth. Dave grabbed his ankles, pulling as he back-crawled. Jack hauled himself to his feet, taking in deep breaths. Above him he could hear Simon singing, a fiddle playing, feet stamping in time. Mart checked his watch. 'I'll go now, man.' Jack stopped him. 'No, we've run out of time for roll call, but let's come back tonight, or we're not going to make it. We can get in here from the orderlies' quarters. I'll get Aub to get it past Mathers. We'll work through.' He was stripping off the work clothes, shaking his head free of spoil, taking the wet cloth from Dave and scrubbing his face and hands. There must be no sign of what he'd been doing.

Auberon was loitering in the spielplatz. They heard him whistle the all-clear. They came out with blankets and a bucket each. 'We're orderlies, after all,' Jack grinned to Auberon. 'We're coming back tonight, or we're not going to make it.'

'What route will you take to get there?' Auberon was pretending to count off the blankets as they walked back to the officers' huts.

'Over the roof, it's easier from our quarters than yours. We've been checking it out.'

'I'll need to clear you being on night shift with the colonel. But if it's a go, I'm coming too.'

Jack, Dave and Mart exchanged a look, and shrugged. Charlie ambled alongside, hiding his filthy hands in his pockets. 'Don't worry, we won't wreck the bloody tunnel,' Jack said.

Auberon grinned. 'That's all right then, because of course that's all I'm interested in, nothing to do with keeping you safe and sound so Evie and Ver don't tear my head off and eat it. So I'm coming. I'll find my own way. No me, no night shift. Your decision.'

Jack stopped, the others continued slowly, listening. Auberon waited with Jack, saying, 'I mean it, Jack. You don't take risks without me.' He came that night and worked alongside them, as he had since the tunnel began, and each time it had made the men grin to think of Bastard Brampton's whelp grubbing in the dirt with them, but each time their respect had increased until any resentment was long gone.

By 4th August the rye was high, the tunnel finished. The first night of the show was scheduled for that evening, and so was the break-out. Auberon had been steadily collecting their escape provisions, to be carried in a sack by each of them. He'd been learning German, and passing on what he could to Jack and the others. Major Dobbs had added himself to the list of escapees at the last minute, which made sixteen. The colonel had been angry, but for the sake of morale he allowed the addition.

Jack felt the tension throughout his body as he made the beds of the six officers he looked after in between his real duties. Charlie, Dave, Mart and Simon did the same. As usual, on the way to appel, Charlie said, nodding towards Roger, 'Not a bad job, is it, being a batman?' He added, 'This time tomorrow.' He nudged Jack. They'd reached their group, and stood to attention as the Kommandant paced the rows. Next to Jack Simon whispered, 'We need to talk.'

Jack smiled. 'You'll be fine, lad.' The sun was beating down on them. The weather was perfect for the final surface breakthrough, which he would make. It meant that his group would be the first out. They just had to remember to keep doubled up and run as though there was a Hun on their tail, which there might well be.

Simon hissed, 'Jack, I'm telling you, I need to talk to you.'

The Feldwebel was on his way. They all stood to attention. Now was not the time to be hauled off on a charge for talking. Jack's mind was racing. He knew Si didn't like the dark, had hated the mine. But he had Evie to get back to, and his parents, his duty. He saw Charlie look at Simon out of the corner of his eye, concern on his face.

Jack concentrated on going through everything in his mind. Auberon had given his parole for walks in the village. He'd checked to see how the river could be forded and noted the shallows, marking it on all the maps on his return. Another officer had been mapping the roads out of the village, and noted the farm with the dogs that barked at anyone who passed. Though their parole would be dishonoured if they escaped while holding their parole card, there was nothing to prevent them observing, noting, and ultimately escaping when off parole.

Appel seemed to last for ever, though in reality it was no longer than usual. Colonel Mathers had ordered that no one was to go near the tunnel, so

Simon and Jack headed for the quarters they needed to clean. It would lighten Roger's load, and cut out some of the grumbling, which they'd be bloody glad to leave behind. As they made Lieutenant Brothers' bed for the last time Jack said, 'Come on, Si, out with it.' Simon tucked in the sheet at the bottom. 'I'm not coming.'

Jack was ready for this. He straightened the sheet. 'It's going to be fine, bonny lad. I'll go in front of you to break us through, and be first out. If I'm seen then you just work your way back. Charlie, Dave, Mart and Aub will be with you. It's boarded solidly, and there's a slope up to the surface. Grab the blanket, there's a good 'un.'

Simon threw it at him. 'Listen for God's sake, Jack. I'm not coming. The major makes it sixteen, and that's not right. I'm giving up my place.'

Jack dropped the blanket on the bed, straightening it as he tried to think. 'You know that the colonel's agreed it, so there's no need to do that. Don't worry, Dave's keeping an eye on Charlie, and Mart'll look after you.'

Simon tucked in the blanket along his side. 'Oh yes, bloody Mart's back, so bloody Mart and you work together to make sure the outsider does as he's told.' He moved to another bed, drawing up the sheet, then the blanket, tucking them in as Jack stared at him, wanting to kick him from here to kingdom come. Instead he called, 'Don't be bloody daft. You're as much a marra as the rest of us. We're not kids, we're trying to get out. You'll get back to see Evie.'

He walked towards him, but Simon moved to the next bed, straightening it, his back to Jack. 'We orderlies will be sent back to the mines if we're recaptured, if we're not beaten senseless in the first place. The officers will just be given a slap on the wrist and brought back here. What the hell are we doing this for when we can just stay put?'

'We won't be caught.' Jack knew it sounded weak. They could be caught, and what Si said was true, but the alternative was to stay here and be shouted at, stuck behind wire, no rights until the end of the war, and when would that be? Besides, it was what men did, and Grace was there, in France. He wanted to see her, needed to see her, and know she was safe.

'You'll see Evie,' he coaxed, reaching for the broom which stood in the corner. Simon turned, fury reddening his face. 'Oh for God's sake, Jack, you're such a bloody child. So you escape, then you're back into the war. You won't be given leave, not for bloody ages. We'll be in the front line. Do yourself a favour and think beyond the next bloody moment, for God's sake. I don't want the war, I want to stay here, where I've got a future.'

Jack swept the dust up into the air. 'Future, here?'

Simon was watching him sweep the same spot again and again, but he had to do something to keep his hands off the little bugger. Simon said, as though choosing words a child would understand, 'I'm working with a Broadway director's son. He thinks I'm good, he'll do things for me after the war. It's my chance, mine, why can't you see that? I can move beyond what I am.'

Jack stared down at the clean patch of floor. This man was his marra, but at the moment the two of them were miles apart. He couldn't understand Simon. 'What about Evie?' he said quietly.

'What about her?' Simon yelled. 'Didn't you hear me? This is *my* chance.'

As soon as the show began Jack, Mart and Dave with Charlie and Auberon wriggled their way down the tunnel, practically naked, to avoid their clothes giving them away with grime and rips the moment they encountered anyone on the outside. Jack powered ahead with the tools, while Mart shoved their two sacks of provisions ahead of him, then Charlie, Dave and Auberon did the same, with Auberon dragging the signal rope. The last of the fifteen, Major Dobbs, would use the bellows. Once the surface was cracked and Jack was out without being shot, Auberon would tug on the rope and everyone else would start down the tunnel. Above them the show would go on for two hours. They should all be through by then.

By the time Jack was working at the surface crust he was bloodied, cut and bruised. Everyone would be the same. Jack had created a small hole two days ago, just to confirm that they were breaking through into the rye, and now he worked by feel, his eyes shut as earth and stones first trickled, and then crashed, through. With them came a great gasp of air. Jack waited a moment, and then hauled himself out into the rye, keeping low. He froze, waiting. No shots. He peered back into the hole, gesturing to Mart. The group scrambled out effortlessly, as the tunnel had been designed to slope up towards the surface. Auberon pulled on the rope twice.

The five of them took their escape clothes from their bags, and keeping near to the ground they dressed before setting out to ford the river at the spot Auberon had spied, to the east of the village. It was a warm and cloudy evening, with not too much light from the moon or stars. Perfect. Jack followed Auberon along the channels between the rows of rye. Auberon was using the compass he'd kept in the heel of his boot all this time. They were going to set out in the opposite direction to the one expected, away from neutral Holland, and swing round at the end of two days' travel.

Jack had told them at lunchtime that Simon had fallen on his sword, and would sacrifice his place in order to allay the suspicion of the Germans, who always attended the concerts.

Mart had said, 'But that had all been worked out, his understudy was so like him, especially with that bloody great moustache . . .'

'Leave it,' Jack had snapped.

Auberon had caught his eye, nodding. 'His

decision,' he said. 'He fell on his sword, that's what we tell Evie.'

Jack thought of Simon warbling, as the owls hooted, and the wind rustled the leaves and the rye, but pushed him from his mind. They must not get caught. They were needed to replace the poor buggers who were face down in the mud at the Somme.

The group of five walked west for two days, and then turned north-east towards Holland. Within another two days they reached a fork in the country road, waiting while Auberon checked his compass and pointed towards a forested area. 'We'll go straight through that, it'll be safer, and quicker.' He indicated the clouds that were looming and rolling. 'We'll need shelter.' They hurried through the deluge which began the moment he'd finished speaking, up a lane and veering off across a ploughed field into the forest. Jack hoped the farmer near the prison camp had finished his harvest. It was becoming clear that Germany needed every bit of grain from the look of the civilians they had passed, none of whom had shown the slightest interest in them. The blockade was effective even if there was a stalemate.

They followed a trail into the wood, seeking shelter, as thunder roared above their heads. Dave grabbed a branch and tore it from a pine. The others followed suit, and soon they were huddling together under the shelter they had created. The scent of the needles was calming somehow, and Jack thought of the cedar tree.

He said, 'Charlie, you'll share a smoke with us under the cedar tree, lad, before you go on to your home when everything is over?'

'That I will, Jack. It seems close now, doesn't it?'

They dug into their almost empty sacks. There was a piece of cheese in Jack's and two tins of bully beef, the same for the others. They used the one knife, held by Aub, to lever one tin open, and shared it, using their filthy fingers. 'Evie wouldn't like it.' It was Mart saying it this time. It had become almost a mantra. Until the weather improved they talked of home, and sleeping for years. Freedom felt good, Jack thought.

They set out at two o'clock, trying to keep beneath the trees because though the rain was no longer torrential, it was steady. They kept alert and made good time, and at dusk they made camp, tearing branches down again. Mart went west to scout the forest for some idea of its size, Auberon and Jack north and Dave and Charlie east. They gave themselves an hour to return. Mart did not.

Auberon insisted they hid their gear and dismantled the tent in case he'd been discovered, and followed his path west. They found him at the bottom of a worked-out quarry at midnight by the light of the moon. It took all night to bring him to the surface, as they had no rope, and then they carried him back to their gear and re-erected the tent before feeling along his limbs to assess the damage. 'You're like a load of bloody elephants, that's me leg you're fiddling with,' Mart hissed. They ignored him.

His femur was broken. Jack thought he knew how to pull it straight. Auberon and Dave held Mart down by his shoulders. Charlie whispered, 'Are you sure, Jack?'

'Nope, but what else can we do, lad?'

'Leave me and get on, that's what you do,' Mart told him. Jack hunkered by his head and said, 'Not again, Mart. Never again.' He nodded to Auberon and Dave, who strengthened their grip on Mart's shoulders while Jack whacked his marra on the chin, knocking him out.

Charlie gasped. He gasped again when Jack pulled Mart's leg just a fraction, but enough for the bone to slip back into place, or so he hoped. He'd done it before in the mine and it had worked.

They splinted the leg, then dug down into the earth for five feet. The soil was friable and dry. They covered the hollow they'd made with pine branches, reinforced by long logs they found and dragged back as dawn broke. They sloped one of the sides, fashioned a stretcher out of branches from the forest and lowered the unconscious Mart into the cave, which was what they'd called it.

Jack dusted off his hands and grinned at the others, who were standing on the lip while he hunkered down beside Mart on the floor of the cave. 'You best get off now. We'll follow in a month or two.'

Auberon looked at Jack. 'By then it will be October, cold, frosty and not a lot of food, if any.'

Charlie gazed around. 'We're in a wood, I'm a gamekeeper familiar with the ways of the poacher. I reckon I'm staying and that you, Jack, need to stop making decisions for me. I'm a big lad now.' He slid down into the cave, dragging his bag behind him.

Auberon said, walking away, 'I'm on watch and I make my own decisions. I'm a boss, remember.'

Dave just said, 'Too much bloody talking, bonny lad. Shove over. I'll take me watch in a couple of hours.'

They waited throughout the rest of August and into September, their beards growing long, wondering if the others had made it, and hoping they'd contact their families for them. They told Mart that they would actually strangle him if he apologised again.

Charlie honed his poacher skills, choosing dry days to snare rabbits and a woodcock, which was bony but tasty. On these occasions, needing to cook, they risked a fire, which burned brightly with little smoke. Only once were they disturbed, hearing guttural voices off to the left, while Aub was on watch to the right. They kicked out the fire and slid down into the cave, holding their breath but what good would that do? The voices faded and Aub emerged from the right, covered in leaves and dirt from digging in under the shrubs. They decided to put two on watch from then on.

Steadily throughout September they had accumulated enough food for two weeks of travelling, and during that time Auberon identified their forest from the map all the escapees had copied from the official one, brought into camp in the lining of a Canadian's uniform. They agreed the route. By now Mart was able to walk, leaning heavily on a thick pine branch cut down and shaped by Dave. On the night of 30th September they set off. They took turns supporting Mart when the going got tough, leaving the forest behind at the end of the first day, and travelling through the night, guided by Auberon's compass readings, illuminated by the hunter's moon. They rested during the day.

After two weeks they reached the River Ems, which ran for two miles on their side of the border. There were barbed-wire entanglements on the riverbank, and guards patrolled infrequently, though one was permanently stationed at the head of the track, which ran to what had presumably once been a ferry point.

Mart said, 'With the best will in the world, lads, I can't hop over that canny wire.' He was thin and gaunt and his beard was long and straggly, but he was not alone in that. They lay in cover, a gully at the side of the bank. Beyond the entanglements, on the other side of the river, the land was flat and exposed. 'I can't run either, so at this point, you lugheads, you really should leave me.' Mart turned on his back and stared up at the sky. 'Some of us must make it, and we're so starved it has to be soon, or we'll all stay this side of the wire for ever, six feet under.'

There was silence as the others stared at the wire, looking along the length of it either way. Auberon whispered, 'The only gap is at the head of the track and that's where one of the sentries stands, permanently.'

'Did you hear me?' hissed Mart.

Jack said, 'We need our jackets to sling over the barbs, then we'll toss Mart.'

'Good idea,' agreed Auberon. 'Even if he lands on his bonce, his skull's so thick it won't hurt.'

Charlie pointed to the left of them. 'Look, a rubbish tip from the farmer's field. I'm going to scout and see what he's chucked.'

He did so, with Dave. Jack watched them, zigzagging, doubled over, towards the rubbish which none of the others had noticed, so distant was it. A sharp-eyed sniper Charlie was, and a poacher. Jack smiled, and murmured to Auberon, 'You could do worse than to employ that lad as gamekeeper. He'll know all the tricks and he's bloody fast.'

'My thoughts exactly, Jack.'

Dave and Charlie were at the tip, rooting about. Their journey back was much slower, and they were dragging something. Jack and Auberon kept a lookout for the guards and saw one coming, but the two foragers had seen them too, and fell to the ground. They arrived back with an old torn tarpaulin, which was far better than their jackets.

They waited until darkness fell before Charlie was given a leg up and over the entanglements, then Dave. Jack and Auberon heaved Mart over. He landed in Dave and Charlie's arms. It was Jack and Auberon's turn, but Charlie hissed, 'Get down.'

They didn't argue, but lay flat on the ground, hoping the tarpaulin wasn't visible, as the moon was high. They saw what Charlie's keen eyes had spotted: a guard lighting a cigarette, strolling towards them. Jack saw Dave tense, ready to spring, but a fish leapt from the water, catching the gleam of the moon. The guard stood watching, and smoking, his rifle slung over his shoulder. No one moved. The guard tossed his stub into the river, turned and strolled back towards the track.

Jack whispered in Auberon's ear, 'Over you go.'

Auberon shook his head. 'Boss goes last, Jacko.'

Jack looked at him for a moment, and smiled. Auberon hoisted him up and over. He landed silently, took Mart's stick and held it over the top of the wire. 'Jump for it, Aub,' he whispered. Auberon did so, and Jack hauled him over. After dislodging the tarpaulin they slid down the bank and into the water, swimming as silently as possible, Jack and Auberon dragging Mart. They clambered up the opposite bank, keeping low at the top, then doubled over, going as fast as they could. It took them two hours to reach the border. Again they waited, watching the patrolling German and Dutch guards until they could cross unseen, unsure if they'd be interned by the Dutch.

Once over the border they walked for three days, keeping out of the way until they reached a small town. They cut one another's beards as close to the skin as possible, with the knife that Jack had used to break through the surface of the field, and dusted off their clothes. Auberon looked at the compass in his hand, then took off his wristwatch and replaced his compass. 'I'd rather sell the watch,' he said. He took it into the town while the others waited on the outskirts. He came back with money, a cheap replacement, and food, enough to get them to Rotterdam. They reached it two days later, having jumped a goods train. Exhausted, they trawled the docks, and finally found a ship that would take them to France and the North Tyne Fusiliers.

At the port they reported to the military. After debriefing and form-filling, with Auberon having to write his reasons for surrendering, they were allowed to telegraph home, Mart was checked out and declared fit enough to kill, the MO said, laughing. Mart wanted to kick him in the balls, he told them as they headed for the showers. Jack telegraphed Grace and received a reply from Rouen to say that she was ecstatic. They were given passes to entrain to their regiment's position, travelling together, then marching with the guns growing louder and louder until they reached Rouen, but there was no time for Jack to see Grace. They travelled further south to Amiens, where C section was in deep reserve. 'Home from bloody home,' murmured Mart as around them the guns crashed, the night sky flared with star shells, the ground shuddered. Yes, they were home, and there were only five former comrades to greet them. The rest had perished on the Somme. Six of their fellow escapees had reached safety and were back in the front line. There was no news of anyone else, including Major Dobbs.

Leave was not a possibility. They were not yet ready to be parted and must renew the battle, if they were to hold up their heads.

Chapter 12

Easterleigh Hall, May 1917

Evie read Grace's letter as she leaned against the cedar tree in her post-breakfast break. Beside her Ron Simmons smoked his pipe. He had discarded cigarettes on his engagement to pretty little Posie Ringrose, a VAD from Lancashire. She didn't mind whether he had a nose or not, but she would not allow cigarettes, so these had gone. Ron was also leaning against the tree, resting his leg as he did when his stump was sore, though he never mentioned the fact. 'It's going well, Commandant Evie.' He raised an eyebrow at her. She grinned. 'Acting only. Veronica had to choose between the acute ward and bossing people about.'

He placed his finger over the bowl and sucked. 'The Hall's solvent, partly because you're managing the shortages. We've all dropped our wages, and Sir Anthony's syndicate have upped their support.'

'Let's not forget Harry's honey,' Evie reminded him, folding the letter. 'Matron is on top of the dressings situation with the sphagnum moss, and we're doing a roaring trade supplying Fenton House, near Newcastle.'

They both peered up through the cedar's branches. The squirrels were leaping about, and somewhere the dogs were yapping. 'Oh God, Ron, I thought America's entry would wriggle the war along.' Evie's voice was flat. In her letter Grace said that she'd seen Jack in the few moments she'd had to spare from the huge influx of wounded from Nivelle's disastrous attack along the Chemin des Dames, and he'd been well. Evie should have been glad, and of course she was, but she wished it had been her seeing Jack the lad she loved more than anyone else in the world, except for Si, of course. But Si had sacrificed his chance to escape, and was safe, and she couldn't remember what he looked and sounded like, and the feel of his arms around her, his lips on hers. She pushed the letter deep down in her pocket. Ron was engaged, Lady Margaret had a lovely little girl, Ver a chubby young lad, even Millie had Tim. What the bloody hell had she?

Ron was tapping his pipe on the huge trunk of the tree. 'The Americans need to build up their army and the Germans will be pushing hard for a victory before they arrive, so it's looking a right bloody-knife edge out there. We'll be busier still at Easterleigh, I fear.'

Evie watched the ash as it fell from the bowl of the pipe. Ron couldn't get the wretched thing to light properly, ever, no matter what he did. Perhaps it was as well, as Dr Nicholls would say. She asked, 'What will happen to the prisoners if they win?'

'The Germans will collect them up, kick us out perhaps, and . . .'

'No, what will happen to ours out there, to Si?'

He looked at her, his nose completely rebuilt now. Work was almost complete on the new Cambridge Military Hospital in Aldershot where Harold Gillies, the facial surgeon, worked. 'I'm sorry, Evie, how foolish of me. The fact is, I don't know. I would imagine they'll be repatriated. Don't worry, he'll come home, with all his bits.' He smiled, then sobered. She knew he was thinking of Jack, Mart, Dave and Charlie and Auberon, who all, so far, remained intact.

'All is not lost,' he said, shoving himself upright and putting his weight back on to his wooden leg. 'Things could swing back our way and until then we go on.'

The German POWs were arriving on the lorry as they walked back across the lawn, ten of them, to work on the vegetable gardens, the pigs and wherever else needed help. Jack had said that the mines had been a home from bloody home, when he'd written. Some of the German POWs felt the same, obviously. Even Mrs Moore talked kindly to them at lunchtime, except for Heine. Neither she nor Evie could abide the blond-haired, blue-eyed, broad-shouldered young man who was from Munich and knew everything, it seemed, while they, mere women, knew nothing.

Evie and Ron walked across the grass, spongy

from last night's rain. Evie waved at the guards, and the prisoners. Ron said, 'Is the strike settled, or perhaps I should say strikes?'

Evie laughed, she couldn't help it. Suddenly something was funny, and her spirits lifted. 'I gather so, and the Bastard has had to up his wages to the prisoners at Auld Maud, Hawton and Seaton, not to mention the steelworks. The union wasn't having peanuts paid to them. They're not monkeys, Jeb told me when I met him at the co-op.'

They were on the drive now, and she could tell from his frown that Ron's stump hurt as the gravel resisted, then slipped and slid beneath his false leg. He said, 'It's remarkable that they care about the enemy at a time like this.'

Evie slipped her arm through his, to steady him as much as anything. 'Oh, thee of a simple mind, they don't, what they care about is that their own men aren't done out of a job and their wages. If Bastard Brampton and other owners can get away with paying practically nothing, how long will our own workers be employed?'

They were in the stable yard now, and Heine was ahead of them, entering the stables, his jacket slung over his shoulder. Several patients were strolling about in their uniform blues, some carrying pigswill in buckets from the kitchen. Millie was heading into the stables after Heine, a bucket in either hand. Stupid girl.

Evie had stopped worrying about it, because if it

wasn't him, it would be someone else, and as Millie now wrote to Jack regularly, took Tim to school before work, helped Evie's mam with the chores at home, and had even stopped glaring at Evie as though she would do her harm, what could she say? Would it be a disaster if she found someone else, anyway? After all, there was Grace waiting for Jack in France, but there was still Tim, and Millie would take him, and that would break Jack's heart, but only if he survived. She shut her mind on the old familiar circle, because it went nowhere.

Ron slipped on the cobbles. Evie took his weight for just that moment. One of the POWs passed, and paused, his hand out. She smiled and shook her head, saying, 'Thank you, but we are all right.' Ron righted himself. 'Have you given more thought to your hotel, Evie?'

They were at the kitchen steps now. 'On and off, but it's pointless. What if we lose?'

'Is that you, Evie? We haven't all day.' Mrs Moore's roar reached them.

They both laughed now, hurrying down the steps and into the kitchen. Today for lunch it was to be chestnut soup, using chicken stock and all the bacon rinds from yesterday, plus the outside leaves of vegetables, onions, apples, even leftover crusts. The soup would be removed by squab pie with a little mutton, apples, onions, and potatoes, covered with a potato crust. It was a favourite. It would be removed by gooseberry crumble, the crumble a mixture of barley and wheat flour with some sugar, liberally dribbled with honey.

As Ron scooted through the kitchen he about-turned, and came close to Evie. 'Bear up, old girl, so far all is well, as your sainted mother says, so very often.' He winked, and she laughed again. Yes, everyone was safe and only when she had been on night duty, ready in the chair by the furnace to provide food and drink, did the world drag on her shoulders.

In June, on a sunny morning, Evie passed groups of patients talking in huddles as she headed back from the herb store at the end of the path running along-side the walled garden. They were officially strolling on crutches, or keeping an eye out for blackfly on the runner beans and the broadies, but in reality they were puffing away on pipes or cigarettes, all the while watching for Dr Nicholls, and talking about the latest news on Haig's Messines Ridge attack, the success of which would help any intended attack on the German lines around Ypres. This could turn the tide, and the excitement was high. Or they might be discussing the success of the convoy system, and the rise in merchant shipping getting through the blockade, as their thoughts were never far from food, or perhaps they were chatting about the latest young women in their lives. The latter was more probable

Evie smiled as they broke off to call to her, and

she refused their offers of help to escort her and her burden back to the kitchen, and a cup of coffee. 'Herbs aren't heavy,' she replied, feeling the sun on her face, 'and today it's bubble and squeak and bullock's heart.' They grimaced, then one said, 'It'll be ambrosia, dearest Evie. It always is. You have a magic wand.'

'Yes, they're called Mrs Moore and Annie,' she shouted back. They laughed. As she entered the garage yard Alfie from Easton was propping up his bicycle against the wall, three glassy-eyed rabbits on the handlebars. He hurried down the steps to the kitchen, shouting, 'Evie, Evie.' She weaved and ducked her way through the flapping sheets the laundry girls had just hung out, and wondered how much he wanted for them this time, the canny little beggar. 'I'm up here,' she called. 'Wait there.'

'Evie, Evie.' He met her in the doorway to the kitchen, with Mrs Moore shouting from the pantry, 'Less of your noise, bonny lad. Give her a chance.' The rabbits hung from his fingers, which were whitening from the pressure of the string. Dark dried blood dribbled from their mouths. 'You should be in school,' she said, trying to pass him. 'Out of the way, now.' He didn't move. Mrs Moore came from the pantry, carrying a huge bowl of chestnuts. There was something ominous in Alfie's face, and he was groping in a pocket with his free hand. 'Note from the parson, Evie. He was in a grand fuss, said you had to read it quickly and come. Crying he was.'

Evie pushed past him, and dropped the herbs on the table. Grace? What? She had her letter, so . . . But that was posted weeks ago. Or Mam? Mam was at home today, with a cold. Da? He wasn't on shift at Auld Maud, he was here.

She grabbed the note from Alfie; it was creased and grubby. Mrs Moore eased the rabbits from his hand, slapped them on the table. Annie came in, saw the blood. 'What the hell's happening, those need to go to the game pantry, not on the table. I've just scrubbed the thing.'

'Hush your noise,' ordered Mrs Moore, rubbing the feeling back into Alfie's fingers but watching Evic, nodding at her. 'Read it, lass.' The gentleness in her tone gave Evie courage to unfold the note. Edward had written, *'Grace is injured, a shell. She was on an ambulance heading back from the front. She is at Rouen Camp Hospital. I should go, but I have so many in need here. Please, please, bring her back. I can't bear her to travel alone. A head injury, burns. You will need to talk to a Dr Sylvester. It is he who wrote the note. I have booked you passage on the ferry. Please, now.'*

Within thirty-six hours Evie was gripping the rail of the pleasure steamer that had been pressed into service as a troopship for the voyage out, and ambulance ship for the return journey. All around were fresh-faced youths, almost doubled over beneath their packs. Some seemed even younger than Harry had been when he first arrived. She turned her head into the wind, clinging to the sight of the land that was steadily taking shape. The sun gleamed on the marquees that straggled along the cliff, endlessly, white and pure, they seemed. But they wouldn't be. She knew it from experience.

She disembarked at Calais, straight into the chaos of shouted orders, khaki uniforms, boots crashing in time as the men were marched away, their packs and gas masks weighing them down, their tin hats slipping sideways, the sergeants shouting. In the distance was the sound of shells. She forced her way through to a naval lieutenant. He directed her to the station. She walked past ambulances, stretchers, stretcher-bearers, VADs, nurses, doctors, padres, filthy, stinking, screaming or silent patients, some with cigarettes, some talking, some staring. No, she didn't know this. She knew the comparative quiet and order of Matron and Easterleigh Hall.

She walked on to the station. There were other women who had disembarked walking alongside her, carrying valises or carpet bags; some were nurses, some relatives. At the station some followed the signs for Rouen. She followed them, and the troops, on to the train, which huffed and puffed, but didn't blow her house down, because it was already falling around her ears. She didn't know any of this, and she had thought she did and her arrogance and ignorance appalled her. The VAD opposite looked beyond tired. Her hands trembled. Evie's did too, but her tiredness was pathetic beside this girl's. 'Are you returning from leave?' Evie asked.

The young woman nodded, then closed her eyes. She didn't open them until the train screeched and wailed into Rouen station, then she gathered her valise and her coat and stepped from the train, her shoulders back, her head high. Evie followed. She asked a Queen Alexandra's Nurse for directions to the camp hospital. 'Follow me.' The older woman spoke crisply, quickly, hurrying along without checking that Evie was with her. Outside there were ambulances discharging their patients, the artillery was louder. The day was drawing to a close; the sky was alight, the ground shuddered. The nurse made for the first ambulance, which was backing out of the station, a large Red Cross on its khaki sides. She flagged it down. 'Two for the camp hospital, Thomas.'

'Yes, Sister Breave,' said the orderly. 'Hop in.'

Sister Breave led the way to the rear, threw in her valise, and pulled herself into the back. Evie followed. They sat on a bench in an ambulance devoid of stretchers but not of the stench of the wounded. There was blood on the floor, an old dressing. The ambulance roared off. It was Evie who closed her eyes now. Was Grace still alive? Had Richard found Jack and telegraphed the news as he had promised? Could he come, or was he in the thick of it at the Messines Ridge near Ypres? Perhaps he was still in deep reserve? Oh God, oh God, she'd thought she'd known, but her brother and his friends were facing these guns, were charging them, in this noise, this dreadful, dreadful noise. Their warm fragile bodies were facing all of this and how could they possibly have survived as long as they had, how could John Neave write cheerful letters, how could any of them?

At the camp hospital Sister Breave pointed her to Grace's marquee. 'Number 14. Give her my love,' she said, her voice gentle now. 'She's lost an ear, has broken ribs, shrapnel, a broken and burned arm. She needs rest and kindness, which she's had in abundance from Slim Sylvester. Make sure she has it from you or I'll hunt you down.' She mimicked a pistol shot with her right hand. She smiled, but her eyes were full of fury and pain.

Evie, carrying her valise, walked along the duckboards past marquee after marquee, from which came sounds that were worse than any at Easterleigh. She had reached number 6. Orderlies and nurses were entering and leaving the marquees, ducking down, flipping up the flaps. Some were overtaking her, some approaching. The duckboards were lit by oil lamps hung on eight-foot poles, around which huge moths fluttered. There was a breeze. The artillery was louder. She had reached number 12. Two more. Number 14. Moths were hitting the lamp outside, casting monstrous shadows.

She walked down the duckboard, hearing her boots clickety-clacking. She drew in a deep breath, and ducked inside. This marquee was divided into ten compartments. In the centre was a table at which sat a nurse. Evie went to her. 'I've come to take Grace Manton home,' she told her. The nurse smiled and stood. The internal oil lamp was attracting moths here too, and even with the artillery Evie could hear the thump as they hit the glass. 'It seems there are quite a lot wanting to see our Gracie,' the nurse said. She pointed to a smaller table almost hidden in the corner. It was in shadow but a voice called, 'By, let the dog see the rabbit, if it isn't our Evie.'

'Mart, oh Mart.' She ran to him, dropping the valise on the way, letting him swing her round and cover her face with kisses. 'I thought I'd never see your ugly mug again, bonny lad, dearest bonny lad. He's here then, our Jack is here?' He put her down, straightening her hat for her, tucking her hair behind her ear.

'Yes, thanks to the boss, but now you're here I have to go. I have a nurse to see. From Tyneside she is, Cathy. Lovely lass, we're made for one another but I've got to make sure she knows that, now I've seen you.' He was off, almost running down the duckboard. 'NO running,' the nurse at the table barked. He did as he was told.

Evie touched her ear as she watched him go. Oh God, Grace. But thank you for getting Jack here. A voice behind her said, 'Do sit down, Evie. You must be very tired.'

That voice. Her hand fell. That voice, the dark of the sea, when . . . Then she felt a touch on her shoulder. 'Please, do sit.'

She turned. Auberon stood there quietly, in the

shadows. 'Aub. Oh Aub.' Suddenly she was crying. 'Oh Aub, I didn't know. I thought I did, but I didn't. How can you bear it, day after day? Oh Aub.' She put her hands to her face and sobbed, quietly, because she must disturb no one, and then she felt him pull her to him. 'Shhh,' he whispered. 'It's all right, Evie, how could you know?'

The tiredness was tearing at her, it had made her weak, but he was here, holding her up, letting her rest, just for a moment. Their boss was here, and she rested against him, and it was as though she was floating in a silent stream, just for a moment. She felt the sobs slow, and cease, and still she leant against him.

Auberon, Jack and Mart watched the ambulance depart. Aub could feel her against him, he could hear her voice, her sobs, and then her silence. And still she hadn't moved from him, until Jack came to find her. If he was killed tomorrow he would die happy, because he had held her. He put his arm across Jack's shoulders. 'Grace'll be safe now, and you were there for her.'

'Aye, because of you, bonny lad,' Jack murmured. 'On a charge, are you?'

'It's worth whatever comes,' Aub said, because he had told his major that they were going, though he had forbidden it. They were in deep reserve again and would not be moving back into line for at least a day, Aub had argued. Permission had again been denied. In his billet he had then written down the orders he had given Jack and Martin to entrain for Rouen, and left it with the adjutant. He was going with his remaining men, no matter what, because Jack would need him, especially after they'd buried Dave after the last push, and Charlie was ill with chickenpox, of all things. Yes, he'd keep these two safe with as much light in their life as possible, if it bloody well killed him. It wasn't until they arrived at Rouen that the Sister told them it was Evie, not the parson, coming for Grace.

On their return to Easterleigh Hall Matron took over from Evie, and placed Grace in the conservatory with the other women. The drapes were yellow and cheerful, there were flowers on the central table, and it was quiet. Above all it was quiet, but Grace, who had not said a single word on the journey, still remained silent, as the nurse led her to her bed and drew the curtains around her. When she was changed and had been seen by Dr Nicholls she still said nothing, and only reacted when she heard a man's voice. But it was never her man, he was back in the chaos. Evie spent every spare moment with her. They had seen shell shock before, and would again. If she didn't improve they would have to send her to a special hospital.

Chapter 13

The Western Front, Winter 1917–18

America had joined the Allies in April 1917, but could send no troops until they had built up their armies. In October, as the Germans held firm, committed to rolling over the Western Front before the Americans arrived in force, Jack and Aub hunkered down in their dugout outside Ypres with the village of Passchendaele in their sights, and the poor bloody Canadians bearing the brunt and taking a beating. They were enduring, of course, because that was what they did, in spite of mustard gas. The steady thunder of shells, the rifles, the rat-a-tat of machine guns were just part of life again. Crump. Nearby. Neither man moved. The candle flickered. How many moments had there been like this? Jack finished his letters, one to Millie and Tim, one to Grace. Auberon was also writing. Jack had seen to it that Charlie wrote to his parents, and Mart never stopped writing to Cathy. He smiled. Auberon finished his to Veronica, and started on his second letter. He finished it, and tore it up.

'You always do that,' Jack said. It was the first time he'd mentioned it.

'Ah,' Auberon said, tapping his nose. 'Can't change things now. It's got me this far.' He scattered the pieces on the ground and heeled them into the mud, of which there was no shortage. The glimmer of the candle didn't reach to the ground, and perhaps it was as well, because God knew what had sunk into its depths. The candle was not in a jar. There were none to be had for love nor money. The allies had gained five miles, taken Passchendaele and used all their reserve forces. Jack said, 'I suppose Haig thinks it was worthwhile, must be over hundreds and thousands of us killed, loads of the French buggers, and how many Germans?'

'Ours not to reason why.' Auberon flung down his pencil.

Captain Vivien muttered from the depths of the dugout, where he'd been dozing on a truckle bed, 'Ours just to do or die, old fellow.'

Auberon nodded. 'Best not to think of it, any of it. We're alive, for this minute. Alive and whole.'

'Grace is better,' Jack said quietly, passing his finger through the candle flame. It was a game he and Evie used to play, seeing who could move their finger more slowly. Bloody silly of them. Another crump. The candle flame danced violently this time and debris dropped from the roof. 'But she still can't, or won't, do anything. It would be better if she did, it seems to help them, doesn't it Aub?' He heard his own anxiety.

Auberon smiled at him, reaching for his helmet.

'Leave it to Evie, she'll sort it out, but talking of doing something . . .' He rose, the others with him. 'No-man's-land is waiting for its wiring party, gentlemen.' Jack blew out the candle.

By December the Germans were still pushing hard along the whole Front, especially now that the Russian revolutionaries had deposed the Emperor Nicholas II and withdrawn from the war. At Cambrai, Haig rushed in reinforcements to successfully prevent German counterattacks from breaking through General Byng's line. For the first time the attack was not preceded by a prolonged bombardment, and tanks rumbled into the action, marking an advance in tactics, and using the element of surprise. 'One wonders why it's taken so long,' Auberon had muttered to Jack.

Jack had peered through the trench periscope. 'Might have helped if he'd actually spent some time in the trenches, like that bugger Winston Churchill. If I had to be in a war, I'd want him in charge. He understands, having had the delightful experience of being in the thick of the trenches after the balls-up of Gallipoli.'

The casualties were massive again, the cold intense, trench foot increased, rotting the feet to the bone if it wasn't caught soon enough. Once in the reserve trenches Auberon made sure that every man had a Christmas meal sent up the line, paying for it out of his own pocket. There was a small present for Charlie, who was back from the camp hospital after shrapnel had embedded itself deep into his arm. 'You've been made up to Corporal in your absence,' Jack told him, thinking of Simon, but he pushed the thought of the man from him. After Simon had chosen to stay, Jack didn't like him in his head. He didn't deserve the room. He didn't deserve Evie either, but that was up to the lass.

Grace was more alert now, but Evie had said in her last letter, *'I believe she's hiding because of her looks. She jokes about only needing one earring now, but she also has scars on her neck, and will not think of taking up Gillies' time and having them improved. I can see why, Jack, because we have seen so many far worse, but I don't need to tell you that. You see the doing of it all. I am so proud of you, of you all. Please give my wishes for their safety to Mart, Charlie and Aub. Lovely Major Granville has died. Lady Margaret is bereft but was prepared and shows great fortitude, and of course, there is Penelope, her daughter.'*

This mention of Aub had surprised Jack, when he thought he could no longer be surprised about anything. Christmas passed into January and parcels arrived from Easterleigh Hall if the postal service could find them, as they trudged, still a team of four, still alive and just about kicking in the freezing mud of Ypres, sinking in up to their thighs or further if they slipped on the duckboards. In a push or wiring party they might take shelter in shell holes, clinging to the sides, digging in their toes, desperate to stay above the stinking water at the bottom.

Every damned day there was such damp cold, such thick mists, perfect for advancing, and for penetrating through their clothes. Every hour they were beyond thought and forgot there was another way of living. Death was their neighbour, and no longer a surprise, whatever form it took. They cursed America for taking so long, but understood, and regretted their curses.

Morning and evening Auberon did the rounds of his men, wondering if he'd ever walk upright again, ever walk over meadows with flowers and trees with branches. He thought of the ha-ha at home as he ducked and scrambled, doubled over. This morning he leaned against the sandbagged sides of the trench, smoking a cigarette one of his men, Ben, had given him: a roll-up. It was thin and flopped in the middle and he was grateful for it. Ben was a private from Hawton; he was nineteen, he should be at the Miners' Club, or walking with his young lady, not here, leaning against a trench wall striking his match on the skeletal arm that had been washed free of mud by the overnight rain. It could have belonged to a lad like him.

'Funny old world, Ben,' he murmured as flares lit the sky.

'Bloody hilarious, sir. Bit bloody cold an' all.' The lad was shivering; they all were as the snow began. 'Strange, to think of home. Thought me da was a

299

right old grump when he stopped me from volunteering, but maybe he was a wise old bugger. Home would seem like a nice world now, if I could remember it.'

Mart was keeping his head down as he came towards them, carrying a hot drink. 'For you, sir, tea boiled on our Jacko's magical spirit stove.'

'Tell Jack, thanks.' Auberon passed it to Ben. 'I'm drowning in the stuff.' They could see the steam rising from it, and the snow falling into it. Ben drank it down, gulping it as though he'd not seen tea for decades. Mart nodded, waited, and Auberon watched the lad and smelt the tea. He'd kill for a sip of it.

At Easterleigh Hall in April, Millie was flouncing around the kitchen, scooping up tea towels, getting in the way. Evie snapped, 'We'll bring them through when we're ready. Can't you see they've a few wipes left in them?'

'I know when a tea towel needs boiling, so I do, Evie Forbes, and you can keep your damn great nose out of it.'

Annie shoved her with her elbow. 'Watch your tongue, it's the commandant you're talking to. You've been foul for weeks now.'

Millie flung the tea towels down and they skidded into the pie dishes already lined with pastry for the pig-offal pie. The dishes were waiting for heart, liver and kidneys, and a mountain of herbs and potatoes. One spun off the table on to the floor, where it broke, the pastry falling off. Mrs Moore gasped, they all did. Rationing had been introduced to try and make life fairer but they were still scrimping and saving to keep the men fed, because they now had huts down past the walled garden for the extra cases streaming in, and as quarters for the workers they were employing to ease their disability pensions.

Millie half shouted to Mrs Moore, 'Annie pushed me, it's her fault.' She ran out of the kitchen and up into the garage yard. There was silence, and Marie from Easton, whose day it was to volunteer, cleared up the mess. Evie sighed and followed the wretched girl. Her behaviour might be due to worry over Jack who was still at Ypres, where the German drive to reach the ports of northern France had failed, or it might just be Millie. Evie would safely place a bet on the latter.

In the yard Millie was shouting at the laundry volunteers who were doing their best to peg out the sheets in a raging wind, and Evie took her by the arm and dragged her over to the garage where the older children of the workers played at the weekend. Shouts and laughter greeted them. Evie slotted her arm through Millie's. 'Look at Tim, he's having a great time.'

Millie watched her son. 'He loves your mam more than me.'

Evie shook her head. 'Oh no, you're his mam. He loves his granny but you're his mam.'

Millie was pale as she whispered, 'Lots of people

301

don't have a mam and they're happy.' She waved to her son, and went to him, hugging him tightly.

Later that afternoon, on Evie's break, Matron came to find her in the servants' hall. 'Grace's almost there, Evie. We just need to get her to remove the shawl from her head and put her nursing cap back on.'

'Just?' Evie said. Matron waited. Evie struggled to her feet eventually. 'Your wish is my command.'

'Of course it is,' said Matron. Evie followed her out and fetched Grace from the conservatory. They headed for the bee meadows, glorious in their wild flowers and sunshine. Grace said, 'Never mind the bees, it's the hives that seem to procreate every week. People are bringing so many to us.'

It was the first light-hearted thing she had said in all this time. Evie slipped her arm through hers, squeezing. 'Bee-keepers want to help with provisions, and give the recovering wounded something wholesome to do. Not that getting stung strikes me as wholesome.' Millie was near the hives, which meant that probably Heine was too. Perhaps that was unfair, because three of the laundry girls were there also, keeping their distance and chatting to the POWs and the wounded as they removed the tops of the hives to do whatever bee-keepers did. These helpers were in full bee-keeping outfits, and busy. Grace and Evie could hear the buzzing amongst the flowers and it evoked memories of a time before the war, happier calmer times.

One of the bee-keepers waved at them, and bowed, calling something to Millie, who laughed. It was Heine. Evie stared, wanting to slap the pair of them, and walked on, taking Grace with her. Grace drew the shawl tighter around her head as they passed. 'Grace, the bees aren't about to sting you. They're far too busy, up to their eyeballs in pollen. Let the sun get at your hair.' Evie squeezed her arm tighter.

Grace laughed quietly. 'It's not the sun getting at my hair, it's the bees.'

They walked through the meadows, on to the path that had been left between the ha-ha, which ran along the bottom of the cedar-tree lawn, and the new potato field. Grace still clutched her shawl around her head as Evie waved to the men and land girls earthing up the potatoes. 'The bees have gone,' Evie murmured.

Grace snapped now, shouting, 'I'll decide. Mind your own business, Evie.' She pulled free and strode ahead.

A volunteer looked up, surprised. Evie ran, though she was too bloody tired for all this. She grabbed Grace's arm, swung her round. 'Look around you. Go on, look around you. Who the hell is interested in looking at one mouldy earhole in this den of misfortune and pain? Good grief, we are housing you women in the conservatory, which was to have been the entrance for the wheelchair patients, which is why we have had to devise a ramp at the front entrance which they use in front of everyone, having slogged across the gravel. Do they hide? You really do have to get a grip and start to use your experience for the good of everyone. I've had enough, just about enough of everyone being so damned bad-tempered.'

Evie stamped. It hurt. She stamped again. Grace glared at her and stalked off and Evie let her, dragging her hand through her hair, feeling like the witch she was. She walked back, trying to regain some calm, looking at the POWs coming back from the fields they had de-thistled. She and her family used to do that to earn extra money when her da was without a job, and later, when they were saving for Froggett's cottage.

Evie joined Veronica in the kitchen, where she was helping to prepare dinner. Veronica worked two days on the wards, and half-days the rest of the week in the kitchen and wherever she was needed. 'I tried to get her to take off her shawl,' Evie said. 'I handled it badly.'

Ver hugged her. 'No, you wouldn't have done. Kindness hasn't worked, so blunt speaking might.'

Evie swung round. 'I'm not sure there was much kindness, but certainly there was a huge dollop of the latter.'

Veronica said, shaping the staff rissoles, 'I heard about Millie. Matron too and she knew you'd be annoyed enough to push Grace.'

The next morning there was a banging on the

kitchen door, and Harry Travers stood there, his face bright red with rage. 'Someone's been at my bees, my poor bloody bees. We've lost two hives. Just shoved over, they were. I want everyone lined up. I need to look for stings.'

Richard and Evie wouldn't agree because it would be bad for morale, but all day she and Harry looked for sleeves that were pulled down, though the weather was warm for April. Heine and Millie were amongst those who were wearing their sleeves long. Harry said, 'I'll have their guts for garters. I can understand him, it's his duty in a way to hinder us, but why her?'

They were in the kitchen and Mrs Moore was preparing potato and apple pudding, peeling the apples which Evie and Annie would then force through the sieves. It was the one occasion when they allowed a knife near the apple peel. Later they'd add honey, a pinch of salt, the cooked sieved potatoes, one egg per pie dish, to be baked for half an hour. 'We can't prove it, they might feel the cold. Let's get him sent back to the camp, he's a bad influence, and she might settle down.'

Grace had stood at the window, looking out as Harry and Evie hurried backwards and forwards, looking at people strangely. What on earth was going on? Sarah, who had been badly burned, came to stand beside her. 'Someone knocked over some hives. God knows what those two are doing. What's a few hives when you look around here? You'd think it was life-threatening.'

Sarah was from an industrialist's family and would always be scarred across her back from the fire after a Zeppelin attack. The two women had become friends. Grace leaned her head on the glass, cool now the sun had moved round. Sarah said, 'Perhaps it is. We forget in here that people need to be fed, and have to find their own way to recovery. Young Harry has come a long way. He has no lower leg, he can't fight but he can help. This is what he does. He nurtures his bees, he nurtures his helpers, British and German, he provides honey now sugar is short. He finds a reason to live, to go on, to handle the losses he endures as his friends die.'

Grace heard her words as though from a distance. Sarah said, 'Let me do your hair, please. Come on, take that damned shawl off and let me show you a better way.'

Grace couldn't, not yet. Jack had said at the camp hospital that she was the most beautiful person he knew. Slim Sylvester had held her hand as the ambulance came. 'I am always here for you.'

But she'd looked in the mirror.

That night she dreamed of bees, meadows and the sun glinting, and there was the sound of stamping. Stamp, stamp, stamp, and her anger was roaring in time with Evie's anger. When she woke she was drenched with sweat. She bathed and washed her hair, and returned to the conservatory.

The other girls, the walking wounded, surrounded her. They dried her hair, and though she said no, they arranged it in a low bun, and dragged her to the mirror. 'What do you think of yourself now, my girl?' asked Sarah. Behind her, reflected in the mirror, were faces distorted and scarred from this bloody awful war, and they were smiling, all of them. Grace put her hand to her rich dark hair with its hint of red, now streaked with grey, and stared at herself, seeing her green eyes, her face only slightly marred by a scar across the bridge of her nose and left cheek, ashamed as she had never been. 'I'm so sorry,' she murmured.

Sarah turned her round. 'Never say that, you have been so tired, you have seen so much and it takes time to heal, but the fear just has to be faced.'

They ate breakfast at the central table, and then Grace rose and found Matron in her office. She knocked. 'Enter,' she was told.

She did so, standing before the dreadnought's desk like a naughty schoolgirl. 'I'm ready,' she said. Matron stood, and what passed for a smile crossed her face. 'Of course you are. Sister Newsome will find you a uniform. Welcome back, VAD Manton.'

That was it, so easy, but it wouldn't be, Grace knew that. This was the first step, though.

Sister Newsome was in the acute ward, Veronica too. She saw them exchange a look, and a smile. Grace said, 'I've been Evie'd, haven't I?'

Veronica stroked her face. 'You look wonderful. Well done.'

Sarah told Grace that evening, after her shift, when she came to the conservatory to clear her bed now that she was moving to the nurses' quarters, that Evie had bribed them with a pre-war sponge cake, made with sugar, butter and jam, to create the moment. They would have done it anyway, but hadn't known quite how to, until Evie made her suggestion. They shared the cake with Grace.

In July 1918 the Germans' successful counter-attack faltered. The French, British and US forces were advancing, and the injured were pouring into Easterleigh Hall. Millie was silent, preoccupied, and read letters she had received from Heine repeatedly, but what could Evie do about that? Grace was working, wearing her cap, bustling, busy, and no one admitted to thinking about their men overseas. What was the point?

At the end of July Evie received a black-edged envelope in an unfamiliar hand. She took it to the pantry, away from the splash of onions sautéing on the range for the onion savoury. In the cool and quiet she opened the vellum envelope. Inside was a black-edged letter and she did not want to read another word, but she did. It was from the mother of Captain Neave, telling Evie that 'dearest John' had been killed at Ypres. Evie had to read the letter twice because it was too much, just too much. She could still see him laughing at Lady Margaret's wedding, and being naughty with Harry beneath the cedar tree. Lovely, lovely John. So many injured and dead, so many had passed through their doors to go out into the maelstrom again in France, Turkey, Africa, on the land, sea and air . . . She wiped her face, dried it on her sleeve. *'We're so lucky, our son's body was found and has been buried. He was the most perfect of boys, the most perfect of men. My dear, he spoke of you often, your humour, your loyalty, your hard work, your dreams that you shared with him under that cedar tree he talked of so much. It was the image he took with him to dark places . . .*

'He made provision in his will for you. I will be hearing the details from his solicitor, but it will be a sum sufficient for the purchase of an hotel. May it bring you the peace you deserve, when or if our world finally rights itself. I would be honoured to be a guest, in his place.

'I pray that news of your family and loved ones is good.

'His loving mother, Mavis Neave'

Evie pushed the letter into her pocket and proceeded to visit her patients above stairs, smiling, always smiling, and then descended to make egg custard for one young woman who had been blinded in an ammunition explosion and craved the food her mother used to make. She left the list of other requests for Mrs Moore. 'Just for a moment,' she whispered, her throat too full for other words, and immediately Mrs Moore and her swollen hands pushed her from the kitchen.

She walked steadily to the cedar tree, picking up Harry Travers from the hives, for the two men had shared each other's struggles as they fought to recover. In the shelter of the tree she showed Harry the letter, and held him as he cried and stumbled over his words, talking of the plans he and John had made to travel the Continent, and then the Empire. 'When will this bastard war end, Evie? When?' he sobbed. Neither of them mentioned the money. It was of no importance because it seemed impossible that the war would ever end, and if it did, what on earth would be left?

Chapter 14

Easterleigh Hall, September 1918

A convoy rolled up the drive and discharged its usual cargo, including more and more Australians and South Africans who fought like tigers, so Jack said in his letters. The marquee was still on the lawn, serving as a triage area, but extra huts had been erected to take convalescents. These were not put up in rows, as Dr Nicholls felt they were too much like barracks, but higgledy-piggledy beyond the formal gardens, the walled nursery and the orchard. Richard hurried along with his clipboard, a pencil behind his ear, much as Sergeant Steve Samuels had done. Steve was now serving at a casualty clearing station at the Front and Ver grumbled to Evie, as she watched her husband lick his pencil, standing next to Matron on the steps, 'Steve just left his bad habits behind. My prim and proper husband licking a pencil, for heaven's sake, what would his mother say?'

Evie hugged her. 'The days when he cared what anyone said are long gone. Oh, except you, of course. He most certainly cares what you say.'

Ver hugged her back. 'No, not what *I* say, but he'd

rather cross the battlefield than cross you or Matron. Why call a spade a mere shovel when you can call it a . . .'

Evie put a hand over her friend's mouth. 'Now, now, that's not the language of a lady, you've spent too much time around these soldiers.'

They laughed. Matron turned and smiled. Evie grinned back, because Matron smiled properly these days, such were the advances as the Anglo-French forces pursued the Germans as they withdrew from Amiens to the Hindenburg Line. Elsewhere the US was co-ordinating with the French and British, and sheer force of numbers must surely win the day. So had said Richard, but somehow for Evie there was no winning or losing any more. There was just the numbness of existing in this outrageous folly, and the laughter of friends making life bearable, even enjoyable. 'How can that be?' murmured Evie.

Ver turned to her, her blonde hair shining in the late summer sun. 'How can what be?'

'Oh nothing, just thinking. Is Mart's mum managing with James and Penny, and how is Lady Margaret really, now that lovely man is dead?'

'Now that women over thirty, with property, have the vote she seems to have perked up. I do rather fear that now Granville is gone, she might revert to Lady Margaret, the horselike pain in the neck.'

Evie laughed. She had thought the same thing herself at the Major's funeral, after Lady Margaret referred to 'servants', not the wartime term 'staff', taking up the back rows only. Major Granville would have insisted on the 'staff' intermingling. She knew it had rankled with Veronica, but would it continue to do so after the war, or would everyone revert to type? But that was too far away, and not to be even thought of in the face of this suffering.

She watched as a soldier was taken from triage on a stretcher. The two orderlies carrying him came up the steps past them. The bandage covering his head was blood-stained. Flies buzzed. That was the sound of war, thought Evie, the flies which buzzed and droned in the ambulances as they arrived, so many flies, and came into the Hall with them. She flapped them away as she walked by the side of his stretcher. 'Well, bonny lad, you're safe now. We've a Matron who is more like a dreadnought, and nurses who sometimes resemble angels, and at other times naughty children. It works well.'

The boy's grimy hand, with torn nails and ripped knuckles, was lifting, seeking hers. 'I'd kill for a bloody fag, bonny lass. Probably have, in fact.'

She always kept some Woodbines in her apron pocket, and matches. The orderly nodded. 'Aye, Evie, he's allowed.' They were now in the great hall where there was organised chaos. Sister Newsome would not have any unnecessary noise on her shift, though, or she'd have what was left of everyone's guts for garters, or so she never tired of telling the injured, who laughed, if they could bear the pain, or smiled if they could not. Evie lit a cigarette for the lad, placed it in his mouth, touched his face, and repeated, 'You're safe now. I'll come to see you later.'

Grace hurried through the hall, waving to her, back in harness with more energy than she'd had for a year or two, she'd told Evie. Her hair was arranged in a low bun, allowed by Matron, to cover the absence of 'one of the party' as she so delicately called Agatha, the missing ear. It was a name given by a concussed corporal, loudly, because he had been deafened and had trouble with volume. He'd learn.

Evie went through the baize door, and set off down the stairs. As she did so she passed Millie standing truculently at the entrance lobby to the small store-room which Mr Harvey had seconded as the silver pantry, after the electrification. The larger one, with the safe, now housed the extra linen. He was only parted from his keys while he slept, so he assured everyone. Evie stopped. 'Is there a problem, Millie?'

'Yes, I was on my way to see you. How dare you speak to Captain Richard about the laundry without talking to me first?' Evie shook her head. 'Well, now you're seeing me, and what did I say that upset you?' she replied.

Millie flounced before her, down the stairs, her hands deep into her pockets, her shoulders hunched in fury. Evie wanted to help her on her way with a carefully placed foot, but refrained. 'What do you feel I've done wrong, Millie?' she asked again.

'I heard you telling Captain Richard that the laundry could provide more sheets, more quickly, with winter coming, if washing lines were put up under a covered area. Do you think we haven't enough to do?'

They were walking along the central corridor. Evie said, 'I don't think it would mean you have to do more, it's just that the drying would be easier.'

Polly stuck her head out of the laundry, her hair lank from the steam. 'There you are, Millie. We've a load more to boil, so some of this needs to go out. You said you'd do it.'

'So I will.' Millie pushed the girl aside and swept into the laundry. Polly raised her eyebrows at Evie. 'It's since that damned Hun's been confined to the camp after the hives were pushed over. Been in solitary too, she told us, after he gave that guard a pasting when he heard the Germans were on the run from that salient.' She closed the door and returned to the cauldrons, as the kitchen staff called the huge coppers. Evie started to walk towards Richard's office, then realised she'd forgotten to bring some figures that Ron Simmons needed.

She turned back, rubbing her arms. So much was still the same, but so much seemed to be different with the change in fortunes along the front line. The POWs were restless, uneasy. Yesterday Evie had told some of them as they helped in the herb garden, 'Please, don't worry. You'll be returning home, we won't hurt you.'

Joachim had replied, 'All this suffering, just for defeat.'

Carl had held out her sage. 'Your blockade has

made my mother starving hungry. She is ill, she said in her letter. Ill, do you hear?'

She'd taken the sage from Carl, who was from Berlin. 'But it's been a disaster brought about by your Kaiser, by all those in power I suppose, paid for by us all.'

She'd thought he'd strike her, so quickly had he raised his hand, shouting, 'My Kaiser is without blame.' Tom, a guard, had stepped forward. 'Best be on your way, Evie.'

Carl called after her, 'You would not have won, you English Fräulein, if America had not saved your pretty lives.'

Evie had not replied, she'd been too shaken. Carl, a student in London before the war, had always been so gentle, so relieved to be out of the fighting. But as she thought about it now, entering the comfort of her kitchen, she wondered if perhaps he was feeling guilty. The prisoners would be going home, all of them. They hadn't fought, they were alive, those that survived captivity. Yes, perhaps it was guilt they felt, and the thought clarified something in her mind, but before she could grasp it she saw Millie hurrying along the corridor to the back steps which led up into the yard, her basket laden high with sheets, and she sighed.

Perhaps the girl was right, and she was a busy-body. There was always so much to do, and plan. Well, she couldn't apologise to Carl, because he'd been confined to camp after yesterday, but Millie was Jack's wife, for good or ill. She'd follow and talk to her, but then she saw Mrs Moore trying to heave out a large dish of parsnip pie, perked up with pigeon, with hands obscenely swollen from the rheumatism that had been steadily reappearing. Evie hurried to help her, asking one of the volunteers to remove the other pies from the two larger ranges.

Mrs Moore straightened, and slipped on to her stool, resting her hands in her lap. She had not once reached for the gin bottle as she used to do. Would she when the war was over?

Later that day Evie used her half-hour break to join her mam in the children's nursery in the garage, where there was space to really romp about and create mayhem. They played the quieter games in the indoor nursery beyond Captain Richard's office. Susan Forbes was sitting on an upturned barrel made more comfortable by a cushion. Mart's mam wheeled Margaret's daughter Penny into the yard and sat on another barrel, while James played with the volunteers' children. Well, they had begun by volunteering, but Richard had insisted, after a bequest from one of his parents' friends, that they were paid.

As Evie joined her mam, leaning against an upright at her side, she wondered if she should mention the money that Captain Neave had left her, and which she had banked in Gosforn. But it was tempting fate. Something could go wrong. The war could never end.

Susan put her knitting down, another pair of khaki

socks, reached up and took her hand. 'Tired, bonny lass?'

'Aye Mam, a bit. How are the children? Have you heard from Mart, Mrs Dore?' Evie always enjoyed her visits to the noisy nursery. The garage's service pit had been covered over with huge wooden planks. A small playhouse had been built by two orderlies, painted by Evie and her mother and placed over it. Several of the convalescents had carved cars and created doll's houses, with soft furnishings made by whoever felt like it.

They talked of nothing in particular, and it was good. As she was leaving, her mam said, 'That Millie must have turned over a new leaf, Evie pet. Perhaps it's because the war might be ending. She often comes in and just watches our Tim when he's here after school, as though she's just discovered him. He's a bright lad for six, you know, Evie. Knows his tables, or the two and three times at the least. She was here not an hour ago, with cleaning materials. She's been sorting the attic up top over the last week or two in her off time.' She pointed up to the boarded area where Geoff the chauffeur had slept. 'She meant well, but the first two days she brushed all the dust down through the cracks and we had to take the children into the stables to look at the pigs. Pall after a while, pigs do. They smell, the bairns said, and they weren't wrong.'

They all laughed. Evie stared at the ladder leading to the attic. 'This I've got to see. What is she expecting it to be used for?'

Her mam picked up young Lucy from Hawton, whose mother helped Evie in the kitchen, her desserts a miracle of economy, while Evie climbed the ladder and peered into the space. The floor was clean, and so were the windows. There were sacks neatly stacked at one end, and the bed had been turned on its side. 'She said it would make a good area for a train set for the older ones,' Susan called up, standing with Mrs Dore at the foot of the ladder, James clinging to her skirt.

Evie called down, 'Well, I'm blowed, good girl Millie. We'd have to secure the hatch somehow, and hold that thought, ladies, because I'll be keeping my great hatch of a mouth shut from now on, where Millie's concerned. I speak before I think, perhaps.'

She climbed back down the ladder, almost into her mother's arms. Susan's hug was warm and comforting as she said, 'No you don't. It's just that no one knows quite what to say about anything, any more. It's so strange, all of it. We don't even know what to think, or to feel, or hope.'

When Evie went in, she joined Millie in the laundry, putting her arm round her shoulder, but Millie pulled away. Evie said, 'I'm sorry, I shouldn't have interfered, and it's grand that you're sorting out the attic for the bairns. Tim will love it.'

Millie started to fold the sheets that had been freshly ironed, her back to Evie, 'I've always been a worker, Evie, and it's time you realised you're not the only one in this war. It's hard for us all, really hard. There are so many things to decide.'

Evie sighed. 'Well, you decided well with the attic. It could all be over very soon. Our men will be back, we can all get on with our lives.'

'Oh, go back to work, Evie. I don't need your blathering.'

It was a freezing October and Auberon clung to the side of the shell hole, digging in his toes, hearing Jack shouting into his ear, 'I'm getting too old for this.'

Mart on Auberon's right yelled above the artillery, and machine-gun fire, and snipers, 'Stop bloody grumbling. You're in lovely cold mud, on your way to sliding down into stinking water at the bottom, with heaven knows what bits of which people are floating in it. What could be better?' Zip zip. Crump. Rat-a-tat.

Charlie had stabbed into the side with his rifle barrel. 'I've found a branch,' he yelled from the other side of Jack, nodding at his rifle. Auberon shouted, 'Tell him why it's not a good idea to do that, will you, Jacko.' He checked his watch. They should be following on behind the creeping barrage, not hiding in here. 'Damned Hun machine gun's got us pinned, Don't they know when they're beaten?' Zip zip. Crump. Rat-a-tat.

Mart yelled, 'Well, obviously they're not beaten. It's our wishful thinking, sir.'

Jack was shouting over at Charlie, 'Not a good idea, Corporal, if you're thinking of saving your life by firing the damn rifle. Now all that'll happen is that a lug of mud will block it, it'll explode and you'll go up in a puff of smoke.' Zip zip, rat-a-tat. Crump. Debris flew over them, into the water. Aub heard the splashes.

Froggett's son, Fred, new to it, put his head down on the mud. Auberon yelled, 'It's child's play, Fred. Just keep your head down like that until we tell you otherwise.' No zip zip. No rat-a-tat. Just crump. Auberon dug his toes in harder, balanced himself, and unslung his rifle, thrusting it past Jack to Charlie, who hung on to his 'branch' and grabbed at it. Auberon could afford to lose his rifle, with the extra arsenal he had taken to carrying.

Auberon listened. Still relatively quiet. He withdrew his pistol in readiness for action. 'Less lying about, lads, lots to do, got to get the buggers back beyond the Scheldt river and then the Rhine, so we can get home. Let's all make it in one piece please, can't stand the thought of searching through this mud for bits of you. Too damned messy. No heroics now, out of this hole carefully, discreetly, like a bishop leaving a tart's bedroom.' They eased their way up, then, doubling over, ran zigzagging into the guns.

That evening Auberon wrote a letter to the Froggetts from the German trench they had taken, while the artillery coughed spasmodically. It was what he called a B letter, just an explanation of a leg injury from shrapnel, hopefully a Blighty one, but the medics at base hospital would decide. It would bring good cheer to that small farm, and the farmer who had stood against the Bramptons and sold the cottages to Jack's family, and Grace's, to stop Lord Brampton's monopoly. Quite rightly too.

Jack was writing a similar one, also bound for the Froggetts, hunkering down, resting on a board. Auberon raised his head, examining the trench, which was a bloody great thing with concrete walls. It paid to capture a town like Lille, one which contained concrete works, bloody poor planning by Haig to let the Germans' hog it. 'What the hell are we going to do when we get home, Aub?' Jack said. 'That's if it's on the way to being over. Nothing seems different, so it's hard to tell.'

'What we'll do is take off our uniforms, have a bath, and yes, surely it will be over soon, Jacko.' Auberon grinned, looking up at the sky. Frost was in the air.

Mart muttered, 'What makes you think we'll be let into the house to have a bleedin' bath? They'll hose us down outside, or me mam will. Don't you think your Lady Veronica will be any different. Aye, and Evie will have something to say about you traipsing around stinking the place out, whether you're her boss or not.'

Jack was chewing his pencil. 'You know Evie said Auld Maud had a roof fall a few weeks ago? One of the first things we should do is put the supports much closer together. It might cost more at the start but think of the stoppages these falls cause, as well as the carnage, which is being sorted at Easterleigh as we speak. We could improve on the pumps to keep the methane explosions at bay, and do regular maintenance of all machinery. Makes sense, Aub. D'you think the Bast—' Mart nudged him to a stop. Jack coloured. 'I mean your father, would go for it?'

Charlie looked confused. 'Who's the . . . ?' Now Mart nudged him. Charlie paused, then resumed. 'One minute we're talking about War, Haig and Lille, the next the mine. Well, while we're at it, you should be thinking of bringing shooting parties back to your estate, and controlling the breeding of the game birds again, sir, when the hospital no longer needs them all year round. The grouse could be ready for next year. I could help. I can still do that, I'm sure I can. Or can I? I think perhaps fighting's the only thing I'm good at now. It's what I understand, and not just me, all of us. You too, sir. I don't want us to break up, I mean, what will I do alone? I'd follow you anywhere, sir. We all would, so I'd like to go on working with you.'

Auberon just nodded. He couldn't speak. Mart said, 'I'll get out the bloody violins, shall I?' They laughed. Mart poked at the stock of his rifle, and it was hard for Auberon to imagine him with a pick. Jack had broken the pencil in half and was staring at it, but Aub knew he wasn't seeing it. It was up to him to say something. He tried, but couldn't. He tried again. 'Let's get through this thing first, but I have a plan. Trust me, all of you. Jacko, listen to me. And another thing, you shouldn't think of just following me. We make a team, we follow one

323

another, and you need to remember that, but don't tell Colonel Gerrard, or I'll shoot you myself.'

Before Auberon could feel any more embarrassed Corporal Devlin, who had been with the North Tyne Fusiliers since the Somme, came along with a clutch of steaming tin mugs. He bore the scars most of them carried around the face, shrapnel here and there, a zip of a flesh wound. 'Soup, sir. Sergeant Major's emancipated a spirit stove he found down the end of the trench in the officers' dugout. The Huns left in a hurry, it seems. There's quite a cook-up going on with their bits and bobs until the supplies catch us up. Oxtail it is, from a tin, well, several tins, or so we think. Of course, it might be horse, but either way it'll warm your cockles.'

They hugged the mugs between their hands, and sipped. Auberon knew from Richard that Italy was under pressure, Turkey too, but the men were right, what the hell was going to happen? Would the plan he'd been mulling over work? Would he even live to put it into action? If not, there was always Richard, who had the package he had left in his portmanteau, and a further letter with instructions for the well-being of his men. Across from him Charlie was running his finger around the inside of his mug. No one thought it disgusting, but someone would say it was. Auberon waited. Mart said, 'That's disgusting.'

Jack shared a look with Auberon. They both grinned. So often there was no need for words.

Auberon thought of Simon, safe in the prison camp,

Simon who had not taken the opportunity to leave, to even snatch at a faint chance to see Evie, but had preferred to build up his friendship with the American director's son. But who was he to criticise others; at least Simon would live safely ensconced as an orderly, and therefore at least Evie would live happily. That was something to hold to him as he did most nights, and that was also why the plan must work.

Jack threw a small pebble, and it stung Auberon's leg. 'Hey, watch it.'

'Well, get your lugs working. Did you find out any more about that grey that is being ridden by the major, out on the right flank?' Jack asked.

Auberon flung the pebble back. Jack caught it. 'Yes, and it's not Prancer. But I'm not giving up, he's out there somewhere.' The others looked anywhere but at him. 'I know, I know,' Aub said, 'but I just feel he is. Bit like the cedar tree. He's there, it's there, so life will go on.'

'And all will be well,' muttered Mart. Jack barked out a laugh. They all repeated, as one, 'And all will be well. Bless her huge and kindly heart.' The artillery was still lobbing shells, flares were sent out ahead of them, but they doubted there'd be any wiring parties with the Germans in retreat.

'Just keep your heads down and your wits about you. There's still a lot of damage flying around,' Auberon insisted, desperate to keep them safe, desperate to get them back, himself too, just see Evie's smile, hear her voice. She was life to him.

Chapter 15

Easterleigh Hall, 11th November 1918

The war was over at eleven in the morning, on the eleventh day of the eleventh month of 1918. 'Neat and tidy, then,' Evie murmured, shivering as she and Grace stood on the porticoed steps waiting for the ambulances to arrive. Frost covered the grass, and glinted on the gravel of the drive. 'The war is over.' It seemed to mean nothing. She tried it another way. 'Over is the war.' She tried it again. 'Is over the war.'

Grace smiled at her. 'None of it makes sense and yes, neat and tidy for posterity one thinks, until you look at these ambulances and their cargo.' Her smile faded. 'Please God, our men are safe. We haven't heard differently, but how long does it take for a telegram to come? Because Aub would signal the news, wouldn't he? Unless he himself was killed, then it would be a letter. What do you think, Evie, how long?'

Evie shook her head. 'I don't know, lass. I just don't know.' The ambulances were coming up the drive now, and would keep coming, because men would have been blasted to smithereens until the last minute, and of this they were more than sure. There was the grinding of gears, the crunch of gravel.

'It's teatime,' Grace said. Evie stared at her. 'Teatime,' Grace repeated.

Evie felt panic. 'Teatime, oh my Auntie Fanny.' She leapt down the steps, skirting the first ambulance that was skidding to a halt. As she ran into the stable yard the organised chaos behind her began. More awaited her at the top of the kitchen steps, in the shape of Mrs Moore standing with her arms akimbo, yelling, 'I'll have your guts for garters, so I will, Evie Forbes. Teatime and where the hell are you? Partying already no doubt, when there are gobs to fill with scones, and party food to prepare.'

Evie skirted round her, expecting a clip on the ear, and it was all so normal that she laughed, really laughed, and fled down the steps into the kitchen, Mrs Moore in hot pursuit in spite of her rheumatics, laughing too. 'I'm beginning to believe,' Evie shouted as she entered the kitchen, 'I'm beginning to believe it's over.'

Annie and the downstairs servants were doing some sort of dance around the kitchen table, and the laundry staff joined in, led by Millie, with such a smile on her face that it was as though she'd swallowed the sun, or so Mrs Moore grunted. They wound out into the servants' hall, and then the interior corridor, until Mr Harvey appeared on the stairs leading to the great hall, clapping his hands and shouting. 'I will not have this when we have injured arriving, and work to do. Decorum, please. You will save this until after dinner is cleared, and only then will you celebrate. Then I will expect you to lift the roof.'

He was so old, so thin, so drawn, but his presence was still larger than anyone's in the whole world, Evie thought, looking at him, feeling a great swathe of affection sweep her, and was astonished. She stared around. She had felt affection, even if only for a moment, for now it was gone, but she had feared that feeling was dead within her and it was worthy of celebration that it was not.

That evening, after a dinner of treats such as smoked salmon, lamb cutlets, sponge puddings involving sugar and cream, and finally wine from Lord Brampton's cellars, liberated by Mr Harvey at Veronica's suggestion, there was a mingling of new patients and convalescents, nurses, VADs, orderlies, downstairs staff , wandering here and there, within the wards and great hall, and downstairs. The celebrations spilled out on to the frosty lawn, and into the triage marquee where refreshments were laid out on trestle tables, and could be cleared within moments if a convoy arrived.

Evie was dragged by Harry to the fiddlers, who were recovering pitmen from Auld Maud's roof fall. She sang 'It's a Long Way to Tipperary', 'If You Were the Only Girl in the World', 'Keep the Home Fires Burning' and others until her throat was raw. She danced with Harry, and Ron who was there with Posie. Richard trod on her foot as they clambered through a waltz. 'It's the wine,' he said. 'I have to say, the old man keeps a good cellar. Not sure how Mr Harvey is going to fudge the wine account book to hide this little lot.'

Evie laughed. 'He'll find a way, no doubt, and hopefully Brampton won't be here for a while.'

She saw Richard's face set, and the lines of worry deepen between his eyes. She said, 'What will happen to us all now?'

'My thoughts entirely, Commandant Evie. What indeed?' He tried a turn, which was unsuccessful, and as their balance went Ron spun up, dragging Posie with him, to act as a bulwark, stabilising the situation. Veronica danced past the near disaster in Harry's arms, calling, 'He's your problem for the moment, Evie. No doubt you'll make a dancer of him yet.'

'Never, I know my limitations,' Evie shouted after her, feeling hot from so many bodies, tired from cooking all day, but joyous. Always, every moment, there was joy.

Richard looked down at her. 'Evie, may we just take a breather, out in the cool, and the quiet?'

The fiddlers were playing their hearts out, the wine bottles were laid out on the tables at the entrance, and two beer barrels too. They passed them, Richard's hand on her elbow, partly to help his balance on the lawn, partly as a courtesy. They walked clear of the milling crowds and joined others, less frantic, strolling in the cold, or standing in groups, the men smoking, the few women talking. The sky was frosty clear. Evie looked up, glad there was no cloud, for such a sky made her feel insignificant, as though it expected nothing of her. She was just a speck, and that was how she felt.

Harry was beneath the cedar tree, a wine glass in his hand, beckoning them. They joined him. He had a bottle and glasses at the base of the tree. Evie retrieved two, and poured. They leaned against the tree, silent until Harry said, 'Now we face the fact that the dead are never coming home but those that are left must go on, with absent limbs, faces and minds. It must be so strange on the Continent. There must just be the greatest silence known to man.'

None of them spoke, just drank, and then refilled their glasses.

The party ended at midnight, and Evie took over from Annie in the kitchen, sleeping on one of the armchairs, with Raisin and Currant asleep on the other. She dragged herself awake, as usual, when a VAD came in for beef broth, or the favourite food that was required by a new patient who had just realised that he was alive, and feeling rather better, or one who wanted the food his mother used to cook one last time, perhaps even just the smell of it, before he died.

At four in the morning, she was dragged awake again by something. Had it been a bang? She sat up, looking round. Had a door slammed? She heard voices, and the sound of running, but no one was ever allowed to run. Matron would have their guts for garters. She sat up, the dogs stirred, and barked. There were footsteps on the stairs, shouting. 'Evie, Mr Harvey, Mrs Moore, Mrs Green, quickly, quickly.' It was Ken, the orderly who had drawn the short straw and was manning the desk in the great hall all night. Behind him she could hear Sister Newsome calling, 'We need hoses.'

Evie flew out of the kitchen, along the internal corridor, meeting Ken, panting, at the bottom of the stairs. 'Hoses?' She asked.

'It's the tree, some bugger's blown it up.'

He was already turning, pounding back up the stairs. Evie followed, her cap askew. 'What tree?'

Ken burst into the great hall, where patients were gathering. They wove their way through to the double doors which were flung open, and there behind the marquee were flames, leaping into the sky, whipped by the wind. Harry, Ron and several others were lugging Old Stan's hoses through from the stable yard, Harry calling back to those in the yard, 'Get that water on.'

The noise of the flames and the crackle of the cedar needles reached Evie as she stood on the steps next to Matron, who was in her dressing gown, her hair in a net, her hand to her mouth. There was a whoosh as something else went up and now Evie was leaping down, followed by Veronica, crunching across the gravel, skirting the marquee, the noise getting louder and louder. They reached Harry and helped with the hose, pulling it in the direction of the tree which lay prone, blackened and burning, branches scattered about. 'Bastards, bastards,' Harry was yelling, struggling to control the hose, which was like a live thing. The men hung on grimly, directing the water on the blaze while Ron doused the marquee with another hose to try to stop it going up too. The heat was intense, more so as the wind whipped up the flames.

'Who did this?' Evie shouted, gripping the hose behind the men, her hands and arms soaking wet. 'Who would do this?'

Harry was looking behind him, towards the stables. 'Where the hell is the woman?' he shouted, then turned back as the hose seemed to leap to one side, knocking itself from Evie's hands. She grabbed it again, and now her skirts were soaked but the heat was still blasting at them. 'Where's who?' she shouted back.

'Millie, she was in the garage. I shouted to her and whoever she had with her to haul out the third hose. Bugger it.' Harry yelled to young Kev, 'Get the garage hose, for God's sake. Get Millie to give you a hand, and the bloke with her. We need another to help Ron with the marquee. Which'll be needed tomorrow, bet your bottom dollar.'

Others had started a bucket line and were dousing the marquee as Kev ran to the garage.

By dawn the cedar tree was a smouldering mess.

No one said that it looked like a great dead body, but Evie suspected most were thinking it. She and Harry stood beside it, with Grace, Veronica and Richard. There was nothing to say, because the image of peace and tranquillity that had sustained so many lay destroyed at their feet. Evie said, 'Bless its heart. It stayed strong the whole of the war.' But their tears were close.

Somehow they all worked as usual and lunch was created and removed, a convoy arrived, the laundry was hung out, and it was only then that Polly came into the kitchen. 'Millie hasn't arrived for her shift. Old Stan said she wasn't at the pickup point. I expect she's faffing about now the war's over. Young Kev didn't find her at the garage either, last night, and I reckon she'd just cycled home, lazy cow.'

Evie's head was aching from the wine and tiredness, everyone's was, but they had all arrived, they had all smiled because the war was over. Soon it would sink in, and the joy would remain and never depart. She smiled at Polly. 'I'll ask Mam when she comes. She'll be biking in after fetching Tim from school. He'll be crammed into that little seat, grumbling all the way.'

Mr Harvey knocked and entered, panting and even paler than usual. 'Just to warn you, Lord Brampton has arrived, with her ladyship. They were in the area, intent on arriving this evening, so they say, but have arrived earlier to inspect the damage. A small convoy is expected at any moment, but in spite of this they require tea in the officers' sitting room for four. Lady Veronica and Captain Richard will be joining them. The officers have been heaved out into the enlisted men's day room, not that it seems to be a hardship to them. They've simply carried their playing cards through with them. Fortunately I have already had Lord Brampton's empty wine bottles removed to a place of safety.' Mrs Green arrived with tea towels. 'The bottles are safely stored down in the bothy, Mr Harvey.'

Mrs Moore called, 'Come and sit, both of you, while we prepare a tray for Mr Harvey to take.'

Evie was already pouring boiling water into the teapot, and instead of scones they set out fancies, which had been part of the feast prepared yesterday. Annie laid the tray with plates, serviettes, cups, milk, and some of the precious sugar.

Veronica thanked Mr Harvey as he placed the tray on the side table at her left hand. She and Richard sat together, with James on Richard's knee. 'Shall I be mother?' she said to her stepmother, who winced at such a lower class question. Veronica poured, smiling slightly. Mr Harvey handed around the cups, and then the fancies. No one even looked. He replaced the plate on the tray, bowing when Lord Brampton waved him away without even a glance. Veronica said, 'Thank you so much, Mr Harvey, what would we do without you? Indeed, what would we have done without you over these last terrible years?'

'Thank you, madam.' He backed out, and almost shut the door, almost, as Veronica had known he would. She looked at her father, waiting, because he had come for something.

He said, 'I have tried to find a buyer for this white elephant. I have failed. Therefore, when the last patient leaves, which I insist must be by the last day of January 1919, I am razing it to the ground as so many of my friends are forced to do, in the face of the taxes inherent on such properties.'

There was triumph in every inch of his body. Veronica felt the words as though they were a body blow. Beside her Richard stirred. 'I have used most of my assets on keeping Easterleigh Hall as a sanctuary for our wounded, as has Sir Anthony Travers, and Auberon. Would you, however, allow me more time to try and raise enough to buy this wonderful home from you?' He was almost begging, and Veronica had never loved him more than at this moment, because she knew what this pleading must have cost him. James reached out and pulled his father's nose. 'For the sake of your grandson,' Richard added.

'It's too late,' Lord Brampton said, 'for such humble pie. Did you really think, Veronica, that your behaviour, when your husband sent me away like some common criminal, would be forgotten by me, or your stepmother? So now you will understand the reality of consequences. You will all have to find your own damned homes, and these overfamiliar servants must find other jobs. Razed it will be, much as that infernal tree has been, which seemed to give you and your brother, and the late unlamented interfering governess of yours, Miss Wainton such pleasure. The matter is in the hands of my solicitors.' He raised his voice. 'Stop skulking at the door, Harvey, and load up the silver. You'll have kept it neat and tidy in your safe and now it will be even safer in my keeping. Have it deposited in the Rolls. Meanwhile I will be inspecting the wine, because this will also be collected in due course. I will remove the wine cellar accounts today.'

There was a click as the door shut.

Evie dropped the pan of potatoes she was just about to put on to boil as Mr Harvey staggered into the kitchen, holding his chest, his face ashen and sweating. 'Mrs Moore, quick,' Evie called. Mrs Moore peered out from the scullery, with Maudie at her elbow. She ran across and together they helped him to the armchair which Raisin vacated reluctantly, helped on his way by Evie. Mrs Moore yelled, 'Maudie, get Dr Nicholls, and then Lady Veronica.' She loosened Mr Harvey's wing collar. He was gasping, and holding out an envelope. 'Don't try and talk,' Mrs Moore soothed him. 'No, don't talk, my love.' She stroked his hair, and he leaned against her. Evie was on her knees next to him, holding his hand, shouting after Maudie, 'Hurry, for God's sake hurry.'

'The silver,' he gasped. 'The silver. The small pieces, all gone.'

Mrs Moore and Evie stared at one another, not understanding. He was pushing the envelope at Evie. She took it, and saw her name on the envelope in Millie's writing, and fear dragged at her. She ripped it open, still on her knees, as Dr Nicholls rushed in, his bag in one hand, Matron puffing in behind, with two orderlies carrying a stretcher.

'Out of the way, Evie, for God's sake,' Dr Nicholls roared. Evie was reading Millie's words. 'Out, out.' Dr Nicholls shook her shoulder. She looked up and scrambled to her feet, backing away as they all worked on her beloved Mr Harvey. Veronica flew in. 'Evie?' Evie pointed to Mr Harvey, and continued to back away until the table stopped her, the letter still in her hand. Veronica said, 'Evie?'

Evie showed her the letter.

Well, Evie

The tree is my goodbye present for you. I said I'd get you, but you probably still don't know why. It's because you're just so smug, so bloody perfect with your hotel plans, with your do-gooding. You and your family is always at it, and so I got to do it as well and will have to go on doing it, if I stay, because you'll get your hotel, you see if you don't, and I'll have to do the laundry, or something.

It's been hell, working in a freak show. And it's not over, because Jack will come home, and we'll have his bleeding shouting all night and who knows what he'll look like, and if you're daft enough to think them Bramptons will still be friendly and nice, when they don't need us, you got another think coming. They'll be back to the masters and we'll be the servants.

I have a right to a whole man, with nice skin, no blue scars, and I'm going to have him. Heine likes me, and I will make him love me. I will. And we've got our start in life, thanks to the bloody Bramptons. We're going on a boat, but you won't know where and now things will work for me. Just look after Tim because Heine doesn't want him. I had to choose. You Forbes took him away from me, anyway. He loved his gran more than me, so now you lot can do the donkey work and anyway, Jack loved the bairn, not me. Don't think I didn't know that. Just like you he is, the big person helping the little people. Well, get on with it and thank you for the silver. I hid it in the garage attic, so you got that wrong. But I was right, it will make a good train play area. Put up a plaque with my name, Millie Forbes

Jack, Martin, Charlie and Auberon marched through Albert, each full of their own thoughts. It was the end of November and not a shot had been fired since eleven o'clock on the eleventh. Jack found the quiet unnerving and strange, and knowing that they could walk erect, and light as many cigarettes as they wished without a sniper finding his target when the third match was struck, took some getting used to. Only a few birds sang because there were no trees, just stumps. There were few houses but a load of bloody ruins, and even the leaning Virgin on top of the Basilica of Notre-Dame de Brebières had gone, shelled by the British to stop the Germans from using the tower as an observation post. What the hell must it be like to look on this if it was your home?

He shook his head clear of the thought, because it wasn't a million miles from Bastard Brampton's intentions. He knew Evie's letter about Millie almost by heart, knew that he was free to be with Grace now and that was still something that he couldn't quite grasp, for he had thought it impossible. He had written to her, telling her again of his love, and that he was hers, and Agatha's, if she would have him, but saying that he came with a son, and that was not negotiable. She had telegraphed back. *Agatha says yes stop so I will have to come too stop your son is my son too stop*

Mart came alongside, hitching his rifle. 'Are you going to tell the boss about Evie's thoughts for Easterleigh Hall?'

'It's not my place, man,' Jack muttered, throwing his cigarette end to the ground. Along the sides of the roads the French were clearing the rubble, and stopped to cheer as they passed.

'It's not your place?' Mart laughed out loud, waving at the children, and tossing them his last tin of bully beef. 'That truly is such a load of bollocks. When has Jack Forbes ever known his place?'

A Frenchwoman was coming towards them, a basket on her arm. She stopped, dug into the basket and brought out apples for them. They took them, and Jack insisted, in French, that she had a packet of cigarettes for her husband. *'Il est mort,'* she said, but took the cigarettes anyway. The men marched on towards the billet, two miles further down the long straight road.

That evening Jack and Auberon did rounds of the men billeted out of town and under tents in an area previously cleared of unexploded shells. The talk was of those who would not come home, and what the future would bring in a Britain fit for heroes, as Lloyd George had promised, and the stunned acknowledgement that they themselves had survived. When they returned, Mart and Charlie were heating water over a small fire, and levering open cans of bully beef. Mart looked up. 'Will you share a tea with us, sir, before you go on for your feast?' His tone was ironic, not bitter.

Aub shrugged. 'I'd kill for one.'

Charlie shook his head. 'Naughty naughty, no need to do that now.'

There was a faint laugh all round. They hunkered round the fire, holding the tin mugs between their hands. Mart threw on some sticks, and one more for luck. They all watched it smoulder before bursting into flames. 'I still can't believe it,' Auberon said. 'That great cedar tree down, just like that. They think the pair of them found a ship bound for America, or so Richard has been told by Brampton, who's had the police track them as far as he can. I presume you won't be taking off after them, Jack?'

His face was all innocence. Jack watched the fire,

wanting to grin. 'I think I'll forgo that pleasure, sir, but if your father has his thugs search my parents' house one more time, I'll rip his head off.'

'Pleased to hear it.' Auberon sipped his tea. Mart coughed. Jack glared. Auberon was watching them both. 'Out with it.' He checked his watch. 'I have to be at dinner in ten minutes.'

Mart said, 'You know Jack heard from Evie yesterday, well . . .'

Charlie interrupted, 'Amazing how postie finds us out here, really amazing.'

Jack watched Auberon watching them, one eyebrow raised. Jack gave in. 'Well, what she said was that your da's going to raze Easterleigh to the ground, but she reckons it'd make a grand hotel. Harry Travers thinks there are enough of the ex-patients to spread the word and you'd get plenty to stay. It's her dream, you know, running a hotel, but reckon I've already told you that, and, aye, it'd be a grand place, with grand food. But then he won't sell to you, will he? So that's that, unless someone else could head it up. She's looking elsewhere because she doesn't think it could ever happen. A dream is just a dream, she says.'

There was a long silence, as they all threw on the fire what small pieces of wood they'd gathered in this disturbed and treeless area. Jack wondered what the cedar tree had sounded like as it burned, and what pain Evie had felt, and he wanted to put his arms around her and tell her all would be well. He laughed grimly. Would it? What about Simon? What about the hotel? What about her future? He had one, in the mine, but what about his grand beautiful sister? What of her?

Finally Auberon rose, dusting down his trousers, peering at his unpolished boots. He had replaced the compass in the heel, and refused to remove it, even now. 'That's of great interest. The final piece in a puzzle I've been working on, Jack. Try not to worry about Evie, I think I can see a way through. But in the meantime I've heard from Richard. He's had you all designated as miners, you too, Charlie. This allows you the green card as pivotal workers and a swift demobilisation. You will be amongst the first home. He is sending to Simon's prison camp and we will have him and Roger home before they know where they are, and that should bring a smile to your sister's face.'

Jack saw the tiredness suddenly drench his captain, and stood as Auberon swayed. 'Sir.' He put out his hand. Auberon smiled, stiffened. 'Do you know, I think I could quite sleep on my feet, but what's new about that, eh, and soon you'll be home, between sheets and not expected into work until you've had some weeks off. Now, Charlie, come and find me at Easterleigh Hall before the end of January, and let's see what we can sort out. Off for din-dins, now.'

He turned, started to walk away, then stopped and called over his shoulder, 'I'm leaving at first light and won't be back for a while. I have things I need to do in Rotterdam, but tell those at home I've been held up at HQ, there's good chaps.'

Jack watched him go, seeing him stumble in the darkness, recover and head off to the officers' mess, which was lit inside with oil lamps, and outside with two lamps hung from poles. Auberon looked so alone that Jack started after him, running, pulling him to a halt. 'Do you need us, sir, in Rotterdam? We're in no hurry.' It was a lie.

Auberon smiled, patted Jack's shoulder. 'I need you to trust me, Jack, that's what I need. Really trust me because I hope I get it right, this time, for us all.'

Mart and Charlie had joined them. Charlie said, 'But you can't go, not without us.'

Jack shook his head. 'Charlie, let the man do what he has to do. He'll come back and you'll be staying with me when you've seen your mam, and will see him then.'

Jack saluted his captain. 'We made it, sir.'

Auberon returned the salute. 'We wouldn't have, without you, Sergeant.'

Jack replied, 'Nor without you, Aub.'

Mart said, 'For the love of God, you'll be kissing next.'

Auberon laughed. 'You take care, Jacko.' He shook them all by the hand. 'God speed,' he said. 'Give my regards to everyone at home.'

Chapter 16

Easterleigh Hall, mid December 1918

Evie sat opposite Edward Manton in the trap, heading away from Easton towards Easterleigh Hall. It was a crisp bright day and the shorn wheat and barley fields glinted behind cobwebbed leafless hedges glistening with frost. Ice pooled in tiny shell holes, as Harry had called them when they came this way last week with her da's cart piled high with sea coal. They had looked at one another and he'd muttered that they'd have to get used to rethinking the images that had become natural. That was when they had really begun to believe that the war was over.

Two days ago she walked over to her mam, at Harry and Ron Simmons' insistence. They said, 'You need to get out and see some hotels, Evie, because it's clear that Lord Brampton is never going to change his mind. We heard Veronica and Richard talking in the office; worried to death they are.'

She had spent two nights with her mam and today Edward had taken her to view a hotel which was for sale in Gosforn. Its clientele were commercial travellers. The whole thing had depressed her, but with a lick of paint it could be brightened up and at least there would be a job for Simon, when he finally arrived, but not for Jack. It was this that hauled her down into blackness. It would be the mine again for him, when he finally returned.

Edward flicked the reins and Sally snorted, tossing her head. He asked, 'Has Grace replied to Jack yet?'

He was staring out at the fields as though they were the most interesting thing on earth as they approached the crossroads. She followed his gaze but there were just a few rooks, gleaning what tiny morsels were left from the harvest. She said, 'She's hesitating now and insists that he needs to see her and Agatha. He needs to understand that she will look like this for ever, not just the duration of the war. She thinks that in the war we accept things, feeling that with peace all will revert back to normal; the dead will live again and return, injuries will go as though they were never here.'

Sally huffed, her breath visible. Edward pulled on the left rein and she turned on to the road leading to Easterleigh Hall, which was visible through the leafless branches. Edward continued, hunched over the reins, 'She's right, of course. My parishioners are beginning to comprehend the permanency of pain and loss, the exhaustion of war, but yours isn't over yet, is it, Evie? Still patients are arriving.'

Evie nodded. 'There's talk of Spanish flu too, though not here, yet. Dr Nicholls says it's because everyone's so tired and we've no resistance, particularly the men, and it's like a bloody scythe, begging your pardon, Parson. As though the world hasn't been through enough.'

Edward shrugged, and broke Sally into a trot. 'She likes to stretch her legs, Evie. She might be a bit of an old girl but she has a sparkle in her. Bit like your Mrs Moore, who had a soft spot for Mr Harvey, I gather.'

Evie grinned, holding on to the sides of the trap as it lurched into a hole, then out. 'Thankfully, it's reciprocal, the dear old things. They're taking it slowly though, which perhaps isn't wise, given their years.' She waited a moment as they turned into the tradesmen's entrance and Edward slowed Sally to a walk. She said, 'We can use the drive, you know. We all do now.'

Edward shrugged. 'I forgot, but we're here now.'

They clipped on, and she said, 'But what of Grace and Jack, Edward? There can be no marriage, as who knows where Millie is, even if a divorce were possible?'

They continued alongside the yew hedge quietly now, as Sally walked on yew mulch. Edward shrugged again. 'After the last four years, my dear, I think we need what happiness we can find. Perhaps they can jump over a broom or something meaningful. Either way Tim needs a mother, Gracie needs her Jack, and Jack needs her. So the equation seems simple, and I can't see the good folk of Easton, or God himself, bothering unduly, can you? What needs

346

to happen is for Lord Brampton to stop worrying Grace and your family as to Millie's whereabouts, as though they'd know. He wants his silver back, but that's only to be expected, I suppose.'

They were turning into the stable yard. 'Have you yet mentioned the hotel idea to Lady Veronica and Captain Richard?' Edward asked, pulling Sally to a halt, and jumping down from the trap. He held out his hands to Evie, who let him swing her to the ground in an arc, a smile on his face. With the demands of war he seemed to have found a sense of informality, or was it normality? She shook her head. 'I've said nothing. What is the point when the Hall is to come down? The fight seems to have gone out of everyone with the cedar tree gone, and Brampton as he is. We're all going to disperse to who knows where, and the men aren't even home yet, though they're crucial workers and have been in the war from the start. Oh, I don't know, Edward. We've clung to the idea of peace and of course it's the most wonderful thing . . .' She stopped, her voice shaking.

Edward was nodding, but not at her. She began to turn, seeing someone on the periphery of her vision, but Edward grabbed her shoulders, making her face him. She resisted. 'What . . . ?

Hands came down over her eyes. 'Jack? Simon?' she said.

'Oh damn, Evie, I didn't think.' It was Ron. She was confused. 'Turn round,' Ron ordered. 'Thank you, Parson, for getting the timing right.'

Edward said, 'There've been a lot involved, young man.'

Ron was turning her round, his hands still over her eyes. She said, 'So that's why we came the back way. Just what are you up to? No good, I imagine.' She was laughing.

Harry said from her right, and Edward from her left, 'Steady now. Let us guide you.' They each took an arm. She could see light through the slits where Ron's fingers met, and felt the cold of his hands. She hesitated to put a foot forward, but Harry and Edward steadied her, pulled her gently along. Around her the dogs yapped. Ron shouted, 'Bugger off, you two, for heaven's sake.'

The cobbles became gravel, which slid and crunched beneath her boots. Around she could hear a murmuring of voices. Were her men home? All of them, Jack, Simon and Aub? Was it them? She strained to hear but there was just the murmuring, and a laugh. It was Tim, and that was James crying, and Angela Dore, soothing him.

She turned her head. 'Let me see,' she demanded. 'Not yet,' Ron insisted. They were on the lawn now, and she thought that to the left would be the marquee which was still up, though quite why, no one knew. It just seemed to be tempting fate to remove it, though Old Stan wanted it gone, so the grass could recover. They stopped. 'Now.' It was Captain Richard.

'Yes, sir,' Ron said. He took his hands away. For a moment she could see nothing, the light was so bright.

She looked down, blinking as Harry and Edward released her arms, and now there was clapping all around. She lifted her head, and in place of the huge cedar tree was another, a quarter of the size, planted in, strong and firm with pine props supporting it against the winter winds. It was young, fresh, beautiful, graceful and motionless even in the wind that was moving the branches of the other trees edging the lawn.

The burned grass was gone, and turfs had been cut from elsewhere and bedded in its place; sand had been scattered. Would the tree grow in the winter? Her throat hurt, her eyes were stinging.

Lady Veronica came to her and said, 'You've been our strength, just as much as the cedar tree. So this is for you. Stan says the turfs will overwinter with care, and the tree is best planted now, in the dormant season.'

She took Evie's hands and whispered, 'It is a gesture of faith. Somehow we will survive. Auberon has today sent a telegram and asks for our trust. He has a plan and is with Father now.'

Ron put his arm around Evie's shoulders and in front of everyone she sobbed: for the men who would never return, for those who would spend their lives damaged beyond repair, for these friends whom she could not bear to lose, for the whole damned crime of the war. But most of all for this wonderful tree that somehow must flourish.

Two days later Evie was preparing chicken casserole alongside Mrs Moore and Annie when there was a thunderous knocking at the back kitchen door. 'Come in, and then plug the hole. We're not living in a barn,' she shouted, cutting the chickens into joints and passing them along to Annie to be rolled in flour. Mrs Moore was sautéing them on the range, prior to slow cooking in the ovens.

In the scullery Maudie and Joyce were banging and crashing the pans, but Evie managed to hear the thud of the boots. Lifting her head, she turned, and there was Jack, her bonny lad, with Mart beside him. She flew at them, hugging them both, kissing them in turn, and again, and again, until they held her off. 'By, lass, steady on, you'll have us over, you will and all,' Jack laughed. They were so thin, so old, so scarred, but they were here. They dropped their packs on Mrs Moore's clean floor. 'You'll have your backsides tanned,' Evie whispered.

'Aye, you will that.' Mrs Moore was beside her now, wiping her hands on her hessian apron, then patting the men, then wiping her hands before patting them again. Mart flung his arms round her, kissing her until she squealed. Evie shouted, 'Annie, leave the chicken, go and get Grace.' Annie beamed at Jack and Mart before hurrying off. The noise from the scullery stopped and the girls appeared at the kitchen door, their hands red from the soda.

Jack's arms were round Evie, holding her so tightly that she thought she'd never breathe again. 'By, lass, I never thought I'd get here.' He'd knocked her cap sideways but what did it matter. 'We were stuck waiting and waiting at Calais for the demob permissions to come through, then we got ours but there was something wrong with Charlie's and we wouldn't embark until his was sorted. He's at his mam's but is then coming here.'

'Aub?' she asked, looking behind her brother. Jack muttered, 'He said he'd go to see the Bastard.'

'Aye, I forgot. Lady Veronica said something.' She was reaching out her hand to Mart, who lifted it and kissed it, his eyes dark-rimmed with tiredness. Evie said, 'Mrs Moore, we need his mam down here from the nursery. She's doing such a grand job, Mart. There's just James at the moment, Penny has been away with Lady Margaret.'

Mrs Moore patted both men again and left, and the scullery maids scuttled back into their lair. As they did so, Grace came to the kitchen door, Annie behind her. Jack released Evie and stood up straight. He faced Grace full on. She wore her VAD uniform, and her hair in a loose bun over Agatha. 'Well, bonny lass. I expected to have heard better from you.' His voice was cold. 'Is it going to be like last time, then, because I can't take that.'

Evie looked from one to the other, then at Mart, who raised his eyebrows. She tugged at Jack's arm, but then moved to the range, pulling off the sautéed chicken which Mrs Moore had left on the heat. 'Don't be so damned silly, the pair of you.' She tipped the chicken into several large casserole dishes, checking the clock because there were still patients to feed, and more expected. The steam rose in her face as she poked the chicken down into the gravy, concentrating on it, but talking too. 'Let me explain in words you can understand, Jack,' she said. 'Grace is worried about Agatha and the scarring in the cold light of peace, and fears that someone as unblemished as you will find her distasteful.'

Evie straightened up, pointing to the dishes of sautéed chicken, and the uncooked joints beside them. 'That's what's distasteful, luncheon waiting to be cooked, with no wine to add as the Bastard has collected the cellar load; it is not the absence of an ear. Now you're back, Annie, you take that gormless great lump called Mart into the servants' hall, and keep him occupied until his mam gets here, then come back. We have luncheon to prepare. Jack, you take Agatha's mistress to the garage to see Tim and Mam, but sort this woman out before you get there.' She threw flour-dusted chicken joints into the sauté pan, turned her back and continued with lunch. Her heart was full, and soon they'd all be home. It was only then she realised she hadn't asked about Simon. She turned over the chicken joints. Well, of course she hadn't. He and Roger would be coming from the prison camp, so why would he be with them?

It was two days later, as Evie was standing at the cedar tree, stroking its low branches and telling it that it must survive and bring great good luck, that she saw Ted's taxi crunching up the drive. It skidded to a halt in front of the portico steps. The door opened and there he was, clambering out in the blue-grey coat given to returning POWs, his red hair glinting, while Ted hauled his new kitbag from the boot. Simon looked older, but not as drawn as Jack, or scarred, but why would he be? He had been an orderly, safe behind bars, when the others had returned to the fray.

She stood, unable to move. Simon was here and she'd waited so long and she couldn't believe it. Yes, that was what it was. She just couldn't believe he was here. 'Evie.' His voice was the same. Now she ran, tearing across the new turf, the gravel, and into his arms, and they were the same arms, his lips were the same, his eyes still so blue. It was she who was different, her mind in a turmoil.

He picked her up and swung her round. He had grown, filled out. Easterleigh Hall had received released prisoners of war who were skeletal, damaged after years of mistreatment, without an arm, or leg. But he was strong, and still handsome. She said against his mouth. 'You must see your mam and da too. I'll get time off.'

'I have, we stopped there first.' He put her down. 'You don't mind, do you?'

She shook her head, holding his face between her hands, kissing his mouth. 'Of course I don't mind.' But she did.

Roger was coming round from the other side of the car, his coat rather too large. He looked thin, feverish, and stopped to lean on the back of the taxi as Ted hauled out his kitbag now. Neither bag was full, but what did they have after years in captivity? Ted was clambering back in.

Simon said, 'Auberon arranged for our speedy repatriation. You do know that I gave up my place on the escape, don't you? I thought I would be of more use distracting the Germans. They loved the show. We had to play it for a further night. It was only then they realised some had gone missing, but they never found the tunnel, thank God. It would have been the end of the drama company.' He hesitated, as though remembering something, his blue eyes searching his mind. Then, 'More importantly, we got more people out. Not bad, eh?'

Sister Newsome was standing or the front steps, taking the air, accompanied by other staff.

Roger fell on the drive as the taxi ground its gears and moved off. She ran to him, felt his forehead. She screamed above the sound of the disappearing car, 'Get the orderly to help, Si. Come on, don't just stand there.' Bloody bloody Roger, he had brought the flu, poor bugger. She was pretty sure of it. There was the sound of running feet across the gravel. Sister Newsome reached them first and put her hands out to the orderlies and the two VADs behind her. 'Only two of you, and then into the isolation ward with him.' The isolation ward had been set up in the conservatory because it had a separate door. The women patients had all gone home.

Simon stood where she had left him, staring. He called, 'It's bloody catching, isn't it?'

In Rotterdam Auberon had thought how neutrality became the place. In his hotel room he had practised his father's signature until he felt it close to perfect. He then wrote the letter of authorisation on Easterleigh Hall headed notepaper that Richard had sent across, without question, in response to his telegram, which promised a plan to save Easterleigh, perhaps.

He arrived at the bank that held his father's safety-deposit box, the one that had been mentioned in the stack of paperwork he had leafed through before he left the Hall a lifetime ago. The manager greeted him with a reserve appropriate to his station, but his coolness faded in response to the letter, which passed muster, thank God. Auberon forced himself to accept a sherry and sit in one of the plush leather chairs set in front of a roaring fire, to discuss the progress of the peace talks, and the power the Americans would now wield in the world after winning the war. 'Well, not quite, old chap,' Auberon said, gripping his sherry glass too tightly. 'I rather feel the plethora of Continental and Empire dead had something to do with it.'

His remark was received in frosty silence. Auberon reined himself in, remarking on the fineness of the artwork that hung about the wood-panelled office, and the excellent eye the manager must have. He checked his watch, drained his glass, placed it on the table. 'Regretfully, I have a ship to board once I have attended to my father's business,' he murmured. 'I am under orders from my father, you understand.' The manager smiled sympathetically. 'Ah yes, I know of Lord Brampton's impatience.' They laughed, man to man.

Auberon surreptitiously wiped his hand. He was sweating with tension. They shook hands at the door, and the manager called into the anteroom, 'De Vries, escort Lord Brampton's son, if you please.'

De Vries led him down wide marble steps, down and down. They reached a barred walkway. De Vries unlocked the gate and locked it behind him. The keys were attached by a chain to his belt. There were many and they clinked when he moved. The walls were white-tiled and reflected the gas lighting. They reached a heavy steel door. De Vries unlocked this, and came into the safety-deposit vault with Auberon, locking the door behind them.

He noted the number on the letter of authorisation that Auberon held out to him, his hand shaking. De Vries looked at him closely. Auberon shrugged. 'Forgive, too many shells.' De Vries nodded. 'I understand.' It was clear that he did.

He unlocked the locker, and drew out a black metal box. Auberon expected that the manager would appear at any moment, having somehow rethought the validity of the letter. Auberon felt sorry for him, momentarily, for his father would not let this lie. De Vries was opening the box. He stood back. 'You understand that your letter does not authorise you to remove anything? It merely states that you have access to peruse.'

Richard had explained that it would be easier to gain access to the box in this way. Auberon smiled, drew out his cigarette case. 'Indeed,' he said.

De Vries shook his head at the cigarette case. 'This is not allowed, smoking, that is.'

'Ah.' Auberon rested it on the edge of the table. He leafed through the papers. 'My father asked me to confirm that he had placed a certain document in the file, as I was so close to Rotterdam.' He laughed. 'Well, one is when one has been fighting.'

As he talked he bent over the box, searching for figures, accounts, letters. He found what he needed and took them from the box, holding them up, examining them closely. He nudged his cigarette case with his hip. It spun to the floor at De Vries' feet. The man stooped to reclaim it. Auberon folded the relevant sheets and stuffed them into his pocket, then rifled again amongst the remaining papers before replacing them in the box. De Vries laid the cigarette case on the table, carefully. Auberon stood straight, his hands open, saying helplessly, 'Well, it's not here. It must be in his office. At least we know where to look now.'

He slipped the cigarette case into his pocket. There was a reason for a bulge now. He waited while De Vries relocked the box, the locker, the vault, the barred gate. Auberon counted the steps as he mounted them alongside the clerk. He shook his hand before walking across the shiny marble floor, reaching the revolving doors, exiting into the fresh cold air and the sound of gulls and ships' hooters, feeling as though his legs would give way as he walked towards his ship. Part one completed.

Three days later he was in London, leaving his Pall Mall club for pre-dinner drinks at his father's house, with his uniform smartly pressed and his boots gleaming. In the heel was the compass, still. He walked to Eaton Place. How strange to be here, in peacetime. How strange peace was, full stop. How quiet, how drab, how wonderful.

He was admitted by his father's new butler, Mr Aston, who waited to take his cap, document case and swagger stick. Auberon refused because he would need to leave pretty smartly, and knew all about the need for speed in a retreat. He followed Mr Aston upstairs, passing portraits of his stepmama's ancestors. He touched his pocket. The slight crackle of paper reassured him. He walked along Indian carpets to the drawing room, entering as Mr Aston announced him. His father stood by the roaring fire, a brandy in one hand, a cigar in the other. The munitions industry had done him proud. The wallpaper was cream silk, there were more ancestors on the wall. How many did the woman have, for God's sake? Chippendale furniture was scattered about, just as at Easterleigh Hall.

Auberon bowed to his stepmother who sat, a cocktail in her hand. She sipped. The drink didn't touch her lips. She inclined her head slightly. Auberon stopped a yard from his father, who barked, 'Brandy for my son, Aston.'

Auberon put up his hand. 'No thank you, Aston, I have a train to catch. This is a fleeting visit.'

'Nonsense,' his father said. 'We have much to talk of. You are expected to dine.' The ash on his cigar was as huge and brash as he.

Auberon repeated, 'No, I have no time to dine. I have business to attend to in the north. Stepmama, you might like to leave the room, you too, Aston.'

His father gaped, and the ash fell to the Indian carpet. What was it with the man and his Indian rugs? Was it he, or his stepmama, who was so devoid of imagination that each house had to replicate the other?

Auberon continued, 'Or I'm perfectly happy to discuss this in front of the butler and my mother's replacement.'

His father was bulling up, on to his toes. Auberon had faced far too much to feel even a flicker of the fear he once had. He merely stared straight into his eyes. 'It really would be best,' he said quietly.

It was his father who dropped his gaze first, waving Aston and his wife from the room. Auberon waited until he heard the door close with a click. His father still held his brandy glass, and now took a quick drink. His cigar ash was growing again.

From his document case, Auberon drew out photographs of the letters and accounts he had taken from the deposit box. 'Perhaps you would like to put your glass down, and your cigar. I have papers which will be of interest to you.' He held up the photograph of the letter confirming the sale of cordite to Germany, via agents in Rotterdam, *after* the declaration of war and when Britain was in dire need of it, and then others of the accounts.

He handed them to his father who paled. Sweat broke out on his forehead, his hands shook. Auberon knew all about the symptoms of panic and fear. His father turned and groped for the mantelpiece, placing his glass on it, throwing his cigar on to the flames, staring at the photographs and then into the fire for a moment. Auberon could almost hear his brain working, but there was no way out for this traitor and bastard, thank God.

Auberon said, when his father turned to face him, a degree of arrogance back, 'I have the originals. I will ruin you without a second thought and just as you warned your daughter of the consequences of her actions, I now point out yours.'

'What do you want?' his father said, planting his feet wide apart, his hands behind his back. Auberon had to give him credit for his courage.

'Easterleigh Hall and its estate and farms, Easton and Hawton pits, and my mother's money which is in trust until I am twenty-five. I am twenty-eight. Veronica requires her money, in trust until her marriage. She is married. Miss Wainton left us the money that my mother left her. We require that money. This is to happen within the next two days. Is that agreeable to you?'

There was silence except for the ticking of the French clock on the mantelpiece. It would chime seven in five minutes. His father cleared his throat and nodded, saying, 'You will then hand me the originals.'

'Just two more things,' Auberon said, watching as his father threw the photographs on to the fire. They flared, curled, and died. It was like the war all over again. 'The first is that I know you have recruited an agent to pursue Millie Forbes for the return of your silver and harass the Forbes family. This ceases from today.'

His father took a step forward. 'Outrageous, that little bitch took some of your stepmother's ancestral silver, and don't think the Forbes are uninvolved. That boy has worked against me in the mine, stirring up the unions, and as for that kitchen slut . . .'

Auberon held up his hand. 'Jack protested on behalf of the workers and that was before the war. He has no involvement in this whatsoever. Evie . . . Well, it stops, do you understand? They both deserve peace, the whole family do.' At last his father nodded.

Auberon breathed heavily, because he had thought the Forbes' demand might just push his father beyond the bounds of common sense. 'The second is Miss Wainton. What happened, the truth now? You dismissed her, but did she jump? Did she really?' He took a step closer to his father, his swagger stick in his hand. His father watched that, and only that.

'It was an accident,' he said. 'She made me angry because she argued, for God's sake. I walked from her on to the balcony and she came after me. I had made it quite clear I had finished, quite finished with the whole conversation. She pulled at my arm and I threw her off, and over she went. It was an accident.' His eyes were as though glued to the swagger stick. It was then Auberon realised that his father was frightened. Perhaps he always had been. He thought of his grandfather, bluff, but with big hands and hard eyes, the man who had built the steelworks, the brickworks, the mines. He said, 'Did Grandfather hit you, Father, as you hit me?'

His father dragged his eyes from the swagger stick, and nodded.

Auberon said, 'Do you miss my mother?'

His father swallowed. 'With all my heart. She was a good woman, not a lady like your stepmama, but a doctor's daughter and a good woman. She made me a better man.'

Auberon knew a woman like that. He turned on his heel. His father called after him, 'I'm sorry, Auberon. I'm sorry for it all.'

Auberon reached for the door. 'So am I, Father, but you are quite safe as long as you keep your distance from us, and do nothing to harm us in any way. I have the papers safely where you will never find them. Two days, remember, by which time I will be home. Send a telegram to me at my club in Durham, with your lawyer's confirmation.'

Auberon travelled to Durham, and waited. Once confirmation arrived he drove in his new car to Easterleigh Hall, having heard from Veronica by telegram that morning that flu had arrived in the shape of Roger. He had replied to say that he would be arriving at eleven o'clock. Would Evie produce coffee, as there were things to discuss?

Chapter 17

Easterleigh Hall, a few days later

Evie and Mrs Moore had cleared the end of the table nearest to the door, and Veronica and Richard sat there, watching the clock. Evie concentrated on preparing luncheon at the other end because hungry stomachs waited for no man, while Mrs Moore collected herbs from the store. They were down to half the patients now, but the flu was spreading so Matron and Sister Newsome feared that the numbers would rise again, as the villagers had need of the hospital. Evie wondered how Roger was today. It seemed, with this flu, that you died quickly, or you lived. Though, true to the pattern of his life, Roger wasn't doing either, he was just comatose, poor bugger. His mother was dead, it seemed, and that was why he'd come to Easterleigh. The Hall was like a flame that drew moths, and her heart ached for the future. What was to become of all these souls?

Just this morning a demobbed soldier and ex-patient, Sid Yoland, had arrived on the kitchen doorstep. The length of his thigh bone had shortened since amputation but the medical board would not remeasure it, and his original pension was still being paid though he deserved more. Richard was receiving letters almost daily, still, asking for help. Veronica called him the pensioners' friend, and he was happy with the title. Now that the war had ended, several such pensioners had found their way back to Easterleigh for advice.

Evie had given Sid hot cocoa because in her opinion that sorted a world of problems, and hoofed Mrs Moore off her stool nearest to the ranges. Si, who had been reading the *Daily Sketch* at the table and getting in everyone's way, had raised his eyebrows. 'Cocoa,' he had scoffed. 'A beer, more like.'

Sid, who had been a private slogging along the wide plank road in Ypres when he'd been hurt, had shaken his head, ducking to sip the hot brew held between white frozen hands. 'By, lass, this is the best.'

Annie had notified Ron, as Richard was checking the accounts, and he'd collected Sid and taken him through to his small office, calling back, 'Chocolate for visitors only, is it then, Evie? Bad show, that.'

She'd grinned, but Simon hadn't. 'It's all right for those who sat out the war here, I suppose. It's given them time to get cheeky.'

Evie had reminded him that Old Stan wanted to show him the rose Simon had planted for Bernie, last time he was here, and had some hyacinths for his mam, if he cared to get them to her. He'd left

Mr Harvey's newspaper on the table, hugged Evie, and said into her hair, 'I'll cycle the hyacinths down to Mam. She'll be right pleased.'

Evie had been relieved to see him gone, and then felt guilty because of it. She would make time for him this afternoon.

At eleven sharp, the sound of a car driving into the garage yard was heard in the kitchen. Did Aub come bearing news of their eviction? Could they hope for anything different? What the hell was going on? Veronica gripped her husband's hand. Richard seemed to know something, but not enough to tell them anything, or so he'd just said.

'Then tell us what do you know,' his wife yelled, just as Auberon walked into the kitchen. He had said to prepare coffee for eleven, and eleven it was. Simon had remarked before he left to meet Old Stan, 'Taking orders from the boss again, are you, Evie? They don't have that sort of thing in America.' She was sick to death of hearing about America and his friend Den, and had snapped, 'Just go and see Old Stan, he needs you.'

Auberon brought in the cold, in a great wave. He shut the door, and removed his driving cap. His mufti coat was grey and well tailored. 'The Tourer is quite the thing, but damned cold,' he told them. He unwrapped his scarf and rammed it into his cap, just in time, for Veronica was hurling herself into his arms. He hugged her, looking over her shoulder to Evie. He grinned, and Evie smiled, feeling a great warmth. Richard was on his feet, pumping Auberon's hand while Veronica still clung to him. 'Just in time for Christmas, how wonderful, and to have you safe, and what on earth have you been up to?'

Evie bustled to the range, removing the coffee pot from the brick warmer, and filling the cups ready on the tray. Auberon pulled clear of his sister, going to Evie. 'Are you well, Evie? Let me take this.' He picked up the tray and moved to the other end of the table, where the biscuits she had baked after breakfast waited on one of the best china plates. 'You've made enough for Mrs Moore, I hope?'

Evie laughed. 'I'd be in trouble if I hadn't.'

He placed the tray on the table as Veronica sat on her stool, and Richard on his, like schoolchildren waiting for their lessons, Evie thought. Auberon stood, pulling off his gloves and pushing them into his pocket, looking at her. Had his eyes always been so blue? Surely his hair was fairer, and it still flopped over his left eye. He was so thin, drawn, scarred, tired. He spoke, looking only at her, and she remembered that moment in the camp hospital, the feeling of his arms around her, the sense that she was about to learn something. It had brought back the sea, the day she almost drowned. 'Simon is home safely? Jack, Mart and Charlie too?'

The memory was being chased away. She said, 'Thanks to you. They start their first shift back tomorrow. Charlie is helping Simon and Old Stan at the moment. Poor Roger is ill . . .'

'For heaven's sake, darling Aub, sit down and tell why you've called us here.' Veronica was tapping the table with impatience.

He gestured to the stool to his right. 'Please sit, Evie. This is your domain, and you're Commandant.' He turned as the kitchen door opened. 'And here's my old friend Mrs Moore, soon to be Mrs Harvey, I dare say.'

Mrs Moore dropped her herbs, blushed to the roots of her white hair, and flapped her hands at him as he picked up the rosemary and sage. 'Oh, Mr Auberon, I can't believe you're here at last.'

'Please sit,' he said and did the same, settling himself on the stool at the head of the table. 'Easterleigh is safe, and ours. All we need to do is to keep it solvent. I am to run the mines, Father keeps all his other concerns. We have the estate and Home Farm, and the tenant farmers are now our responsibility.'

Solvent, that word rang in the air, along with the burbling of the kettle. Evie sat on her hands as the others looked at one another. 'Solvent? Presumably the rents from the farms and the income from the pits will cover that?' Richard pondered.

'Hardly,' Auberon replied, his eyes on Evie. He called to her, as she started to respond to the kettle which was simmering, but soon to boil. 'Leave it for a moment, Evie, because Jack tells me you have a first-class idea. You wrote him about it.' His smile was gentle. He had a scar across his eyebrow; how close it had come to his eye, Evie thought. Yes, she had an idea but now the moment was here she could hardly speak.

Auberon took a biscuit. 'Come on, dig in, everyone. Let's listen.'

Veronica was looking at her, eagerness in her face. 'Evie, what have you up your sleeve? Come on, out with it.' Mrs Moore nudged her. 'Come on, Evie, or I will. It's a perfect idea. Harry and Ron both think so, so does your Jack.'

Veronica looked taken aback. 'Oh, they know? Why haven't you shared it with us?'

Auberon sighed. 'Do be quiet, Ver, let the girl speak.' He passed the biscuits to Mrs Moore, who took one, checking the clock as she did so. 'Quickly now, we must get on.'

Evie drew a deep breath. 'My dream has been to run a hotel and Easterleigh Hall will be perfect, and what have we been doing for the last four years if not making things better for people, changing beds, providing food? It would only be a short step to changing our role, once we have restored the house, and after the last patient has gone. Harry said that many of them would return as guests; what's more, they would spread the word, and their families already love it and have often said that they would like to be a patient here themselves. You've heard them, Ver?'

There was a pause. Veronica looked at Richard, and gripped his hand. Auberon was grinning at them all. Veronica said, 'It's perfect, quite perfect. Of course, of course. Perfect.'

It was as though a dam had broken and words rushed around the kitchen, with Auberon pacing, and Veronica at his side. Richard joined them. Evie and Mrs Moore looked at the clock. Finally Evie shouted through her laughter, 'Enough. We have luncheon to prepare, why not take yourselves into the garage yard to see the Tourer, and talk it through even further.' Mrs Moore was dabbing her face with her handkerchief, then she flapped it at them. 'Yes, we need to feed the five thousand.'

Veronica spun round. 'Evie, you are a diamond among women, isn't she, Aub?' She gave him no time to reply but ran on, 'Please, you, and Mrs Moore, must know that you will be the most important of our staff, there will always be a job for you both, and we really need your cooking.'

Evie's laughter died. She felt as though the water of the dam had drenched and frozen her. So. So. Peace was here. Mrs Moore touched her arm, her face also cold, disappointment in every pore of her skin. Veronica stood there, her hand on her brother's arm, looking from Evie to Mrs Moore. 'What? What have I said?'

Auberon had halted on his way to the door and he was watching Evie. Well, let him bloody watch. She drew herself up on to the balls of her feet, as

Jack had always done before one of his bare-fist fights. She said, 'I have money. Captain Neave left me some, as you well know, Lady Veronica. I will stay at Easterleigh Hall, but not as a servant, only as a partner.' She swept her arm towards Mrs Moore. 'Our days in that position were over at the start of this war, surely you can see that, all of you?'

She looked from Auberon, to Veronica, to Richard. They coloured, and avoided her eyes. Evie continued, 'My cooking alone would make me worthy of a partnership, and Mrs Moore too. The downstairs staff have done just as much to make the hospital function as the medical staff, and they have learned that out there, in the big wide world, there are other forms of work. I know that now the war is ended the munitions factories will close, and men will want their jobs back, but men and women won't be prepared to give up their freedom to be servants. If I stay I insist on a partnership. I insist that the staff are treated as staff, not servants. Surely if running this hospital has shown you anything it is that patients, or guests in this case, want the same faces around them. To that end you must encourage loyalty, give the staff some reason to stay. That means an annual share of the profits.'

They were all motionless, looking at the floor, apart from Auberon, who was staring at her, and listening closely. She gripped her hands into fists, knowing she might as well be hung for a sheep as a lamb. 'Things shouldn't go back to the way they were before the war, with the class division written in stone, and if they do, then I wish you well, but I will leave, and I daresay there'll be a load of people along with me. Now, please, Mrs Moore and I have lunch to prepare, so leave the kitchen, Captain Auberon, Lady Veronica and Captain Williams.'

She turned her back on them, her mouth dry. She reached for the oven cloth and checked the state of the stuffed bullocks' hearts. One day good food would be plentiful again, but not yet. She heard them leave, felt Mrs Moore's hand on her shoulder, and only then did she smile, ruefully, and lay her head on Mrs Moore's shoulder. 'I thought better of them,' she murmured.

Mrs Moore held her close, patting her. 'They're learning. Let's see what happens, bonny lass. Remember that Mr Auberon has been through a great deal like everyone else, and from the look of him is bone bloody weary. He's been running around like a blue-arsed fly just recently, and has achieved much. Trust him. I do, now.'

Luncheon was served. It was vegetable soup, removed by stuffed bullock's heart, removed by rhubarb crumble with custard. The Bramptons ate in Lady Veronica's suite, as Evie made herself call her mistress now. Were they complaining about the jumped-up cook, she wondered, as the kitchen staff ate with the off-duty nurses, VADs and orderlies in the servants' hall.

In the afternoon Evie walked in the arboretum

with Simon, who had returned in time for luncheon. He had come in the cart, his bicycle laid on top of the sea coal he and his father had collected, as Alec was on the back shift. He asked how the meeting had gone. She told him. There was silence. He held her hand lightly. 'You're right, you know. In America there aren't servants, not like ours. There isn't this hierarchy, you can make it good.'

Evie sighed. 'America? You and Den talked a lot then, in the camp? He's the one whose da is something on Broadway?'

Simon kissed her hand, looking over it and laughing. 'Not his da, his *father*, Evie. Not everyone is from a pit village.'

She wanted to slap him. Instead she said, 'Well I am, and you are, or have you forgotten?'

'I'd like to, because if we want to get on, we have to.' Their pace had increased. She said, 'But people coming to our hotel will want to hear you sing, and want to admire your garden, wherever it is. I spoke for you too this morning, bonny lad.'

Simon was looking at jackdaws high in the branches of the birch and sycamore. 'I know you did, but . . .' He stopped.

She didn't want to know what he meant. She said, 'I hope Jack and Grace have sorted themselves out. They're made for one another.'

Simon kissed her hand again. 'Like us, Evie. Just like us.' He drew her to him and his kiss was hard, his hands on her body urgent, and slowly she felt herself respond. 'It's been such a long time,' he murmured into her neck. 'It's so strange not to be fenced in, surrounded by guards shouting, with beds to make, lines to learn. I just can't get used to it.'

She held him. 'None of us can. Here, we still have a foot in the war with the convalescents arriving daily, but on the other hand, the guns have stopped. It's as though we don't know what to do any more.'

He held her shoulders, stood away and looked at her, really looked. 'You do know, Evie. You always know what to do. Look how you set about them this morning. You're like Jack, so certain, so strong. Some of us aren't, you know. Some of us . . . Oh, I don't know.' He held her close again. She said into his shoulder, 'I'm only certain about some things. Others I just don't understand at all.' She touched his hair, his lovely red hair which she had once loved, but about which she felt little, now.

After dinner had been cleared in the evening, Mrs Moore declared that she was too tired to face a lot of argy-bargy and swept into the central corridor. 'Enjoy your evening with Mr Harvey,' Evie called. Mrs Green had passed along the corridor, on her way from the laundry to the linen store, and smiled wearily above her pile of sheets. Mrs Moore called, 'Have a glass of sherry with us, Mrs Green?'

'Thank you, Mrs Moore.'

Evie watched them walk along the corridor together. Mrs Green's hair was quite white now, and matched Mrs Moore's exactly. What was going to happen to these dear loyal efficient people? Would they stay or go? If they stayed, would they be paid properly, receive shares, be treated with respect?

Lady Veronica had said they would be down at nine, when James was settled and Lady Margaret would have returned from her visit to her parents with Penelope. Evie couldn't understand what it had to do with Lady Margaret, but no doubt it would be explained.

Beef tea was available for any patient who needed it, and as always there were bowls ready should egg custard be requested. Evie wiped over the dresser, and checked that Maudie and Joyce were getting on with the pots and pans. She collected those that were dried and polished, and rehung them above the deal table. The furnace was gurgling quietly. At eight forty-five she released the scullery maids from their duties and they headed into the servants' hall. Maudie muttered, 'Can't get used to sitting there with no knitting on the go. I dream about balaclavas and ruddy khaki socks.'

At nine sharp Captain Auberon, Lady Veronica and Captain Richard entered the kitchen. Captain Auberon carried a tray with brandy goblets and a decanter. He set these on the table. Evie said, 'Someone about to faint?'

At last they met her eyes, at last Veronica laughed.

Lady Margaret came along the central corridor and entered, closing the door, the chill clinging to her, a few snowflakes caught on her hat, and in the black fur collar of her coat. She had moved into one of the estate cottages when half the VADs left last week. Marion Walters, her new housemaid, had in fact moved her in, while she was with her parents. She was rubbing her hands. 'I received your letter, Auberon, and have given the matter thought. Heavens, I only arrived back an hour ago; thankfully the cottage had been warmed through by Walters.'

Veronica pointed to a stool. 'So lovely to see you, Margaret. As you know, we're here to discuss the hotel that Evie has suggested. You did say after the brouhaha with Father that if there was a rescue mission you would like to participate. Well, this is it, Margaret.'

Lady Margaret was wrenching off her black leather gloves with her teeth. It made her look even more like a horse. Evie stared, fascinated, then saw that Auberon was doing the same, and probably making the same comparison. For a moment their eyes met, and the laughter almost screeched out of his, as she knew it did from hers. She looked away, and down at the table, listening as Lady Veronica outlined the idea of the hotel, and the conditions as laid down by Evie.

There was a pause. Evie looked from one to another, refusing to be cowed. Lady Veronica ended by saying, 'I think we each need to say what we feel, honestly and briefly. Aub, would you begin?'

'In a moment, let's pour the brandy first. I need

a tot if no one else does. There should no longer be shells popping off every five minutes, but it feels as though there might be.' Auberon poured. They all watched as though he was creating a masterpiece. The kettle burbled on the range, some damp coal hissed in the furnace. He handed out the brandy glasses. Evie saw the scars on his hands, the gouge across three fingers. Shrapnel, which had cut to the bone?

He said, lifting his glass and studying the amber liquid, swirling it within the glass, 'I applaud Evie's ideas and apologise without reservation for my reaction. It's strange how you leave one situation and arrive in another, one so different that it defies belief and changes, fundamentally, everything one has been brought up to adhere to. I refer, of course, to the war. However, at this point I pause, because you and I, Ver, were brought up by Mother and Wainey to respect others as people. I had forgotten that, but in war I found it again, thanks, primarily, to yet another member of the Forbes family. At the outbreak of peace one returns to the old world, and assumes the old attitudes all too easily. Forgive me, Evie. I think your idea of shares is inspired and I accept with eagerness a partnership with you, Mrs Moore, Uncle Tom Cobley and all. My name is Auberon, I do not require Mr, just to be quite clear.' He raised his glass to her.

Richard looked from him to his wife. 'Your turn, Ver.'

She gripped his hand. 'Aub's thoughts are ours entirely, aren't they, Richard? Nothing changes, we are as we were, friends, and now partners, and I couldn't be happier, or more excited.' She and Richard raised their glasses, grinning.

Lady Margaret was running her finger around the edge of her glass, her colour high. Perhaps she should remove her coat, Evie thought, and suggested as much.

Lady Margaret declined, and turned to Veronica. 'I know that you and I have always held different opinions regarding the ability of the lower orders, Veronica. You and Evie followed Sylvia Pankhurst's universal suffrage ideals, while I supported Christabel and Emmeline's more selective and realistic policies. I concur with their thoughts and feel that only those of certain breeding, means and education can handle information and behave with intelligence in positions of authority. If you all cast your mind back to February of this year you will remember that the vote was awarded to women over thirty, and those who were property owners, a clear indication that this situation is recognised and supported by our government. There is sense to the old order. In our society, you and I, dearest Veronica, have the education to guide those less able. I am fond of Evie, as you know my dear.' She smiled at Evie. 'Indeed, my late husband enjoyed the many hours he spent with you, in here, laughing and joking, leaving me alone, to my own devices.'

She was smoothing her gloves now. Evie watched, remembering Major Granville who would remove his mask and just sit and talk, because his lower jaw and tongue were whole, and his face, though an initial shock, was something that became unremarkable. She hadn't known that Lady Margaret was lonely, and missed his company. Lady Margaret continued, 'But I can only be involved in something which I respect.'

There was silence. Auberon said eventually, 'So you vote against a partnership, even though Evie took over as commandant to make life easier for Veronica, and has most ably fulfilled that role?'

'At the present time, yes, I do. During extraordinary circumstances, ordinary people rise to the occasion, but cannot sustain their role. We need to restore the traditional order in our efforts to return to normality,' Lady Margaret insisted, stabbing the table with her forefinger.

Evie concentrated on the kettle. The furnace was no longer hissing. It would need more coal soon. The armchair beside it looked appealing. It would ease her backache, or that of the incoming cook who would take her place, but she'd have to turf off the dogs. She half smiled and looked around at the spotless cupboards, then up at the gleaming copper pans, all the result of hard work by the scullery and kitchen maids. They had learned their skills and carried them out, flawlessly, above and beyond the call of duty, ordinary people in extraordinary circumstances be damned. Her fury was building.

She breathed deeply, concentrating on this room, her hub, her powerhouse. Everything was so much brighter now that it was electrified. The new cook would approve, but how many would stay to help her in her work? What of the upper servants, those dear loyal souls? She pushed her glass towards the centre of the table, and began to stand. Auberon was waving her down. She remained standing.

'No, I . . .'

Auberon looked at her, his eyes so blue, so serious. 'Trust me. Please, sit, just for a moment, Evie.' She did so, as he glanced at Veronica and Richard. They nodded. He said, 'Thank you for your honesty, Margaret, and we are sorry that you won't be part of our new adventure, and wish you well. You are of course welcome to remain in the cottage until you have found other accommodation.'

That was all. It was enough. Lady Margaret flushed even deeper, her breath coming in short gasps. She stood, confused. Veronica went to her, slipped her arm through hers and led her from the kitchen, down the central corridor, stopping to talk to Mrs Green who smiled a smile that the Cheshire cat would envy. Then they disappeared up the stairs to the great hall.

Auberon lifted his glass to Evie and Richard. 'Now let's sort out the contract, and settle on plans. Ron and Harry want to be part of this, and agree totally with the co-operative idea, especially as it is likely that times will become hard, and jobs scarce for even our able-bodied lads returning to "a land fit for heroes". We need to make sure that we continue to do our bit.'

Evie sipped her brandy, watching Auberon, his face alive, warm, beautiful. Yes, she'd trust him, to the ends of the earth and back again.

Jack waited outside Grace's house, watching the gas lighting in her bedroom flutter. It seemed that he had stood here so often, his heart breaking. He screwed up his cap, the cold bitter on his head but he had to have something to do with his hands. He wore the greatcoat he could have handed over at the demob centre in return for a couple of quid, but it was a good coat, and would come in useful. He, Mart and Charlie had hung about until their de-mob suits were ready, though they had to keep their uniforms, as they were still on the Z reserve.

He moved from foot to foot as the breeze got up. Snow was falling, but lightly. They said every snow-flake had a different pattern. How could that be? Who was it who'd told him that? Ah yes, Tommy Evans, as the mud sucked at their boots, and over their boots to their puttees, one foot in front of the other. One foot. One step. Another. Another. Bugger fatigue. Keep walking, one foot. One foot. Towards the Menin Gate, the stink of stagnant water, the broken teeth of the buildings, the slip slide of the limbers with their guns on the planked Ypres road.

He remembered the feel of the rope when they'd all had to pitch in to haul one of the bloody things out of the mud.

Must have been one hundred men there, their packs dragging at their backs, the rope as muddy as hell, their hands slipping on it, burning off the skin, their boots slipping as they hauled, hauled, bloody hauled. They'd got it back on the road, the sky alight with the flashes of field guns, the sounds pounding and racketing around their heads. Yes, they'd got it back, Charlie in front, Mart and Aub behind, while all the other officers stood and shouted orders.

Where was Tommy now? Ah, yes, he could picture the back of the aid station they'd taken him to after a sniper had got him on a wiring party. They hadn't expected him to die, but it was shock, the orderly said. They'd both written to his mam.

He flicked his cigarette to the ground now, drew a deep breath. He was alone and he missed them; all of them, every minute of every day, because they were his marras and he didn't have any focus now, any real reason for . . . He walked through the front gate. It more than squeaked, it screamed. He reached the porch, and the front door opened. She was there, she was his, and now his arms were round her, but still he felt alone, because no one but his marras knew what he felt, what he dreamed, what he remembered, what he smelled.

He cried then, great wracking sobs, because he

loved this woman who had said she would live with him. She said, 'I know what it's like. I've felt it, I've nursed it, I know what it's like and it will get better.'

She led him up the stairs because Edward was out, having decided that he must sit with a parishioner. She led him into the bedroom whose light he had stood and watched so often. Now he saw that the wallpaper had roses, the counterpane was pink. She was in her dressing gown. She removed his coat and let it drop on the floor. She undid his shirt, and now he was frantically helping, and she allowed her gown to fall at her feet and they fell on the bed and at last they were together, and she was as soft and wonderful under his rough and scarred hands as he had thought she would be.

Afterwards he slept, and though he dreamed it was of sunshine, and the cedar tree, the older tree to begin with, but then his old friend the darkness slunk and then roared into his world as it always did. When he woke he lay looking at the sun streaming through the windows. He had slept the night through, and in his mind had been the young cedar tree, which would grow and become strong, as he would, again.

Later that morning Jack was in Evie's kitchen, telling her of Grace's decision that after the trial run of last night, the parsonage was large enough to cope with Tim and Jack, and that though there was no need of a tin bath, his back would still have to be scrubbed.

Evie held up her hand. 'Stop, go no further. I am far too innocent.'

He perched on the edge of the table and turned when Grace hurried in, her VAD uniform as pristine as always. 'Evie, Roger's asking for you. He's not going to make it. Will you come? He's most insistent. Hold a handkerchief to your face, though what good that will do, I don't know. We're going down like flies.' She blew a kiss to Jack and spun out again. Jack grinned after her and Evie raised an eyebrow, holding up her hand again. 'No, not a word, I don't want to know.'

She hurried after Grace, waved to one of the two remaining orderlies, and asked after Matron, who had gone down yesterday with the flu. Grace muttered, 'She's seen it off. Well, would you stand against her?' It didn't require an answer.

Evie took one of the sphagnum moss sachets from the basket outside the conservatory. It had been sprayed with disinfectant. She held it to her face as she entered. All the drapes were down and the furnace was roaring to keep the temperature up in this glass building. Outside the snow lay at least three inches on the ground. She hoped Simon had his jerkin on, even though he was in the warmth of the glasshouses nurturing the overwintering plants.

Roger was nearest the door, his colour grey. His hair had turned quite white. She sat beside him, pity moving her, for he had no one else to care or visit.

'How are you, Roger?' she said, her voice low to keep the mood calm and quiet for the other patients.

'Bloody dying, you daft cow.' He opened his eyes briefly, his laugh turning into a cough. She smiled. She'd never known him to joke before, and it was a bit bloody late. She didn't share that thought. He said, 'It's about that Millie, you know. I did her a bad turn, and she's gone on to better things, but there's still the boy.'

Evie tensed, because this man had threatened he would take the boy from Jack. She said, 'Tim's happy with my mam and da, and Jack. You have no claim. You're not on the birth certifi—'

'Hush your noise, Evie. You know as well as I do that I'm bloody dying, haven't I just said so.' He coughed again. Evie held the moss sachet tighter to her face. 'I've money, that's all. Me pay while I was a POW, me pay while I was valet, and this, that and the other.' He coughed again, and she could almost feel the pain it caused him and didn't know what this, that and the other entailed. Please God, not a deathbed confession. He started again. 'I've money. I wrote a will. It's in my pack. We all did it. It's for him. Tell him it's from his dad. It's good to know you were loved by your real dad, wish I had been. Or don't tell him. You can decide, or your Jack. Matron knows the details.' His voice was fading, his eyes closing. Evie held his hand; it was just skin and bone, poor wee man. She wanted to ask what name to use on the headstone, Roger or Francis Smith, but how could you shove that in a dying man's face? He coughed, opened his eyes, gave a funny breath, long, outgoing. Gracie touched her shoulder. 'He's gone, Evie. I'm glad he wasn't alone. It was good of you to be with him, after all he's done.'

Evie sat for a moment, looking at him. 'No, it was nothing. Life makes us what we are.'

Chapter 18

Easterleigh Hall, 24th December 1918

The tree was up in the great hall but not decorated. Work had stopped for Roger's funeral, conducted by Edward. The church was full, not out of affection but because of sadness for one so disliked. They buried him using the name Francis Smith, which seemed only right. Evie sat in the front with her mam and da, Tim clutching Mam's hand. It had been decided that he should not be told who his real father was at this time, especially after the departure of his mother, whom he still expected to return at any minute.

Simon spoke about Roger from the lectern. 'He was an excellent orderly, and showed me the tricks of the trade while we were incarcerated in the Offizier Gefangenenlager. He was interested in butterflies, and we discussed many times the plants and bushes that gave them succour. Somehow we became friends, perhaps because we were the ones left behind: I because I gave up my place for another, he because he felt the price to pay for an enlisted man if recaptured was too high.'

Tim was wriggling. Jack stroked the boy's head with something close to fury in his face. Evie stared at him. Was he angry because Roger had left money? Now Edward was speaking, and Simon was entering the pew, reaching for her hand. 'Was that all right?' he whispered. 'Of course,' she replied, but something was wrong. She looked towards Veronica and saw that Auberon, standing next to Charlie and Mart, was thin-lipped; in fact they all were. There was no funeral tea, because it was Christmas Eve and yet more staff had gone down with influenza, and more patients had arrived, to be housed in the huts. Dr Nicholls had sent for extra nurses in order to cope.

Simon helped to decorate the tree, along with Jack, Charlie and Mart, before going home to spend the night in his parents' house. They would all be here for lunch tomorrow but it would be in the servants' hall, because Mrs Moore wasn't having Mr Harvey messing about trying to squeeze tables into the ward as Mr Auberon had insisted in 1914; not with his back. The patients would be served first, and then it would be the turn of the servants, so they could put their feet up, or use them to dance. It would be a cold supper for those who felt like it.

Christmas Day dawned deep and crisp and even, with snow a foot deep, and the wind blowing it into drifts against any wall or tree it could find. Evie took a moment to go out, wrapped in her comfortable threadbare coat given to her years ago by Grace, and with a shawl around her head. She stood beneath the shelter of the young cedar tree. 'Keep warm, keep safe,' she murmured, the wind beating and battering its branches. Auberon spoke from behind her. 'Let's hope it has as gallant a heart as its predecessor.'

His head just cleared a branch. 'It was good of Harry and Ron to organise this for you.'

She leaned back against the trunk, her arms crossed against the cold. 'It wasn't for me, really. It was for everyone. It has become a talisman, I think.'

Auberon looked skyward. Some snowflakes fell through the branches to lie on his lashes, cheeks and hair. He wore his khaki greatcoat, stained, worn but a familiar part of him now. 'It was for us, a talisman I mean. But they did it for you, they told me. They hold you in high esteem. You seemed to be everywhere, making sure that everyone had all they could possibly need.' He looked at her now. 'What about you, Evie Forbes? Have you everything you could possibly need?'

In the darkness of the tree she remembered the camp hospital, the feel of his arms around her, the war stench of his coat, his eyes, the safety. She pushed herself free of the trunk, straightened her shoulders. 'Yes, Simon is home and we're going to make a wonderful hotel here, Aub, thanks to you. And I have to thank you too for bringing everyone home safely.' She reached out her hand. It was frozen from clutching her shawl. He took it, kissed it. 'I forgot my gloves also, Evie, so we're both too cold for our own good. We should return to the warmth, don't you think?'

He waved her before him. They walked together across the lawn, creating new footprints, the snow squeaking as they did so. She hurried across the gravel towards the kitchen. He went up the steps, waiting at the top, watching her, hoping his love hadn't shown, nor his despair. But all he wanted was her happiness, he reminded himself, and that was what she had now. It was time he moved on.

On Boxing Day morning Auberon called into the parsonage. He had walked in the snow, now at least eighteen inches thick, and his trousers were saturated above his boots, and bloody freezing. Charlie had arrived last night and was staying with Jack and Grace, and Mart had obviously been here a while as he was warm and dry. They were all gathered around the kitchen table. Grace had tea on the go and said, 'I know you wanted the meeting here, Aub, away from the chaos of the Hall with all the flu cases, but I hope you don't mind the kitchen. It's the warmest room in the house.' She led him through the hall into the gas-lit kitchen.

Auberon sat on the cushioned carver chair at the head of the table, with Jack at the other end. 'Someone should tell Evie she needs cushions on the kitchen stools,' he said. They looked at one another, then at him, ironic pity on their faces. Grace said, 'It would be like telling Matron that perhaps she needs to improve her patient care, so we'll leave you to charge those particular guns, Aub. We'll patch you up afterwards.'

Auberon laughed. 'Perhaps I'll not mention the cushions, but I need to talk to you all seriously now.' He stirred his tea, but why? There was no sugar. There was a pot of honey though, and Jack pushed this towards him. It was Easterleigh Hall's and the label was impressive, with a pen and ink drawing of the cedar tree, the old one. The new one would grow into its likeness, with Evic guarding its progress. He stopped himself. Enough of Evie, her future in the hotel was assured.

He took a spoonful of honey and held it over the tea, watching it run from the spoon. As it did so he said, 'I think it's a lost cause to suggest Jack and Mart leave the pits altogether?'

He checked they were listening. They were, and nodding. 'The rumour mill will have told you by now that Ver, Richard and I own the pits, and I propose that you, Jack, and you, Mart work three days a week at Auld Maud and Hawton, and attend a course the other two days for two years to gain your Certificate of Competence. This means that when Davies at Easton, and Montgomery at Hawton retire, which will be in three years, you can take over the running of a pit each. That should end the endless complaints against the bosses.'

He placed his teaspoon in the saucer and sipped his tea, watching them over the rim. They were looking at one another, dumbfounded. Good, he'd made them speechless at last. He smiled, adding, 'Of course you will be paid throughout, and I will carry the cost of the study. We need people who physically understand the mines here, and you two do, and might I say that you deserve every moment of the success I know you will have, and will create the safest pits in the whole history of the mining industry, and no doubt tread on numerous toes while doing so.' He laughed.

Jack muttered, 'Aye, been under enough falls to read Auld Maud like a bloody book.' But he too was laughing. Grace gripped his hand, her face alight with relief. 'They needed something to focus on, Aub. But you'll know that, with the hotel to build. It'll keep you out of mischief.'

Mart said, 'Hawton would be like a home from bloody home. Same seam line. But I reckon Jack would just make a balls-up on his own at Auld Maud, so we'll stick together there. Be time enough to wear suits and strut off to work when we've got the certificate in our hands. It'll be grand, bonny lad. Bloody grand.' They came to him. Aub stood. 'I'll do my best for you, Aub,' Jack said, pumping his hand.

'I know you will, Jacko.' Mart was there too, taking over the pumping. 'You'll have the best and safest bloody couple of pits in the region, bonny lad, and no doubt be looking over my shoulder every step of the way,' he told Auberon.

They resumed their seats. Charlie was staring into his cup, as though he could see Australia. Auberon said, 'Now, young Charlie. It seems to me that your idea of organising shooting parties for the hotel guests is a very good one. Of course, unlike your wartime activities you will not be wearing a sniper's badge, but it will be up to you and our gamekeeper, Thomas, to protect and increase the numbers of our pheasant, partridge and every other damn game bird under the sun. You will stay in the under-gardeners' house, if that suits you, and that will give these two a bit of time alone.'

It suited Charlie very well, and as always he was the one who put into words what the others found they could not. He said, 'You've saved us again, Auberon. It's going to get hard with the soldiers coming home, and the world in chaos. Work will be scarce. But now, we'll live to see many beautiful days together. All of us together.' He came to the head of the table, his hand out, pumping Auberon's and then hugging him. The others watched and Auberon heard a lot of coughing going on and smiled to himself, his own heart full. He hugged Charlie back, feeling his ribs. 'You need just a bit more feeding up, lad. Make sure you make a friend of Evie, not to mention Mrs Moore.'

Charlie released him finally, returning to his seat. Grace poured more tea. Charlie finished his in two gulps. 'Bit small, these cups, Gracie.'

'Come on, I'll give you a refill.' She did so, as

Charlie watched, and then asked, 'But what about Simon? Is he going to be head gardener when Old Stan goes?'

There was a general shifting, and Jack said, 'What more can he want? He has my sister's love, and the hotel; the gardens to tend, and the guests to entertain. Old Stan'll be around for a while yet. It would kill him to have to leave, especially now his son and grandson are six foot under.'

Auberon spooned honey into his refreshed tea. 'I feel just that, Jack. There really is nothing more I can offer a man with so much.'

Grace was pushing ginger biscuits towards him, watching him closely, but she said nothing. A minute passed. He could think of nothing to say, no way to leave. Jack leaned forward. 'Evie sent these when she heard that you had asked for a meeting. Rustled 'em up in no time. She knows they're your favourite. Have one, or I'll tell her you turned your nose up.'

He smiled then, and took one, placing it on his plate. Grace said, 'What of you, Auberon? Will you help with the renovation of Easterleigh Hall when the last patients leave?'

Auberon had known this would come, and checked his watch. 'Good heavens, is that the time?'

He snatched up the biscuit, 'I'll eat it as I go.' He looked around the table; Charlie with colour in his cheeks, just a bit, Mart eager now to face the future, Grace staring, a puzzled look on her face. Jack was hot on his heels as he hurried to the front door, helping him on with his coat, heaving himself into his own. Aub put the biscuit in his pocket and helped settle Jack's coat on his shoulders. 'There's no need, Jack. Stay in the warm.'

'I need some air.' Jack's tone was final. In a way, Auberon was glad. He opened the door and the cold gushed in. He turned. Grace, Charlie and Mart were in the hall. 'See you tomorrow, boss,' called Mart.

Aub looked for a long moment, then nodded and set off down the path, with Jack as his shadow. The wind was biting into them, carrying more snow, he didn't doubt. The smell of sulphur from the slag heap hung heavy; the smoke was more like steam. Auberon looked around, as though drinking it in. 'Home from bloody home,' he murmured. 'You take care of your family, eh Jack. Make a good life for yourself, now it's all over.' Jack pulled him round. 'What's going on, Aub?'

Auberon was dragging on his gloves. 'I'm going away, back to the Somme.'

Jack stared, then said very quietly, 'In search of tranquillity? It's a bloody ruin, man.'

'Not all of it, only along the front line. The river remains, and it's long, and full of carp. There are villages to the east with *estaminets*. Maybe I'll find something, or someone, there.'

'For how long?'

'Ah, Jacko, how long is a piece of string?' Auberon smiled, but it was a strained, weary, sad smile.

Jack gripped his arm. 'But you're our marra, my

marra. We're home. You're home. I need you. I'll miss you, for God's sake. You're part of what I fought for.'

Auberon couldn't look at this man whom he respected above all others, who he felt was like the other half of him. 'You're my marra, just know that, always. I understand, now, exactly what that means.'

Veronica stood beside Auberon on the bottom step, looking down the drive. Richard was on Auberon's other side. No Ted and his rumble-tumble taxi, as James called it. 'You've everything you need, darling Aub?' she asked, determined that she would not cry. He was safe, the war was over, he was just going on a journey. But why, she wanted to scream.

He kicked at his kitbag. 'It got me through the war, it'll get me through the peace.' There had been no snow last night after all, but the cold was bitter. 'Do go inside, Ver. No need to catch a chill with this influenza in full flood.' He drew out his cigarette case, offered it to Richard, his eyes on the cedar tree now. Snow decorated its branches. 'It looks as though it belongs on the Christmas cake Evie baked,' Veronica murmured.

He patted the end of his cigarette on the case, which he slipped back into his pocket, lit his cigarette and drew deeply, watching the smoke he exhaled as it drifted straight up. They all watched it. Was he working out a sniper's sighting? Veronica heard him at night, in the room next to hers. Sometimes he shouted, sometimes screamed. Grace said that Jack did too. Well, it was no more than they had been living with at Easterleigh Hall for such a long time. 'Stay,' she said. 'Here, where you are loved.'

'It will grow,' he said, flicking his hand towards the tree. 'Give it time.'

She clung to his arm. 'Aub, you sound as though it's for ever. Please, I love you, we all love you. Come home to us.'

He patted her hand, his eyes still on the tree. 'You can write through my bank. They'll know where I am as I send for money. I just need some time, Ver. It's been so long since I've been alone, just to think, to find a way . . .'

'Let him go, darling. I know what he means.' Richard put his arm around Aub's shoulders. 'Come back, old lad.'

Ted's taxi was turning into the drive. They watched as it stalled between the gateposts and laughed gently as Ted got out, slammed the door shut and cranked the engine. They could imagine the language.

Behind them the doors opened. Evie came to them, a hamper in her arms. 'If you must go, Aub, you will take some remnants of Christmas, and if I find the cake in crumbs on the drive as a feast for the birds, I will hunt you down, with another piece. Is that quite clear?'

Veronica laughed as Auberon threw his cigarette on to the snow-covered drive and took the hamper, placing it on top of his kitbag. 'I wouldn't dare,' he said.

Evie was shivering. 'By, it's a cold day for you to be going off fishing, Aub. I think I'd prefer a fire and a scone, myself.'

She stood there rubbing her arms, her hessian apron flour-dusted, her cheeks red from the range. Veronica brushed some flour from her cheek. 'Quite,' she agreed.

Ted had at last restarted the car and all four of them watched as the wheels skidded on the snow, and then gripped, coming towards them. Auberon carried the kitbag and hamper down on to the drive. Veronica wanted the engine to stall again and never restart. She felt Evie's hand in hers, squeezing, then they both hurried down the steps to stand with him. Ted getting nearer. Evie stood in front of Auberon now, looking up at him. 'You take care, bonny lad. We'll be here when you return, unchanged, the hotel on its way. It had better not be for too long, you hear? Our Jack says you're one of his, and they need you back. Be safe, be lucky.'

Veronica saw that her eyes were full, as her own were. Auberon just nodded, then said, 'Look after yourself and Simon. You have your dream, live it. Be happy, for you deserve every second.'

They heard Mrs Moore then, shouting from the entrance to the stable yard, 'There are vegetables shrivelling as you three loiter, let the pair of them be, lass, or you'll end up being put in the boot with the kitbag.'

Evie waited a moment, then reached up and

touched Auberon's cheek for a second, and rushed away. Veronica watched her, and then her brother, as Evie disappeared from view. She had never forgotten the diary entry and it was only now that she knew why he was leaving, and her heart broke for Auberon, but what could she say?

Ted chugged up, turning a circle, keeping the engine running as he clambered out. He was even more grumpy than usual, the black shiny cap which he insisted on wearing when he came to the big house slipping to one side. He was murmuring under his breath, 'Bloody old bag, that's what she is, got no manners, not one.' He meant his car.

He carried the hamper to the boot. His cap slipped right off, into the snow. 'Bloody bloody cap . . .' Veronica, Richard and Auberon exchanged a laugh, a quiet one. 'Look after everyone,' Auberon told Veronica, and held her.

She said into his coat, 'You know very well who does all the looking after in this establishment, a monstrous regiment of one.'

He smiled down at her. 'Then look after her, and everyone else will be all right.'

He shook Richard's hand. Richard said, 'We'll miss you, old chap. Really we will.'

Suddenly the steps were crowded with nurses, VADs, orderlies, Dr Nicholls, Matron, and staff who used to be called servants, Veronica said to herself, glad of the change. They were calling, 'God speed,' 'Come back to us,' 'Goodbye, good luck.' There was one last wave from Auberon, and then he was in the car, and Ted was chugging off towards the road. Veronica looked towards the stable yard. There were all the kitchen staff with Mrs Moore, Evie and Simon, waving with tea towels. Veronica wanted to strangle Simon with one of them, because he had the happiness that her brother deserved.

Chapter 19

Easterleigh Hall, 1919

As January turned to February, many of the wounded had now recovered enough to be moved to convalescent homes in their own areas, or to be discharged completely. Millie had sent a card from America for Tim's eighth birthday, saying that she and Heine were well and would see him again one day. In the meantime he was to be a good boy for Jack. Grace sat next to him on Susan and Bob Forbes' sofa after they'd had tea and said to Tim, 'Sometimes something happens in a life and a person has to go away. It doesn't mean she doesn't love you.'

Tim looked from her to Susan Forbes, who had been there, always. He held up the drawing he had done of one of Grandad's pigeons. 'It's a belter, isn't it, Granny? Mam's all right. She'll be back if she wants. She always does what she wants, doesn't she?'

Influenza was still raging world-wide, and that included Easterleigh Hall, where it was taking lives. Returning POWs were arriving, skeletal, with injuries often resembling those of miners, which was what many of them had been in the hands of the Germans. Throughout the country there was discontent at the slowness of demobilisation. Yet again Evie blessed Auberon and Richard for bringing their men home so quickly, but Richard wouldn't want her thanks again as he and Veronica suffered with influenza in their suite of rooms. Angela Dore kept James well away in her own quarters, which were now in the cottage that Lady Margaret had vacated.

Matron insisted at the morning meeting around the kitchen table that today, 10th February and her birthday, was the day on which as many VADs as possible must be given notice of release, and nurses too, because they were also getting demobilisation fever, and she had enough to deal with without a load of hysterical females cluttering up the place.

She added, 'I, however, will remain until the end, because I feel that the huts erected beyond the formal gardens could still be used for anyone in need of convalescence, when you start considering accommodation for your hotel clientele.'

Evie looked up from her note-taking, Ron too. 'Go on,' she encouraged. Matron's look made it clear that she had every intention of so doing. 'Well, it's common sense, isn't it? Our wounded are not just going to disappear from the earth in a puff of smoke. They will exist until the day they die, with injuries that will change their lives. We should be here to look after them. Young Harry feels his father's fund-raising group would be prepared to provide money for their care, and indeed, their families, should they wish to come too. These people may come for holidays, for help with false limbs, for whatever is needed, or for longer stays. I hope that whoever else cares to be involved will remain here, at Easterleigh, in that rather nice little cottage which is at present almost derelict. Dr Nicholls has agreed that there is a need, and has intimated he is happy to be involved, as has Sister Newsome. Grace will be happy to join us, on a day-to-day basis.'

Evie and Ron looked at one another. Would Dr Nicholls dare not to be happy to be involved? He was sitting opposite Evie, looking older than his sixty years. His shirts, waistcoats and jackets did up with no difficulty now, so hard had he worked, so little sugar had he downed in these days of rationing. He sighed, nodded and then smiled. 'I think it's a quite wonderful idea. The war is over, but its consequences remain.'

Ron dug his finger into Evie's thigh. She nodded. He said, 'I think, don't you, Evie, that this is an excellent idea, especially if Harry's father will handle the economics. Where is Harry?'

Mrs Moore spoke from the end of the table. 'He's taken Simon out to the hives. He's worried about the cold, and they've lugged some straw to put around them as insulation.' She had been strangely quiet, and now Evie saw that her eyes were over-bright, and sweat beaded her cheeks and forehead.

Matron saw it too, and pointed to the door. 'To bed, now. Evie, rum.'

It was the only cure that seemed to do any good. No one knew how else to deal with this virulent strain, but as Dr Nicholls had said more than once, the world was exhausted from more than four years of hell, so had no defence.

Evie nursed Mrs Moore and Mr Harvey herself, for what happened to one, happened to the other; out of love, Evie thought. She tended them both throughout the night, traipsing from one bedroom to the other, with damp facecloths and cool water. They survived but then, as Mr Harvey said, they'd had the best food that Easterleigh Hall could offer.

Richard had hidden more than half Brampton's wine and spirits before Lord Brampton's chauffeur came to collect the contents of the cellar. He had announced the fact only at the end of the war, when Matron and Dr Nicholls had decreed that rum was the answer to influenza. Veronica had actually slapped him, but across his false arm, bemoaning all the times when a bit of wine would have perked up a casserole enormously. Evie had then slapped her for demeaning her cooking. Richard had redeemed himself by uncorking a bottle of burgundy and sharing it between the four of them, because of course Simon was included.

Mrs Moore and Mr Harvey rallied out of danger within the week, and Simon returned to Easterleigh Hall after caring for his parents, who had gone down with it. They had also recovered. Veronica and Richard also recovered. Veronica appeared in the kitchen at the end of February, pale but determined. 'We need to complete our plans, Evie,' she said, taking her place at the morning meeting. This time it was Simon who was glassy-eyed and sweating as he came in from checking the hives with Harry.

Evie led him to her bed up in the attic, and nursed him day and night. She sat beside him on the old attic chair, making him sip water, or rum, calling Matron from her room along the corridor at two o'clock one morning, when he was delirious, calling for Denny, his American friend, singing, then laughing. Together they stripped him, and bathed the fever down, and down, and down, until with the dawn he was calm, and finally slept. Sitting by him as the day grew cold and bright, Evie realised that it was the first time she had heard him laugh, the first time he had sung with joy since his return. She understood, now, that Denny had become his marra.

Simon was slow to recover, and Evie handed much of the cooking to Annie and her mam, who came from the village to stay at the Hall. Mrs Moore was allowed in the kitchen only to make the scones for tea until she was back to full strength. This was Mrs Green's job, but Mrs Green was ill, and failing to thrive. When Simon became more aware on the sixth day Evie propped him up on pillows, and knitted a navy blue scarf for him, or read to him from Mr

Harvey's *Daily Sketch*. She had tried Richard's *Times* but it had irritated Simon.

On the eighth day Evie had read the newspaper to him, cover to cover, and started a pullover for Tim, in green. Outside the room the clock chimed midday. She was needed downstairs, but Simon protested. The fire was glowing. It would have broken Lord Brampton's heart to have heat in the servants' quarters, now known as the staff attic. The sky was blue, though it was that pale blue which denoted arctic temperatures. Perhaps she could tempt Simon to check on the bees in a few days, he needed fresh air.

She looked at him. 'How are you, bonny lad? Shall we try to get you up? Matron says it's time.' He looked up from the song he was writing. 'Knitting's for old women, Evie.'

She laughed. 'No it isn't, it's what we had to do in the war and I don't like to sit and do nothing.'

'Well, you remind me of my mam, sitting there, knit knit knitting.' He was pale, lacklustre, his hair no longer shone. She took his hand. 'I love you.'

'Then put down your bloody knitting, and show me.' Flu made people bad-tempered, she knew that, but she still wanted to clip his ear.

She let the knitting drop to the floor, knelt by his bed and kissed him. His lips were dry. She stroked his hair, kissed his eyes, his forehead and again his lips. He brought his arms around her, tightly, his mouth opening, his tongue searching, and she wanted to draw back as he grabbed her breast, then ripped down her apron and unbuttoned her uniform blouse. She tried to pull away. He held her with one arm, saying, 'Show me you're not an old woman, show me you're hot-blooded. I love you, I need you.'

She weakened and kissed him fiercely now. This was the man she'd loved, the man she'd waited for, the man . . . She shut down her mind as his hand stroked her skin, but the thought grew. Did she really still love him? His hand was clawing at her skirt now, dragging it up. She tried to pull free. He gripped her tightly. 'You're my lass,' he said. 'Show me you're my lass.' His face was red, his hand was moving on her thigh, up, up, his eyes were shut. 'Show me, let me love you, show me you love me. Let's do it Evie, it's been too long to wait. Others do, come on.'

She felt something like passion stir, some great need, but something was wrong. She wrenched free and stumbled to her feet, looking down at the man who had been her lovely lad. 'No,' she said. 'Let's marry. To have a child without . . . Well, it wouldn't be right. Look at Millie.'

He flung his arm over his eyes as she pulled her skirt straight, 'So what are you saying, Evie Forbes? I'm just another Roger, am I? Where does love come into all of this? I've been patient, haven't I?' She tried to adjust her apron, but her fingers seemed to have a mind of their own and wouldn't co-operate. 'Evie, you're not being fair, you're leaving me out of your life, just like Jack and the others do,' Simon complained.

She stared down at him. 'Not being fair? I've nursed you day and night, you have a hotel to help run, you will have guests to entertain, a garden to create, a partnership that will flourish.'

He lurched up on to an elbow. 'It's your partnership, Evie, not mine. You never asked what I wanted.'

She walked to the window and stared out across the hills to the sea at Fordington. The waves would be crashing, the sea coal would be there for the picking. Wasn't the hotel their dream? She rubbed her forehead. It always had been, hadn't it? What else would bring them security and a chance for him to sing? She couldn't think any more.

She turned, and smiled. 'I think you miss Denny. He's your marra. Can't we try and get hold of him? He might like to come and stay, what do you think?'

Simon turned on his side, away from her. 'He said he'd telegraph by the end of February. Fat liar, he is.'

'It's only the first week of March, bonny lad. He'll contact you, and then we can arrange a visit, if you like.'

There was no answer, and she left. The kitchen needed her. It was easier to cook than to try and see inside someone's head, including her own.

On 10th March Simon received a letter from Denny. He came into the kitchen reading it, his face alight.

As she looked up from her breadmaking Evie recognised that it was the same look that had lit up those blue eyes when he had been with her, before the war. 'He's worked it, his father wants to meet me, give me a chance, on Broadway,' he told her.

Opposite Evie Mrs Moore stopped in her kneading. Evie went on kneading at the same pace, refusing to pound the dough again and again as everything in her screamed for her to do.

Simon came to her, slipping his arm around her. 'It's my chance, Evie. Can you see that? I'll be back in no time, then we can sort out what we do. We could live in America, how would you like that?' It was then that Evie knew that *this* was his dream, not the hotel. She held her hands in the air, the dough sticky on them, and hugged him with her arms alone. 'You must go, of course I see that.'

He left from his parents' house. Evie, Jack, Mart and Charlie came to see him off. He slung his kitbag into the back of the cart and they shook his hand, patted his back and Jack told him to come home soon. Evie just smiled, hugged him tightly, and waved him away. 'He'll be home, bonny lass,' Jack said.

'Aye, he'll see his friend Denny and perhaps realise that his friends are here, and he's not always the outsider,' Charlie said.

Jack and Evie watched the cart disappear down Wenton Street in the lee of the slag heap that was still spewing sulphur, the winding gear of the pit

beyond. Mart said, 'Not still on about that, is he?
He chose . . .' Jack cut across him. 'He'll have a grand
time and get it out of his system and see just what
he's got waiting for him here, a bossy lass with a
bloody good hotel in the making.'

Evie went on looking in the direction that Simon
had gone. She had no idea what she felt.

In April Mrs Moore and Mr Harvey tied the knot,
with Edward Manton officiating. Mrs Moore had
wanted Mrs Green to be her matron of honour but
the influenza had claimed her, to the deep sorrow
of everyone who knew her, so it was Evie who
walked down behind her and Jack, who was giving
Mrs Moore away.

'We're not love's young dream,' Mr Harvey said
at the wedding tea in the marquee which was set
up on the front lawn again, because the last of the
patients had been moved to the huts, and work had
begun on restoring the Hall to something of its
former grandeur. 'But our love is deep, nonetheless.'

Richard gave the best man's speech. He said that
Mrs Moore was a treasure to behold, at which she
flapped her serviette, and that Mr Harvey was the
person he most respected in the world, a man of
honour and courage. He concluded with the words,
'Mr Auberon sent his very best wishes and hopes
to see you very soon. He knows, though not as
clearly as I, that we could not have weathered the
war without you.'

Evie looked askance at Veronica, who shook her

head, whispering, 'No, he's making it up, we haven't heard a word, and has Simon written again?'

Evie had heard twice, first a telegram informing her of his safe arrival, and then a letter describing the auditions, the excitement, the roar of Broadway, the fun he was having with Denny and his family. She wrote weekly, but of course she had more time than he, now that she only had the family, the staff, and those in the huts to cook for. She shook her head.

After the wedding tea Ted's taxi arrived bedecked with white ribbons, and bows on the door handles. The bridal pair were holidaying in Scarborough while the conversion of the hunters' stable into a ground-floor apartment and an upstairs apartment was completed. It only needed decorating, so they would return in two weeks.

Jack and Martin tied cans to the taxi, which clanked off along the drive while they all waved farewell, Evie and Veronica laughing together about Ted's mutterings as they departed. Richard put his arm around his wife, and murmured, 'I give it till the crossroads and then he'll be out of that car and ripping them off.'

After changing into her cook's uniform, Evie checked that the cold supper was ready to be taken to the huts before joining Richard, Ron, Veronica and Harry. They were in the virtually empty ballroom, poring over the plans, which were set up on the long table. The chandeliers would in time be rehung but there was work to be done before then. Their architect, Barry Jones, was the one-armed husband of the new housekeeper, Helen. They had accommodation in one of the huts.

It was hoped that Easterleigh Hall Hotel would open for guests in the autumn of this year, to take advantage of the shooting now that Charlie and the gamekeeper were working so hard and making great inroads. But it was only a hope. Ted's surviving son had agreed that he would help his father with his taxi business, taking guests on trips on the moors and along the coast as well as collecting them from the station. Tactfully Ron had suggested that Ted purchase a spanking new limousine, funded by a low-interest loan, which could be repaid from the fee that Easterleigh Hall would pay for Ted's son's exclusive services.

Builders, carpenters, plumbers and electricians had converged on Easterleigh Hall after Richard had advertised for workmen at the Newcastle demob depot, and were working practically round the clock, in shifts. The men were desperate for jobs in this post-war country that was struggling to create any sort of world, let alone one fit for heroes. Richard had sufficient skilled men to train the unskilled he insisted on taking on and those who arrived seeking his help to fill in forms and establish their disabled pensions.

Evie's da had retired in January and she was using some of John Neave's bequest to pay for him and

Tom Wilson, the blacksmith, to spend two months at the artificial-limb unit at Roehampton, in order to bring themselves up to date on the world of prosthetics. Once back, they wanted to work with the amputees who came to stay in the huts for some respite from their daily lives.

Veronica waved Evie over. 'Barry Jones has suggested some changes to the plans. Look, if we knock through from our two rooms upstairs and incorporate half the bedroom next door, we have an apartment. You and Simon can then form an enclave with us and have the adjoining group of rooms, or would you prefer to be with the lovebirds in the stable conversion?'

'I think perhaps Si would prefer the stables. More fresh air and closer to the gardens, and it might be an idea for me to be halfway between the house and the huts, to be able to work between the two. I think Barry's idea of creating a kitchen in the first hut, with covered walkways between all the huts, is ideal, and my money will easily cover it.' She put up her hand. 'No, Ver, I want to invest financially as well. My skill only goes so far. But listen, what about the apartment for Aub, when he returns?' She pointed to another set of three rooms on the second floor and said into the silence that had fallen, 'Have you heard anything?'

'Nothing, though his bank, having received an update from him, says all is well. The fishing is good and the river runs calmly. He is fly-fishing, to the amusement of the French, who prefer a pole.'

Evie nodded. 'As long as he is finding some peace.'

Harry slipped to her side. 'What about you, Evie, is there any news of Simon's return yet?'

'No, but why would there be, when he's on Broadway?'

Again there was a silence, again Richard made the offer he had made last week. 'Let us pay for you to sail over and attend a performance.'

Again she declined. 'I think he, like Aub, needs this time to himself, and if I went, I could afford to pay for myself, but thank you.'

She pored over the plans again, listening as Veronica announced that she was about to advertise for Prancer. 'He might have survived and his return could tempt Auberon back. Jack said that he was forever on the lookout for him in the war.'

Yes. Yes. Prancer could do that, and the headache that had drummed in the background since their men had left, lifted for a moment.

In mid May Auberon stood in his waders as the river Somme swirled around his legs. He cast again with the new fly he had made yesterday evening. Midges swirled above the clear water, and a woodpecker was busy knocking hell out of one of the hazel trees along the opposite bank. Behind the hazel trees a farmer and his family and most of the village were scything the hay, delayed this year, so heavy had been the rain in the last month. But they had just enjoyed a week of sun, and Monsieur Allard had decreed in the *estaminet* yesterday that the scything would begin at dawn. The *estaminet* had emptied, with the men shaking their heads at the idea of work.

Monsieur Allard had stood in the doorway, calling after the hurrying men, lifting his glass of rough red wine, *'Aujourd'hui à moi, demain à toi.'* Today me, tomorrow thee. They turned up at dawn, Auberon as well. Aristide Allard had shaken his hand and said in French, 'My friend, a few hours will be sufficient for those with untried backs and hands, and then you must drink wine with us this evening.'

Indeed, a few hours had been sufficient, because Auberon's back was breaking and his hands blistered. This afternoon, he held the rod loosely, pulled back the line with his fingers and cast again. He had named the fly Evie IV. Perhaps one day it would be Adelaide or Marie-Thérèse, but he doubted it. How could anyone compare to that extraordinary woman?

He flicked back his rod, and cast yet again. The plop on the water did not disturb the midges, or the carp, but occasionally the carp rose to the bait. 'Today you're failing me, Evie,' he said.

He waded to the bank and sat on the grass, his basket floating empty of catch in the river, except for minnows that swam through the netting. All around the trees were clothed in soft green leaves and they were a joy, because they were whole and the village was untouched, physically. Not emotionally, of course, and once a month Monsieur Allard journeyed to the battleground and joined the men

415

who were attempting to clear the unexploded shells, so that agriculture could begin again, and life continue. Last month he had taken Auberon in his cart. They had travelled for some hours, and spent the night at Allard's cousin's house. There were pockmarks in the walls, and the church had lost its steeple, but it functioned. Nearer the line the churches and villages did not.

The next day, with some ex-soldiers, they had probed, searched and lifted, with the utmost delicacy; much had already been done by servicemen not yet demobbed, but more needed doing. Tomorrow, a month to the day, they would go again, while others continued with the scything. Monsieur Allard had said, when Auberon asked why he went, '*Aujourd'hui à toi, demain à moi.*' Today thee, tomorrow me. It was enough. Auberon shook himself. Allard said this too often, but that was what life was, just enough, and that sentiment helped him through the day.

The next morning Monsieur Allard was waiting in his farmyard, a basket of pâté and bread in the back prepared by Madame Allard, enough for an army but actually just for the pair of them. They set off, the geese squawking and following them in bursts out of the farmyard and down the lane, their necks forward, their wings arched.

Allard was not given to talking, and his cigarettes were too strong for Auberon, so he smoked his own. The sun had dried the ruts on the tracks, and they lurched in and out. Auberon wore a panama, his host a beret. In the back several jugs of wine slopped in a bucket of cool water from the well. They stopped for lunch and drank several glasses. The mule knew the way to Allard's cousin, fortunately, because they both slept, their heads lolling on their chests, lulled by the lurching cart. They woke to fields of red: poppies growing in profusion in the area south of Albert. '*C'est approprié*,' muttered Auberon.

'*Oui, Monsieur*.'

They drank more wine at Allard's cousin's property. He was also an Allard. Monsieur Aristide Allard insisted that now he and Auberon would call one another by their given names. It made things simpler. Indeed it did, especially by the time they had finished three of the bottles. Monsieur François Allard lived in the barn which was all that was left standing, and to which he had returned a few months ago, leaving his wife in Poitiers where she had family. They had lost their son at Verdun. The men slept on the straw and this time there were no dreams or nightmares which had plagued Auberon since November 1918, just a raging thirst and a head fit to split apart in the morning. He preferred the headache.

They travelled, all three together in the cart, to clear a small section of François' land, both the Frenchmen in berets, their faces dark from the sun, their moustaches long, their eyes half closed. Auberon half closed his too. God, his head. The cart lurched.

Oh God, he was going to be sick. He felt a tap on his leg. François held out a flagon of water. Auberon downed it desperately. François said something to Aristide, and both men laughed. Auberon had missed it but frankly didn't give a shit. He just wanted to die, and thought of the time Mart and Jack had taken him to an *estaminet* and the same thing had happened. He was a lightweight, Jack had said then, and would say again today.

He closed his eyes and must have slept, because he woke and feared he'd dribbled. He wiped his mouth, thank God he hadn't, and his head was marginally better, but the sun was even hotter. Aristide had pulled up the cart and the two of them were eating cheese this time, with bread. François handed him some, his hands as strong and blunt as Jack's. It made him feel at home. He ate, and felt better, though shook his head at the offer of more wine. Dear God, no. He asked François when he felt he could farm his land again. The Gallic shrug was familiar, because the toxins from the munitions raised a question mark about it all.

They travelled on along tracks leading through poppies waving in the breeze. Auberon searched the terrain, as he had the first time he came. They must have marched through here, step by step by step, dragging their feet, ducking, sleeping on their feet. He didn't recognise it particularly, just the shell holes, the churned-up earth, and always the poppies. Was there one for every soul?

'Tonight we will sleep in the cart, under the stars,' Aristide said, 'dreaming of beautiful women, but first we will work.' They pulled up. 'First we will work.'

There was a working party several yards from the track, several ex-soldiers among them. One man waved, spreading his arm to indicate the area they were to search. All three of them nodded, carefully, because of their heads. They gathered up their long prodding sticks and worked for hours, under the baking sun, and by then Auberon felt he understood van Gogh's style of painting, because his headache was so appalling he could barely see. They had called for the ex-soldiers several times when their sticks had met resistance, and each time a shell had been carefully exhumed and carried to the dump near the track.

He stretched his back as the sun began to slip down towards the horizon. Another shell was carried past by one of the ex-soldiers. 'Soon, my friend,' Auberon called across to François. 'Soon you can farm here again, and bring life to it.'

Auberon gently drove his stick into the earth, a second behind François. He heard nothing, but felt the gust. It tore the stick from his hand, he tried to think, he rocked on his feet, his head screamed, his ears were pulsing, pulsing, a wave drowned him, the explosion tore into his body, the pain, and now the roar, the sound, the smell, the pain, the nothingness.

Chapter 20

Auld Maud, May 1919

'Mart, pick your bloody feet up, you're kicking up enough dust to drown us.' Jack dipped down lower and lower as the gradient increased, and the roof lowered, but it was only for fifty feet. They were heading out of their cutting towards the main drag. They'd picked a good allotment when they'd drawn the cavil with a pure load at the club the other night. Jeb, the union rep, had a smile on his ugly face for once, because Davies was allowed sufficient money to provide enough decent props, and a rescue station positioned between Hawton and Easton. Sidon and therefore the Lea End lot, what remained of them, were to be a party to it. Dave would have been pleased.

'Done your homework, have you?' Jack puffed. His chest hadn't been the same since that waft of mustard gas had caught them at Passchendaele, and enough had caught Mart to give him a snifter too.

Mart was panting as he said, 'Enough to treat meself to a beer. Bloody hell.' He ducked smartly, but the sharp edge in the roof caught him. 'There you are. If you stopped talking, I'd stop knocking me bonce.' They were approaching the cage now, and joined the queue waiting for their turn. Mart wiped his forehead and muttered into Jack's ear, 'Bloody glad we're doing the certificate. It's not the same, not quite the home from bloody home it was with this chest of mine.'

'Aye, I'm with you there.' Jack eased his back. He couldn't wait to get home to Grace, to have her scrub his back, kiss his mouth, laugh and tug his hair. Then he'd read to Tim, and spend the rest of the evening with his bonny lass. It was murder when he was on the back shift and they barely saw one another, let alone lay in bed together, as far from Edward's room as possible. He wiped the dust from his mouth.

'Where the hell is Auberon?' Mart muttered, worry creasing his forehead.

'No news is good news. He's still drawing money from the bank and he did say we wouldn't hear a ruddy word.' Jack was trying to talk himself down, as well as Mart, who wouldn't give it a rest, tapping his bait tin as he said, 'Aye, but he's not said whether he's coming for the hotel launch, and that's not too many months away. I don't like him there, alone at the Somme. He's one of us. He's ours.'

Eric was feeding the men into the cages efficiently for once, after Jack and Mart had told Davies that the bugger needed to up his game and the men didn't want his dilly-dallying after a long shift. He was on a warning, the little rat, and it had given Jack the greatest pleasure to be allotted the task of spelling it out to him, with Jeb's permission. Eric had been the only one to bad-mouth Da after he'd gone up to Deputy, and had had to join Brampton's lodge, not the union.

As Eric clanged the chain across the cage, he glared at Jack, who laughed. One tap. They creaked and groaned up towards the light. 'What about Si?' Mart shouted above the noise. 'He'll be back, surely?' Jack just shrugged, and they shared a look which said he'd better bloody be, for Evie's sake. Mart muttered into his ear now, not wanting to be heard by the others, who were crammed close, 'We should tell her that he wanted to stay for his own sake, not for this blather he keeps on about. He'll give himself a medal soon.'

Jack shook his head. 'He could straighten out, become a man.'

Evie and Veronica stood in front of Lady Margaret's stables, as they'd recently been christened, in memory of her attempt to burn them down as part of Christabel Pankhurst's pre-war campaign of destruction. Work was complete on the two apartments, except for a touch up here and there. The foreman called, 'Clock is ticking, got to get on, lots more work needed around the place.'

Evie replied, 'Carry on, we're on our way to the Captain Neave wing.' They lingered, though. The wood had been replaced with brick from Brampton's brickworks, which he'd offered at a discounted price, via his manager. Richard and Ron had dug about for a catch, but there seemed none. They knew that any sniff of a rift within the family would not have enhanced an image already besmirched by Brampton's munitions gains. The press were having a fine old time whingeing about the profiteers, now the war was over.

Not one to let an opportunity go by, Richard had grabbed the moment and ordered more bricks, because Evie had decided on Barry Jones' advice to dismantle the wooden huts and rebuild them in brick, and had sufficient funds to do so. It just meant moving the men and the nurses from one place to another until the work was finished. They were also building a small annexe where Evie's da and the blacksmith could work on their various limbs.

Ver slipped her arm through Evie's. 'I'm so pleased Mrs Moore . . . No, Mrs Harvey decided on the ground-floor apartment. The thought of the stairs after her retirement worried the life out of both Richard and me.'

Evie glanced up at the building. It looked clean but severe, though honeysuckle growing up it would remedy that. She should feel excitement, but she felt nothing. 'Si will be pleased to live here, I know he will.'

She knew nothing of the sort any more, because he seldom wrote. She wrote weekly, but with news about the hotel when she should have written words of love, words that failed to come. There was just a sort of anger, a disappointment, a fatigue at the thought of cajoling him as she had so often done.

The first Sunday after the Treaty of Versailles was signed, at the end of June, Edward held a memorial service in Easterleigh Hall's church. People arrived carrying white chrysanthemums and lilies, Evie and her parents amongst them, Grace, Tim, and Jack too. The scent was overpowering, and cleansing. The Forbes family sat with Richard, Veronica, and James, who objected to sitting on his mother's knee and preferred to clamber on to Tim's. Harry sat with Annie, and they held hands beneath the folds of her uniform. What would Sir Anthony Travers think of that, Evie wondered. Well, at the launch they might find out. Charlie sat with Mart, who was squashed against Maisie, the nurse who worked with the men who skipped from hut to hut, one step ahead of the builders. Matron sat with Mr Harvey and Mrs Moore, who had sighed at the last meeting, as everyone tried to remember to call her Mrs Harvey, 'For goodness sake, call me Mrs Moore. It's who I still am, if you get my meaning. Nothing's changed.' But it had. There was a bloom about her that Evie envied.

The service began, and it was conducted jointly by Edward and Davy Evans, from the chapel at Easton. The church was so crowded that people stood outside, with the windows and doors open so that they could hear. The choir sang a hymn composed by Harry's mother, with Evie as the soloist. For a moment, as she gazed out across the packed congregation, holding pristine white flowers for those who had not returned, she felt something stir, and it was a sense of great loss.

Richard spoke of the courage of the patients at Easterleigh Hall, and of the staff with their enduring compassion. Jack spoke of the war, the larks that flew over the fields when away from the front, the ruin of the land as it now was, the kindness of some of the German guards which had made life tolerable. He spoke finally of Auberon.

Evie watched as her brother faltered, searching for words, and for composure. 'He became one of us. He fought with us, and for us. He watched our backs and we his. He is a grand man, a man of honour, one who returned to make good the promises he made to himself. I repeat that he is one of ours and we miss him, and want the silly bugger back here again.'

The congregation laughed, and it was laughter that rolled out through the windows and doors to be joined by that of those outside.

In September the invitations for the launch in November were sent out, though there was still decorating to be done, with no furniture yet reinstated. It was a gamble, but with a definite date they'd just have to make it.

Veronica and Evie sat over stewed cups of tea in the kitchen with Harry, who had asked for the meeting just to check on a few details about the launch. Harry was to be front of house, operating from Lord Brampton's old desk placed where the orderly's station had been in the great hall. He poured himself some more tea and scoffed a scone, loaded with honey. 'Trust me,' he said. 'I've put the word about to all Father's connections. The newspaper editors say they'll send reporters, and they might, though they're not known for reliability. It all depends if an actress is caught with a cabinet minister in a state of undress.' He was talking with his mouth full. Crumbs landed on the table. Evie said, 'Don't be disgusting.'

He laughed, and more crumbs showered out. 'I'm not, it's the sort of thing that does happen.'

Veronica said, 'She meant the crumbs, naughty boy.'

He swallowed, and wiped his mouth, then flicked at the table with a serviette. Evie sighed. 'Ver, can we possibly have this urchin as front of house?'

Veronica shook her head. 'He'll have to show some improvement or Mr Manners will have something to say, indeed he will.'

Harry grinned, and shoved a list across to the two women. 'Have a look. I've sent to these, in my very best handwriting, ma'am.'

At the top of the list were Lord and Lady Brampton. Evie and Veronica looked up, appalled.

426

Harry held their stare, though his colour rose. 'We have to, or it will look strange to our guests. It is still, to all intents and purposes, perceived as his house.' Evie recognised the set of his chin. She had seen it so often when he struggled with his wooden leg. He would not move on this, and it was too late anyway.

Veronica said, 'Richard knows of this?'

'No, it is my province and I thought you two should know first.' He reached for the last scone, but at the last minute offered it to them. They declined, letting him lather it with honey and watching, fascinated, as it went in whole. Then they read down the list. Everyone who should have received an invitation was there. Beneath Lord and Lady Brampton was Auberon. Beneath him, Simon.

'Now we wait,' Harry said.

Two days later Evie woke at midnight in her attic room, her head and heart pounding. She drank a little water, but her hand trembled and more spilt down her nightdress. She slept until a banging on her door woke her. 'Evie, it's late, it's eight o'clock, breakfast is finished.' It was Annie. Evie couldn't speak, she couldn't move, her body ached, her lungs were full of water, she was drowning, swimming amongst reeds. Someone was touching her forehead. It hurt. Just the touch hurt.

Matron was there. 'Sit up, lass.'

No, she couldn't move, she was drowning. She

felt an arm under her, it hurt. She was being lifted. No, it hurt. 'Drink.' The glass against her lips hurt. No. It was being forced. Rum scalded her throat. She swallowed. It hurt. No. No more. But there was more. It scalded.

They laid her down, let her drift, let her swim and the waves were there, twisting and turning, throwing her up and then down, the sand was scraping her, hurting her. 'No.'

'It's to cool you down, bonny lass.' It was Mam, here in the water too.

'No.'

'Come on, darling, just a sip.' It was Ver, and it scalded. No.

She was alone at last. The waves pulled her towards shore, and then away, further, further, deeper and colder, deeper, colder, into a place where there were no voices, no one tugging but then Jack came, through the sea. 'Come on, bonny lass. One sip, just one.' No.

'Try, lass, try to breathe.'

I'm tired, Da. I'm just tired, let me be. I'm tired and I'm alone and it's quiet. Now it's quiet.

'We need you, pet. Come along now.'

No, Mrs Moore. I'm just too tired and I like it here, away in the deep of the sea, away from the roar of the surf, and the scratching of the sand, away from your newly-wed bloom which makes me happy and then sad, so sad. It's dark here, in the river. Yes, it's a river, not the sea. It's softly flowing where no waves move me. I'm just floating, through pictures, fragments, lots of fragments. There's Mam's kitchen and the proggy rug. In and out with the strips, not the green there, Mam says. Not there, pet. Here's Grace, digging in her garden, earthing up the potatoes. Jack, you're in the water, why are you digging too? Timmie, you're painting your soldiers. They're grand, bonny lad.

'No, Evie, no. You must not do this. You must try.' It was Ver, too loud, too harsh. No.

Mrs Moore was reading her recipe bible. There she is, her finger running along the page, her poor swollen finger. There are the fancies that Mrs Green should make but I do, for them, Veronica and . . . and . . .

Jack smiled as he swam through the tendrils, and Timmie and there were no blue-black scars and it was cool and dark and no voices called. It was quiet, at last it was quiet and she could let the air from her lungs, and let her chest rest, let her heart rest, let everything stop.

She was on her bike, the air was sweet, the larks sang, the sheep were in the meadows, the cows in the corn and little boy blue . . .

'No, I won't have it, do you hear.' Ver was shouting.

Be quiet, I like the quiet. Little boy blue . . . Such blue eyes. So very blue, so kind.

The water was kind, Jack was kind, swimming close, and she could feel his breath on her cheek.

Timmie was close, and there was someone. Who? Who? There was someone in the shadows, and he was waving and calling, and she'd missed him. Her heart was empty because he had gone but he was calling her now, and she could hear him, faintly, and she could see him, faintly and he was smiling, and his eyes were blue, so blue in the darkness and he was moving upwards towards the light, and his hair was shining, yellow like the sun, and he was calling her up, to the surface and she must hurry, or she would lose him, this man who could fill and warm her heart.

She broke the surface, gasped, dragged in the air, and the light was too bright, shiny and bright. Where . . . ? Where . . . ? Her head ached. Evie gulped in more air. 'Where is he?' she whispered. 'Where is Aub?' But there was no one there to hear her.

She slept.

Jack and Mart acted as guides on 7th November, the day that Easterleigh Hall Hotel opened its doors. The press came in force, photographers set up their cameras and Lord and Lady Brampton were photographed shaking hands with Richard, Veronica, Evie and Mrs Moore on the front steps. Lord Brampton's eyes glazed as he found himself looking into the face of a Forbes, but Evie merely said, 'I'm so pleased you could attend the launch of our hotel, Your Lordship.'

Jack was grinning in the crowd, which clapped

when Harry finished the welcome speech. 'Short and without crumbs,' Veronica whispered to Evie

He was to be assisted in his role by Steve Briggs, the demobbed orderly, who looked as smart as a new pin. His suit had come out of the hotel expenses, and worth every penny, Matron was heard to bark. Though it was November it was a clear bright day, and in the distance the rattle of guns could be heard as one of the shooting parties fired their first salvos.

People thronged the lawns, the formal gardens, and explored the house, and the Captain Neave wing, which was what the brick-built huts had been named. This gave his mother great pleasure, she insisted on telling everyone. Lady Margaret arrived with her parents, and Penny. Several people made a point of addressing her as Lady Margaret, even Veronica and Richard, which perplexed her parents, and Lord and Lady Brampton.

'Who the hell cares,' whispered Richard to Evie. 'You look a million dollars, as they would say on Broadway.'

Evie's elegant pale green silk dress had been made by the seamstress who had run up the dining room gold and cream curtains. Richard led her to a quiet spot in the great hall. 'Do you really not mind that Simon has married that American girl? Denny's sister, did you say?'

'No, it's perfectly all right. How could I have left Easterleigh and moved to New York? This is my

home, it's my peace and perhaps one day he'll . . .'
She stopped, and shrugged. Richard prompted,
'He'll . . . ?'

'Never mind. We have people to see, people to
talk to, Richard. But thank you.'

She was still weak, but calm. It was as though
something had lifted, and the light had entered her
life, in a way it had never done before. Light and
certainty, and if he, Auberon, never returned, what
did it matter? She loved him, and it was enough
that *she* knew. Easterleigh Hall, her dream hotel,
would suffice, because it had to.

She walked out into the cold, and across to the
cedar tree. Mrs Neave was there, with Harry, her
hand slipped under his arm. She smiled at Evie.
'Thank you, my dear. He lives on.'

Evie gripped her outstretched hand. 'Indeed he
does. He was such a good man, and Harry's particular friend.'

'Yours too, I believe, my dear Evie,' Mrs Neave
said. 'I feel he would never love another woman
quite as he loved you, but I suspect you knew that.'

Evie hadn't known, and moved on, touching the
branches as she made a point of doing every day,
insisting that the tree grew strong and firm. Old Stan
said she was a daft beggar, and it would do its little
best, with or without her help.

Lord Brampton and Sir Anthony were drinking
champagne, donated by Brampton, on the other side
of the tree. The Bastard was less bumptious, Evie

thought, looking at him. She moved closer. He was saying, 'Of course, all this nonsense about squeezing the Huns until they squeak is nonsense. They can never pay the reparations, look at the mess they're in, and the Versailles Conference must have known that. It's window-dressing. The Kaiser has gone to live in Holland, there's chaos in Germany with faction fighting faction. Trouble is the people don't know they lost, because we didn't follow them in and wave it in their faces. They think they've been sold out, to use a ghastly American expression, and mark my words, they will want revenge. There will be war again. Good for business.' He sipped his champagne.

Sir Anthony looked back at the Hall. 'I do hope not, or we'll be needing beds in here again, with more youngsters to patch up.'

Evie moved on, past the Easton and Hawton brass band in full blow. Ron and Steve had draped bunting across the front of the house. Lady Brampton had declared it working class and worthy of the seafront. Veronica had said, 'Do you go often?'

That had successfully ended that conversation.

She made for the kitchen, wondering where Auberon was, hoping he was safe, but perhaps they'd never know. Jack caught up with her as she was checking that there was sufficient food to replenish the buffet set up in the marquee. 'You know we know, don't you, pet?'

Evie was confused. 'Know what?'

'You were talking when you were ill. We all know

that it's Auberon you love, and Ver has just told us that in the diary he left at the start of the war, he wrote of his love for you.'

For a moment Evie thought she had not heard correctly. Jack repeated it as though she was a penny short of a shilling, and then common sense came to her rescue. 'Well, Jacko,' she smiled, 'that was the start of the war, and a boy who knew no better. War changes people, as we well know.'

Mart ran down the steps from the stable yard and burst into the kitchen. 'I've just checked with Veronica. No one's heard from Aub except the bank, and that's not as often as it used to be. It's daft and I've had enough, because Ver's just heard on the telephone that Prancer's still with us. She's bought him off the major who was stuck in supplies, lucky beggar. Well, the bloody horse is coming home, so Aub needs to damn well come back too. I vote we go, Jack, drag him back by the balls, beggin' your pardon, Evie, if we have to.'

Three days later Jack and Mart took leave of absence from the course, and the mine. Charlie had to stay behind to fume at Easterleigh Hall, because he was needed for the shooting parties. They paid Ted to drive them to Gosforn and were gone from England by the 12th November. The bank would give out no details but they knew he'd have headed for Picardie, and the Somme, and they would march the bloody length of it, if it came to it.

They took the ferry to Calais. There were no longer any tents on the cliffs, though the cobbles were the same when they disembarked. They entrained, heading for the Somme via Albert, asking for an Englishman called Brampton as he had said he would be back one day to see if the virgin had been restored. They carried on to Amiens, which was a stone's throw from the river. Albert had looked like broken teeth in a destroyed mouth, and Amiens, for so long a quiet rest area, had been bombed and shelled towards the end of the war, so it, too, had ended up damaged and torn, but infinitely more whole than Albert.

They asked at the town hall for an Englishman called Brampton. Heads were shaken. 'It's walking the river for us, then,' Jack said, hitching up his pack.

They marched together, falling into step as though it was as natural as breathing, past relatives who were searching for graves, for answers, for something to take away the silence of their lives. On, out of town, in the direction of the river, in boots they had worn in the war because they had struggled and toiled for many miles around this area, and it seemed right that they use the same footwear again. Besides, they had been worn in to the point that they felt like slippers. Mart looked about. 'Poor Frenchies. The Channel is a good old moat for us British, you know, lad. Keeps the enemy at bay.'

They found the river and walked towards the west, eating the almond-paste biscuits, *macarons d'Amiens*, which the baker explained were a rarity because of the shortages, but which he made from time to time. They had bought six and asked if an Englishman had been seen fishing the Somme, and the Gallic shrug said it all.

'Once we get to the mouth we'll head back until we reach the source. It could take weeks,' Jack said. 'So, it takes weeks, bonny lad,' Mart said, humming. They saw churned-up land and stumps of trees if they looked over to the north, so instead they looked at the river, slow-running and carp-filled. Soon they saw green fields and undamaged villages into which they diverted, always asking, 'Have you seen an Englishman fishing, called Brampton?' Always the answer was no.

They walked for three weeks, and then turned back, paying a lorry to take them as far as Amiens. Before making for the source, they turned towards the front line. It was in the second village that they found him.

Evie waited by the cedar tree with Veronica. It was Christmas Eve and guests were enjoying dinner, and those patients and ex-patients in need of limbs and respite had joined them. Evie was to sing later. Simon had hoped that he would be here; he had telegraphed saying, *Evie stop I have made mistake stop I want to come home in time for Christmas stop we can be together again stop*

She had replied, *Simon stop you must live with your decision stop I have another life stop I wish you well stop*

Jack had not said a precise time, it depended on the train on a night like this, with the snow on the line. Veronica said, 'He actually told us nothing, just that they were bringing him home. What the hell does that mean?'

Evie was straining to see the lights of a car. 'We'll find out.'

Harry came out of the main doors, down the steps, across the gravel to the lawn, a lit cigarette in his hand. He stood by her. 'Do you remember the first Christmas of the war, Evie? You waited, you, Millie, and Veronica, and they came. They'll come again and he'll still love you. Just you wait and see.'

There were headlights at the entrance now, and the cough and splutter of Ted's old taxi. The engine died. The lights went out. The car doors opened and closed. How many? Two? What did that mean? Two people, or was it three? Bugger Jack, why couldn't he have said more? Did Auberon still love her? Ver was sure he did from the look on his face when he left. But why had it been so long with no word? How could he? Did he love her? How could he? The thoughts were chasing one another like Currant and Raisin. She could see the bobbing of lit cigarette ends. Three. Surely there were three?

Prancer whinnied from his stall next to Tinker. She heard him kicking. He neighed now. Figures were emerging from the darkness. Three, the middle one Aub. Veronica clutched her arm. 'It's him, but so slow. Oh great heavens, Evie, so slow.'

Evie was running then, wrenching free of Veronica, seeing, on the edge of her vision, Harry reaching for Veronica, holding her back, saying, 'No, this is Evie's time.'

She ran, her feet slipping on the snow, crunching the gravel beneath it, closer and closer, and then she was there, standing so near that her dress touched his suit. He smiled, throwing his cigarette away, his face full and free of fatigue, his eyes so blue, his hair yellow even in this dull light. He said, 'I will love you for ever, Evie Forbes, if you will let me.'

She clung to him, feeling him reel just slightly. 'If you ever go away again and leave me alone, I will kill you myself, bonny lad.' His arms were round her and he was kissing her. Mart and Jack stayed with them.

'Why didn't you come?' she said against his mouth, which felt as she had dreamed it would. She reached up and stroked his hair. Still her brother and Mart were there, and then she realised it was because they were propping him up.

Auberon said, 'I wasn't well enough. I needed time to heal, my mind and my body.' She stepped back, holding his arms, seeing his cane, now held by Mart. 'How much damage?' she asked, because whatever it was she could cope.

He lifted her hand to his lips. 'Very little. I'm just a bit hard of hearing, and have a leg that is in a spot of bother.'

'It will have to come off?'

He gripped her hand and pulled her close. 'It has already gone, dearest Evie, and now it just needs you, Easterleigh and your da. I have a rather clunky peg leg and healing stump, which are in need of his and Tom's tender mercies.'

Prancer was neighing. 'Can you hear that?' she asked. He was grinning as his horse neighed again. 'We're coming,' he called, kissing her again. 'Sometimes life is too wonderful to be real, but you know what, dearest Evie, when I've said hello to Prancer I would so love to walk to the kitchen and sit down on one of Mrs Moore's stools, if there is a cushion?'

The seamstress had made them only last month. Her three men walked up the drive with her, and they met Veronica and Harry halfway. Auberon was limping badly now, but clutching her hand and Jack was at his side, his hand under his arm. They stopped to look at the cedar tree. Auberon murmured, 'We search and search but it's so often here, laid under our feet like a cloth of gold.'

Mart said, 'Aye lad, a home from bloody home.'

Jack told them, 'All will be well.' They laughed, and Auberon's arm was round her and she had never known such tranquillity.

Also available in Arrow

Easterleigh Hall

Margaret Graham

**Her life began in the service of others.
Her future would be hers.**

When Evie Forbes starts as an assistant cook at Easterleigh Hall,
she goes against her family's wishes. For ruthless Lord Brampton
also owns the mine where Evie's father and brothers work and
there is animosity between the two families.

But Evie is determined to better herself. And her training at the
hall offers her a way out of a life below stairs.

Evie works hard and gains a valued place in the household.
And her dream of running a small hotel grows ever closer.

Then war is declared and all their lives are thrown into turmoil.

arrow books